For my sister, because she always has my back.

**Rave reviews for Diana Rowland's
White Trash Zombie novels:**

"The third outing in Rowland's marvelous series takes new zombie Angel Crawford deeper into a deadly conspiracy where zombie research and testing has taken some horrific turns. Rising star Rowland has created such a compelling and charming heroine, building reader investment throughout this truly outstanding series!"
—*RT Book Reviews* (top pick)

"So far, this has been an incredibly fun series, and a breath of fresh air in an increasingly crowded field. While there's no denying that the basic premise is fascinating and entertaining, the real draw here is Angel's personal journey of growth and self-discovery. . . . Angel's a heroine worth cheering for."   —Tor.com

"If you haven't discovered this series, you're in for a treat. Angel is one of my favorite heroines in urban fantasy right now, and I can't wait to see what she's up to next!"   —My Bookish Ways

"An intriguing mystery and a hilarious mix of the horrific and mundane aspects of zombie life open a promising new series from Rowland. . . . Humor and gore are balanced by surprisingly touching moments as Angel tries to turn her (un)life around."
—*Publishers Weekly*

"Rowland's delightful novel jumps genre lines with a little something for everyone—mystery, horror, humor, and even a smattering of romance. Not to be missed—all that's required is a high tolerance for gray matter. For true zombiephiles, of course, that's a no brainer."   —*Library Journal*

"Every bit as fun and trashy as the brilliant cover. The story is gory and gorgeous with plenty of humor and a great new protagonist to root for. There is also a tightly written murder mystery too that shocked me by the end. No word yet on the next book in the *White Trash Zombie* series, but I'm already feeling the Hunger."
—All Things Urban Fantasy

Also by Diana Rowland:

SECRETS OF THE DEMON

SINS OF THE DEMON

TOUCH OF THE DEMON

FURY OF THE DEMON

VENGEANCE OF THE DEMON*

MY LIFE AS A WHITE TRASH ZOMBIE

EVEN WHITE TRASH ZOMBIES
GET THE BLUES

WHITE TRASH ZOMBIE APOCALYPSE

HOW THE WHITE TRASH ZOMBIE
GOT HER GROOVE BACK

*Coming in 2015 from DAW

HOW THE WHITE TRASH ZOMBIE GOT HER GROOVE BACK

DIANA ROWLAND

DAW BOOKS, INC.

DONALD A. WOLLHEIM, FOUNDER

375 Hudson Street, New York, NY 10014

ELIZABETH R. WOLLHEIM
SHEILA E. GILBERT
PUBLISHERS

www.dawbooks.com

ACKNOWLEDGMENTS

In no particular order, enormous thanks are due (and overdue!) to Anna Hoffstadt, Kat Johnson, Steve Wages, Andy Rogers, Mary Robinette Kowal, Google Street View, Matt Bialer, Mrs. Mary Biernacki, ibuprofen and cyclobenzaprine, Cathy Rathbun, Lindsay Ribar, Roman White, the entire Hoffstadt clan, John and Tara Palmer, Wikipedia, Jordan Ellinger, Nils Onsager, Moses Siregar, Joshua Essoe, chocolate, Jaye Wells, Eddie and Cindy Schmidt, Matt Saver, Bill and Ann Jacobson, Scott Knight, those exercise band thingies that you hook over a door, Daniel and Kat Abraham, Dan Dos Santos, Jodi Levine, bacon, Marylou Capes-Platt, Jill Smith, John and Kristine Scalzi, Myke Cole, Betsy Wollheim, Kevin Hearne, Paul and Julie Wood, Joshua Starr, Peter Stampfel, Jack Hoffstadt, George R.R. Martin, Sherry Rowland, the entire DAW staff, and everyone else who helped keep me in one piece this past year.

Chapter 1

Sweat dribbled into my eyes and my ribs ached, but I stood my ground against the burly man in front of me. He flexed his hands as we slowly circled each other, his teeth bared in a sneer framed by a truly majestic beard.

His hand shot out to seize my sleeve. I twisted to break his grip, but he merely shifted to grab my shoulder with his other hand. Within about two seconds he spun, slammed his butt into my hips, hoisted me up and sent me flying.

I landed hard on the mat, breath whooshing out of my lungs before I remembered to slap my hand down.

"No, no, Angel, the slap is *part* of the fall." That was my *sensei*, his voice laced with three months of frustration from trying to teach me the most basic aspects of *jiu jitsu*.

"Right," I wheezed. "Got it."

My brawny opponent reached down and grabbed the front of my *gi*, then hoisted me up to set me on my feet as easily as picking up a kitten.

"C'mon," he rumbled. "Try it on me. It's all about balance."

All about balance, my ass. I weighed barely a hundred pounds, and Freddie easily topped three hundred. Lips drawn back in a snarl, I seized his sleeve, grabbed his shoulder with my other hand, then spun and tried to slam my scrawny ass into his groin in an attempt to copy the move he'd performed on me.

"You're not going to get him onto your back using brute strength," my sensei lectured as Freddie remained immobile. "Try a different move. Try *osoto gari*."

I gave him a blank look, and he sighed. " 'Trip the Drunk Guy,' " he said, supplying my own nickname for the move.

"Gotcha!" Why did they have to use so many weird names for things? And yes, I knew it was Japanese, a beautiful and elegant language that wasn't weird in the slightest, but I still had trouble with parts of the *English* language. Expecting me to remember a bunch of foreign words was asking way too much of my brain. Of course, for all I knew *osoto gari* actually meant Trip the Drunk Guy.

I adjusted my grip, yanked on Freddie's arm to try and get his weight onto one leg, then shot my own leg forward and slammed it back into his to sweep it.

Like kicking a tree trunk.

"Pull on the arm," *sensei* suggested, oh-so-helpfully.

"I *am*," I growled, then added a belated, "sir."

I continued to yank and pull and grip and kick and sweep until finally Freddie tumbled to the ground—with a perfect slap and fall—though I was pretty sure he'd simply taken pity on me. Sensei probably suspected the same thing, but he looked more relieved than anything. Poor guy. It wasn't his fault that I wasn't exactly the best learner in the world.

After my brilliant demonstration, it was my turn to stand back and observe humongous Freddie and normal size Chance go at it. My ego recovered slightly as I watched Chance get taken down over and over, though when he fell he slapped the mat and did shit right instead of flopping like a sack of flour the way I did. About a month ago I'd snapped something in my ankle because of my horrible form, but a quick snack of brains healed the damage right up. That was one awesome thing about being a zombie. As long as I had my "protein shake" in my bag—with its super special ingredient—no one, especially my sensei, ever needed to know I was hurt.

Sensei gave the two men some critiques on form, then turned to me. "Rollouts, Angel," he instructed, gesturing to the length of the mat. "Both sides, back and forth twice, then you're done."

"Yes, sir!" I said with a cheerful grin, then proceeded to throw myself at the mat in the most spaztastic rolls any *jiu jitsu* dojo had ever seen.

I wasn't sure, but I think *sensei* might have wept a little.

"Cherry red face."

The skin parted beneath my scalpel as I let out a soft snort of derision. "Oh, please. Give me a hard one. Carbon monoxide poisoning."

Dr. Leblanc smiled from where he leaned against the counter. Fifty-something, with thinning grey-blond hair, glasses perched halfway down his nose, and more flab than muscle around his middle, he wouldn't stand out in a crowd, but I didn't care about that one little bit. The pathologist for the St. Edwards Parish Coroner's Office was one of my all-time favorite people in the world, mostly because he seemed to have absolute faith that I was capable of all sorts of great things. I didn't always believe him, but I sure tried my best to live up to his expectations. Barely an hour earlier I'd been spazzing my way through *jiu jitsu*, and one of the reasons I hadn't given up weeks ago was because, shortly after I started training, Dr. Leblanc had remarked that he would be honored if I would invite him to attend my belt ceremony once I earned my yellow belt. *Honored.* Before I was turned into a zombie, I'd been a drug addicted high school dropout with a felony conviction who couldn't hold a job. And Dr. Leblanc couldn't have cared less about any of that.

"All right," Dr. Leblanc said, "let's stick with the carbon monoxide subject." He tipped his head back as he contemplated my next challenge. "Your decedent has second and third degree burns over ninety percent of his body. No evidence of other trauma. Tox scan comes back clean. Carboxyhemoglobin level is five percent. How does that level corroborate your decedent's death by fire?"

I drew the scalpel down the woman's abdomen to finish the Y-incision as I thought. "It doesn't," I said after a moment. "Poor dude probably got himself killed, and the murderer tried to use the fire to cover it up."

"Are you sure?" He leveled a stern look at me.

"Yes," I said, with mock-seriousness. "Well, not about the murder part," I amended, "but about the dead-before-the-fire-started part. With only five percent on the . . ." I faltered. I knew what the damn test measured, but I had a hell of a time spouting off the word. "With a carboxy-hemidoodamajigger level of only five percent, there's no way he was alive when the fire started, otherwise it'd be way higher from breathing carbon monoxide." The hamster raced on its wheel in my head. "Could be he died of a heart attack and dropped a cigarette onto a pile of newspapers. Five percent would be pretty normal in a smoker." I shrugged. "Murder or accident, dude didn't die from the fire or its smoke."

His smile returned. "I should probably say I'm impressed, but the truth is, I'm not."

"Huh?"

"To be impressed I'd have to be surprised by how well you've absorbed the material," he said. "And I'm not surprised at all."

Flushing with pleasure, I returned my attention to the body and finished separating skin and flesh from ribs. "I still have a long way to go." I set the scalpel aside and picked up the big pruning shears—the same kind I used to snip branches at my house. Not that I actually did much in the way of yard maintenance besides shoving a lawnmower around every few weeks.

"But every piece of knowledge is one more step down that long path," he replied. He watched me snip through ribs to remove the triangle-shaped section, then pushed off the counter to step forward and peer into the chest cavity. "And one day you will look at that long path and find only a few steps left."

"Keep being so wise, and I'm going to start calling you Most Honorable Master Leblanc," I teased as I wiped down the shears. "You'd look awesome with a long white beard and moustache to twirl."

He laughed. "I suppose I do sound a bit pompous."

"Nah, it's cool," I said with a grin. "Just don't ask me to punch through boards or anything."

"I can promise you that's not likely to happen," he replied, then picked up a scalpel and began his examination of the throat, chest, and abdomen.

Funny thing was that I *had* punched through boards before—not all that long ago, in fact. A flash flood had washed my house away this past summer, and with my dad and me trapped in the attic, I'd punched and kicked my way through the plywood and tar paper and shingles to give us a way out.

Nobody knew about that, though, except my dad. It wasn't the sort of thing any normal person could do, and especially not one like me—barely a hundred pounds of skinny bitch who sure as hell didn't look tough enough to break a toothpick, much less rip through a roof.

Then again, I wasn't normal. Not one bit.

I moved to the end of the table and began work on the young woman's head. Mid-twenties, pretty in a girl-next-door sort of way. Sarah Lynn Harper. The name didn't ring a bell, but I couldn't shake the nagging feeling I'd seen her before, when she was alive.

Scalpel in hand, I made a slice from ear to ear on top of her head, then peeled the scalp back to expose her skull. Trading scalpel for bone saw, I cut a neat circle all the way around, like a bowl cut gone wrong, then took a chisel-like tool called a skullcracker, shoved it into the groove and twisted. The bone gave a satisfying *crack*, followed by a wet *sllrrkk* sound as I pulled the top of the skull off to expose the pink and grey convolutions of the brain.

The weird and gross music of the morgue, I thought with amusement, then took a deep breath and inhaled. The lovely scent of that brain filled me, but I resisted the urge to grab a handful and stuff it into my mouth. I wasn't all that hungry, but *yummm,* fresh brains. I'd chow down later when there weren't witnesses to how very *not* normal I was.

My desire to munch on brain matter wasn't because I was crazy. No doubt there were people who'd argue that I had a mental twitch or three, but that was beside the point. About a year ago I woke up in the ER with memories of horrible injuries yet not a scratch on me. I soon discovered that an anonymous benefactor had arranged for me to get a job with the Coroner's Office, and I'd been harvesting brains out of body bags ever since. I wanted the brains—hell, *needed* the brains—because I was host to a truly bizarre parasite. As long as I ate a brain every week and a half or so, I was fine. The parasite stayed happy, and would even fix me up if I got hurt or sick, though that required more brain-fuel. However, if I didn't give my parasite enough brains, I'd start to fall apart—literally. Not only would I rot, but I'd lose my ability to think clearly and, worst of all, I'd get hungry. Really hungry. Hungry enough to kill for the brains I needed.

Fortunately, my job as a morgue tech kept me well stocked on brains. No need for any murderous rampages today.

The creak of the door jerked me out of my thoughts, and I glanced over my shoulder to see Allen Prejean, the Coroner's Office Chief Investigator, step into the cutting room, a clipboard in his gloved hands.

Yanking my gaze away, I returned my attention to my work as he and Dr. Leblanc exchanged pleasantries. Allen didn't like me. He'd made that very clear from day one by giving me everything from crap schedules to undisguised sneers and offhand comments about work ethics and unsavory lifestyles. There were plenty of people who didn't like me or who saw only what they expected to see—high school dropout, former felon, and recovering drug addict. In other words, a loser. Most of the time I had no problem blowing it off when I got the stink-eye. In the past year I'd worked my ass off to leave my loser self behind, and if there were some people who couldn't see it, well, screw 'em.

Allen's barely hidden contempt hadn't really bothered me until last summer when I'd accidentally sliced my hand open right here in the morgue. If Dr. Leblanc hadn't been in the room it wouldn't have been a big deal, but I couldn't exactly say, "Don't worry, Doc. I'll slurp down a baggie of brains and my zombie parasite will have me fixed up in no time!" I was forced to play it out like a normal person. To save me the hassle and paperwork of the emergency room, Allen stitched it up—and not only was he vaguely decent to me while he did so, but he let slip that he tended to use his vacation time to go on Doctors Without Borders missions. Admirable shit. And in a flash I went from not giving a rat's ass that he hated me to being bugged by it.

That's his *problem*, I told myself for the billionth time. So what if he and I weren't BFFs? He couldn't fire me without cause, and I did my damnedest not to give him any.

I removed the brain and set it on the scale while Allen peered at the body. A few seconds later he made a mark on his clipboard, then turned away to inspect the body bag Sarah Lynn had occupied. Checking up on me, I knew. Several months ago there'd been a stink about missing jewelry, and ever since then Allen had instituted spot checks like this one to make sure personal property was removed and properly logged.

Keeping my face expressionless, I continued my work. He had yet to ding me for a single screwup, real or imagined, and I intended to keep it that way. Head down, do my work, don't make waves. Be a good little Angel.

"Allen, did you hear Angel's news?" Dr. Leblanc suddenly asked as he set a kidney on the scale. I dutifully recorded the weight on the white board on the wall behind him, while I wondered what the hell the pathologist was talking about.

Allen's eyes narrowed ever so faintly. "News?" His gaze swung to me, and I noted a hint of curiosity in his eyes. Probably wondering if it was something he could add to his Angel Shitlist.

Dr. Leblanc removed the kidney from the scale and began to section it. "Angel passed her GED last week," he announced with a broad smile. "The sky's the limit for her now."

Yep, I'd finally managed to scrape out a passing grade on the GED—after hours and hours of free tutoring from my coworker, Nick, along with quite a few more hours of not-free tutoring that focused on my recently diagnosed dyslexia.

I braced myself for some sort of eye roll or dismissive snort from Allen, but he managed to force a smile—for Dr. Leblanc's benefit, no doubt. "Congrats, Angel," he said with as much enthusiasm as a garden slug. "You'll be heading off to college soon then, I take it?"

Heat crawled up my face at his tone and the unspoken *No fucking way will you make it through a real school. This is as far as you'll ever go in life.*

"Actually, I'm going to register for a couple of classes at Tucker Point Community College next term," I shot back before my brain could engage itself. Crap. I'd toyed with the idea and even made it as far as checking out the college website, but I'd been too . . . well, okay, I'd been too chicken to do anything more. I'd passed the GED by the skin of my teeth—by one damn point, to be exact—and only managed that because I was allowed extra time because of my dyslexia. How the hell could I make it through *college?*

Yet I'd gone and said it, which meant that now I was stuck. No way would I give Allen the satisfaction of being right about me, and no way would I disappoint Dr. Leblanc, not with that proud smile on his face.

"Sounds good, Angel," Allen commented without so much as a glance my way. He made another note on his clipboard, gave Dr. Leblanc a slight nod, and then departed without another word.

The pathologist removed the woman's heart, weighed it, and set it on his cutting board. "I suppose I don't need to suggest that you get in there and show everyone what you're made of?"

I snorted, forced the fierce smile Dr. Leblanc expected from me. "Nah. Got that covered."

Shit. Looked like I was going to college.

"Now isn't that interesting," Dr. Leblanc murmured, frowning down at the sectioned heart.

I peered over at the abnormally thickened wall of her left ventricle. "Ventricular hypertrophy?" We saw it all the time in cases of heart disease and high blood pressure, but hardly ever in someone this young. And certainly not where there was barely any space in the ventricle at all.

"I think we can be more specific," he said. "Cardiomegaly, young, signs of pulmonary edema, asymmetric septal and ventricular hypertrophy." He ran the probe over the septum in the cross section. "See?"

Not only did I see, but I actually understood everything he'd said. Hot damn! Of course it helped that I was almost positive we'd seen this once before in an autopsy—

Oh, shit. We *had* seen this before, and now I knew why the woman looked familiar. She'd been one of the extras—a zombie cheerleader—for a movie that had been filmed in the area this past summer: *High School Zombie Apocalypse!!* Another female extra, Brenda Barnes, had died from the very same condition.

"We had a case like this a few months ago," I said around the sudden chill that gripped my throat.

"Hypertrophic cardiomyopathy," he said, expression turning grave. "Two cases in a short span of time, and this one just as perplexing as the first."

An echocardiogram from a few months prior to Brenda Barnes's death had shown no sign of the heart condition, yet she'd died of it all the same. After quite a bit of frustrated puzzling, Dr. Leblanc had finally decided that either there'd been a mixup in medical records or a mistake was made in the echo.

Unfortunately, I had another theory. Several months ago Saberton Corporation was busy performing pseudo-zombie experimentation. They needed a large group of test subjects, and the movie extras fit the bill perfectly. Makeup hid side effects of rot, and behavioral issues were chalked up to acting like, well, zombies. And, of course, none of the extras knew they were part of an unethical, horrible, and utterly evil experiment to test fake brains and who knew what else.

But maybe Sarah Lynn was different and already had the heart condition? The thought that more people would die months down the road because of Saberton's bullshit made my stomach turn. "Anything in her records about it?" I asked, clinging to the slim hope.

"Nothing about any sort of heart condition in any of her records," he said, dashing my hopes to the ground and stepping on them. "And she has a *lot* of medical records. Lymphoma . . . and two months ago she went into remission." He let out a sigh.

"She traded cancer for a fatal heart problem?" I didn't like the direction of my thoughts, but I couldn't share them with Dr. Leblanc.

"It does appear to be a supremely tragic twist of fate," he said. "It's possible some aspect of her treatment contributed to the heart condition. But I'll check everything out thoroughly, especially with the similarity to the previous case."

And what if he discovers that both were extras in the movie? The thought unsettled me deeply. Would he report the link to authorities? Would they in turn dig up Saberton and its zombie research? As much as I hated the idea of the Saberton assholes getting away with murder, the last thing the zombie community needed was prying from outsiders.

He picked up a scalpel and carefully sectioned the heart while I busied myself with sewing up the incision. As much as I liked Dr. Leblanc, all I wanted right now was to get away so I could process this crap.

Chapter 2

After we finished, I returned Sarah Lynn to her body bag and placed the clear plastic bag of organs between her legs. Under normal conditions I'd wait until I was alone in the morgue, then go into the cooler and collect that brain for my own dining pleasure. But not this one. It would stay right there in the bag with the liver and kidneys and other organs. I wasn't about to risk screwing up my zombie parasite by eating a Saberton-contaminated brain. It might as well have been a lump of sawdust for all the appeal it had now.

I tucked the body away in the cooler, cleaned up the morgue and readied everything for the next day's autopsies. With that done, I grabbed my phone from my purse then headed outside and to the other side of the back parking lot. Dr. Ariston Nikas ran the zombie research lab where I worked part-time, twice a week. If anyone had answers about autopsies and zombie research, it would be him, but I wasn't about to risk that someone might overhear.

Dr. Nikas answered on the second ring. "Hello, Angel," he said, a smile in his pleasantly accented voice. "I was about to call you."

"Oh? What do you need?"

"No, you go ahead first," he said. "It must be important if you are calling."

I checked around me, then lowered my voice. "You remember the movie extra who died from the Saberton experiments a few months back? We just had another case. Sarah Lynn Harper. She was an extra too. Twenty something with hypertrophic cardiomyopathy that wasn't there two months ago."

"Oh, dear."

With those two words my hopes for a non-Saberton explanation sank. "You think the experiments caused it?"

"That would be my first theory," he replied solemnly "It's unprecedented for that condition to develop in such a short time frame. The common denominator for both victims is Saberton."

"There were a couple of hundred extras," I said, stomach knotting with anger and dread. Most of the extras had been unemployed, laid off from a factory Saberton bought and closed. The company had promised to rehire everyone once Saberton got some big juicy defense contract, but that had yet to happen. "*All* of those people could die or get screwed up? We have to do something!"

"Philip smuggled enough of the Saberton research data to me that I may be able to develop a counter agent," he said, referring to Philip Reinhardt, a Saberton employee I'd been forced to turn into a zombie when I was a prisoner in Dr. Kristi Charish's secret lab. Philip turned out to be an undercover operative working for Pietro Ivanov—the head of the local "Tribe" of zombies—and it was because of heroic efforts on Philip's part that Dr. Nikas was able to stay a step ahead of most of Saberton's bullshit.

Dr. Nikas released a sigh heavily tinged with regret. "I'd truly hoped the death of Brenda Barnes had been an isolated incident."

"I'm with you there." I began to pace in the parking lot to vent some of my anger and frustration. "But there's something else. Sarah had lymphoma that went into remission after the filming, and when we autopsied her, it was like she never had it. The same shit that killed her, cured her."

Dr. Nikas fell silent for a moment before answering. "That would be my conjecture. It apparently mimicked the zombie parasite's healing ability, which is . . . remarkable."

"It'd be cool if it didn't come with the whole dying thing," I kicked savagely at a pine cone in my way. "Saberton hasn't stopped, have they? They're still experimenting."

"They have too much invested to stop," he stated. "They aren't operating in south Louisiana anymore, but I have no doubt they're forging ahead with some form of zombie research. Without Philip undercover with them anymore, my information is sketchy."

A number of curse words leapt to mind, but I held them back for Dr. Nikas's sake. "So, what were you going to call me about?"

"I have a new protocol ready for Philip that I'd like to start as soon as possible, balancing his parasite with yours. Would you be able to come in at two this afternoon?"

I stopped pacing and tried to think if there was anything I needed to do after work. The drive to Dr. Nikas's lab took about half an hour and burned up gas I could barely afford, but I was willing to do it if it would help out my zombie-baby, Philip. Dr. Charish's stupid fake brains had badly screwed up Philip's zombie parasite, and without Dr. Nikas's work to repair the damage and stabilize him, Philip would've been dead ten times over. In fact, about once a week I volunteered blood and time so that Dr. Nikas could use the zombie mama-baby connection to develop treatments for him.

My left arm began to itch, as if in response to my thoughts about blood samples. The needles the lab used had a special coating on them to keep the parasite from closing the skin and clogging the needle, and ever since I'd started giving blood frequently, a few months back, I'd had this stupid itch. On the other hand, Philip had improved tremendously in that time, which made it worth putting up with a relatively minor annoyance.

"I can come at two," I said. "But aren't you going out with Pietro today?"

"It's a late day," he replied. "We're doing dinner instead of lunch, so no worries."

"That's good," I said, relieved to hear the "date" hadn't been cancelled. Dr. Nikas didn't get out much, and the occasional outings with Pietro always seemed to do him good. "I clock out of here at noon, so I'll run home and change after that, and see you a bit before two."

After we said our goodbyes I returned inside and settled in to work on organizing and labeling the shelves in the supply room. Although this sort of busy work usually distracted me pretty well from various troubles and worries, it sure as hell didn't work this time. By the time Nick walked in a half hour later, I'd labeled every shelf, arranged protective gear by color, and lined up scalpel blades by size.

Nick the Prick. That's what I'd secretly—and sometimes not so secretly—called him for the first several months of my time with the Coroner's Office. At some point this past spring he'd become plain old Nick to me. He still had his pompous, know-it-all moments—lots of them—but he'd also patiently tutored me for my GED without asking for any sort of payment, and had been unexpectedly kick butt helpful and supportive after I lost everything in the flood.

He stood in the doorway now and surveyed my handiwork. "Everything okay?" he asked.

"Sure!" I chirped. "Couldn't be better."

"Right." He nodded slowly, lips pursed. "Is that why you labeled that box of gloves 'Hand Cover Things'?"

Shit. I gave a weak chuckle and ripped the offending label off the box. "I wonder how that happened."

His mouth tightened into a worried frown. "Maybe your dyslexia has developed into preliminary dementia."

For a second I thought he was serious, then I rolled my eyes and flicked the wadded-up label at him. "You are such an ass."

"I think that's been established," he said with a trace of amusement in his green eyes. "And ass or not, I don't believe you."

"Yeah, sorry," I said, sighing. "I have some things on my mind and can't focus worth shit."

"Think you can focus on walking and carrying?" I gave him a baffled look, and he continued, "Doc is swamped, and I thought he could use a cappuccino. Me too, for that matter. You want to go to Dear John's Café with me to help carry?"

"You mean stop this whirlwind of inaccurate labeling?" I asked even as I dumped the label maker into a drawer. I doubted he really needed help carrying stuff, but rescuing me from my self-inflicted mental misery was the kind of gesture that had lost him his prickhood.

"I'm sure the morgue will survive," he said, then turned and headed for the door in quick strides. Halfway there he hesitated, as if remembering he should have waited for me, and I smiled to myself and hurried after him. As if to make up for running off without me, he held the door and flashed a genuine smile. He wasn't a big guy, only a few inches taller than my not-quite five foot three, but he carried enough attitude for a guy the size of Andre the Giant. I hadn't seen much of Nick since the GED tutoring finished. He usually worked a different shift, but since my awesome partner Derrel was off on vacation to the Bahamas for the next ten days, Nick was filling in for him.

Even though we'd worked together for close to a year, I didn't know all that much about Nick. Aside from making sure people knew he was a pre-med student, he didn't volunteer much personal information. Every now and then I'd ask about his family or what his childhood was like, and each time he would either suddenly realize he had something else he needed to do, or he'd quickly change the subject.

Maybe the two of us weren't all that different. Not that he'd been a loser addict dropout or anything, but maybe being a pompous prick was his way of putting something in his past behind him and saying, "Fuck y'all. I'm here, and I'm cool no matter what."

Or maybe I was just making shit up to hear myself think.

Outside, a cool breeze made me wish I'd grabbed my jacket. It wasn't cold enough to bother going back for it, but it left no doubt the Louisiana summer was over. We took a shortcut across the back lot then skirted the St. Edwards Parish Courthouse to put us on Dead End Way, a busy avenue that had long outgrown its name.

"Anything I can help with?" Nick asked after we crossed and started down the side street toward the shop.

It took me a second to realize he was referring to my lack of focus. "Nah," I said. "Personal stuff. I'll get over it, but thanks anyway." I couldn't exactly tell him I was worried about the long term effects of unethical zombie research on innocent people.

"You always shake bad shit off in no time, so I bet you'll be doing better before the day's out." For an instant he looked embarrassed by his own words of encouragement, then he cleared his throat. "Maybe some hot chocolate will perk you up. My treat."

I gave him a warm smile. For all his Nickitude, I appreciated the decent person and friend under it all. I kind of suspected he liked me, but he seemed to be totally respectful of my relationship with Marcus, and he'd never said or done anything to make me feel uncomfortable.

"Thanks," I said. "Don't mind me. I'm just moody." I hesitated, then forged on into scary territory. "I sorta told Doc I was going to sign up for college classes next term."

His head snapped around. "At TPCC? That's a big step."

I stuffed my hands in my pockets, his shock confirming my suspicion that it was a big and *stupid* step. "Yeah. I should probably back out and wait until I have more tutoring under my belt with Jennifer." And that could be a while since the dyslexia specialist cost a fortune. I had to space out my sessions in order to pay for them. Hell, for that matter, how was I supposed to pay for college?

"No!" Nick commanded, bringing my near escape from college to a screeching halt. "You can do it. No point in putting it off. And, uh . . ." He trailed off and seemed to find the sidewalk ahead very interesting.

The guy could be kind of cute when he got flustered. I hid a smile. "And what?"

"Maybe I could help out," he blurted a little too eagerly, then backpedaled to a more casual, doesn't-matter-to-me tone. "I mean, you know, if you get stuck on something."

My smile slipped out as this particular worry faded away. "I'd like that," I said and meant it. "Though I still don't know how I can afford tuition."

"Financial aid," he said firmly. "Grants, scholarships, loans. I'll help you with the applications."

Well, there went my last remaining excuse. "Okay, so do you

think I should take Introduction to Life Sciences or Biology one-oh-one?"

"If you want the credits to really mean something, take one-oh-one. Life Sciences won't transfer to a four year school."

"Wait." I blinked, then shook my head. "A four-year? I haven't even thought about that."

Nick shrugged and lifted his chin in his I-know-all-about-this posture. "No point in wasting time," he declared. "Better to have credits that transfer than not. It's the only smart choice."

I gulped. One-oh-one was sure to be a lot harder than Life Sciences. "I guess that makes sense," I said weakly, wishing it didn't.

"Of course it does," he said as he opened the door to the shop. A delicious mix of smells flooded out—coffee and chocolate and all sorts of baked gooey things. "I'll order. You want anything besides hot chocolate?"

"Since you're buying, I'll have one of those cherry cream cheese pastries," I replied with a grin. "I love those things."

"You got it," he said and joined the line by the counter.

Dear John's Café offered good beverages, pastry, and snacks, along with plentiful booths and decent free Wi-Fi. But its claim to local fame was the paper enshrined on the wall near the register—a Dear John letter that actually started off with "Dear John." The letter had been written to the owner, John Hickey, ten years ago by his wife when she left him for his brother's ex-wife. According to local legend, after a heavy drinking binge and a night in jail, John realized it was the best thing that had ever happened to him, quit his insurance sales gig, traded in his Lexus for a Toyota, downsized his house, and invested everything in the café. Who the hell knew if any of it was true, but it made a good story, and great coffee and a solid business model made for a booming business.

"Angel," a woman called from the far end of the shop.

I looked toward the voice and saw Pietro Ivanov and Jane Pennington cozied up in a half-circle booth by the back wall. Jane gave me a warm smile and gestured for me to come over. A pleased tingle ran through me as I waved and returned the smile. It still floored me that anyone as cool as *Congresswoman* Jane Pennington wanted anything to do with little old me. She even called me on occasion when she wanted to poll "ordinary, everyday people" for opinions. I was far from either, but I wasn't about to tell her that.

I tapped Nick on the shoulder. "Hey, I'm going to be by that booth by the back wall," I told him. "Come find me when you're done? I have some people I want you to meet."

He nodded acknowledgment, and I headed back toward Pietro and Jane. Pietro was a rich-as-fuck local businessman, and also uncle to my boyfriend, Marcus Ivanov. But more importantly, Pietro as head of the local group of zombies, devoted himself to their survival and welfare, at times by whatever means necessary. I didn't always agree with the "necessary means" Pietro and his organization used, but I'd also learned that none of the issues they dealt with were black and white.

Plus, I didn't have much room to talk. Less than five months ago I'd bashed a man's head in with a baseball bat and then feasted on his brains. Sure, he'd been shooting me seconds before, but there was no denying I'd used *necessary means* to remove the threat.

Pietro watched me approach, a relaxed smile on his face that only seemed to make its appearance around Jane. Sixtyish-looking, stocky but fit, he complemented her effortless elegance perfectly. Half-finished cups of coffee and the remains of a shared pastry sat on the table in front of them. I gave Pietro a nod of greeting then smiled to Jane. "I didn't know you were in town."

"I'm not really," she said with a quiet laugh. "Only passing through to take care of a little business in my district and see Pietro."

I glanced over as Nick approached. "This is my friend Nick Galatas," I told them. "He's one of the death investigators at the Coroner's Office, and he's also totally responsible for me finally passing the GED." I grinned. "Nick, this is Congresswoman Jane Pennington and Pietro Ivanov." I didn't try to hide the hint of smugness in my tone that I knew such cool people. If the situation was reversed, Nick would be all over it.

Nick did the handshake thing with both of them, seeming totally confident and comfortable. "I helped a little with Angel's preparation and studying," he said, "but Angel was the one in the test room. She worked hard and earned it."

A little heat rose in my face at the praise. I *had* worked hard, dammit, but it was still cool to have it recognized. "It's too bad you can't be here a little longer," I said to Jane. "You're going to miss the oh-so-awesome Nutria Festival this weekend."

Pained amusement lit her eyes. "Believe it or not, I gave a speech there last year on the condition of our wetlands."

Pietro laid his hand over hers on the table, gave it a squeeze. "We met at an incredibly tedious fundraiser only a few days after that. Jane stopped me from slitting my wrist with a broken champagne glass to escape the boredom."

A *joke* from Pietro? If he didn't watch out, having Jane as a girlfriend was going to turn him into a normal person.

Jane laughed. "I'm not sure it was quite so dramatic," she said.

"You were still a state senator then, if I'm not mistaken?" Nick asked.

Pietro smiled broadly. "Right up until the now *former* Congressman Dale Grubbs was caught taking kickbacks."

"I couldn't have possibly won the special election to replace him without your help and support," she told Pietro, voice warm with affection, then gave me a smile. "And as much as I regret missing out on nutria jambalaya," she shuddered, "I'm off to New York this afternoon for a few engagements before The Child Find League Fundraiser Saturday, then back to DC. Committee meetings, staff meetings, and more meetings." She shuddered once again.

"You're on the House Judiciary Committee, right?" Nick asked, in a way that made it clear he already knew the answer. At Jane's nod he continued with a smile, "Congratulations on that. Impressive feat for a freshman Congresswoman to score a spot on such an influential committee, but I suppose having doctorates in Political Science and Law helped considerably."

I tried not to look as surprised as I was at the two doctorates thing. And here I'd assumed she was a medical doctor. Duh.

Jane chuckled. "It certainly didn't hurt, though I'm still getting used to the maneuverings and behind-the-scene deals that aren't taught in the classroom."

Nick gave a knowing nod. "Your detractors who are complaining that you're not doing enough to secure a defense contract for Saberton don't understand how the system works."

An expression of true regret swept over her face. "I would love to wave a magic wand and reopen the factory so that all those people could be rehired," she said, referring to the employees laid off after Saberton bought a farm machinery company and then failed to obtain a hoped-for defense contract. "But the sad and brutal truth is that in order to ensure Saberton lands that contract, I would have to expend every bit of political capital I've acquired in the past few months, and owe quite a few favors besides." She sighed. "I can't afford to 'blow my wad' on the Saberton contract."

Nick nodded again. "Not when there are bills coming up for programs and funding that have far more impact on this area," he said. "Wetlands, drilling rights, flood control. It would be a short term fix with long term issues."

I glanced over at Nick, probably with my mouth hanging open, impressed and surprised that he had a clue. Hell, more than a clue. I caught the gist of what they were talking about, and as much as I wanted to see those factory jobs come back, I had a hard time getting behind anything that helped Saberton Corporation in any way. I figured Pietro couldn't either, not with their track record of fuck-y'all exploitation of both zombies and regular people. Yet Jane's reasoning seemed logical and sound, and not at all based on an "I Hate Saberton" point of view. Then again, as far as I knew, Jane still knew nothing about the zombies. I had no idea if or when Pietro planned to tell her, but that sort of thing was *waaay* into the sort of none-of-my-business that I actually abided by.

Jane smiled at Nick, genuine and appreciative. "You know my pain. Damned if I do, damned if I don't. I'm going to have to find other solutions for the unemployment situation." She sighed. "It's a frustrating dance."

Pietro leaned in and gave her a kiss on the cheek. "One you do with poise and grace, my dear."

Jane gave Pietro a warm smile accompanied by a soft-eyed look that left no doubt how she felt about him.

Time for Nick and me to leave the lovebirds to do their thing. "We should get going," I said. "It was great running into you two."

Jane reached and touched my arm. "It was wonderful to see you, Angel, and a pleasure to meet you, Nick."

We made our goodbyes and headed to the counter. I picked up the box with pastries and glanced over at Nick. "How did you know so much about that stuff?"

"I read a lot," he said with a shrug as he collected the carrier with the drinks. "And this is a hot topic, locally."

"I'm saving up for a computer," I said as we headed to the door. "Maybe I can watch news videos or something." A gust of wind sent leaves scuttling along the sidewalk as we stepped out.

"It's important to keep up with what's going on," he replied with a knowing nod.

"By the way, thanks for asking me to come with you. I needed the distraction."

He shot me a smug look. "I know."

Laughing, I punched him in the arm, hard enough for him to feel it, but not hard enough to spill the coffee and chocolate he carried. I had my priorities.

He made a show of rubbing his arm, but we were both smiling when we returned to the office.

Chapter 3

The living room was empty when I walked through my front door, but I heard the shower—our *only* shower—running. Crap.

"Hey, dad," I yelled through the bathroom door. "You gonna be much longer?"

"Be a coupla minutes," he hollered back. "I just got in."

Double crap. No way could I fake it and go to the lab without a full shower. Not with bone dust in my hair and the smell of *yuck* clinging to me. "I gotta be somewhere," I shouted. "And I'm all dirty from the morgue."

"Yeah, well, if you stop shouting at me I'll be a lot faster," he shot back.

Sighing, I bit back an obnoxious comeback. He'd only get revenge by staying in the shower even longer. Stripping off my clothes as I went, I headed to my room and killed some time finding stuff to change into once I no longer reeked of morgue-funk. Well, killed a couple of minutes. Didn't take long to go through my miniscule wardrobe. So far I'd managed to replace the necessities I lost in the flood: work uniforms, bras and undies, socks, a couple of pairs of jeans and some miscellaneous shirts. And I had exactly one nice outfit—a butt-hugging skirt and a silky blouse, with some fuck-me pumps that I'd scooped up on clearance, beating out a busty red-head who'd been reaching for them.

I resisted the very silly urge to put on the skirt and blouse and pumps since they'd be incredibly inappropriate for going to the lab, and pushed down the totally crazy bit of wondering how Philip would react to me in the outfit—and where the hell had *that* come from anyway? Instead I found jeans and a long-sleeved t-shirt. But with my clothes all nicely laid out, I had nothing left to do except wait with increasing aggravation as the shower continued to run. And now my dad was singing. *Singing!* Scowling, I wrapped a towel around me and marched back down the hall.

"C'mon, Dad!" I yelled with an accompanying pound on the door. "I'm gonna be late! What the hell's taking you so long?"

"I'm washing my goddamn hair!"

"Y'only got about twelve hairs on that head of yours!"

His response was to start singing again. Loudly and badly.

It was war.

I tested the doorknob. Locked, and I had a feeling he'd nipped out and done so while I was going through my clothing. Sneaky bastard. But I could be devious too. I ran to the kitchen and turned the cold water on full blast, then went to the half-bathroom near the front of the house, turned *that* water on, and flushed the toilet for good measure. Listening, I waited, and about fifteen seconds a yelp and cursing rewarded my efforts, followed by the shower going off.

I quickly turned the water off in the bathroom and kitchen, then returned to the hallway outside the main bathroom, leaned against the wall and folded my arms over my towel-covered chest. I heard grumbling and muttering, but also a rustle of sound that I hoped was a towel drying flesh.

My dad yanked the door open and gave me a dark scowl, but I thought I detected a gleam of appreciation in his eye. "You're lucky I got somewhere to be, Angel," he huffed, then marched off toward his bedroom with the towel wrapped around his waist, leaving a trail of wet footprints down the hallway.

With a smug smile, I claimed the shower, and didn't even mind that I had to clean out the drain first.

Since I was already running late, I made do with a quickie shower that was enough to wash the smell of death off me. Probably a good thing I raced through it, since even at super speed the water temp edged toward not-even-close-to-hot by the time I rinsed off. I dressed quickly, shoved my fingers through my wet hair along with a bit of gel, swiped some mascara across my lashes, grabbed my purse, and headed for the door.

Then stopped dead at the sight of my dad standing in the kitchen, buttoning his cuffs and *whistling*. I sniffed. Cologne? And, wait, cuffs? Not a t-shirt or sweatshirt?

Nope, Dad had on black denim pants—not raggedy jeans—a

plaid shirt that actually looked stylish, and cowboy boots. His hair was combed, and his face free from stubble.

"Do you have a job interview?" I asked.

His smile was nothing sort of *smug*. "Nope. Got me a date."

It took me a second to re-engage my brain, and I barely stopped myself from saying, *With a woman?* "With who?" I managed instead.

"Tammy Elwood," he replied. "She tends bar down at Kaster's."

"I don't know her," I said, unable to keep the suspicion out of my voice.

The look he gave me was tinged with amusement. "I bet I know lots of people you don't, Angelkins."

I knew I was being silly, but damn it, my dad simply didn't *date*. "How long have you known her?" I asked, trying a different tack.

He slipped a jacket on. "Not long. It's actually a double date with Belluci and his lady. They're kinda settin' us up together."

Oh, lordy. Rick Belluci was a loud redneck with a huge beer gut who seemed to know every racist, sexist, and otherwise inappropriate joke in existence. He and my dad used to be drinking buddies, staying out every Thursday night until the bars closed or kicked them out. I could only imagine what kind of woman Belluci would think was right for my dad.

"Are y'all going to a bar?" I asked, trying hard to be casual, but I heard the edge of worry in my voice. Dad had been doing pretty good with controlling his drinking lately, and I wanted it to stay that way.

He gave me a faint smile, understanding in his eyes. "We're just gonna go see a movie and maybe get a bite after, I promise."

"Well, call me if you're gonna be out too late."

To his credit he didn't laugh. "Only if you promise to do the same."

That was fair, I supposed. "Deal." I moved to him, gave him a kiss on the cheek. God, but we'd come so far. He responded with a hug, then left the house, a spring in his step that I didn't think I'd ever seen before.

My dad has a date. How weird was that?

Chapter 4

I wanted a distraction from my worries about Saberton's experimentation, and the universe happily obliged. I rubbed my arms against the frigid air of what I called the Head Room as I peered into the vat. About two feet across, the container looked like an oversized stainless steel crock pot, but I sure as hell didn't want to eat what was cooking in it.

"*That*," I said with a shiver of disgust and delight, "is seriously gross."

Thick, dark pink liquid like blood-tinged mucus oozed its way around the vat, while something resembling a deformed fetus drifted below the surface of the snot. Stubby little hands curled up by its chest, and misshapen lumps like developing organs formed a weird pot-belly. Uneven legs splayed out in opposite directions. No umbilical cord, and the heart wasn't beating, but I had the weirdest impression the entire thing was vibrating, like a buzz from a bee-hive.

From neck to butt, the fetus-thing was about two inches long, but the truly weird and gross part was the full-sized head. Wisps of dark hair clung to the skull, waving sluggishly in the thick liquid. The face had Korean features, though it was hard to tell right now with the blotchy grey and shriveled skin.

Kang. The first zombie I ever knew, besides myself. Or rather, the first zombie I ever knew who I *knew* was a zombie. Kang had taught me a lot about survival as a zombie: how often I'd need to eat human brains, how exertion increased the hunger, and how my mental faculties would degrade along with my body if I went too long without eating brains. But Kang hadn't listened to me when it counted, and he'd ended up the victim of a serial killer who'd been targeting zombies and chopping their heads off.

And *that* was one hell of a seriously complicated story.

I pulled my gaze away from fetus-Kang. His vat was one of six in the dimly lit room. A pale and thin man with dark wavy hair crouched by a control panel as he made adjustments—Jacques Leroux, the lab tech and Dr. Nikas's assistant. On the other side of Kang's vat stood Pietro, the relaxed smile of earlier now hard and flat as he looked down at Kang.

Dr. Nikas stood next to Pietro, his arms folded loosely over his chest as he peered into the vat. Average height and unimposing, the director of the lab had light brown eyes set in a kind face, and brown hair pulled back in a ponytail that hung to his shoulder blades. I didn't know exactly what Dr. Nikas was a doctor of, but I figured it was a lot of different things, especially since I had a strong suspicion he'd been around for more than a few centuries, even though he didn't look older than late forties. While Pietro ran things, Dr. Nikas was the heart and soul of the lab and, from what I'd seen, had final say on what happened within it. On the outside, the lab was a drab industrial building smack dab in the middle of Nowhere, Louisiana with nothing but pines and swamp for miles in any direction. However, within those boring walls was a high tech research lab and small medical facility, like something out of a science fiction movie.

"Kang grew that much in only one day?" I asked Dr. Nikas. "I changed the fluid yesterday morning and he was still a prune-skinned head. Same as he's been for months."

"Amazing, isn't it?" Dr. Nikas said. "My theory is that he hasn't been quiescent at all, but rather, preparing." He leaned over the vat and peered with avid delight at the deformed thing that could have been straight out of a horror flick. "Assessing resources and checking the DNA blueprints one might say." He lifted his head and gave me a warm smile.

The hard line of Pietro's mouth flattened even more. "Ari, how long before you know if the memory is intact?"

Dr. Nikas straightened. "I don't know when I'll be able to determine anything about *his* memory or cognitive function," he said, and I didn't miss the emphasis on "his." This wasn't an impersonal lab experiment to Dr. Nikas. Each vat in here contained a severed zombie head, and every single one was a person with their name on the vat handwritten on a card in elegant script. Little personal touches like that told me Dr. Nikas gave a shit. "It may not be until he fully regrows," he added.

"How long will that take?" I gestured at fetus-Kang. "I mean, this happened in less than a day."

"It's one of the many things we still don't know," Dr. Nikas said with gentle indulgence. "This growth happened very quickly, but he has been in stasis again for the last six hours." He spread his hands. "It may come in spurts. Or it may not happen again until we move him into the full vat where he has ample resources." He gestured in the direction of the new coffin-looking container on the other side of the room. "It's all very new territory. Theoretically, the potential is there for full regrowth to happen quickly—perhaps within weeks. We'll know more after he grows again."

Jacques moved around the vat to check another control panel, and I stepped back and out of his way. "You'll, uh, track the rate of growth over time and then make a projection from that?" I asked Dr. Nikas. A year ago—hell, six months ago—I wouldn't have known what any of that meant.

Dr. Nikas's smile widened. "That's right, Angel," he said. "Jacques can show you how to access the charts and raw data on one of the workstations. You can see our current projections and watch as they adjust with additional data."

Pietro frowned in obvious impatience. "Can't the EEG give you some indication of what memory or cognitive function Kang will come back with?"

Annoyance whispered across Dr. Nikas's face. "It shows us nothing more than it did before the growth," he stated. "With the parasite fully encapsulating his brain, this is what we get." He nodded toward a screen that showed flat lines alternating with wild spikes every few seconds. Even I could tell it was screwy. "Until the parasite activity returns to baseline, I can't tell what Kang's functional level is." He exhaled. "Remember, he came in from Kristi, and her initial preservation and handling was far from optimal."

I didn't bother hiding my sneer. Dr. Kristi Charish was the neurobiologist who'd kidnapped me then used me for her psycho zombie experiments. She'd been under Pietro's house arrest ever since he'd captured her after the secret lab fiasco and, like Dr. Nikas, lived at the lab 24/7. However, unlike the good doctor, she wore a tracking anklet and had round the clock supervision by one of her three assigned guards. Kristi had shown herself to be an unstable, reckless, and treacherous bitch, and had broken more laws than I could count, but we couldn't exactly turn her over to the cops. *Yes, officer, this respected scientist kidnapped me and made me chew on a couple of almost dead guys. Why? Oh, y'see, I'm a zombie and eat human brains, and she . . . Wait, what are you doing with that Taser? Hey, stop! Ow!*

It would only go downhill from there.

She was currently working with Dr. Nikas to develop a nutritional substitute—a.k.a. fake brains—that zombies could survive off of instead of human brains. I had little doubt that if Kristi wasn't such a sharp researcher Pietro would have made her disappear rather than keeping her, and I suspected that was the only reason Dr. Nikas tolerated the outright slavery under his roof. Setting her free simply wasn't an option.

Dr. Nikas gave me a nod. "You can close it now, Angel."

Pietro backed away from the vat as I replaced the lid, but his gaze lingered on fetus-Kang for another few seconds before shifting to Ari. "I want to be kept apprised of *any* changes," he stated, then pivoted and briskly exited the room.

Dr. Nikas and I followed him out, leaving Jacques to finish his adjustments.

"Angel, I'll meet you at the central lab in about five minutes," Dr. Nikas said tightly as we reached a cross-corridor. "I need to have a brief *chat* with Pietro."

"Gotcha." I didn't mind being left out of that particular chat. I continued straight while Dr. Nikas turned left, but when I passed the door to the lounge off the central lab, I spied Pietro's head of security, Brian Archer, sitting on the couch and flipping through a decade-old magazine.

"Hey, you missed the freak show," I said, ducking into the lounge. "Kang's head is *way* gross."

Brian set the magazine aside. "I think I get enough *freak show* without an extra dose," he said with a casual smile. Brian didn't have the kind of looks that turned heads, but he made up for it in presence. He looked like he was in his forties, but he once told me he'd been a zombie for a little over fifteen years, and I'd never worked up the nerve to ask him his age. I'd never seen him looking sloppy or dressed casually, and today was no different. Dark navy suit, cream-colored shirt with a tie that coordinated without calling attention to itself. Short brown hair and deep brown eyes. Nails neatly trimmed. No jewelry of any sort. Not a man to be fucked with.

"Yeah, I guess you do," I said with a laugh as I flopped into a chair. "What are you doing out here? Haven't seen you in a while."

"I have a security meeting not far from here in a little while," he explained, then tapped his upper chest. "I figured now was a good time for Dr. Nikas to check out my port and test a new mod."

I'd only found out about ports and mods a few months ago, but I was seriously considering putting them on my Christmas list. Mods—modifiers—were specialized drugs that revved up or toned down parasite activity as needed. The port itself was implanted beneath the skin and provided an easy way to get a mod into the body. With a port, mods could either be delivered quickly, dumping into the system all at once, or the drug could be stored and set to release slowly. Mods could have some pretty awesome effects, such as more efficient brain usage, or better senses, or resistance to the kind of tranquilizers that worked on zombies. All sorts of useful stuff.

The drawback was that only one or two mods could be used at the same time, and some couldn't be mixed at all without big side effects. They were a lot like regular human drugs in that respect.

"Everything go okay with that?" I asked.

"Some kinks with the mod still, but it's looking promising," he said. "It's designed to be a short term turbo charge of zombie abilities. Speed, strength, reflexes, senses, that sort of thing. Would be nice to have for emergencies." He stretched and stifled a yawn. "But right now I'm simply waiting to see if Mr. Ivanov has anything for me before I take off."

"Don't let the excitement of it all overwhelm you," I said with a grin. "How's everything else going?"

"Business as usual in the zombie security world," he said, which I figured was his way of saying he couldn't talk about anything. "Never a dull moment with the Tribe."

The Tribe. Pietro Ivanov's organization was actually a number of corporations—a chain of funeral homes, real estate, construction, and even health care clinics that disguised the zombie research. And probably a ton I didn't have a clue about as well. Up until a couple of months ago I'd privately referred to the whole deal as "The Zombie Mafia," yet after some time working steadily in the lab, I discovered that the people *in* the organization—humans and zombies alike—referred to it as "the Tribe." After some thought—and with the greater knowledge I had of Pietro, his people, and his goals—the reality of the whole common-ties-common-support thing settled in, and I grudgingly agreed that Tribe was a better nickname.

Most of the time, at least. There were reasons the whole Mafia tag had come up in the first place, and that undercurrent was still alive and kicking.

I peered at Brian. "Don't you ever get to go off and play on your own?"

Brian's eyes widened in exaggerated wonder. "You mean . . . not be on call?" Then he laughed. "I have down time, sure, but I'm never truly off duty."

"Well, that sucks," I said, narrowing my eyes. "When do you get to be your own person?"

"I'm doing what I want to do," he said, giving me a reassuring smile. "I have a couple of hobbies to fill in the gaps. I can't imagine a different lifestyle."

I wondered about the gaps. As far as I knew, he didn't have a girlfriend. At one time he'd seemed seriously interested in my best friend, Naomi—formerly known as Heather—but that fell flat when she hooked up with Kyle Griffin, one of Brian's top security guys.

Brian seemed content enough, though, and I knew it really wasn't any of my business. Not that I'd ever let that whole "none of my business" thing stop me from being a nosy buttinsky before.

"Well," I said, "if you're okay with your schedule, I guess I won't need to have strong words with Pietro after all."

Brian grimaced, obviously not *entirely* sure I was teasing. "Not on my account."

"I'll behave," I said. "Don't worry."

He wiped his brow in mock-relief, though maybe not totally *mock*. "Don't go getting me into trouble," he said, then stood as a tall, black woman with braids that hung to mid back entered the room. Radiating ultra-confidence with a dash of scary calm, Rachel Delancey was Brian's second in command, and one of the few female zombies Pietro had working for him.

Her gaze slid over me as if I was a steaming pile of dog shit on the carpet before it came to rest on Brian. Yeah. We weren't going to be best buds anytime soon. Her idea of security probably didn't include a new zombie like me hanging around at the super secret lab. But I had a niggling feeling there was more to it than that. She'd seemed okay with me at first, then gradually went colder than a polar bear's ass. I'd tried a few times to be friendly but got nowhere. The only thing I could figure was that she'd found out about my loser past and thought I was a security risk. Or maybe she thought I was going to take advantage of Marcus or Pietro or Dr. Nikas. Whatever the deal was, I couldn't see any way to change her opinion of me. Oh, well. Her loss.

"Everything set for Dr. Charish's transfer?" Brian asked her, and I realized he was referring to the mental health breaks that Dr. Nikas insisted be provided for Kristi. Pietro would've been fine with Kristi chained to a lab station and locked in a cell at night, but that shit wouldn't fly with Dr. Nikas. At his insistence, and despite Pietro's grumbling, Kristi was allowed to spend two days every few weeks at one of Pietro's remote hunting lodges.

Rachel shot a quick and disapproving glance my way as if she really didn't want to say anything with me in the room. I kept my smile on my face and resisted the urge to roll my eyes. Who the hell did she think I'd blab to?

"We're good to go," she told Brian. "Simon is driving Chris and Dr. Charish, then the other two on her guard rotation will meet them at the lodge after the security meeting." She passed him a paper. "Here's the full schedule."

Brian looked over the schedule then passed it back to her. "You're aware that Mr. Ivanov will be heading up there as well?" She replied with an affirmative, and he glanced at his watch. "Everything looks good then. I'll see you in about half an hour for the meeting."

Rachel gave a crisp nod and threw one last disapproving glance my way before sweeping out.

I made my best *Bite Me* face at her back. "I can't get over how warm and fuzzy she is to me. The constant adoration is getting a little embarrassing."

Brian stifled a laugh. "She's opinionated but efficient as hell and damn good at what she does." He abruptly stood, eyes on the doorway. A few seconds later a scowling Pietro stepped in. Damn, Brian either had a super-senses mod working or was seriously tanked on brains. I hadn't heard, seen, or smelled whatever Brian had. But in the next instant I remembered the dude had a wicked sense of smell. Like, *crazy* good—he could even tell by scent alone if someone was lying.

"Any changes, sir?" Brian asked Pietro.

Pietro shook his head. Whatever the chat with Dr. Nikas had been about, it hadn't left him in a sunny mood. "I'll meet with Kristi at the lodge as usual, then go out to dinner with Ari. I'll call you after I leave Kristi, as we need to discuss some matters."

"Yes, sir. I'll be clear of the security meeting before you leave the lodge." Brian checked his watch again. "Speaking of which, I should get going unless you have anything else for me, sir."

Pietro responded with a vague wave of dismissal. Brian gave him a respectful nod, shot a quick smile my way, then departed.

Pietro wiped the frown from his face as he shifted his focus to me. "Angel, we didn't have a chance to speak earlier," he said. "Ari tells me you're doing very well here at the lab. Is it something you want to continue with?"

"Yeah, totally!" I replied, doing my best not to grin like an idiot at the praise from Dr. Nikas.

"Good. We'll talk in a few days about making your position here more permanent, though in an arrangement that will fit in around your morgue work."

"That would be awesome," I said fervently, though I clearly heard the unspoken reminder that I was allowed to work at the lab only because Pietro allowed it. I worked for *him,* not Dr. Nikas, and he didn't want me to forget that. "And, um, I'm going to be taking a couple of college classes next term. Is it okay to work my schedule around that too?"

He raised his eyebrows. "That's excellent, Angel. We'll certainly discuss that as well."

"I really appreciate it," I said in relief, meaning every word. Not only did I enjoy the hell out of the work, but I also had a fairly hefty loan from Pietro to pay off. When my dad and I lost everything in the flood after the spillway collapsed, we only recovered because I was able to borrow money from Pietro to buy a new place, along with cars, clothes, and all the other shit that comes in handy when dealing with Life.

"You're welcome," Pietro said with a slight nod as if I'd said exactly what I was supposed to say. "I'll call." And with that he turned and headed out.

I wandered back to the central hub of the lab to see if Dr. Nikas was ready for me, but found it unoccupied and quiet other than the soft ping of one of the workstations with an analysis in progress. This domed circular room formed the heart of the complex, with several corridors and doors going off in different directions, and thick sliding glass security doors that led toward the exit. Fancy equipment lined the walls, and a semi-circular island in the middle of the room held even more machines and computer workstations.

Not more than half a minute later, Dr. Nikas stepped out of the hallway that led to his office, looking somewhat harried. I had a strong feeling he'd waited for Pietro to leave first.

"Everything okay?" I asked.

He blew out a breath. "Forgive me. He gets to me sometimes," he said, then shook his head. "Nothing to worry about. My full focus is now on you and Philip and the parasite-balancing procedure I wish to attempt."

"If this is a bad time to, er, balance my parasite we can always do it tomorrow," I said.

"It isn't a bad time." He gave me a reassuring smile. "Philip will be here any minute, and he needs this," he added. "I have a few things to get ready, but I won't keep you two waiting long."

"It's cool." I held up my phone. "I brought a book." Well, an audiobook. My reading speed was somewhere between garden-slug-slow and oh-my-god-glaciers-are-faster, but thanks to the local library's audio lending program I was gradually catching up on all sorts of books that were "should" reads, as well as a good number that were just plain fun.

"Excellent," Dr. Nikas murmured as he turned to leave, though I wasn't sure he actually heard me. Already he had the familiar unfocused look in his eyes that told me he was sorting through a new research problem.

I dropped into a chair at one of the computer workstations, stuck my earbuds in and settled down with the book—a purely fun one, and a few minutes later Philip Reinhardt entered through the glass doors. He had a smile on his face but also a heaviness in his step as though the movement took effort. Philip was a good looking guy, with blond hair cut close above a ruggedly handsome face, but his blue eyes revealed the pain he tried to hide. I hit pause on the book and yanked my earbuds out.

"Hey, Zombie Mama," he said with a grin. "Ready for another day of excitement?" He rubbed his arm. "Jacques just stuck me about a dozen times. I think half of them were just for fun."

"I feel ya! He got me earlier. I'm starting to think he's more vampire than zombie." I rubbed at the itchy place on my arm.

"A vampire zombie." He laughed softly. "Now that would be a rough life. He'd need blood *and* brains."

"Well, Jacques is in the right place for it." I gave Philip a thoughtful look and made a point of stroking my chin. "Coincidence? Hmmm . . . got a stake handy?"

"I could probably find a pencil around here, but if the parasite heals the stake wound, it could get ugly." He did his own thoughtful chin-stroke. "You'd need a stake to the heart and a bullet to the brainstem at the same time."

"You've thought about this."

He gave me an innocent smile. "Who wouldn't?"

"Most normal people?" I suggested.

"That counts us out."

I couldn't argue with that.

Together we headed into the treatment room to wait for Dr. Nikas. Power lights glowed on several of the devices on the counter, and Dr. Nikas's odd shorthand covered half the whiteboard on the wall beside the cabinets. A near-empty glass of sparkling grape juice beside a stack of computer print outs told me he'd already been working in here this morning.

The procedure chair looked like a cross between a recliner and a torture device, but I plopped into it anyway. Its position gave the best view of the awesome mural that covered the entire far wall—a scene of a rolling grassy meadow and a distant mountain with brilliant blue sky above. Philip leaned against the exam table, and I surreptitiously studied him. Adjusting to life as a zombie wasn't a breeze under the best conditions, and his had been pure crap. His parasite was damaged from the bad fake brains Kristi had fed him shortly after he was turned, and as a result he suffered excruciating chronic pain, muscle spasms, and other unpleasant symptoms—a mess of afflictions we simply called the Plague. Much of that had been brought under control or was improving with the treatments, but he still wasn't anywhere near a hundred percent.

"Your color is better," I remarked. "But you look worn out."

He nodded, unoffended by the observation. "My sleep has been off, and the leg pain hasn't let up," he admitted, "but otherwise it's been a decent week." He snorted and quirked a faint smile. "I puked my guts out after the last treatment, but luckily it didn't last long. I'm all for no puking this time."

I grimaced. "Yeah, that sucks. I wish there was more I could do."

"I'm not complaining," he assured me. "I promise. Without you helping I doubt I'd have made it this long."

"Gotta take care of my zombie baby," I said with a smile that masked a persistent sick fear. After eating the bad brains Philip had turned two of the Saberton guards into zombies, and both had died within three months of being captured by Pietro's people, despite Dr. Nikas's best efforts to save them. My blood helped in treatments for Philip, but I still worried. What if the treatments stopped working? What if my blood stopped making a difference?

I took a deep breath and tried to focus my worry into anger at the one who'd done this to him. None of this would have happened without Kristi Fucking Charish.

Philip's gaze went to the door as it opened, and he pushed off the exam table. Speak of the devil. "Good morning, Kristi," he said with a pleasant smile to the slim, auburn-haired woman who entered.

She gave a slightly tremulous smile in return and kept her eyes away from me as she moved closer to Philip. "You're waiting for the new treatment?" she asked, reaching toward him as if for reassurance.

He took her hand and gave it a comforting squeeze. "We are indeed." He glanced toward the door again as Rachel entered, then he returned his attention to Kristi. "This must be an outing day," he noted.

"Outing weekend," Rachel stated, tone brisk but pleasant enough with Philip. "Chris will be leaving with Dr. Charish in a few minutes, but she wanted to see you first."

Philip gave a low chuckle and tucked a stray wisp of hair behind Kristi's ear. "Of course you did."

I watched in stony silence. Philip had no reason to like Kristi, and every reason to hate her fucking guts. Yet they sure as hell looked buddy-buddy.

No, not like buddies, I decided. More like . . . a master and his dog. I didn't have the warm fuzzies for Kristi either, but this docile version seriously creeped me out. I'd seen her like this before and had assumed she was medicated, but now I realized that wasn't likely. After all, Pietro kept her alive because she was useful and clever, and she wouldn't be either if she was drugged to the gills.

A man with bright green eyes and about a billion freckles stepped into the doorway and leaned against the frame. "Philip, you're hogging all the beautiful women," he said with an infectious grin. Chris Peterson, another member of the security team.

"Can you blame me?" Philip replied. Kristi turned and gave Chris a bright and genuine smile.

"Not one bit!" Chris stuffed his hands into the pockets of a faded leather bomber-style jacket and gave me a nod and Kristi a quick wink, but the smile he turned on Rachel had a lot more heat behind it. To my surprise her expression softened, and she responded with a look that could only be described as *sultry*. Hot damn, tough as nails Rachel wanted to get nailed?

A laugh tried to escape me, and I jerked my attention back to Chris. He wasn't *handsome*, but he was kind and funny and light-hearted. Nothing at all like Rachel—but maybe that's what she liked about him? He kept himself in good shape, and though he wasn't Mr. Suit And Tie like Brian, he dressed well. Today he had on a dark red oxford-style shirt and pressed khaki pants, and of course the awesome leather jacket. He shifted, and I noticed a pair of aviator sunglasses tucked into the front pocket of his shirt.

"Do you fly?" I asked. "Or do you just like the accessories?" I abruptly realized that my second question could be taken as a bit snide. "Crap, I mean—"

Chris simply laughed and held up his hand to stop me from digging myself any deeper. "Both!" he declared. "Been flying for close to twenty years. I actually had to stop about eight years back. Developed Type 1 diabetes, and they grounded me." What seemed like grief briefly shadowed his eyes, and I realized that being unable to fly must have been a devastating loss. Then he brightened again. "I got back in the air as soon as possible after I was turned, trust me."

"That's so cool," I said fervently, ridiculously pleased that the zombie thing had given that back to him. "I've never been in a plane," I confessed.

"Yeah?" He cocked his head. "I'll take you up sometime. I fly a couple of times a week." He shifted his gaze back to Rachel. "You ready to go up with me yet?" he asked her, the double meaning practically screaming through the room.

Briefly flustered, she dropped her eyes to the papers in her hand and began to shuffle needlessly through them. "I, um, would need to check my schedule." She cleared her throat and recovered her bearing, straightening her shoulders. "Is your driver ready? You need to get going soon."

He pushed off the door frame. "Simon has the car ready and waiting."

Rachel nodded. "I'll probably be up there later this evening for a security check."

Security check, my ass, I thought with ridiculous glee.

"You got it," Chris replied. "And then you can take a day off next Tuesday and fly with me." He gave her a teasing chuckle. "Maybe we can join the mile high club."

Her mouth dropped open, and a flush climbed up her cheeks, visible even beneath her dark skin. A pained expression came over Chris's face as he no doubt realized he'd gone too far with the flirting, especially in front of us.

"I . . . need to get to the security meeting," Rachel blurted, then hurried out of the room.

Chris winced as he watched her go. "I shouldn't have said that. Rachel takes this job really seriously." He heaved out a sigh. "I'll buy her a big box of chocolates to apologize."

I snorted. "A gift card to a boxing studio might be better choice, and not *quite* as sexist."

"Oh. Yeah. Your idea is better, especially since I kind of sexually harassed her just now." He grimaced, clearly annoyed with himself.

"Y'think?"

"Not often enough, obviously!" He glanced to Kristi. "You ready, Doc?"

Kristi gave Philip a questioning look, as if seeking permission. Philip nodded. "You go and have a nice time off, and I'll see you when you get back," he said, then released her hand. Kristi gave him another hesitant smile, then left the room with Chris.

I waited until the door had closed again before clearing my throat. "You and Kristi are awfully, um, friendly," I remarked.

He dropped into a chair, face scrunching as if he smelled rotten eggs. "I've done a lot of *work* with her," he said.

I narrowed my eyes. "What kind of work?"

"The kind that encourages compliance." He looked briefly pained. "She's a risky asset."

Compliance. I shuddered. Some sort of conditioning, probably, and I had zero desire for details about how that worked. I knew Philip had some sort of military or special ops background, but I didn't know any specifics, which was fine with me. "She's lucky Dr. Nikas insists on the mental health breaks."

"Her living arrangements here are comfortable, but none of the rooms have windows." He made a face. "I've been crashing here since you extracted me from Saberton, but at least I get to go outside when I want. I'd go nuts if I couldn't feel the sun on my face."

"Then it's a damn good thing I made you a zombie and not a vampire."

Chapter 5

Dr. Nikas entered carrying a tray the size of a cookie sheet, with Jacques right behind him pushing a cart full of electronic doodads, wires, and I had no idea what else.

"Ah, not there, Angel," Dr. Nikas said as he spied me in the procedure chair. "I need you and Philip much closer for this."

"How close?" I asked, then gave Philip an exaggerated wink. "Holding hands close or spooning close?"

Philip chuckled, but Dr. Nikas had already slipped into his intense focus and completely missed my attempt at humor. "Sitting back to back will do," he said as he set the cookie sheet down on a counter. To my dismay there wasn't a single damn cookie on the thing. Nothing but syringes full of various colored liquids. Lots and lots of syringes. Yikes. Good thing I lost my fear of needles when I got turned.

Dr. Nikas moved to me and, without warning, firmly drew his index finger down my cheek, then stepped to Philip and did the same, this time with his middle finger. While Philip and I exchanged bemused glances, Dr. Nikas touched both fingers to his tongue, frowned, and looked off into space. Taste diagnostics, he called it, and the weird-as-hell process apparently gave him a ton of information in a few seconds. I didn't know how it worked, but I'd seen him do it a few dozen times, and it always yielded impressive results.

Dr. Nikas muttered something then proceeded to add incomprehensible symbols to the whiteboard. Jacques brought two ordinary rolling stools into the room, and I plunked myself down on one, gave it a good spin, and pulled my feet up. Once around. Twice. Three times. The thing had smooth action. Four and slowing. I caught a glimpse of the exasperated look on Jacques face, and slammed my feet down to bring my spectacular test drive to a stop then flashed him an innocent smile. Probably better not to piss off the Needle Vampire.

Without a word, he gestured for me to sit back to back with Philip, then lowered Philip's stool so we were closer to the same height. No way was I going to complain about having Philip as a backrest.

Once we were positioned properly, Jacques placed an IV catheter in Philip's right arm and then another in mine, which I assumed was so all of the weird stuff on the cookie sheet could be injected. Once that was done he began attaching monitoring equipment to us: EKG pads, straps around our heads, the little finger clampy thingies that measure blood oxygen and pulse, blood pressure cuffs, and several other things with trailing wires. I had *no* idea what the wire-thingies measured and was more than a little afraid to ask.

Lastly, he moved over to the cart and returned with a roll of duct tape. I watched him warily. "What's *that* for?" I asked.

He gave me a thin, triumphant smile as he crouched beside me, then proceeded to tape the wheels of my stool to the floor. The bastard *had* to have brought it in specifically for this reason.

"Aw, c'mon!" I said. "I only broke one little thingamabobby the other day."

His face grew more grim than usual as he taped the last two wheels, but when he finished and straightened, his eyes told a different story. Large, hazel, and amazingly expressive, they'd become my best gauge for whether I'd amused him, annoyed him, or Really Pissed Him Off. Whew. I was still in the safe zone.

All the attached junk made it awkward to get comfortable while perched on a stool. I swiveled the seat a bit and shifted against Philip's back. "It's a good thing I like you," I murmured to him.

"Of course you like me," he murmured right back. "Only an idiot wouldn't like me. I'm dangerously likable."

I began to snicker, but some monitor beeped, and Dr. Nikas's worried frown reminded me to behave.

After some fiddling with equipment, Dr. Nikas picked up two syringes with blue contents, passed one to Jacques, and then Dr. Nikas injected me as Jacques injected Philip. They repeated this process three more times with yellow, green, and milky pink. Finally just Philip received an injection of a colorless liquid.

"What exactly is this going to do?" I asked.

"We are attempting to remind Philip's parasite how to operate optimally by imprinting it on yours."

I processed that. "Imprinting? Like ducklings?"

Dr. Nikas smiled. "In a manner of speaking. I'll be stimulating both sets of parasites into a bit of a frenzy, and as yours copes, Philip's will hopefully follow suit." Dr. Nikas placed the empty syringes in a sharps disposal container. "How do you feel?"

"My teeth are buzzing," I said with a grimace. "Like they're full of bees." It didn't *hurt*, but it was mighty unpleasant.

"Mine too," Philip said, his voice rough. "And my throat is getting scratchy."

Dr. Nikas pursed his lips and moved back to the cookie tray, mumbled distractedly as he picked up a syringe with red contents, then shook his head and replaced it. His expression grew thoughtful but after a moment it cleared. He retrieved two syringes that contained what looked like chocolate pudding and passed one to Jacques. Apparently the consistency was pudding-like too, because the needle looked more like one of those turkey baster injector things. Except about twice as big.

Dr. Nikas crouched before me. "Lift your shirt, please?"

Wary, I lifted it to right below my boobs. Apparently that was high enough, because Dr. Nikas placed a cool hand on my stomach and set the needle about an inch above my belly button. "This might be a bit uncomfortable," he said and then drove the needle into my gut.

A tiny yelp escaped me, and it was with some small relief that I felt Philip stiffen behind me as Jacques did the same pipe-to-the-gut move. It took at least a minute to inject the substance, during which I breathed in shallow pants against the pain. *A bit uncomfortable, my ass.* "Dr. Nikas, this *sucks*. I'll stick with the buzzing teeth."

"Give it a moment, Angel," he murmured.

About ten seconds later the bee-teeth sensation faded. "That's better," I breathed. Unfortunately, rather than echoing my sigh of relief Philip groaned and jerked against my back.

Monitor wires caught at me as I tried to twist to see what happened. Jacques slapped the intercom on the phone and shouted, "Reg!" to call in the other lab tech, then moved to us and wrapped an arm around Philip to keep him upright. Philip twitched and let out a shuddering cry. I swiveled the chair, not caring that clips and patches pulled off, and stared at Philip.

"Angel!" Dr. Nikas said with urgency. "Turn around. Stay *still*."

I didn't. I couldn't. Not with the side of Philip's face looking as if a billion ants crawled under the skin. In seconds, the flesh split as an ugly patch of rot formed and deepened, exposing bone and teeth. Zombie stench, distinctively heavier and sweeter than cadaver stink, rolled over me in a sickening wave. I stared, shocked. We'd had trouble during treatments before, but this—

Dr. Nikas took me firmly by the shoulders in an unexpectedly strong grip and turned me with the stool until I faced away from Philip again. He pressed me back until I could feel Philip jerking and shaking against me, and held me there.

"Angel, I need you to stay right here," he said, voice calm and reassuring. "He's going to be fine, but I need you to help me by remaining still and keeping in contact with him. It's important. You have it?"

Gulping, I met his eyes and nodded. "I got it. Sorry," I said. "That was seriously freaky."

He squeezed my shoulders, then released me and turned away to work with the vials and syringes on the tray. Dr. Nikas always fixed things, but that didn't keep my heart from trying to thump its way out of my chest. Philip gurgled and twitched, and I held my back against his. "You're gonna be okay," I said, as much to reassure myself as him.

A tall and angular man with close-cropped red hair slid to a stop in the doorway—Reg, his head swiveling this way and that as he took in the scene. Jacques barked out a couple of orders for an ice pack and "brain formula ninety-nine," and Reg disappeared again.

My cheek started itching, and I fought the urge to scratch it—partly because I wasn't supposed to move and mostly because of the fear it would be gross and rotten like Philip's.

Dr. Nikas returned to us with three syringes in his hand then injected them, one after another, into Philip's IV. I waited anxiously for them to work and let out a breath of relief when Philip relaxed about a minute later. Reg entered with the needed items in hand and passed the ice pack to Jacques.

"Philip, count backward from one hundred. Odd numbers only," Dr. Nikas said.

"Ninety-nine, ninety-seven, ninety-five," Philip responded, voice a little rough but steady.

"Good," Dr. Nikas said. "Reg has brains for you with additives. Eat both packets and hold the ice pack on your jaw for about ten minutes, and you should feel much better."

Calm and collected as though nothing happened, Jacques moved to me and began reattaching the wires I'd pulled loose. All in a day's work. Reg efficiently tidied the counter top and straightened the remaining syringes, then departed as silently as a ninja. A zombie ninja.

"What happened?" I asked.

Dr. Nikas released a breath. "An overreaction by Philip's parasite to the stimulation by your parasite," he explained as he took a syringe from Jacques. "With the imprint link between you two, Philip's parasite reflected the reaction of yours but, because of its damaged state, it responded inappropriately. That said, the whole episode helped me understand better how to assist his parasite to normalize."

"You mean the whole face falling off thing was good?" I asked doubtfully.

"Not much fun," he replied with a slight smile, "but, yes, it was good since it was under controlled conditions and gave me a great deal of information. I've made adjustments and suspect it will be smooth sailing through the remainder of the procedure."

"I'm all for smooth," I assured him. "That was enough excitement for one day."

"I understand completely, Angel," Dr. Nikas said. "The good news is that there's nothing you need to do but be still for about half an hour while the parasites commune."

"What's the bad news?"

"You'll need to be still for about half an hour while the parasites commune." His eyes flashed with amusement.

"Are you accusing me of being fidgety?" I made a show of trying to roll my duct taped chair. "Jacques made sure I wouldn't break anything this time."

Dr. Nikas laughed and shook his head, then moved off to check the monitoring equipment. "Philip, how are you feeling now?"

"Good. I had a killer headache during the procedure, but now I feel better than when I came in," he said, his voice clear again. "The leg pain is gone, and I'm not as tired."

"Excellent." Dr. Nikas made notes on the whiteboard and muttered to himself. "Excellent," he repeated a moment later as he stepped back to take in the whole of what he'd written. "Thank you, Jacques. That's all I need for now." The lab tech nodded and departed, and Dr. Nikas glanced our way. "Everything appears stable, so at the moment we're simply waiting. Philip, keep the ice pack on your jaw."

His cell phone rang, and he answered with a simple "Yes?" then listened for a few seconds. "Now?" He frowned, glanced back at us, then to the whiteboard. "Are you—? Yes, all right." He slipped the phone back into his pocket, glanced at us and gave a vague smile, then departed.

"You sure you're okay?" I asked Philip.

"Bright and shiny, Zombie Mama," he said. "I wouldn't want to do that every day, but if it helps me, I'm not going to complain."

"Good deal," I said, truly relieved. "You sure are full of surprises."

He snorted. "If I heard right, it was *your* parasite that overreacted."

"And *yours* that couldn't cope," I teased. Laughing at the horror of it made it easier not to freak about it.

"Angel, you need to hold still," Philip reminded me, and I realized I'd started fidgeting and swiveling the seat. I needed something to distract me.

"Damn," I muttered. "I left my phone with my audiobook in the central lab."

"What are you listening to?" Philip asked.

"Uh . . ." I racked my brain for something that didn't sound as stupid as what I was actually listening to. "Moby Dick," I blurted.

There was a moment of pregnant silence before Philip spoke again. "Really?"

I groaned. "No. I lasted about five minutes into that book before I gave up on it. Now I'm listening to *Passion of the Viking*."

He made a strange cough that I knew damn well was him choking back a laugh. "Is his helmet *horny*?"

"Shut up."

"Does he go all *berserker* with her?"

"I swear to god, I will cut you."

He snickered, but wisely held back any more commentary.

I busied myself by counting tiles on the floor, then tiles on the ceiling. Thankfully, Jacques entered right about the time I was trying to figure out how many speckles each floor tile had. I gave him an expectant look, but his full focus was on the readings on the computer screen. Not that I expected him to be all chatty. He wasn't exactly known for being overly talkative. But it was still better than counting tile specks.

"Almost done?" I asked hopefully.

"Forty seconds," he murmured, eyes glued to the screen.

"Good," I said with a sigh of relief. "I'm starving for some real food."

I felt Philip shift at my back. "You want to grab a bite?" he asked. "There's a great cafe in Tucker Point, and I'm heading that way."

"Sure thing!" I replied.

"Time," Jacques said and began to turn off and disconnect the various monitors.

"It's not fancy," Philip continued, "but the food is good."

I gave Jacques a smile of thanks as he removed the IV and the last of the other stuff. "Good food works for me." But my eyes went to Jacques as he returned to stare at the whiteboard. "Everything cool, Jacques?"

His brow furrowed, gaze remaining on the whiteboard for another few seconds, then he moved to the cookie sheet of injectables to check what was there. He finally looked up and gave me a nod. "You can go."

I stood and stretched to work out the kinks in my back. "Is Dr. Nikas still around?"

"No, he left to meet Mr. Ivanov," Jacques replied with a tiny smile. "Forgot to tell me he was leaving. Again."

I snorted, smiled. "I guess that happens often?"

"Often enough over the years," he replied with a resigned shrug.

"Well, tell him to give me a buzz if he needs anything more from me."

Jacques gave a distracted nod, brow furrowing as he looked at the whiteboard.

"That was almost a conversation," Philip said as we headed out.

"I could barely get a word in edgewise."

We exited the security doors. Philip stuck sunglasses on as soon as we were outside. "So far I'm not sick," he said. "That's promising."

"It's a good sign," I agreed. "But if you do get sick, warn me so I can avoid splatter, okay?"

Philip winked. "Where's the fun in that?"

"I can think of all sorts of things that are more fun without puke splatter," I shot back. "Where are we going?"

"Nice little café called Top Cow," he said, and somehow I kept my expression even. That was the first place Marcus and I ever had lunch together, though we hadn't been *together*-together at the time.

As if the thought of him had been a summons, my phone rang with the Marcus ringtone.

I glanced at Philip as I pulled it out of my purse. "Hold that thought?" He nodded, and I stepped a few feet away before answering, even though I knew it was silly to be self-conscious about talking to my boyfriend in front of Philip.

"Hey, babe," I said as I answered. "What's up?"

"Just checking on my favorite zombie," Marcus said, a smile in his voice.

"Ooh, do I even outrank your uncle on that scale?"

He laughed. "Well, I know which one I'd rather see naked."

"Jeez, now I have a mental image."

"Sorry," he said, though he didn't sound sorry at all. "Actually, I was calling to see if you wanted to grab an early supper."

"Perfect timing." I winced as soon as I said it. "I mean, I'm leaving the lab right now, and Philip and I were about to head to Top Cow Café since we're kind of starving. Would you be okay with joining us?"

"Yes, sure thing," he replied quickly, but I heard the slight catch in his voice. He'd never been to the lab—had never even been invited. I also knew he wasn't exactly thrilled to pieces about my spending time with Philip. It didn't even matter that it wasn't a whole lot of time. Philip was, well, Philip.

"We should be there in about twenty," I told him. "Meet us there?"

"Will do," he said. "Love you."

"Love you too." The words tripped from me with the ease of habit. I hung up and turned back to Philip. "Marcus is going to meet us there. I hope that's okay?"

He smiled beneath the sunglasses. "Totally." I tried to hear if there was anything beneath his words—jealousy, resentment, annoyance—but he seemed completely fine, and I couldn't decide if I was relieved or disappointed.

Oh, god, I groaned to myself. *I'm going to lunch with my hunky boyfriend and my also-hunky zombie kid. Awkward City, party of three.* I kept the smile on my face, but the second I was in my car and on the road I stuck my headset in my ear and hit the dial for "Naomi Comtesse." Naomi worked for Pietro, but she wasn't a zombie. Hell, she wasn't really "Naomi" either.

I'd first met her when she was stalking me—taking pictures and generally being kind of suspicious. After I confronted her she told me her name was Heather Miller, however, it turned out she was really Julia Saber, daughter of Nicole Saber, the CEO of Saberton Corporation. Following in her grandfather Richard Saber's footsteps, Julia worked industrial espionage for Saberton as Heather Miller for nearly a decade. In fact, a little over four years ago, it was Heather who stole documents from Pietro that allowed Saberton to learn of the existence of zombies. She came to regret that, big time, after she stumbled onto the uglier side of Saberton's zombie research, and in a tangled twist of events during the filming of a zombie movie, she defected from Saberton, came into the Tribe, and became Naomi Comtesse.

But more importantly, she became my best friend.

"Hey, chick," she said with a bright lilt to her voice. "Calling to hear me gloat about my trip to Tahiti? Totally magical, I tell you!"

"Oh, sure," I replied sourly. "Please do tell me all about your tan lines, or lack thereof. But later. Right now I need your help."

"What's wrong?" she asked, instantly completely serious.

"I'm about to have lunch with Philip and Marcus. Together," I said. "I need you there. And maybe Kyle should be there too. And it might not hurt to pick up some of the day workers hanging out in front of the hardware store to bring along for some more manpower."

"You . . ." She laughed. "How the *hell* did you get yourself in that situation?"

Scowling, I gave her a quick explanation. "C'mon," I whined. "Don't you owe me some favors?"

"Under any other circumstance, being the human shield between two testosterone factories would burn up any and all favors owed, but I wouldn't miss this for the world." Amusement resonated in her tone. "I'll roust Kyle, and we'll meet you there."

"You are beyond wonderful," I said fervently.

"And you're pathetic," she shot back.

"Guilty!"

Chapter 6

The Parking Gods decided to be nice and left a spot on the street open for me less than a block from the restaurant. They even placed it near the corner so that I didn't have to embarrass myself by demonstrating to the world that my parallel parking skills sucked ass. Totally cool of them, and I offered a heartfelt prayer of thanks as I slid my car into the space.

Unfortunately, the Car Gods didn't like me anywhere near as much, as demonstrated by the way my car lurched and died before I could turn the ignition off. And, when I tried to start it again, it clicked and nothing more. *I'll deal with it after I eat*, I told myself while silently praying that, whatever the issue, it wouldn't cost more to fix than the car was worth.

I grabbed my purse and left my stupid dead car behind. Marcus was already there, waiting outside and leaning against the wall beneath the Top Cow Café logo. The restaurant sign had been repainted at some point in the last year, but I suspected the painter had been high or drunk. The cow looked more like a blotchy meerkat on its hind legs, and the top hat perched on its—were those supposed to be horns?—looked more like a crouching walrus.

The restaurant itself was a hole-in-the-wall, with tables and chairs crammed so close together the waitresses barely had room to squeeze through. Apparently the tight quarters made it impossible for the servers to carry any sort of pleasant attitude as well, and it was widely known that one came to Top Cow for the excellent food, not sunny dispositions and bright smiling faces. If the waitress cursed you out, you probably deserved it and, even if you didn't deserve it, the food was still good, so shut up and get over it.

"My car died," I told Marcus when I reached him. "I may need a ride home. Or a flamethrower."

He chuckled and gave me a kiss. "Ride, yes. Flamethrower, not so much," he said. "I put us on the waiting list. Should only be a couple of minutes, since we're early for the supper rush."

"Thanks, but it's going to be five of us now," I said with an apologetic wince. "Naomi and Kyle are coming as well."

A wave of obvious relief passed over his face, and I realized he knew damn well how uncomfortable it might've been with only the original three. *One point to me for inviting the others!*

"Not a problem," he said. "I'll go tell the hostess." He slipped past the other waiting people and inside, then returned about half a minute later, though he kept twisting his head awkwardly to look behind him.

"What's wrong?" I asked.

"Do I still have an ass?" He grinned. "I think the hostess just chewed half of it off."

"I'll be glad to check later," I offered with an appropriate leer.

He opened his mouth to say something that I knew would be nice and naughty, but then he closed it, expression shifting to polite and bland as Philip walked up.

"You snagged the last parking place in three blocks," Philip said to me, then turned to Marcus. "Hey, man. Good to see you."

"You too," Marcus replied, acting for all the world as if Philip was a guy pal he hung out with all the time. Which I didn't *think* they were. Were they? That would be weird as all hell. Or, was I reading too much into their reactions to each other? The whole "two hunky guys must obviously be jealous of each other because of me" thing *was* a bit conceited and self-centered, if I stopped and thought about it.

The hostess hollered Marcus's name, and we obediently followed her to a round table in the corner set for five. Marcus and Philip started some silent jockeying for who would get to sit with their back to the wall, which I solved by scooting forward and claiming the wall-seat for myself.

The two men exchanged a look that clearly meant *Great. Now we're all fucked if terrorists storm the restaurant,* but managed to seat themselves without overt conflict—Marcus to my left, and Philip across from us with an empty chair on either side of him. Smart man.

A waitress with purple streaks in her hair and rings in her eyebrows slapped menus onto the table and tapped her foot impatiently as we gave her our drink orders. As she stalked off, Naomi bopped in with a mischievous gleam in her blue eyes that told me she was ready to stir up some shit. Six or seven years older than me, she'd seen the world a hundred times over and had plenty of opportunities to perfect her troublemaking skills. Defecting from Saberton had meant faking her death and a Pietro-funded change in appearance. Hair color, facial plastic surgery, and even a tasteful boob job. Her Heather identity had worn hazel contact lenses, but she'd fiercely refused to even consider shifting to green or brown for the Naomi persona, declaring that contacts were too much of a pain in the ass to bother with. She was one of a handful of non-zombies who worked for Pietro. Philip had been another until I'd turned him. I knew there were several others scattered throughout the organization, but I had yet to meet any of them since their jobs tended to be fairly specialized.

As Naomi made her way toward us, she gathered her chestnut hair into a ponytail and wrapped it with a scrunchie. Kyle moved more sedately in Naomi's wake, tall and lanky with dark skin and smooth, catlike movement, calmly exuding an air of danger without even trying. The other patrons in the restaurant edged away from him, probably not even aware they were doing so. He scared me a bit as well, but I totally approved of the way he looked at Naomi—caring and thoughtful and deeply affectionate.

"Move, Zoldier," Naomi said with a teasing grin to Philip. "I wanna sit next to Kyle." Pietro had even bought her a new voice, a little deeper and throatier. I hadn't even known that was possible.

She plopped down in the empty chair beside Marcus. Crap. Of course Philip was too nice to stand his ground and tell her to piss off, which meant he shifted over to the only available seat—beside *me*. I fixed a smile on my face and gave Naomi an exasperated *You were supposed to HELP! You did that on purpose!* look which she acknowledged with a wink. Just my luck to land a BestFriendForever who thought trouble and mayhem were fun.

The waitress dropped a plate of biscuits on the table and took Naomi's and Kyle's drink orders. As soon as she left I grabbed a biscuit and proceeded to stuff it with butter.

"What's your weekend looking like?" Naomi asked me as she followed suit.

"Can you believe I actually have it off?" I said around butter and biscuit. "I think this is the first weekend in about a zillion years that I haven't even been on call."

Her smile widened. "Cool. I talked Kyle into going to Paintball Palisades on Saturday if I can find worthy teammates." Her gaze raked Marcus, Philip, and me. "Or *opponents*."

Marcus leaned back in his chair, brow puckering. "Paintball, huh? That sounds like it could be interesting." Beneath the table he found my hand and gave it a light squeeze. I squeezed it right back. Marcus was a *beast* at paintball, but he obviously didn't want the others to know. A little hustle action? I hid a smile. His secret was safe with me.

"Y'all would wipe the floor with me," I said, not lying one bit. "Me no have grunt grunt combat skills." My *jiu jitsu sensei* could attest to that. Sadly, I would most likely never become a zombie ninja.

Naomi leveled a stern glare at me. "No combat skills? I've seen you hold your own a time or two for realsies."

Marcus squeezed my hand again. "Plus, Angel's getting to be a pretty good shot," he surprised me by saying. "She might be harder to wipe the floor with than you think."

"What about you?" Kyle said, looking over at Philip with a slight smile of challenge. "I have some floors that need wiping. Are you a man or a mop?"

Philip simply shrugged. "Haven't you heard? I'm an invalid. Damaged. I doubt I'm worth your time." Yet his eyes said the opposite.

Kyle leaned forward a few inches, eyes still on Philip. "You'll have Angel and Marcus to protect you . . . for a few seconds."

Marcus stiffened, and I tightened my grip on his hand. I knew—or rather *hoped*—that Kyle hadn't intended to insult Marcus by implying he'd pose as little threat as I would.

Unfortunately, Kyle seemed unaware, as did Philip. "That's all I'll need," he responded, also leaning forward.

Tension vibrated through Marcus's body, even though he kept his face composed. More composed than I'd have been in a similar position. *Shit.* I caught Naomi's eye. Her smile was fixed, and a wince hovered just below the surface. She knew, even if the other two men were oblivious.

I abruptly grabbed the neckline of my shirt, pulled it out and peered down at my chest. "Oh my god! I think I just sprouted a chest hair from all the excess testosterone at the table."

Naomi let out a laugh, bless her, and Kyle and Philip broke their eye contact and sat back in their seats. Philip glanced my way, and I saw the shift in his expression when he noted the tension in Marcus. He opened his mouth to speak, but I gave a micro-shake of my head. Saying anything now would only make it worse.

To my undying relief the waitress arrived at that moment to bring drinks and take food orders. Marcus shifted his attention to the waitress and rolled his eyes as usual when I ordered the Philly Cheesesteak without bell peppers. Everyone else found that amusing as well, despite my insistence that bell peppers were nasty, and the tension leached away. Naomi made small talk about some innocuous and forgettable topic, and all of us relaxed into her banter. She had an inexplicable talent for putting zombies at ease, sometimes enough to spill their deepest secrets. That, paired with her natural intuition, made her one sharp cookie. By the time the waitress delivered food everyone seemed to be a shitload less stressed.

Kyle's phone buzzed as the waitress took our orders for pie. He answered with a low, "Griffin," then listened in silence for almost half a minute during which time the waitress gave up on him and flounced off in impatience. "Got it," he finally said, hung up and looked over at Naomi. "We need to go."

She dug money out of her purse and dropped some bills on the table. "Duty calls," she said with a smile as she and Kyle stood. "Y'all play nice, and yes, you can have my pie."

"If you're going back to Tahiti, I don't want to know," I told her.

She simply laughed, tucked her arm through Kyle's and threaded through the tables to the exit.

Philip cleared his throat softly. "I should probably be on my way as well," he said, also dropping money to cover his share. I was pretty sure he didn't have anywhere he needed to be, but he was gracious enough to recognize his third wheel status. "I'll catch you later, Angel," he said. I responded with something similar, and after giving Marcus a parting guy-nod thing, he departed.

Since people were waiting for tables, Marcus and I didn't linger much longer—only enough to scarf down pie, pay the bill, and overtip the waitress with the excess the others had left. By the time we stepped outside the sun had dropped below the buildings, and the western sky glowed with orange and purple. The temperature had dropped as well, and I hugged my arms around myself.

"Sorry that turned out kind of weird," I said as we walked down the street to where my car was parked.

"It's okay." His expression was a mix of tired and resigned, but he dropped his arm over my shoulders and pulled me close in reassurance. "It helped me clear out some doubts."

I gave him a puzzled look. "What do you mean? Doubts about what?"

He took a deep breath and let it out in a rush. "I'm quitting the sheriff's office."

That stopped me in my tracks, but once I had a second or two to process his statement, I realized it wasn't all that surprising. "Okay,"

I said, walking again. "I know you didn't want to be a cop forever, but do you have something else planned?"

A smile touched his mouth. "I got accepted into law school."

Squealing, I threw my arms around him. "Oh my god! Law school? Marcus, that's fantastic!" I knew he'd wanted to go to law school close to a decade ago, but he put that on hold and became a cop when his mother developed breast cancer.

He hugged me close. "I probably should've gone that direction a few years ago, but then I'd have missed getting together with you."

"I didn't even know you were applying." I grinned up at him. "I'm so happy for you! Wow, law school!"

"It's only in New Orleans, which means we don't have to move a long distance away," he continued, smiling. "I know you'd hate to be far from your dad and friends."

The fuck? My grin disintegrated, and I pulled back. My phone buzzed in my pocket, and I sent it to voicemail without even looking at it. "Wait. Marcus, don't you think we should *discuss* moving?" Hell, we weren't even officially living together. There'd been some preliminary "wouldn't it be cool if" discussion, but that was about it.

"Okay, I guess I jumped the gun on that, but I figured since it was just to New Orleans . . ." He sighed. "Sorry."

My dismay climbed higher. New Orleans was over two hours away. This wasn't as if he'd suggested a move across town. "Marcus, I love you," I said, "but I don't want to move. I'm just starting to get my life figured out."

Exhaling, he pulled me close again. "Okay, okay. Sorry. We'll make it work. I don't think two hours even qualifies as a long distance relationship."

I hugged him back, but suddenly it was as if he'd left a box of bait open and all the thoughts and worries and uncertainties began to worm their way out. Law school was a big deal, yet he'd never even told me he was applying. And for him to simply assume we'd move in together—in a different city, no less—with zero warning or discussion . . .

A weird fatigue settled on me. The same relationship problems kept popping up, over and over. We were in a rut, and while it was usually a pleasant one, the banks only seemed to be getting steeper. I'd been in a rut with my ex-boyfriend, Randy, as well, one I'd stayed in for almost four years before being turned into a zombie shocked me out of it. The nature of that rut had been different, consisting more of the habit of being together and a lack of desire to change what worked well enough most of the time. Yet, weirdly enough, even though my time with Randy had been unhealthy on a number of levels, I knew there was no way in hell he'd have ever made a big decision for me like this.

"I don't want a long distance relationship," I heard myself say as my thoughts finally settled.

"It wouldn't be," he insisted. "Sure, we wouldn't see each other as often, but . . ." He trailed off, and it was obvious he didn't want a long distance relationship either. "Angel," he said, obviously torn. "I *need* to do this, but I don't want to lose you."

"I know," I said, "and I want you to go to law school and kick all the ass. But I think that if we try and do the long distance thing, it'll fall apart. Us, I mean." I kissed him lightly. "I think we would do better being the absolute best of friends than we would being long distance boyfriend and girlfriend." Bizarre relief bloomed within me. A way out of the rut?

Shock spread over his face. "Angel—"

"Marcus," I said quietly, "I don't ever want us to get to the point where we break up and never want to see each other again. I don't ever want to *not* be around you. Does that make sense?"

"I wish to hell it didn't." He let out a heavy breath and tightened his arms around me. "I think I've just been dumped," he murmured.

Hugging him close, I leaned my head against his chest. "No. You've been gently placed on a soft cushion so that you'll still be all shiny and pretty when it's time to play with you again."

Marcus snorted. "Better be a damn nice pillow."

"It's an *awesome* pillow," I assured him.

"I believe you." He hugged me tighter before releasing me. "You still want a ride home, or do you want to try and get your car fixed now?"

"Crap, I forgot about my car." I wrinkled my nose. "A ride home, if you don't mind. I don't want to deal with the car in the dark, and no one's going to mess with it here."

Taking my hand again, he walked me down the street to his truck. "This is going to take some getting used to," he said, glancing down at our hands before releasing me and opening the truck door.

I'd taken his hand just as automatically. Best friends probably didn't do that sort of thing. "It would've been a big change either way," I said, hating the question in my voice.

He gave me a hand as I climbed in. "They say change is good." He managed a wry smile. "I'm not so sure."

"If you don't change you die," I replied glibly.

"No chance of that." He kept the smile, but I knew him well enough to see how hard he was working to keep the hurt from showing. "Let's get you home," he said and closed the door for me.

Chapter 7

Marcus pulled into my driveway, put the truck in park and killed the engine.

"I guess this is it," he said, voice low and rough.

I gave him a light punch on the shoulder. "It's not like we're never going to see each other again," I pointed out. "We're still best buds. And I'm not giving you back your mix tapes or anything."

A brief chuckle escaped him. "I've never in my life made a mix tape. Don't lay that on me." He let out a long breath. "This isn't at all how I pictured things going."

I mirrored his sigh. "I know, but you keep forgetting to let me be a part of drawing that picture."

"I get it. I really do," he said. "I'm glad we're still friends."

"I am too," I said, though I wondered how much he really did get it. It wasn't the first time this issue had cropped up. At the same time, I was glad he still wanted to be friends. That was way better than pissed and distant, which would have made the break up a billion times harder. "Marcus, I know this is gonna sound pompous and preachy, but I'm really glad you're taking control of your life and going to law school."

"Uncle Pietro has been after me to do it for ages." A corner of his mouth quirked up. "Looks like we've come full circle. A year ago I was the one getting you to take control of your life."

I snorted and filed away the fact that Pietro had been nagging him. Another thing he hadn't bothered to share with me. "I'm not sure me telling you to go to law school after you'd already been accepted compares to everything you did for me, but I'll take the credit if you're going to offer it."

He laughed. "Sure, what the hell."

"Do you know where you're going to live?"

"I'll drive to the city tomorrow and start hunting apartments," he said.

Without me. "I think you're going to fucking shine," I said.

He leaned over and kissed me, chaste and sweet enough to make tears spring to my eyes. "So will you—"

Whatever else he was going to say got cut off as the truck door on my side flew open. Yanked open, I realized as I let out a stupid girly shriek and jerked back against Marcus. "What the shit?" I yelled, bringing my legs up to kick out at the attacker, even though all I could see was a looming shadow.

Marcus grabbed his gun from the console and was out the door in a flash to draw down on the assailant. "Back off!"

"Wait!" I yelled, then dropped my legs and leaned forward. Holy shit, it was Philip, face flushed and one hand gripping the truck door so hard I was shocked he didn't dent it. "Jesus, dude, are you all right?"

Philip's lips pulled back from his teeth, and he shot a hand toward me, even as survival instinct had me scrabbling back toward the driver's side door. He got hold of my ankle for a second, then released it and staggered back several feet, hands held out as if for balance, and face pinched with an expression I knew too well as his splitting-headache face.

Marcus came around the front of the truck to my door. "Angel, you okay?" he asked, continuing to cover Philip.

"Yeah, I'm good." I quickly slid out of the truck. "But something's wrong with him."

"No. No . . . nothing's wrong," Philip said, fighting to straighten. His throat worked as he swallowed, and then he plastered a sickly smile onto his face. "I was . . . worried about you. I called you, but you didn't answer." He held up his left arm, and the dim light from the truck revealed a mottled patch of skin above his elbow. "I, uh, had a reaction. I put a call in to Dr. Nikas, but I was worried about you."

Marcus frowned and lowered his gun. Dread rising, I yanked my sleeve up. "Aw, crap." My arm held a discolored spot in a matching location, and when I poked it with my finger I found it grossly spongy. Pre-rot. But how could I be rotting when I wasn't hungry for brains?

Worry bloomed on Marcus's face as his gaze shifted back and forth between us. "What does this mean?"

"I'm sure it's nothing," Philip said, shaking his head. "I over-reacted because Angel didn't answer, that's all."

He's covering. He needed to talk to me on my own, and he knew there was no way Marcus would leave if he knew Philip hadn't exactly been himself when he came at me a few minutes earlier. On top of that, Philip obviously didn't want Marcus to be jealous. Perfectly natural for a nice guy like him, especially since he didn't know we'd just broken up.

A pang went through me. Broken up, and Marcus was moving away, at least for a couple of years. Marcus and I had been through a number of ups and downs over the past year and had broken up and gotten back together more than once. But he'd always been around. Near. He'd made me a zombie, saved my life. And he'd been a part of that life ever since.

"I feel perfectly fine," I told him. "What did Dr. Nikas say?"

"I left a message," Philip said. "I'm waiting for him to call me back."

"I'd like to hear what he has to say when he does."

Marcus twitched his hand toward mine then pulled it back. "You sure you're all right?"

"Totally," I reassured him.

His eyes went to Philip and stayed there for several seconds, no doubt assessing and deciding whether it was safe to leave me with him. Philip looked perfectly fine now, though a little pale.

Marcus drew a breath and released it. *He* was the third wheel now, I realized with a sharp pang, and he knew it.

"I'll call you tomorrow," he said. "If that's all right, that is."

"It is," I replied. "Thanks for the ride home."

He leaned in and brushed his lips against my cheek, cast a hard look at Philip that clearly held all sorts of *Hurt her and I will destroy you* type messages, and then turned away, climbed into his truck, and drove off.

I waited until his tail lights disappeared around the bend of the road, then rounded on Philip. "What the *hell* was that?" I demanded.

Philip exhaled. "I came by to see if you were home yet. I didn't see your car, so I called, but you didn't answer. I decided to wait a bit to see if you'd come by." He lifted his chin toward the end of the driveway. "You pulled in, and I had every intention of waiting until Marcus was gone, and then—" His face lost all color. "It was like I was watching myself go and yank the truck door open," he continued. "No way to stop it and no idea what was coming next. Like being a backseat passenger in my own body." He shook his head. "Then it was gone. Left me dizzy and with a headache like the one at the lab this morning, but worse. The headache's almost gone now, at least."

Well, that sounded like all sorts of suck. "What about this?" I asked and pointed to the blotch on my arm. "You don't have any brains on you?"

Philip exhaled. "Angel, that's the problem. I'm tanked. It doesn't touch it."

Permanent rot? An ugly twist of fear curled through me, and I had to fight the urge to rub at my arm. "We should call the lab and try and get hold of Dr. Nikas again," I said.

He nodded agreement. "I left the voicemail earlier when I noticed the rot, but shit's going downhill."

"Yeah, weird freakout episodes justify another call," I said with a glower. "Come on in. I'll make the call, and we can go from there." I led the way up the driveway and inside.

"Okay if I use your bathroom?" Philip asked.

"Yeah, no prob," I replied and tried not to think about what condition the bathroom might be in. Horrific, most likely, even though I'd cleaned the toilet only last week, with possible nastiness that ranged from hair in the shower drain to Dad's skid-mark underwear hanging from the toilet flush handle, with a dying roach in the sink for added ambience. Best not to even think of it. "Since you've already left a voicemail for Dr. Nikas, I'll try Jacques or Reg," I added.

"Sure thing," Philip said. "I'll be right out."

Detouring to the bedroom, I snagged a bottle of brains out of the fridge. A few gulps later, I peered at my arm in dismay as Absolutely Nothing happened. Shit. Double triple quadruple shit.

Returning to the living room, I hit the lab's number. Jacques picked up on the first ring.

"Leroux," he snapped out.

"Hey, Jacques, it's Angel."

"Oh. Angel," he said with unmistakable disappointment. Who was he expecting at this time of night? A hot exotic dancer? "What do you need?"

"Philip had a freaky episode, and we both have matching pre-rot patches on our arms," I explained. "He left a message for Dr. Nikas, but that was before he pulled a caveman stunt and tried to drag me out of Marcus's truck." Philip came out of the bathroom with a hopeful look. I shook my head and mouthed *Jacques,* and he grimaced in disappointment. "It's not his normal Plague stuff," I continued to Jacques. "I think it's a reaction to the procedure this morning. Is Dr. Nikas around?"

Jacques remained silent for a moment. "He's not available," he finally said then cleared his throat as though choking down the urge to say more.

I frowned. Not even a *Maybe I can help you,* or *Come on in*? "Jacques, we need help, sooner rather than later." Whether Dr. Nikas was available or not, I'd feel better at the lab in case anything else happened with Philip. "We'll head over now."

"Now? Wait. Hold on." A second later an onslaught of tinny elevator music screeched through the phone.

I glanced at Philip. "I'm on hold, and Jacques's acting weird."

The music stopped and a female voice said, "Angel?"

"*Naomi?*" I replied. "What the hell is going on? Why is Jacques all stressed out, and why are you at the lab this late?"

"Kyle and I are assigned here tonight," she said, an intense edge in her voice. "Jacques said you and Philip need to come in for an assessment?"

"Yeah. What's the deal?"

"Not on the phone," she said. "You can come on in, but we changed the codes for the doors. Ready to hear them?"

"Did something happen to Dr. Nikas?"

"We'll talk when you get here," she insisted, her tone no-nonsense. "These are based on the weapons locker code. The first one, add a twenty-three to the end. The second one, add a seventy-six to the beginning. Got it?"

"Weapons locker. Twenty-three at the end for the first, seventy-six at the beginning for the second," I repeated, and a nod from Philip told me he knew the sequence. "We'll be there in about a half an hour, and no more dodging the questions."

"You got it," she said. "See you in a bit."

I jammed the phone into my purse and headed for the door. "Something serious is up. Let's go."

Kyle and Naomi's silver SUV was in front of the building when Philip pulled into the lot. He parked beside it, and as soon as the car stopped I threw open the door and clambered out. "What's the weapons locker code?"

"Three-seven-seven-six-zero-eight-four-one," he rattled off as he noted mileage in his log book.

I hurried to the door, punched in up to the sixty-eight and called back, "What were the last two?"

"Four-one," he said though the open door.

I entered that then added the twenty-three, and enjoyed an irrational sense of satisfaction as the lock buzzed. It wasn't as if I'd cracked the damn code myself or anything. I pulled the door open and glanced back. "Philip, come on."

He still sat behind the wheel, his head lowered, writing. I frowned. No, not writing. His head lolled to the side. Alarm shot through me. "Philip!?"

He jerked and sat upright as though waking from sleep, a bewildered look on his face. I released the door handle and rushed back to the car. "Dude, what happened?"

"I don't know," he said as he scrubbed a hand over his face. "I greyed out, but I feel fine now."

"The fucking Plague strikes again," I said with a worried scowl. "Let's get your ass inside."

Philip climbed out of the car, swayed a bit, then steadied. "I'm okay. That sucked."

The door clicked open, and Naomi stuck her head out. "You two okay? The code dinged, then you didn't come in."

"Sorry," I said, heading her way. "Philip had another episode."

She opened the door wide. "Get inside. I'm not wishing bad stuff on you, but it'll be good for Jacques to have something to do."

We passed through the drab reception area that I was certain was meant to convince anyone who managed to get through the outer door that they were most certainly *not* at a super secret high tech zombie lab.

"Enough of the riddle shit," I said as Naomi punched the code into the next security door. "Why does Jacques need distraction? *What* is going on?"

The door clicked open, and we passed through. "Trouble," Naomi said as she waved at the mirrored glass in the next small room, the last security checkpoint before entering the lab complex. "Hang on, I'll explain everything as soon as we're through."

The heavy door on the far wall buzzed, and we passed through into a wide corridor. Ahead of us were the thick sliding glass doors to the central lab, with the medical wing and security office off to the right. Naomi continued forward as the glass doors slid open, and we followed her into the lab. Kyle lounged at a station, calmly reading a fat paperback, though he paused long enough to give us a nod.

Naomi finally turned to us. "You know when Kyle got that call at Top Cow? It was the alert that Mr. Ivanov, Dr. Nikas, and others were gone. Abducted."

I stopped dead, feeling as though my whole world tilted. "What? How?"

Philip cursed softly behind me.

She took a steadying breath. "Mr. Ivanov and his driver, Simon Sirtis. Kristi Charish, along with Chris Peterson, and their driver, Ken Godwin. Plus Lawrence Hawkins, the security guard at the Retreat Lodge. All missing."

I processed that as she spoke. I knew every one of those people except Lawrence. "Does Brian know who did this?"

Naomi's face hardened. "*Brian* took Dr. Nikas in broad daylight, out front."

Chapter 8

Cold crept through me at Naomi's words. "Wait. You mean Brian took Dr. Nikas to a safe place?" Nothing else made sense.

"I wish." She pulled out her phone and thumbed through a couple of screens. "It sucks. Tranqed him and threw him in the back of his car. Check it out." She held the phone so we could see a segment of surveillance video.

I watched in numb shock as Brian spoke on the phone in the driver's seat of his SUV outside the front door of the lab, then dropped the phone onto the seat and waited. A moment later, Dr. Nikas came out the door, leaned into the passenger window to talk to Brian. About ten seconds later, Dr. Nikas turned back toward the building, and if Naomi hadn't replayed the section, I'd have missed it.

Brian shifted in the front seat, a small motion. Dr. Nikas jerked, then swayed as if about to faint. Brian leapt out of the passenger door, caught Dr. Nikas as he sagged, and hustled him into the back seat. The door closed, Brian got behind the wheel again, then peeled out of the lot.

Naomi tucked the phone away. "You can see the tranq gun better from the other camera view."

Brian? *Brian*? He'd have been at the very bottom of my list of People Who Would Betray Pietro.

"No one watching the security cameras *noticed* this?" I asked, shaken.

"You saw how quickly Brian moved," Naomi said. "They all thought he was leaving with Brian voluntarily." She raked her fingers through her hair, aggravated and pissed. "It was *Brian*. Beyond suspicion. *No one* knew anything was wrong until Dr. Nikas's driver showed up to take him to dinner with Mr. Ivanov. Then suddenly they couldn't get hold of anyone to check in, and security started digging."

"Do you have any idea where they are?"

She shook her head, grim. "Not at this time. If any ransom demands were made, we weren't informed. Kyle and I are here to back up Raul and Dan. For extra security."

I flicked a glance at Kyle as he turned a page in his book. How the hell could he possibly be so calm?

"Angel," Philip said. "Brian was on the phone in the vid. The time stamp puts it before we left here earlier today."

I turned to him, eyes wide. "That was the call Dr. Nikas got during our treatment." I grimaced as another realization hit. "He didn't leave us by choice, which meant the procedure wasn't finished properly. No wonder you're a mess, and we're doing synchronized rotting." I touched the spot on my arm, certain it was uglier and squishier than before. "We need to see Jacques."

"He's in the treatment room with Reg," Naomi told me. "Last I saw him he was going through Dr. Nikas's notes from this morning."

Philip headed off that way, jaw set. I leaned closer to Naomi. "It must be Saberton Corporation behind this."

Distress shimmered in her eyes even as Kyle's gaze locked onto me over his book. Anything about Saberton hit close to home with Naomi. Everything had turned upside down for her a few months back when she stumbled onto Saberton's cruel zombie experimentation, and she ended up killing one of the researchers to protect a vivisected zombie test subject. When she informed her brother, Andrew, that she was done with the bullshit, he threatened to tell their mother about the murder if Naomi didn't get her act together for Saberton. Instead, Naomi broke his nose, hogtied him with a sheet and fled.

As I watched, Naomi pushed the distress aside and lifted her chin, face fierce like some sort of warrior princess. "I'm certain they're behind it," she said with conviction. "My mother is desperate enough these days to plan a stunt like this. I only wish she'd been careless enough to screw it up." She smacked the counter with her hand. "I can't *believe* I used to think of this as a big game."

"The Tribe screwed up Saberton's movie zombie experiment pretty badly," I said. "You think your mom might have grabbed Pietro for revenge?"

"I wouldn't put it past her," she said, eyes narrowing. "With the company in trouble since granddad died, she's lost moral perspective." Her mouth twisted in a scowl. "With family *and* business. Don't get me wrong, she was never very motherly. But she wasn't so cutthroat or vindictive, and she wouldn't . . ." She trailed off as she ran her fingers over her cheekbone, a deep sadness in her eyes and voice. "What other daughter has to go through *this* to keep their mother from hunting them down and killing them . . . or worse?"

A changed appearance and a faked death. Sure, it kept Julia/Naomi safe from Nicole Saber, but it also meant isolation from her family, however crappy that family was.

"It sucks big time," I agreed. "All we can do now is focus on getting our people back. Who's on it? Rachel? I bet she'll tap you to get the inside scoop on what you think Saberton's next move is."

"She hasn't yet. I should probably call her." Naomi gave me a determined, closed-lip smile. "Rachel doesn't much like me, but I know a lot of shit about Saberton."

"Yeah, you do," I said. "And welcome to the Rachel Hates Me club." I gave her a quick hug. "I'm going to see if Jacques has a fix for Philip and me. I'm not too happy with the permanent rot thing."

Naomi made a face. "I'm with you on that one."

I left her and made my way to the treatment room where I found Jacques drawing a blood sample from Philip, while the other tech, Reg, worked at a computer on a counter nearby.

"Dr. Nikas didn't document what he was doing," Jacques said, face pale and voice unsteady. "He was adjusting as he went. He often works that way." He pulled the needle from Philip's arm. "Some notes. Nothing clear."

This was an absolute fountain of words from the man. "It's cool. We trust you," I said, but I heard the high, thin worry in my tone. "It's cool," I repeated. Reg glanced over from the computer station and gave me a somewhat steadier smile, though his eyes held plenty of concern as well.

Jacques took the blood samples over to another table and began doing stuff with vials and machines. "He *never* leaves before a procedure is finished," he muttered, distressed. "I never would have let you leave. I assumed it was complete. I should have known, should have realized something was wrong."

"Hindsight is some awesomely useless shit," I stated firmly.

"None of us could have known," Philip said at the same time.

Jacques gave a slight nod, though the level of anxiety in his eyes remained the same. "I'll run these and we'll go from there. It'll take about twenty minutes." He gathered up the vials and moved to the adjoining room.

Philip took the small cup of pureed brains Reg offered him and downed it. The tiny mark from the injection faded, but the rotted areas stubbornly remained. He murmured a thanks to Reg and handed the cup back, then gave my shoulder a bump with his. Though, with the height difference, it was more like my shoulder met his bicep. "C'mon, ZeeEm, we can wait in the main room," he said. "The lab boys don't need us hovering over them."

I turned with him toward the door. "ZeeEm? Seriously? Zombie Mama?"

A smile twitched. "You don't like it?"

Tilting my head, I pretended to consider. "Y'know, it's not bad. And I kinda like the idea of calling you ZeeBee."

"Zombie Baby," he groaned, then chuckled. "Okay, I deserved that."

Grateful for the humor, I bumped my shoulder against him. But even with the brief distraction, the severity of the situation didn't stay away for long. "Surely there's someplace we can start looking," I said as we made our way down the corridor. "There's a crime scene somewhere, right? Wherever Pietro and the others were kidnapped?"

"We can check with Kyle and Naomi, but I'm sure security's been on that all day."

"And how much training do they have on crime scene investigation?" I asked with a frown.

A faint grimace touched his mouth. "Basic, but they won't be calling in any experts."

"Why not? If they report it to the police, do they *have* to mention that Pietro and the others are zombies?" My frown deepened. "The cops have a lot more equipment and training and connections. They'd stand a better chance of finding out what really happened." But even as I said it I knew it couldn't possibly work out that way. "Shit, no. If the cops investigated they'd find out about the rest. It's why I didn't report it when Saberton's goons took my dad."

Philip nodded. "The risks are too great. As bad as the abductions are, exposure is worse."

We entered the central lab. Kyle was still reading his book, and Naomi studied maps on one of the work station computers.

"So in the meantime we wait." I *sucked* at waiting, being patient, and most other things that were supposed to come with that whole maturity thing.

"I doubt the Tribe is sitting on their hands," Philip said. "What *we* do is another matter." Worry tightened his expression, and I saw his gaze flick to the darkened patch on his arm.

"We need to see what Jacques comes up with first," I said. How much help could either of us be if we couldn't control the rot? And I didn't want to think about Philip's weird fit and his greyout in the parking lot.

I flopped into one of the chairs and amused myself by slowly spinning around. Kyle glanced at me once, snorted very softly, and then returned his attention to his book. Fine, I'd be picking him last for my hallway office chair bobsled team.

The glass doors slid open as Raul leaned in from the outer hallway. He swept his gaze around before it came to rest on Kyle. "Hey, Griffin, could I see you for a minute in the security office?"

Kyle carefully marked his page with a scrap of paper, set his book on the counter, and moved lithely to the door. Raul gave the rest of us a nod, then the doors slid closed behind the two.

I spun my chair again. "How long has it been?" I whined.

Philip leaned against a counter and folded his arms over his chest. "I think we're up to a whole five minutes." He straightened and patted his pocket. "Crap. Left my phone in the treatment room. Be right back." With that he headed back the way we'd come.

Pushing off against the desk, I sent my chair careening across the floor. "I just want to *dooooo* something." My eyes fell on Kyle's book, and I scooped it up to peer at the cover, which had a cool painting of a sword with dragons carved into the hilt. I began to flip through to see if I could find out more about the dragons, then jerked my head toward the main corridor at the unmistakable sound of a gunshot.

Naomi bolted upright. "Kyle!"

Shoving up from the chair, I sent it skittering back across the room as I ran to the door. It obligingly slid open before I realized that if people were shooting, opening the door might not be the safest thing to do though by then it was too late to change my mind.

Across the hall and a little to the left the door to the security room stood open, giving me a perfect view of Raul crumpled against the wall, gurgling and clutching at his throat while blood poured between his fingers. Dan stood beside him with a tranq gun in one hand and a real one in the other, both leveled at Kyle who already had one dart sticking from his lower stomach. As I took all this in, Dan fired the tranq twice more. Kyle staggered as the darts struck but still managed to lift the gun in his hand and squeeze the trigger. Dan jerked and bared his teeth as the round took him in the shoulder, even as Kyle slumped back against the desk and slid to the floor.

All of this happened in the couple of seconds that it took me to cross the hall. "What the *fuck?*" I stopped in the doorway and stared at the completely unexpected scene.

"Angel, stay back," Dan ordered, keeping both guns on Kyle.

"Kyle!" Naomi pushed past me and hurried to him.

"What happened?" I demanded. "Why'd you shoot him?"

"We need to take him into custody," Dan replied, jaw tight and tense.

Teeth bared, Kyle fought to lift his gun. "Take . . . him . . . out."

Take *Dan* out? "Goddammit," I snarled, "who's the fucking bad guy here?"

Naomi jerked around to shoot me an *Are you fucking kidding me?* look an instant before she spun and drew her own weapon on Dan.

Dan didn't waver, but I saw the hesitation in his eyes. Shooting Naomi with a tranq would kill her—the powerful drugs designed to stop a zombie in seconds were lethal to humans in the same amount of time—but Dan obviously didn't want to shoot her with a regular gun either. "It's orders," he said through clenched teeth. "He's been implicated in today's actions and we're detaining him. That's all."

"Shit," I breathed. Naomi trusted Kyle, but the fact that they were lovers probably had her a teensy bit biased. I clenched my hands in frustration, and realized I still held Kyle's book.

Raul let out a gurgling cough, his color already grey as the parasite used resources to keep him alive, and Dan flicked a quick glance at him. I turned as if to move back, then slung the book as hard as I could at Dan.

Holy hell, but I hope I'm not making a huge fucking mistake, I thought as it arced through the air, closely followed by the hope that Naomi could take some sort of advantage of the distraction.

Fortunately, the last thing Dan expected was a thick book with a big sword on the cover to bean him in the head. He let out a startled yelp and staggered, but that was all Naomi needed. She launched up and drove a shoulder into his gut, seized the tranq gun, twisted, and shot him twice.

Dan tried to bring his other gun up, but between my literary attack and the tranqs, Naomi had no problem relieving him of that weapon as well.

"What the hell's going on, Naomi?" I all but shouted as Dan crumpled. "Tell me why I threw a book at Dan's head."

"Angel!"

I looked back down the hallway to see Philip running my way with Jacques some distance behind him. "Angel, I heard shots!" He slid to a stop and took in the scene in the room. It was a sign of his experience and training that he didn't say anything stupid like "What the hell's going on?" or "Who's the fucking bad guy?"

Instead he moved toward Raul while pulling a packet of brains out of his pocket. "Jacques!" he called over his shoulder. "We need more brains here."

Philip crouched by Raul and began feeding him brains to stabilize him and keep him from going into too much rot, even going so far as to press some into the wound. Naomi stepped back from Dan and looked over at me.

"I don't care what they say," she said with a lift of her chin. "Kyle didn't have anything to do with the abductions." She pivoted back to Kyle and began to carefully extract the darts from him.

Philip glanced back at me. "Angel, Raul had this in his hand." He tossed me a phone, which I managed to catch. "See what's on it or if he had someone on the line. *Something* instigated this."

A number of pictures had recently been texted. I scrolled through and fought to make sense of them. Four showed different angles of Chris Peterson, half in and half out of what could only be a shallow grave in a heavily wooded area. The lower half of his body was covered in dirt, but it looked like he'd partially sat up, then collapsed to the side. A cell phone lay on the ground by his hand. Bloody face, ligature marks around his throat, and an ugly hole at the base of his skull—a fatal wound for a zombie. A fifth picture was of nothing but the ground, and the last was of Rachel crouched beside the exhumed body, one hand on his chest, glaring into the camera with an *I'll destroy whoever did this* look on her face and her eyes scarily demon-red in the flash.

"Oh my god," I breathed. "It's Chris. He's dead."

Naomi sucked in a breath. "And Rachel's saying Kyle did it? It's a lie!"

"Would you chill?" I snapped. "Let's figure out why anyone would think that."

Jacques stepped in to take over the care of Raul. Philip came over by me to look at the photos. Face grim, he examined each one carefully, then moved to a cabinet and removed zip ties and a set of handcuffs.

"For now we'll lock all three down," he said, then shot a stern look at Naomi as she began to protest. "You too if you don't settle."

"That seems more than fair," I said. "At least until we know more."

Philip handcuffed Kyle's hands behind his back and ziptied his ankles, then moved to Dan and Raul and ziptied them both at wrists and ankles. As soon as he finished, Jacques administered tranq an-

tidotes to both Dan and Kyle. Dan began to perk up almost immediately, but Kyle was slower to recover, probably because he'd been
tranqed three times. Raul's wound had closed, and he was breathing
more easily but was still terribly pale with a grey cast to his skin.

Jacques murmured something about finishing the blood analysis
then departed. Philip took the phone from me and once again
looked through the pictures.

"Rachel will be on her way out here soon, or will send someone," Philip said, half to himself. "Hopefully all this shit will get
straightened out then."

"You want me to throw a book at her head too?" I asked cheek-
ily, but he wisely ignored me and instead crouched before Raul.

"Give me your report," he asked Raul, calm and all business.

"The pics." Raul licked dry lips. "About half an hour ago, Chris
phoned Rachel but all she heard was scuffling noises and wheezing.
It went quiet, but the line was still open. She traced the GPS, and
when she went out she found what you see there." He nodded toward
the phone in Philip's hand. "He'd been garroted in a double loop—"
His eyes flicked to Kyle and then back to Philip. "—stabbed in the
brainstem and then buried in a shallow grave. But apparently he survived long enough to claw his way out and try and call Rachel." He
took a deeper breath, color slowly improving. "Rachel sent me the
pictures then called and told us to detain Kyle for investigation."

"I don't understand why that points to Kyle," I said, confused.

"Kyle's signature move is a garrote looped twice," Philip said
quietly.

Raul shifted his attention to me, nodding in agreement with
Philip. "Yes, but it's the fifth picture that's the most damning."

"The one that's just dirt?" I asked, even more baffled.

"Zoom in," Raul said. "To the right of the pine cone."

I peered over Philip's shoulder as he did so.

"It's K-Y," Raul said. "Chris scratched that in the dirt and started
another letter before he died."

Crap. Somehow I doubted Chris had been asking for lube. My
mind raced as I tried to sort everything out—raced right to K-Y-L-E
but didn't stop there. Naomi still crouched by Kyle like a lioness
guarding her cub, obviously not entertaining even a whisper of
doubt. Philip slowly scrolled through the pictures again, meticulously examining each one.

"I don't think Kyle's stupid," I blurted.

Not in a snide way, Philip asked, "What's your point, Angel?"
without looking up.

"Well," I began, "if he's not stupid—which I'm pretty sure he's not since he's this hot shit operative with all sorts of experience and skills—why would he make it so goddamn obvious it's his work and then come bebopping back here?" I shrugged. "I mean if *I* was going to fuck over the Tribe and then return here, I'd at least make sure that there was no possible way it could ever be traced back to me. And I'd sure as hell make sure the zombie I killed stayed dead."

"Those are all good points," Philip said. "But standard procedure is to detain and then investigate." He jerked his head toward Kyle. "He knows that."

I clung stubbornly to the fact that he didn't specifically say he was going to actually *follow* the standard procedure. "Uh huh, but detention locks down one of our top guys. If it's a setup it's a good one, because it really fucks us up and slows us down." I gestured around the room and at the three restrained men as evidence of that.

"We'll see what Kyle has to say when he can speak," Philip said. The front door *dinged,* and Philip glanced back with a slight frown. "Rachel's here already?"

I stepped over to the monitor that showed the drab waiting room, then sucked in a sharp breath. "That's not Rachel!" Four men in black tactical gear poured through the outer door and on into the short hallway to the next secured door. With pistols at their belts and automatic weapons in their hands, they didn't have "Saberton" stenciled on the back of their shirts, but they might as well have. I recognized the overall look all too well.

Shock coursed through me as one of the men lifted a scrap of paper and began inputting a code on the number pad. "Philip! They're getting in!"

Already up and moving, he dove to slam a hand on the remote door lock, but the second door clicked open the instant before he could hit it. Easily visible now through the broad window, the four moved on to the next door. I backed away from it even though I knew it was several inches thick. One of the men crouched by the door and dug in a small backpack while another held a cell phone to his ear and kept his eyes on the window. Even though I knew he couldn't see me, it was still unnerving as all hell. The other two men stood by, their weapons ready. They definitely weren't stopping by for a beer.

Philip swept a quick look around the room. "Naomi, grab weapons," he snapped, jerking his head toward the weapons locker. "We'll set up in the hall so that these guys aren't sitting ducks." He flicked a hand at the three secured zombies.

Naomi leaped into action, surprising me a bit that she didn't argue that Kyle should be released to help fight. Maybe she realized there wasn't time for that shit.

"They don't have a code for this door," I announced. Backpack Guy had pried the front panel off and hooked an electronic thingy to it.

Philip spared a quick look. "They'll have it open in less than a minute," he said grimly, quickly donning the ballistic vest Naomi tossed his way and seizing up weapons. I looked back at Naomi, taken slightly aback at the sight of her in ballistic armor and helmet, looking badass as fuck. No doubt at all, she was ready for action.

"Jacques and Reg!" I spun back to Philip. "Saberton must be trying to get them as well, since they already have Dr. Nikas." Another hideous thought hit me. "And the heads. Shit."

"Kang," Naomi breathed. They'd been close friends before he was murdered.

"Run," Philip ordered. He took my arm and propelled me to the hallway. "Get them and you barricaded up and safe. We'll handle these guys."

Naomi slammed and locked the door to the security room behind her. "We got this, chick," she said when I hesitated. The main door beeped, and she gave me a shove. "Go!"

She and Philip turned to the door, flattened against the wall with Naomi crouched low, and lifted weapons.

They knew what the hell they were doing, so I did what the hell I knew how to do.

I turned and ran.

Shouts and the sound of gunfire followed me as I raced through the central lab rotunda and down the hallway to find Jacques, but all the noise was drowned out by the thoughts screaming through my head. *They had the codes. They used the codes to get through the first two doors.*

Those codes were barely two hours old, which meant that Brian wasn't the only insider. Naomi had set the codes. Who else had them besides Philip and me? Probably Raul, Dan, Kyle, maybe Rachel. *Kyle.* Shit. There were plenty of other possibilities, but I didn't like his name on the list.

I slammed doors in my wake and locked or jammed each one as best I could in the hopes of buying myself more time. To my relief Jacques was in the first place I looked for him, in the treatment room. "Jacques!" I tried to catch my breath without success. "Bad guys . . . here to get you . . . and Reg . . . and heads . . . I think."

He turned, and now I saw that he was on the phone. "It's Angel," he said, apparently answering a question of who was speaking to him. "She thinks they're here for the heads or for Reg and me."

I moved toward him. "Who are you talking to, Jacques?"

He lowered the mouthpiece a couple of inches. "It's Rachel. She's on her way here."

I yanked the phone from his grasp and hung it up. "Someone gave these guys the codes to get in," I explained as he gaped at me in shock. "That means Brian wasn't the only insider, and we don't know who to trust."

Eyes wide, he visibly swallowed. "Oh, dear."

"We need to get you and Reg and the heads to a safe place," I said. "Is there a room y'all could barricade in? Y'know, like a safe or a bomb shelter?" I threw the last two in in an attempt at humor, then blinked in surprise when he actually nodded.

"We have an emergency bunker," he said hesitantly.

"Really? That's awesome!" I didn't hear gunshots anymore, but I had no way of knowing if it was a pause in fighting or if one side had been defeated. "C'mon, let's get y'all tucked away."

Looking more than a little dazed, Jacques hit the intercom button on the phone. "Reg, meet me in the regrowth lab. Now. With gurneys."

The intercom crackled. "Roger that." Good ol' Reg, as go-with-the-flow as anyone I'd ever met.

I strained to hear if anyone was trying to get through my lame-ass attempts at barricades. I thought I heard some thuds and thumps, but that could've been my paranoia working overtime. "Is there anything you need from here?"

The phone rang. Jacques began to reach for it then stopped and looked at me uncertainly. "It's from outside the lab."

"It's probably Rachel calling back," I said. "Let's pack up fast and move."

"The bunker is stocked," he said, looking and sounding shaken. He glanced once again to the ringing phone then headed to the hallway. "I'll get what I need for the heads from their lab."

I picked up the phone and hung it up again, then followed him at a jog. Reg was in the room with the heads when we arrived. I gave him a terse rundown of the situation as I helped disconnect vats and transfer them to the gurneys.

The muffled sound of more gunshots spurred us all to move faster. In less than five minutes we had all the vats loaded up, along with a cart filled with supplies and equipment, and were pushing it all down a narrow corridor that I'd passed a billion times but never been down. At the end of the hall stood an extremely solid-looking door with a heavy handle.

"Holy shit," I said as Jacques heaved it open. The damn door was nearly a foot thick. "Y'all could survive a nuclear war in here."

Lights flickered on within, and Jacques stepped in and tugged a gurney after him. "Barring a direct strike, yes," he said matter-of-factly.

I wanted to gawk and poke around and see what a bunker really looked like, but I knew I was running out of time. I helped get the gurneys and cart into the bunker, then gave Jacques a troubled look.

"I don't know who we can trust," I told him. "Promise me you won't open the door until you hear from me, or Pietro, or Dr. Nikas, or . . ." I struggled to come up with anyone else who I knew could be trusted without a shadow of a doubt. Guilt flickered that I couldn't put Philip or Naomi in that category, but I swallowed it down to let it sit like a rock in my gut.

"We'll lock it down," Jacques said as he worked quickly to get the vats reconnected to power. "No one can open it from the outside if we seal it from within. Ari . . ." His voice faltered. The pain and distress on his face nearly brought me to tears, and I realized I'd never heard him call Dr. Nikas by his first name before. "You have to get him back," he went on when he could speak again. "He can't tolerate being out."

A thick lump of emotion lodged itself in my throat. I didn't know his history, but I'd picked up that Jacques had worked with Dr. Nikas for *decades*. He needed Dr. Nikas as much as a zombie needed brains.

"I will," I said around the lump. "I promise. I won't come back without him." I stepped outside and looked back at the two men. "Good luck."

Jacques took hold of the handle and gave me a sad, tragic smile. "Thanks, Angel," he said then tugged the door to close heavily.

I stood there for a moment and listened to the grinding *chunks* and *whirrs* of the door as it sealed, then pulled out my phone to text Philip.

Who won?

The reply came within seconds. *Zombies rule.*

Chapter 9

Loaded down with two coolers full of scavenged brain packets, I ran back to the security room. Signs of battle marred the walls and floor: bullet holes, scorch marks, thick smears of blood, and drag marks that led to a stack of black-uniformed bodies farther down the corridor. Breathless, I slid to a stop in the doorway. "Rachel's on her way, Jacques and Reg are locked in the bunker, I grabbed as many brains as I could carry, and we need to get the hell out of here."

To my complete shock, no one asked me to explain any of that.

Philip jerked his head toward the desk where four big baggies were neatly lined up, a whole brain in each one. "Will those fit in the coolers?"

"Three of them will, for sure," I said after a second or two of thought. My mouth watered at the sight and delicious scent as I stuffed three baggies into the coolers. The fourth went into a small duffel I found under the desk, and I had no doubt the brain it held would be eaten long before it had a chance to spoil.

Philip stepped over Raul and Dan, heaved Kyle up to his feet, then hooked an arm around him for support. Naomi grabbed the coolers, and I scooped up every available handgun and tranq I could find, stuffed them into the duffel, then followed Philip to the front.

"Uncuff him," Naomi said to Philip with a frown. "It'll be easier."

"Not until we're away from here and can get some perspective," Philip replied in a that's-my-final-word tone.

A mulish expression formed on Naomi's face, but I took her

arm. "C'mon, it's going to be okay," I told her. She glowered, but didn't make any further protests.

A quick peek out the front door showed that Rachel and the rest of the backup hadn't yet arrived.

"We'll take my car," Philip announced as he headed in that direction. "Kyle, anything in yours we need to grab or should know about?"

"Jump . . . bag," he slurred. "Trunk."

"Mine's in there too," Naomi added.

Philip fished the keys from Kyle's pocket and tossed them to me. I impressed myself by not dropping them, then ran to the car and popped the trunk. The only things within were a pair of black backpacks, each a bit larger than a school bag. I grabbed them, closed the trunk and ran back as Philip was folding Kyle into the back seat of his car.

"This what you meant?"

"Yesh." He gave a lopsided nod. Naomi opened the back door on the other side, but Philip straightened and shook his head.

"Naomi, you're up front with me," he said in the same uncompromising tone he'd used earlier. Jaw set, she complied, but it was clear she was getting dangerously close to not putting up with this shit. However, Philip didn't appear to give a flying fuck about her attitude or morale. He turned to me, pressed a tranq gun into my hand and met my eyes. "You can handle the back?"

I gulped. "Yeah." I could, couldn't I?

Naomi opened her mouth to protest, but Philip speared her with a *look* that made the hardness of his voice seem as soft as fluffy cotton rabbit butts. She sat in the front, then glanced back at Kyle with a frown. "This is crazy."

"No." Kyle managed to shake his head. "Is . . . warr . . . anted. I would . . . do same."

Naomi subsided at that. Philip and I climbed in, and then we got the hell out of there. When we made it to the highway without encountering Rachel and her team, every one of us let out a breath of relief.

Philip hung a right and floored it. "With any luck the mess we left at the lab will delay pursuit," he said. "I figure we have about half an hour lead before they figure out how to track us." He glanced in the rear view mirror at Kyle and got a nod of agreement. "I'll head to the spillway, and then we can reevaluate."

"Shit!" I dug in my pocket for my phone. "I don't know if Marcus has heard about his uncle."

"He needs to know," Philip agreed.

To my annoyance, my call to him rang four times then went to voicemail. After the beep I left a message that was somewhat vague about how his uncle had gone on an "unexpected trip" and that he *really* needed to call me as soon as possible. My shoulders sagged as the weight of the entire screwed up day finally came crashing in. Back in my old, pre-zombie life, I'd have popped a couple of Percocet or Xanax to take the edge off and make the bad shit seem not so bad. Those sort of meds didn't work on me anymore, but every now and then there was a tiny part of me that wished they did. Not that I wanted to go back to being a druggie—hell no!—but having the parasite also meant that I couldn't use legitimately prescribed meds for anxiety or insomnia or anything like that. Yet, at the end of the day, I had to admit it was better that none of that shit affected me anymore, thanks to my parasite. It had sure made kicking the habit easy.

Some nice, fresh brain would help take my mind off our crappy situation. I fished the brain out of the duffel, cut it into manageable pieces and divvied them up. Philip and I chowed down as he drove, while Naomi fed chunks to Kyle.

Philip slid a look at me. "Don't overdo it," he warned. "We need you fully alert."

"Oberwoo?" I asked around a mouthful of brains.

"Tanking up puts you at your peak of zombie senses and abilities with no consequences," he explained. "Over-tank and you'll get a Super Zombie feeling, but then you'll crash as your parasite utilizes excess resources."

"Oh." No wonder I always needed a nap after sucking down a big load of brains when I wasn't Hungry, hurt, or super active. I'd always figured it was the same as the human desire to sleep after a big meal. I swallowed the bite and gave him a smile. "I'm good," I assured him. Okay, maybe I was a teensy bit over-tanked. Reluctantly, I dropped the remaining two chunks of brain back in the baggie and passed it back to Naomi. After being hit with three tranqs, Kyle could probably use the extra.

We rode in silence for another fifteen minutes or so before we pulled into the deserted gravel parking area by the river and the spillway.

"Now what?" I asked after Philip killed the engine.

Kyle made a low noise in his throat. "Kill me . . . or free me."

"No one is killing anyone," Naomi snapped. Philip pulled a phone from his jacket pocket and started flicking through the pictures.

I gave Kyle a baffled look. "Why the hell would we kill you?"

"It's what happens to traitors," he said, voice almost back to normal. "Right, Philip?"

Philip didn't respond and simply continued looking through the pictures on the phone. Raul's phone, I realized. Naomi had gone very still, barely seeming to breathe.

"Are you a traitor?" I asked Kyle, uneasy and unsettled at the tension in the car.

"No," he replied evenly. "But my opinion isn't the one that counts."

"Well, then stop talking about us killing you," I said sharply.

Philip turned in his seat and held the phone so that Kyle could see the picture on it. The one with K Y drawn in the dirt by Chris. "What do you think?"

Kyle's eyes went flat as he looked at the pic. "I appear to be a traitor," he replied.

Philip didn't move. "The physical evidence points that way. The code leak points that way." His focus remained on Kyle, and I had a feeling he was weighing Kyle's reactions against my earlier argument in his favor.

"It's a setup!" Naomi cried. "Kyle didn't do this."

"Naomi," I said through gritted teeth as I watched the two men, "would you please be *quiet* for a few minutes?"

She drew back, as stung as if I'd told her to shut the fuck up, but she remained silent.

"Everything points to it," Kyle agreed, and for the first time I heard the tension in his voice. "I'm not the insider, but I have nothing other than my word."

My utter hatred of this entire scenario rose to unbearable levels. "Philip, can I talk to you a sec?" Before he could reply I swung my attention to Naomi. "And can you *please* promise to chill and not do anything outrageous and, well, Angel-like until I finish talking to Philip?"

She folded her arms over her chest and stuck her chin out. "For now."

I waited until I was out of the car before rolling my eyes at her reaction. To my relief Philip stepped out and joined me about twenty feet from the car.

"What do you *really* think?" I asked him, voice low.

He grimaced and rubbed the back of his neck. "It looks bad," he admitted. "But what stops me is that Peterson wasn't dead. Kyle isn't sloppy or careless."

"That bugged me too," I said, nodding. "It fucking points to him, hard. *Too* hard. If Saberton wanted to really fuck us up, this was a perfect way to it."

He glanced toward the car. "So ninety percent he's clean," he said softly, "and ten percent he's a knife in the dark."

I mulled the whole thing over for a moment, then met Philip's eyes and lowered my voice even more. "No matter what, we *can't* kill Kyle." The mere thought twisted my gut so hard I knew there was no fucking way in hell I could let that happen. I had no idea if Philip felt the same way or simply felt my utter resistance to that option, but he gave a slight nod. "And if we lock him up somewhere until we figure out what's going on," I continued, "we'd have to lock up Naomi too. If this is a Saberton setup, we'd be doing their dirty work for them."

"All right. We let him go and keep our eyes open." He shook his head. "It's a risk, but my gut says he didn't do it."

"I agree," I said, to both parts.

Naomi and Kyle watched our approach as we returned to the car. "Okay, we believe you," I said.

Naomi sagged in relief, and I realized she'd known what the stakes were for her as well. Something flickered in Kyle's eyes—disappointment or grief, though neither made sense—but he gave a slight nod and smile. "You mean the odds fell in my favor."

"Whatever you want to call it." I said with a shrug. Damn, but I hoped we weren't making a huge mistake. "Now, can we please figure out what the hell to do now?"

I stepped back as Philip helped Kyle out of the car and removed the cuffs. Kyle breathed a sigh of what I guessed was relief and rubbed his wrists.

"I appreciate your trust," he said.

Philip opened his mouth to reply, then closed it. A shudder crawled over him, right before he shot a hand out to seize my arm in a hard grip. I staggered, taken by surprise and off balance as he yanked me behind him.

To my horror, Philip pulled his gun and leveled it at Kyle and Naomi. "Get out of here!" he ordered, voice strained and laced with stress. "Both of you, get the hell away from here!"

"Philip, no!" *Just like the incident by my house!* His finger on the trigger stopped me from grabbing his arm. Kyle could survive most bullet wounds, but Naomi was a shitload more fragile. "Philip, please, stop!" I shot Kyle a frantic look. He remained stone still, assessing everything. Behind him I saw Naomi edging toward the tranq gun I'd left in the back seat. I caught her eye and shook my head. No guarantee the tranq would work on him with his altered parasite, and every chance it could make him worse.

"Go!" he shouted, teeth bared. I shifted to stand beside him, placed a hand gently on his arm while my heart pounded like crazy.

"Philip, no, they can't go," I said. "We need them. Don't hurt them."

He blinked, and I watched him come back to himself. Horror and dismay crawled over his face as he looked down at the gun and saw where it was aimed. Swallowing hard, he lowered it and took a shaky half-step back. "Damn."

"Philip, give me the gun please," I said, voice quavering.

He flipped the safety on and passed it to me, butt first. "Damn," he repeated.

"What was that all about?" Kyle asked, dark eyes on Philip.

Philip's expression turned grim and bleak. "It's an adverse effect of a treatment I had this morning. Dr. Nikas was abducted before he could finish it and isn't here now to correct the problem." Hands tight at his sides and back tense, he turned away and walked to the edge of the parking lot, misery practically rolling off him.

Aching for him, I carefully held the gun and tried not to show how much my hands were trembling. *If he'd shot Naomi . . .* I shoved the unwelcome thought away. "We need to find Dr. Nikas before someone gets really hurt," I said. Sick worry rose in a choking wave. "We need to find Pietro and the others too. *We* need to. We don't know if Rachel and Dan and the rest of them are going to try—especially for the two drivers and the security guard—and even if they do, we *know* there's an insider. *Someone* gave those Saberton thugs the codes to get in."

Kyle's gaze remained on Philip's back. "Without Mr. Ivanov, the Tribe will falter," he stated. "And without Brian," he shook his head, "the organization of the remaining security and teams is crippled."

And what will happen to me if the Tribe falls apart? I selfishly wondered. It was more than a cool part-time job. It was security that went beyond money or brains. Once Marcus moved away, would I have anyone around who understood me? I knew I was being crazily self-centered, but fuck, sometimes it was called for, right?

I moved to Philip, not caring that the others were watching or could hear me. "We need you," I murmured, and bumped him with my shoulder. "We'll get through this. Don't make me bite you again."

A weak snort of laughter escaped him. During the mayhem that occurred at the filming of *High School Zombie Apocalypse!!*, Philip went berserk, and I'd followed through on a bizarre urge to sink my teeth into his shoulder. Weird as hell, but it calmed him right down.

He bumped that shoulder into mine, then turned and walked back with me to Kyle and Naomi.

"How do we find Pietro and the others?" I asked. "Do we have even the slightest clue where they might be?"

"It would most likely be Dallas or New York," Naomi said.

Kyle gave a solemn nod in response. "They weren't taken for ransom, and Saberton has major operations in both cities."

"Great," I said. "How do we know which city?"

"The R&D labs are in Dallas," Naomi said, forehead creased in contemplation. She tapped her chin as she considered. "And the corporate offices are in New York. No lab though."

"All right, so we go to Dallas?" I asked.

"The immediate use is likely for research," Philip said. "Dallas certainly makes the most sense."

But Naomi held up a hand. "You're right—the two drivers and the guard are most likely in Dallas. Probably Dr. Charish as well However, there's a solid chance that my mother ordered Mr. Ivanov taken for retribution or some other personal reason. If so, then he *might* be in New York, since that's where she stays this time of year."

Great. Everyone had some bit of personal knowledge to help except me. I wanted to ask questions, but I had a feeling I'd end up being one of those people who asks the stupid questions that everyone already knows the answers to and simply ends up slowing the whole thing down.

"We don't have enough manpower to check both," Kyle said, then lifted his head and snapped his fingers. "Flight plans. They'd have flown him to New York if they took him there. Naomi, how hard would it be to check if a Saberton jet left here and, if so, where it went?"

She smiled. "Not hard at all." She walked a few feet away and started doing stuff on her phone. I moved off in another direction and once again tried to call Marcus. Again it rang and then went to voicemail. Frustrated I hung up without leaving a message and instead simply texted him. *Something happened 2 ur uncle n doc. Need to talk 2 u ASAP!!!!*

My heart leaped when it dinged with a reply message. *I know. Pursuing possible lead and keeping head down. You ok?*

Relieved, I quickly thumbed in a reply. *I'm ok. with some others. where r u? need to join up.*

Can't join up. Risky. About to leave town. Will explain later. Need to turn off phone soon. Stay safe. I love you.

I stared at the last three words, heart in my throat. Even after being dumped, he still cared. Finally I texted my reply. *Love you too.*

"It's New York," Naomi crowed in triumph, jogging back to the others. "Flight plans confirmed it. Time to get serious now. First things first, we need to ditch all the phones."

"Phones can be tracked," Kyle said with a nod of agreement.

"Right." I tore my eyes from Marcus's text. "I'll turn mine off."

"Not good enough," Naomi said and held out her hand. "With the right technology it can still be tracked, even without a battery. Hand it over."

The look in her eyes stopped me. "What are you going to do?" I asked, suspicious.

"Smash and toss," she said.

"Are you *crazy?*" I clutched my phone to my chest. "This is a brand new phone!"

Philip looked at me, expression grave. "And we're talking about our lives. A phone is replaceable. You aren't."

"Yeah, well I bet you three make a fuckload more money than I do!" I retorted. "Y'all can smash your phones, but I don't see why I can't hide mine somewhere so I can get it back after all this shit is over."

"It's just a phone," Naomi said with a roll of her eyes.

"Did the Tribe give you your phone?" I demanded.

"Well, yes—"

"And the rest of you?" I stabbed the two men with my glare, and they gave grudging nods. I swung my attention back to Naomi. "I'm not as stupid as you seem to think, and I get that we need to ditch the phones, but shit's only *replaceable* if you have the money to replace it. I have a goddamn mountain of debt right now because I had to replace *everything*." My stomach roiled with tension at the memory of the flood and the aftermath. "I'd rather not make that mountain any fucking higher, so forgive me if I'm not all excited about tossing away something that isn't exactly cheap. I spent half a week's salary for my phone." I started to go on about the fact that I had two pairs of jeans to my name because, instead of buying a third pair, I decided to buy dishes that actually matched each other, but Naomi jerked her hand up to stop me.

"Okay, fine, I get it," she snapped, and I had the sense she was more annoyed that I was making her feel guilty about her financial status. Well, what the fuck was I supposed to do about that? Not my fault she had no clue what it was like to be poor.

"Where do you want to hide it?" she asked with an impatient gesture around her. "Need to do it sooner rather than later so we can get moving. And you have to promise not to freak if it's not here when we get back."

My scowl deepened. "I won't freak," I muttered, stung. "I just don't want to destroy it." Part of me knew my freakout about the phone was avoidance to keep from thinking about the scariness of going to New York, but I still felt a weird hurt that Naomi wasn't even trying to understand what it was like to always have to sweat finances.

"There's a post office half a mile down the road," I told the others. "The lobby's open twenty-four/seven, and I can mail it to myself."

Philip nodded slowly. "That's a damn good idea, Angel."

Naomi grumbled something under her breath, but didn't protest, though she made a big production over smashing her own phone and tossing the remains into the water. Philip rolled his eyes at her antics, but he followed suit. As we returned to the car Kyle suggested that it might be best if Philip didn't drive, and, considering the incident moments before, no one argued. Kyle took the wheel and less than ten minutes later my phone was sealed within a priority mail box—addressed to myself at the Coroner's Office, because I didn't trust my neighbors not to steal packages left on my porch. The self-serve machine spit out the correct postage, I dumped the box into the slot, then returned to the car.

"Damn it," I muttered as I climbed back into the car. "I think I forgot to turn it off." When nobody responded I realized the others were focused on Kyle. Still in the driver's seat, he was dialing a number on his phone—which had obviously not yet been destroyed.

"Calling Rachel," Kyle said. "Giving notice."

I shot a baffled look at Naomi but she simply gave a helpless shrug in response. Philip appeared equally confused, so apparently I wasn't the only one operating without a clue.

"Rachel?" Kyle said. "Griffin here."

Kyle must have turned the volume up because I had little trouble hearing Rachel's voice. "Griffin," she snarled. "You need to come in so we can *discuss* this situation."

"That's not happening," he replied. Calm. Assured. "You have an insider. It isn't me. It could be you. Griffin out."

"Me!" Outrage and fury filled her voice. "Griffin, this isn't over.

I swear I'll hunt you down and—" Whatever else she had to say stopped as Kyle crushed the phone in a zombie-strength grip.

There was a moment of silence. "Nice finish," I finally said. "Kind of like dropping the mic and walking off stage."

Kyle and Philip turned bewildered looks my way, but Naomi gave a snort-laugh. "So," I continued. "New York City. We flying there?" I kept my tone as light and casual as possible, though my level of inner freakout climbed a few more degrees. Not only had I never set foot in an airplane, but I didn't even want to think about how much something like that would *cost*.

"We're not flying," Naomi said, to my relief. "It would be too easy to nail us on arrival. We're driving. We were deciding where to pick up a vehicle since we have to ditch this one."

They'd already discussed this, I realized. When I was off mailing my phone. Not that I had anything useful to contribute, but it still bugged me. "You gonna buy a car?"

"No time for that," she said, "and it could still be traced. We'll have to 'borrow' one."

The look I gave her was nothing short of dubious. "You intend to steal a car, and then drive it to New York?"

"I have vehicles stashed in long term storage in a few cities—including New York—for emergencies, but not here," she said, totally matter of fact about having excess cars she didn't use. "None of us have any here," she went on, "so yes, we need to steal one."

My level of *dubious* went up a couple of degrees. "Let me get this straight. You're going to steal a car. And then drive it on roads and through intersections and on highways—"

"Jesus," she interrupted with a scowl, "not a car that's going to be reported any time soon."

"How do you know?" I shot back.

"Because we'll pick it up from an impound lot or long term parking at the airport," she said. "Chances of it being missed over the next week will be miniscule. We'll obey all traffic laws and not give any cop a reason to pull us over."

"But what if it does get reported?" I pressed. "What if we do get pulled over, or get in a fender bender? Hell, what if we go through an intersection that has one of those cameras that's linked to the stolen car database, and the cops get notified?" Jeez, I did *not* want to once again experience the joy of being arrested for possession of stolen property.

Philip glanced my way. "It's a definite risk, but I don't see that we have any other option."

I fell silent and stayed that way for a couple of minutes. I had an idea, but I knew damn well everyone would think it was really stupid. *Screw it.* "I know where we might be able to get a car."

"Where, Angel?" Kyle asked, without a trace of condescension or impatience.

"My ex-boyfriend," I said. "He fixes cars."

Chapter 10

It was true, Randy *did* fix cars. Of course, he also dabbled in various illegal activities related to cars and parts and that sort of thing, but that wasn't worth mentioning. It didn't really matter at the moment, and they could probably figure that part out on their own.

Naomi's eyebrows lifted. "Randy?" she asked, disbelief thick in her voice. She'd heard a few of my tales about my ex. "Why would he help you?"

But Kyle lifted a hand. "Give her a chance to tell us," he said to Naomi, eyes on me.

I shot him a grateful look. "I don't know for sure that he would," I said. "I'd have to feel him out first, but, well, we go way back." I shrugged. "We dated, like, *forever*, and if we could get a car from him, then we wouldn't have to worry about getting hooked for having a stolen car."

"It's worth a try," Philip said, and Kyle gave a nod. "Where do we need to go?"

I rubbed the back of my neck. "It's Friday, so he's probably at Pillar's Bar, on Kapp Street." That was the bar where we used to hang out the most. It was also where some asshole put a date rape drug in my drink, which led to my becoming a zombie in the first place.

"Got it," Philip said, making a turn. About ten minutes later we pulled into the gravel lot. The old neon sign on the roof simply spelled out BAR in big block letters like a beacon to outsiders. Everyone around these parts knew it was Pillar's, so why waste money on the sign? Over thirty cars and pickups crowded the lot, along with half dozen motorcycles up near the entrance. Randy's 1968 red Dodge Charger sat in the first space at the end of the building, where he always parked. Nothing had changed.

An odd curl of nerves wound through my belly. I hadn't set foot in this place in over a year, and I hadn't spoken to most of the people from that old life in just as long, including Randy. "It might be best if I go in by myself," I said.

"Probably so," Philip agreed. He reached into the bag resting on the console and pulled out a packet, handed it to me. "Eat that first. I'll be right outside."

I obediently sucked it down, then scraped my fingers through my hair to get it to lie down in a slightly more orderly fashion. "Wish me luck," I said, then slipped out of the car and headed toward the entrance. I heard a car door close and looked back to see Philip following me.

"I'll be right outside," he repeated.

My nerves eased slightly. "Thanks."

The people clustered by the door gave me a glance then returned to their cigarettes and low conversation. Music poured out when I opened the door, like hot air on a cold day. I quickly stepped inside and pulled the door shut behind me, feeling as if I'd let all the music out if I left it open.

The four piece band on the crude stage against the back wall kicked out a decent version of a Blake Shelton song while a cluster of worn lights flashed to the beat of the music, sending weak pulses of red and blue through the haze of cigarette smoke. Loud conversation, drunken laughter, and the occasional crack of pool balls surrounded me like a comfortable blanket. How much time had I wasted here?

Winding my way through familiar faces with forgotten names, I returned glares and scowls with defensive ones of my own and made my way toward the man behind the bar. He gave an odd double take when he saw me, then pushed a beer toward a regular at the other end of the bar. He took the bills offered and stuffed them into the till, then came over to me and leaned an elbow on the bar.

"Been a while since you been in here, Angel," he said as I racked my mind for his name. Bill. Yeah, that was it. I'd scored Percocet from him a time or two. Bill had pills.

"Yeah," I said, trying to raise my voice enough to be heard over the din without actually shouting. "It's been a weird year. Can I get a beer?"

His mouth twisted into a sneer. "I heard you got Clive busted. Called the cops on him."

Shit. Now I understood all the hostile looks. I narrowed my eyes. "Is that what he told you? That weasely little shitball. I guess he left out the part where he called the cops on *me*. And I can fucking prove that shit. That's on motherfucking nine-one-one."

That took him slightly aback. "He told everyone you set him up," Bill said, expression remaining accusing.

"Why the hell would I set him up?" I demanded. "I was trying to get clean after fucking overdosing. I didn't want to be anywhere near him."

A frown started between his eyebrows. "Huh. Yeah, I heard you almost died." He picked up a rag and swiped at some unknown liquid on the bar.

"You heard right," I said. Kind of *did* die, depending on how you defined it. "Clive was a whiny bitch and was all butthurt 'cause I wouldn't buy from him anymore." It wasn't a total lie. Clive *had* been pissed when I wouldn't steal confiscated drugs from the Coroner's Office and pass them his way. "He called the cops on *me* because he's a little prick, then when the cops came and wouldn't arrest me for his bullshit, he fought with them and got his own ass busted." I couldn't help but smirk. "And of course he had a car full of steroids, so they busted his stupid ass for that too."

Bill's gaze remained hard and distrusting for another moment while the band shifted to a crappy cover of a Garth Brooks song. Finally he reached for a beer, popped the top off and set it in front of me. "Yeah, that sounds like him."

Doing my best not to show relief, I took the bottle and sipped. "He's a fucking moron."

"You still clean?" he asked. He glanced at the bottle in my hand.

"No drugs, no pills in a year," I said then set the bottle down and gave it a tap. "This is as hard as I go anymore, and not much of that."

A smile kicked up one side of Bill's mouth. "That's cool, Angel," he said, and I decided he really meant it. "I got my one month chip last week," he continued, ducking his head a bit as if embarrassed.

"Yeah?" I smiled. "That's fucking awesome. Must be hard to do while working here."

Someone called his name from farther down the bar. He held up a finger to him, then looked back at me and shrugged. "Nah. Not as long as I keep my head on straight. Every day I see how fucked up people can be, and it helps me remember why I'm doing it."

"I get that," I said.

"Look." He leaned slightly closer. "You need to watch your back in here. Pretty much everyone thinks you fucked Clive over." Then his brow furrowed. "What are you doing here, anyway?"

"I'm looking for Randy," I said. "I saw his car out front."

Bill jerked his head toward the back. "He's playing pool. Him and Carol Ann."

At the mention of that woman's name, my face heated in a flush of anger that should've been dead. For the last two years of my relationship with Randy, she'd hung on the edge, trying to slide her loser self between us any time we had one of our breakups.

"They're together?" I asked as nonchalantly as possible.

He shrugged. "According to her."

In Carol Ann's world, that was all that mattered. "Thanks." I pushed a couple of bills across the bar to pay for the beer. "Keep the change. And good luck."

"You too. Watch your back."

With a parting nod I took my beer and headed toward the pool room. Now that I knew the reason for the hostile looks it was easier to glare right back. The band thumped out the last notes of their pathetic ballad and announced a break.

The crowded pool room off to the left of the stage reeked of old cigarette smoke and a hint of sewage, with a touch of chemical-flowery air freshener thrown in for good measure. A chubby guy with flushed cheeks and a bubba buzz cut casually flipped me off as I descended the two steps to the grimy linoleum, then turned away to fish pool balls from the return on the farthest of the three faded tables. Most of the people in here were too focused on their game to give much of a shit about me, and I didn't recognize more than a handful anyway. A few gave me quizzical looks, likely wondering why I deserved a middle finger, then apparently decided it would use up too many brain cells to figure out the mystery. A cluster of barely legal bimbos whispered and giggled by the cue rack, eyeing some young stud. A stud by their standards, at least. Hell, a year or so ago I'd have overlooked his slight beer gut and shaggy mullet too.

I took a fake sip of my beer to hide my smile. Damn. At least I had standards now.

A woman with screaming red hair leaned over a table to get a shot, giving everyone behind her a great look at her red thong underwear as her way-too-short jeans skirt hiked up. Carol Ann Pruitt. She hadn't been "barely legal" in damn near a decade, but she still clung to it with her acrylic nails and over-whitened teeth.

Carol Ann took her shot and missed badly, laughing as she straightened and tugged her skirt down—though only enough to barely cover the cheeks of an age-and-beer-widened ass. She swept a hopeful gaze around, probably to see if anyone was watching her show. Her slightly unsteady looksee went past me, then snapped right back, to my annoyance. Like I had time for this shit.

"You!" She stabbed the pool cue in my direction. "You got some kinda nerve dragging your narc cop-lovin' ugly ass in here!"

I gave her a lazy look and shrugged. "I needed a laugh and figured I'd come see the chunk of hair on the back of your head that you miss every fucking time you do your color. Seriously, do you even own a damn mirror?"

Titters went through the room in a wave, which didn't ease Carol Ann's mood one bit. She tightened her grip on the cue and started toward me with murder in her eyes. Shit. I'd forgotten just how much bigger she was than me.

"I got a mirror, bitch, and I use it to see how much better lookin' I am than you!" she shouted. "Randy don't want nothin' to do with you, so get your skanky ass outta here before I get pissed."

Behind her I saw the men's room door open and Randy step out. My pulse quickened as he saw me, but I was too busy having fun with Carol Ann to spare him a second of attention. "Aw, will you turn green and get big and ugly?" I taunted her. "You got all but the color part down already."

This time the laughter and catcalls were unmistakably in my favor. Narc or not, this was a crowd that loved them some good putdowns. Unfortunately, Carol Ann couldn't appreciate the finer social points of insult-trading. The only comeback she could muster was a rage-sputtered "Stupid bitch!" right before she swung the cue at me as if she was Babe Ruth driving in a homer.

The air seemed to disappear from the room as everyone sucked in a breath. Logic and experience told them that Carol Ann was about to split my head wide open and probably be arrested for murder—or manslaughter at the very least—after which she'd no doubt end up as the head of her own prison girl gang with a few bitches willing to be at her beck and call in exchange for dubious protection from the other mean girls. It'd be a good step up for Carol Ann, an opportunity for her to take a strong leadership role in a way that she'd never been able to manage as a waitress at Jiggy Joe's Truck Stop. She wasn't a smart woman by any stretch, but with a little coaching she could pull off savvy, and after about five years she'd probably get paroled and maybe even go on to speak to underprivileged kids about anger management, being good, and staying in school. Hell, she might be held up as a positive role model—someone who made a terrible mistake in the heat of the moment and then turned her life around to become a good and decent upstanding member of society.

All that went through my head in a flash, followed by: *Pool cue. Coming at my head.* With the help of some good ol' zombie speed I shifted my beer to my left hand, ducked under the stick, then came right back up and drove my right fist into Carol Ann's double chin, killing forever her chances of becoming a reformed murderess. Well, maybe not forever. I doubted this would be the last time she flew off the handle and tried to split a head open.

The cue went flying out of her hand, and several people managed to dance out of its way before it smacked into Bubba Buzz Cut Guy's shin. He let out a yelp and a curse as Carol Ann went down in a totally unattractive sprawl.

"And stay down, bitch!" I said, mostly for effect, since everyone seemed to expect me to say something in that vein. I shook my hand out, even though apparently I'd *finally* managed to learn how to punch without breaking my hand. That was a nice change. *Sensei* would be so fucking proud. Well, maybe not with the whole bar fight thing without a shred of *jiu jitsu.* He'd sigh and get that pained look on his face. But, hey, I'd even kept hold of my beer. Now *that* took skills that weren't taught in a dojo.

I backed away to make room for the people taking cell phone pictures of Carol Ann as she moaned on the floor. I almost felt sorry for her before remembering that *she* had pretty much been the total aggressor and would've probably killed me if not for some *sweet* brain-charged action on my part. So, yeah, a few humiliating pictures on the internet wouldn't kill her, though I did keep half an eye on her to make sure no one in this crowd took the wrong kind of advantage of her. Fortunately—since I really didn't want to babysit the bitch—a couple of her girlfriends rushed over and scooped her up, and gave me reproachful and wary looks while they helped her stumble to the bathroom.

That's right, darlin'. I'll be the leader of my own girl gang.

A hard shove from behind put my internal revels to a harsh end, and I stumbled into a table, bruising my hips. Before I had a chance to react something hit me hard in the back around my left kidney, and in the next instant my vision went white as pain seared through me. And *kept* searing while I fought unsuccessfully to resist or jerk away or anything to get away from the source of the agony.

After several endless seconds the pain stopped as abruptly as a light going off. My legs buckled as much from the pain as from the sudden end of it, and I stumbled sideways to fall hard to the floor.

"And stay down, bitch!" a familiar voice sneered.

Stun gun, I realized as I fought to catch my breath. A lot like the time I was Tasered by Kristi Charish's goons, though not *quite* as sucktastic. And the voice belonged to Debbie Stewart, another Carol Ann crony. I tried to turn to deal with her, but to my surprise Randy stepped between us. Good thing, since I wasn't moving all that well.

"What the *fuck* you think you're doing, Debbie?" Randy challenged.

I managed to push up to a swaying kneel, shifting enough to see Debbie with a stun gun in her hand and a defiant look on her face. Good thing Randy had my back since my left side was a mass of pins and needles thanks to her holding the stun gun on me for so long. If she'd tried to hit me again, there wasn't a damn thing I could've done about it.

Debbie took a step back in the face of Randy's anger, then jerked her chin up. "You saw what that narc whore did to Carol Ann!" she declared, a vicious gleam in her eyes. "We don't take that shit around here."

Seriously? I thought as I accomplished one knee up. Half the stains on the floor were from bar fights. This place was a staph infection's wet dream.

Randy's shoulders tensed. "You just pulled some low shit even for 'round here," he said, words clipped. He only talked like that when he was really riled up. "And, yeah, I saw what she did to Carol Ann." He took a step toward Debbie, and it warmed my heart to see her back away in response. "She kicked Carol Ann's ass, so I'm thinking you best get your ass outta here before Angel gets up."

That sounded like the perfect cue for me to do exactly that, though it probably would've been a lot more impressive if I hadn't been swaying. Damn it, my left side still didn't want to behave, but a familiar ripple of hunger told me my parasite was on the job.

"She ain't gonna do shit," Debbie said, then brandished the stun gun. "And you best back off!" She looked around at the crowd for support, but frowned when she saw that most were simply watching or recording the entire event for future shits and giggles.

A mild stir in the crowd behind her drew my attention long enough for me to see the familiar blond head of Philip. Relief shot through me, quickly followed by worry. The rugged, clean-cut operative and former soldier would stand out in this place like a lion among kittens, and the last thing I needed was for Randy to get spooked or for even *more* fighting to break out. Yet even as I caught Philip's eye and gave him a slight *It's cool* head shake, I realized he wasn't attracting anywhere near the attention I'd expected. He had a bit of a slouch in his shoulders now, and an unhurried air that fit with the overall vibe of the crowd. The instant he caught my signal he smoothly shifted direction to amble to the bar as if he'd been headed that way the entire time.

Fortunately all Debbie saw was that the crowd wasn't as firmly on her side as she'd hoped. Scowling, she swung her attention back to Randy. "Why you have to go get in the middle of things?" she whined. "You should be taking up for poor Carol Ann!"

Randy folded his arms over his chest, ignoring the stun gun completely. "Carol Ann took a lot less hurt than she was planning to give out," he said. "I'd say that's even. It's you buttin' into things now, so you'd best back the fuck off." He sounded laid back again, but I knew him well enough to know he was still pissed. Right now I was fine with letting him handle things. Even though my left side wasn't buzzing anymore, I felt just enough brain hunger to know I wouldn't have any zombie super speed going for me.

Debbie hesitated, defiance flickering in the face of Randy's staunch defense of me along with the lack of overwhelming crowd support. Glaring at Randy, she waved the stun gun in my direction. "She got off easy!" she announced, then turned and flounced off toward the bathroom.

For an instant I considered charging after her to tackle her face first into the grimy linoleum, and even took a step forward to do so, before deciding it wouldn't be the best idea considering my overall goal here. *Eyes on the prize, Angel.*

With the excitement over and no blood to clean up or ogle, the onlookers drifted away to return to their games or conversations or drug deals or whatever the hell they'd been up to before. No one was giving me Fuck You looks anymore, so apparently I'd proved myself by decking Carol Ann. It didn't make a lick of sense, but I understood it all the same.

The bartender said something to Philip and gestured toward the back room. Philip nodded and headed that way without a single glance in my direction as he passed. My guess was that he planned to duck out the back door, though I already saw girls angling in his direction like sharks scenting hunky blood in the water.

I gave Randy a fervent smile. "Thanks."

He shrugged. "There's dirty fighting, and then there's fighting dirty, ya know?"

"Yeah, I know." I rubbed the crook of my left arm where it still had a bit of tingle. "It's okay. I'll get her back someday when she's not expecting it."

Randy chuckled, and the last of the anger slipped away from the set of his shoulders. "Carol Ann's gonna be pissed when she can think straight again," he said, smile tugging at his mouth that told me he didn't really care and that he'd enjoyed the scene as much as any of the others. Probably would've enjoyed it more if we'd ended up in a classic roll-on-the-floor catfight where we ripped each other's clothes off, but I could forgive him that since he'd stepped in when I needed the help.

"What are you doin' down here?" he asked, cocking his head. "Come back for a little of what I got?"

Here I'd been worried that Randy would tell me to fuck off, kind of the way I'd told *him* to fuck off the last time I'd seen him—right after he asked me to steal drugs from the Coroner's Office for Clive to sell. We sure as hell hadn't parted in a nice way. Then again, we'd broken up and got back together so many times over the four years we'd dated, he'd apparently taken it in stride just like all the other breakups, even though it'd been over a year.

Hell, if he really thought I wanted to get back together with him, who was I to set him straight? An uncomfortable tickle of guilt fluttered in my belly for leading him on, and I couldn't entirely push it away. Randy was a loser, sure, but we'd been losers together, and right now he was a loser I needed. So, what the hell did that make me?

I just gotta be careful, that's all, I told myself as I put on a smile for him. "Yeah, something like that." That part wasn't a lie. I *was* back for a little of what he got.

He moved closer. "Where's that cop asshole you been fucking?"

"We broke up," I said and shrugged, doing my best to keep the ache of it off my face.

Lingering tension in his face relaxed in what seemed like relief. "I like the sound of that." He leaned against the post beside me. "You need another beer?"

"I can't stay long," I said, and set the barely touched beer down on a convenient table. "Can I come by your place in a bit? There's something I need to ask you."

Pleased surprise lit his eyes. "Sure you can." He grinned. "I got answers for *all* your questions."

"I bet you do," I said, unable to resist a low chuckle at the good ole Randy charm.

The women's bathroom door opened, and a sniveling Carol Ann came out, flanked and supported by her two cronies. Randy glanced at her then gave me an easy smile. "It's gonna take me a while to clean up the mess here. How 'bout I see you in an hour or so?"

"An hour or so it is." I gave him a wink and a smile, then turned and sauntered out, sashaying as much as my skinny hips would allow. As soon as I made it outside and the door closed behind me I blew out a breath and let myself slump. Philip pushed off from the wall where he'd managed to be damn near invisible in the shadows, judging by the startled reactions of the junkies clustered near the corner of the building. They skittered off like roaches in sunlight when Philip moved toward me.

"You sure you're okay?" he said as he raked an assessing look over me.

"Yeah. Thanks for having my back," I replied, then grinned. "Worth getting zapped to deck that skanky bitch."

Amusement lit his eyes. "I don't doubt it."

"Let's get out of here," I said. "I'm going to his trailer in about an hour."

"He has a vehicle we can use?"

"Dunno yet, but at least he's willing to talk to me."

We returned to where the car was parked on the perimeter of the lot, and I settled in the back with Naomi. Philip climbed into the front passenger seat, then tossed a small handful of cocktail napkins onto the dash before giving Kyle a sly look.

"Seven, in under three minutes."

Kyle gave a dry chuckle. "Nice."

Naomi frowned. "Seven what?"

I leaned forward to peer at the napkins, then laugh-groaned. "Phone numbers of girls who thought Philip was a filet steak in a room full of cafeteria hamburgers."

"Good lord," Naomi breathed. "I'm surprised he made it out alive."

"It was touch and go for a minute there," Philip replied. "Or rather, I felt touches where I didn't want them and knew it was time to *go!*"

And on that note we got the hell out of there.

Once we were away from the bar and headed to the highway I downed some dehydrated brain chips then filled the others in on the conversation with Randy. Naomi remained fairly quiet while I spoke, and I figured she still thought it was a bad idea to ask Randy for help. Hell, she was probably right, but no one else had come up with a better solution. And, no, stealing a random car was *not* a better solution.

"He was cool?" she finally asked. "No jealousy crap?"

"He was cool," I replied. "I think he got turned on when I knocked his girlfriend on her ass."

Kyle made a noise that sounded *almost* like a snort of laughter, but when I looked at him his face was as stoic as ever.

I gave Kyle directions, a little surprised when he knew the roads. Randy didn't exactly live in a high-traffic area of St. Edwards Parish.

At least I thought he knew them. I straightened when he made a right instead of a left onto Locust Lane. "Hey, you went the wrong way. You need to go toward the river."

His gaze was on the rearview mirror but he wasn't looking at me. "Tail," he said and it took me a couple of seconds to understand.

"Shit!" Immediately I craned around in my seat to peer behind us. "How do you know? Maybe it's just someone else going the same way?"

He was nice and didn't give me an *Are you fucking kidding me? I really do know what I'm doing* look and simply said, "Made two turns with us plus this one."

Fair enough. If Kyle said we had a tail, we had a tail. "Can you tell who it is?" *Saberton or Tribe?* I didn't need to say it. We all wondered the same thing.

"Headlights," he said simply. "No details." Then, "Hang on."

He made a sharp turn and floored it, but the other car obviously had a better engine. Within seconds they were right behind us. I clung to the seat, utterly certain that our pursuers were about to ram us and send us flying off the road.

Kyle abruptly did *something* that I couldn't follow at all. I only knew it involved brakes and tight turns and skidding, and at one point we were going backward at what had to be sixty miles-per-hour, but when we straightened out we'd miraculously gained a substantial lead.

"Holy shit, I know this area!" I said as I realized where we were, practically flapping my hands in excitement. "There's a game trail I used to take back in junior high and high school when . . ." I hesitated, then realized these guys wouldn't hold my past against me.

"It leads to a clearing where some of us used to smoke pot. It goes on through to the road that runs past Randy's property." I'd met Randy for the first time in that clearing.

Philip's frown was reflected by the other two. "We're more vulnerable on foot," he said.

"But we'll be off road," Kyle put in. "I doubt they'll have dogs to track us." His eyes met mine. "You sure you can lead the way and not get us stuck in some godforsaken bog?"

"I only know nice god-sanctioned bogs, I promise," I replied. "Turn at the broken signpost right up there." Kyle made a turn that left my stomach behind, and we bounced over rutted and winding dirt road for about a minute. "Here! Stop here!"

Kyle did so, and we quickly grabbed everything we had with us, which wasn't all that much, thankfully. As we bailed out of the car, Philip snagged his jump bag from the trunk, and Kyle looked back toward the main road. "They went past," Kyle said. "The brush is high enough to hide the car from the road, but they'll be coming back to see where we turned off. We have about two minutes to get some distance and then go to ground."

"Not a problem," I insisted, then took off into the chest-high grass with the others close behind. Less than a minute later we heard the sound of tires on the bumpy road.

"Down," Kyle ordered. We dropped to the wet, spongy ground and didn't need another order to tell us to be still as statues. I concentrated on slowing my breathing, listened as the car stopped. The beam of a powerful flashlight skimmed by, but the grass was tall and we'd made it far enough away from the road that they couldn't see any sign of us.

I heard a muttered and angry conversation, filled to the brim with curse words. After some more cursing, the men returned to their car and backed out to the highway. I began to rise, but Philip seized my arm and shook his head. Muscles taut, I listened for any evidence of our pursuers but only heard the retreating sound of their car. Even after it reached the highway and peeled out we remained still in the grass, and it took everything I had not to shriek and leap up when something slithered across my calf.

After what had to be ten minutes Kyle muttered, "Clear."

Philip released my arm, and I shot to my feet. "Snake," I gulped.

Luckily, Philip didn't laugh at my reaction. Good thing, since I'd have decked him like Carol Ann, zombie baby or not. Or at least tried to. Okay, maybe just thought about it really hard.

"Which way?" he asked.

Fighting the deep desire to make a bunch of noise to chase off any lurking snakes, I turned and headed away from the dirt road and toward the thick darker darkness ahead that I knew was the woods. I had a panicked minute when I couldn't locate the game trail, but finally found the dead tree that marked it. Philip pulled out a key-chain LED light and clicked it to red as we started working our way through the brush and trees and sticker bushes. At long last, lights glimmered through the trees, and in another hundred feet the trail opened out onto a road.

"We lost them, so that's good," Naomi remarked. "On the other hand, after that jaunt through the brambles, I have thorns in unmentionable places."

I grinned. "I'm not helping you with those." I pointed to a rusted mailbox about fifty feet down the road. Beyond it the road turned to gravel. "That's Randy's driveway." I brushed at mud and dirt and finally gave up. I couldn't see what I was doing anyway.

"We'll wait here," Kyle said.

"Yeah, I think he'd freak if all four of us trooped up to his door." Naomi gave me a worried look. "Be careful."

I had a feeling she was more worried about my mental well-being than the physical. "I will," I replied, then jogged to Randy's driveway.

Chapter 11

Randy began learning everything there was to know about cars about the time he was old enough to hold a wrench. His mama had run off not long after he was born, and his dad practically raised him in the garage. They worked together until a few years ago when his dad met a lady and moved to Houston. After Randy and I broke up I finally climbed out of the pit of denial I'd been in during most of my time with him, and accepted that much of Randy's business wasn't exactly on the legal end of things.

Right now that didn't really bother me one bit. Hell, only a few months earlier I'd bashed a guy's head in with a baseball bat. I didn't have any room to talk.

My steps slowed as I reached the end of Randy's drive. The gate itself probably hadn't been closed in twenty years and hung crooked and corroded against the barb wire fence. A dilapidated, corrugated-metal garage, held together by rust and wishful thinking, stood beside a huge oak tree. A yellow bug light over the garage door made it impossible to determine the colors of the three fixer-upper cars parked in front of it. Lights inside the trailer and the faint thump of music told me Randy was home, and likely in a Carol Ann-free zone, since only his Charger was parked by the door. He didn't like being on the hook to give someone a ride back to their car in the morning.

He's expecting me, I reminded myself. He wasn't stupid enough to have Carol Ann here when he knew I was coming by. Randy might be totally fine with watching two women fight in a bar, but he didn't like a lot of drama in his own place.

I climbed the three steps and knocked. He opened the door a few seconds later and peered at me through the screen. "What happened to you?"

"Car trouble," I said, keeping my eyes on his face so that I wouldn't have to look down and see the oh-so-sexy view of his old, dingy tighty-whities—the only clothing he had on at the moment. And, knowing Randy, I couldn't even chalk it up to some sort of sad attempt at a come on. It was *completely* normal for him to come home and strip down to underwear.

He pushed open the screen door. "C'mon in and get cleaned up."

"Thanks." I stepped in and took a look around. Not much had changed in the year since I'd last been here. The game system had been upgraded, and the recliner looked brand new, but the rest was as familiar as home. The smell of pot and cigarettes and bacon grease hung in the air. A bong sat on the TV stand beside the big screen, and the remnants of a couple of joints lay in the ashtray on the coffee table. "I just need a wet washcloth," I told him, looking down at my jeans and shirt—both wet and muddy from lying in the marsh. "Not sure how much good it'll do, but worth a try."

"Sure thing." He stepped to the kitchen, pulled a washcloth from a drawer and wet it, then wrung it out and handed it to me. "Where's your car?" he asked as I started wiping the mud off my knees. "Stuck or broke down?"

"Um, well *my* car is parked down the street from Top Cow because I couldn't get it to start earlier today." I worked at cleaning off the worst of the gunk but gave up on getting the ground in stuff. "I was in a different car tonight that sort of got stuck." Sighing, I swiped at my shirt. "It's kind of why I wanted to talk to you. I need to borrow a car."

Randy didn't have any education past high school, but he wasn't stupid. "You mean that's what you came to Pillar's for?" Hurt flickered across his face. "To get a car from me?"

"Yeah." I sighed. Crap. Now I felt like a heel. "I'm sorry for misleading you. A couple of friends of mine are in some really deep trouble, and I, uh, need a car that can't be traced to me." I met his eyes. "I know we didn't break up on the best of terms, but I . . . I hope you don't still hate me."

He reached for a pack of cigarettes. "Well, ain't that some shit."

Grimacing, I rinsed out the washcloth then set it on the counter. "I'm sorry. If you want me to go, I will."

Randy lit the cigarette, took a drag from it. "Who are these friends of yours? And what kind of trouble?"

"Not sure you'd believe me if I told you."

He picked a stained coffee cup off the counter and tapped ash into it. "Why don't you try me."

I remained still for a moment while I ran down my options, possible lies, what portions of the truth I could tell. In a weird way I missed the simplicity of my old life. No big secrets that could destroy other people's lives. Simple goals.

More like no *goals*, I reminded myself. Wanting more out of life was hard work but worth it. "You can't tell *anyone*," I finally said.

His brows drew together. "Shit. What kind of trouble you got yourself into?"

"Swear to me you won't repeat anything I tell you tonight," I said. "I mean not one fucking word to anyone. I'm not exaggerating when I say my life depends on it."

He took a pull off the cigarette then held it out for me. "You know I can keep my mouth shut."

I took the cig and thought about that for a few seconds. Despite his many other faults, he wasn't one to blab secrets.

Well, this would be interesting. I took a drag, not even minding that it would use up brains. "Okay. So, I have this *medical* condition, and I have to take a certain kind of supplement about once a week or I get really messed up," I began. "Problem is that this supplement is illegal, but there's an organization of people who all need this same kind of supplement, and we all work together to get it. But there's also this big corporation who wants to control it and study what it does to us, because some of the stuff about this certain medical condition is kind of good, as long as we get the supplement. I mean, like, we don't really get sick the usual way anymore." God this was all kinds of fucked up, but I was in too deep to stop now. Taking a deep breath, I plowed on. "And now the big corporation has kidnapped the head of our, um, group, as well as the main scientist who studies this medical condition. And if we don't get them back we're all pretty much fucked." I took another drag and handed it back to him.

"Damn." He took the cig, frowned. "You know that sounds crazy, right?"

I gave him a crooked smile. "I toldja you wouldn't believe me."

"Funny thing is, it's too crazy to be made up." The frown stayed on his face. "You know I'm not one for calling the cops, but kidnapping sounds like a big deal."

"Yeah, well, there's that whole *illegal supplement* part of it," I pointed out. "If we call the cops, these guys are in even bigger trouble." Cripes, it sounded like I was working with a cartel. Then again, in some ways I was. Just not the kind of drugs Randy expected.

"Makes sense." He put the cigarette to his lips, then lowered it. He looked suspiciously at it and then to me. "How do I know I haven't caught this shit from you?"

"Doesn't work that way," I told him. "Promise. I mean, it's not contagious just by being around someone or fucking them. It's pretty rare."

Apparently satisfied, he sucked on the cigarette then headed to the hallway. "Y'know, since you're done with that cop, it'd be all right if you hung out here again some." He stopped in front of the dryer, picked a t-shirt and a pair of shorts out of the pile atop it and tugged them on.

I couldn't keep the slight smile off my face. "I appreciate the offer. I'm gonna try being single for a while though. I really haven't been since I was a teenager."

He didn't respond to that, simply walked back to the living room and tamped the cig out in the ashtray on the coffee table. "Let's go find you a car." He dug a ring of keys out of the sofa cushions then headed out the door. I followed, relieved.

He paused to flick a switch at the end of his trailer then continued on. A floodlight above the garage flared on, drowning out the yellow of the bug light. Faded brown paint peeled on the big sliding door.

"What kinda car you need?" he asked over his shoulder as he fiddled with the lock on the garage door.

"I need something big enough for four people, that can get us to . . . Chicago." I caught myself barely in time from giving away our real destination. I trusted Randy, but there were limits to every trust.

He wheeled around, surprise and worry on his face. "Goddamn, Angel. What the hell you gonna do with yourself in a city like that?"

The worry I'd been holding back finally rose up in a smothering wave. "I dunno," I said, slumping. "Stick close to the people I'm with, I guess. Jesus, Randy, I'm scared out of my fucking mind." I could talk to him about this, I realized. "I've never been that far from home before. New Orleans is the biggest city I've ever been to, which isn't saying a whole lot."

He slid the garage door open with a screech of tired metal. "These people you're with, they got your back?"

"Yeah, they do," I said without hesitation. "They're totally cool."

But then I sighed. "I don't know how much help I'll be though. They pretty much *have* to bring me along because of another guy's, er, health condition." I shook my head. "Hard to explain, but I definitely feel like a fifth wheel." I tried to laugh it off, but it came out weak and humorless.

Randy turned to face me. "You'll be okay, Angel," he said with utter conviction. "You always are." One side of his mouth kicked up in a smile. "Just take some of that good ol' Louisiana coonass mojo with you, and those city folk won't know what hit 'em." He pivoted and flicked a light on inside the garage, while I stood there gaping at the completely unexpected show of support.

"This one ain't pretty but it runs good," he continued as he pulled a cloth off a dark green Ford Taurus sedan with a long dented scrape down the driver's side. "Rebuilt engine and new tranny. It'll get you up north."

I quickly wiped my eyes before he could see my sniveling, then stepped up to examine the car. "That's perfect." I slanted a quick look at him. "It's not hot, is it?"

"Nah. This one's cool. You won't get in trouble driving it." His eyes ducked away, obviously remembering the time I drove a car that *wasn't* cool, thanks to him, and got busted for possession of stolen property. "Guy gave it to me couple months ago in exchange for work I did on his truck and other car. Wasn't nothing but a piece of scrap to him. It's legit. Promise. I was gonna get it painted and then sell it." He unwound a key off the ring and handed it to me.

"It might be at least a week before I get it back to you," I said as I took it.

His shoulders lifted in a shrug. "It was just gonna be sitting out here anyway."

I held the key tightly in my hand and gave him a smile. "Randy, thanks for not holding a grudge against me."

"We had some good times." He shrugged again.

He missed me, I realized. He didn't know how to say it, but there it was. And I missed him too, in a weird way. Not in a let's-get-back-together kind of way. At all. No way. But it was silly to think I could simply turn off a whole chapter of my life and stick it in a drawer to never even think of it again. For better or for worse, my time with him helped make me who I was.

And, even though I knew getting back together with him was impossible on any number of levels, I found myself missing some of the closeness we'd shared. Hell, date someone for four years and you fucking get to know them.

"Yeah, we did have some good times." I shoved the key into my pocket, then didn't know what to do or say.

"I guess this is it." He shifted his weight. "You wanna take a few joints for the road?"

I hesitated. "Can't. Sorry. My condition gets a lot worse if I do stuff like that." It was a flat-out lie. Pot burned up less brains than cigarettes, but that wasn't the goddamn point. Thanks to my parasite keeping my system squeaky clean, I could smoke a whole joint and not get even the teensiest hint of a high. Truth was, I didn't want the joints around because they'd only remind me of how fucked up I used to be. Besides, what was the point of having them if they didn't do shit?

"Damn. That sucks," he said, making an appropriately sympathetic face.

"I'm used to it." I knew I needed to leave, but I couldn't let go of the sense that we had unfinished business between us. Being with him had been a seriously unhealthy rut for me. It bugged me that he couldn't—or wouldn't—get out of the rut as well. "Hey, I passed my GED a couple weeks ago," I blurted. "Finally got that high school diploma."

"Well, I'll be damned." A slow smile touched his mouth. "Never seemed you gave a shit about that."

"I didn't give a shit about anything." I shook my head. "I didn't see any reason to. I mean, my life was a fuckup from top to bottom." I dragged a hand through my hair. "It's weird but getting, um, sick was what finally made me realize I could do more with my life."

"You sure look good," Randy said, voice warm. "Don't look sick at all."

"Thanks," I said, "but you don't want to see me if I haven't had the supplement in a while." I glanced at my watch, surprised at how late it was. "Shit. I gotta go. I'm sorry."

"Me too." He lifted a hand to my cheek, stroked his thumb over it, then let his hand drop. "Guess I'll see you when I see you."

I stepped forward and gave him a light kiss. He tasted like beer and nicotine, smelled faintly of motor oil and whatever cologne he'd worn to the bar. Familiar and oddly pleasant.

He returned it just as lightly, then I turned away, got into the car, and left.

The others stepped out of the woods as I left the gravel of Randy's driveway. I gave up the driver's seat to Kyle then joined Naomi in the back.

"Took a long time," Philip said as he took shotgun.

"I hadn't seen him in almost a year," I replied. "I couldn't exactly say, 'Hey, gimme a car. 'Kay, thanks, bye!' "

Naomi looked over at me, a frown line between her eyebrows. "He didn't try anything, did he?"

"Nah, he was cool," I said, and shrugged. "We talked a bit, that's all."

"You okay?" she asked, lowering her voice. "You don't exactly look okay."

"It was weird seeing him again," I confessed.

She sat back. "I've never been in that situation."

I shot her a look of surprise. "Really? No exes?"

"Pathetic, huh?"

"Stop that," I ordered. "It's not pathetic. Hell, if it makes you feel any better, Randy's my *only* ex." Except as soon as I said it I remembered it wasn't true. *Nope, you got two exes now.* I hadn't told Naomi about Marcus yet. Everything had moved so quickly there'd been zero time to slow down and talk. Pour my heart out. Whine. Now wasn't the time either, not in a crowded car when a hell of a lot more than my love life was at stake.

"I also have half a decade on you," she pointed out, but she had a bit of a smile now.

"And last time I checked, it wasn't a contest," I shot back along with a light punch to her arm.

She chuckled softly, then looked ahead at Kyle. "I'm not going to be trying to win the ex competition, that's for sure."

I reached and gave her hand a squeeze. "Good plan. And I think you're safe there."

"Damn straight." She lifted her chin. "Okay, folks," she said at a more normal volume, "let's get the hell out of town."

Chapter 12

I knew better than to ask if we could swing by my house so I could throw some stuff into a bag for the trip. Maybe I wasn't a hotshit experienced operative like the other three, but I had enough brainpower to know the Tribe most likely had my house staked out. Of course, if I'd been a hotshit operative like the other three, I'd have had a jump bag packed like the others, and wouldn't be silently trying to figure out how the hell I was going to buy basic toiletries and enough clothing for several days with the eighteen dollars and ninety-four cents I currently had in my purse.

As stealthily as possible, I counted my money again, clinging to the stubborn hope that one of the bills would magically turn into a hundred dollar bill, or even a twenty. When that failed to happen, I quietly dug through my purse, searching every nook and cranny for cash.

Crap. Eighteen dollars and ninety-four cents wasn't going to get me very far. "I know y'all are going to say No," I said, "but I need to hit an ATM. I won't ask to do it again after this, I promise."

Kyle met my eyes in the rear view mirror. "Not a problem, Angel. We're still close enough to Tucker Point that the location won't give anything away."

Naomi turned to look at me, frowning slightly. "But you don't need to. I can cover anything."

"I have money," I replied, a bit defensively. "I don't have much cash on me, that's all. I need to get it out of the bank."

A hint of annoyance crept into her expression. "Okay, but we haven't even been on the interstate five minutes."

"Which bank?" Kyle asked, not exactly ignoring Naomi, but not quite taking her comment under consideration either.

"Lake Pearl Bank," I said, avoiding Naomi's eyes. "But any ATM'll do."

Naomi gave Kyle a *Seriously?* look, then made a small frustrated noise in her throat and flopped back into her seat.

What the hell was her issue? I didn't think I was being obnoxious by insisting on paying my fair share, but I was so out of my depth I couldn't be sure. Where was the line between being a moocher and accepting help?

"There's a BigShopMart about ten minutes ahead," Kyle said, "You can use the ATM, and we can pick up a few supplies at the same time."

"Thanks," I said, relieved, and even Naomi seemed somewhat mollified.

We made it off the interstate and to the store without incident. The others headed off to shop while I stopped at the ATM.

I stuck my card in and hit the button for express withdrawal of two hundred dollars, then stared at the "Insufficient funds available for this transaction" screen, which might as well have said "Haha! Fuck you, loser!"

A second attempt for a hundred dollars got the same obnoxious screen. Baffled, I did a balance check—which I probably should've done in the first place, but I'd thought for sure I had close to three hundred dollars in my account. Sure, I'd paid some bills recently, but those checks had all cleared, hadn't they?

The slip of paper spat out at me like a tongue, with $13.42 listed as my balance.

I crumpled the paper and flung it into the trash can, then grabbed a handheld shopping basket and stalked into the store. For a bizarre several seconds I felt like I was back in high school, trying to scrape out a way to buy clothing that didn't suck, and knowing that the cool kids would snicker behind their hands at me. Hell, the uncool kids as well.

Scowling, I shook off the memory. I wasn't poor anymore. I was *broke*, and there was a big difference between the two. However, growing up dirt poor had taught me a few things—some bad, like how to shoplift, and some good, like how to scrape by until Dad's next disability check came in.

I only considered the shoplifting angle for a second. Or two. Instead I scooped up cheap travel size toiletries at a dollar each, found a two-pack of underwear that I knew would crawl right up my ass, but hey, it was a buck ninety-nine for both, then scrounged up sweat pants and a t-shirt that wouldn't survive three washings, but hopefully, I wouldn't need them to.

Naomi and Kyle were already in line to check out when I approached the registers. I had absolutely no idea how they'd managed in such a short time, but their cart was piled high: Snacks and drinks, miscellaneous clothing and jackets, duffel bags, a large suitcase, and other every day necessities such as rope and zip ties and duct tape.

I joined a line a few registers down, sternly telling myself I didn't need to be self-conscious about how little I had in my basket. Someone got in line behind me a few seconds later, and I couldn't help but smile when he murmured, "Hey, ZeeEm."

"Hey, ZeeBee," I replied. "You doing okay?"

"Five by five." He leaned over my shoulder and peered into my basket. "You get everything you needed?"

The lie leaped to my lips, but I swallowed it back down and shook my head. "I couldn't get any money from the ATM," I told him, fighting down a wave of embarrassment. Damn it, harder to shake off those old ghosts than I thought. "I got a toothbrush and deodorant and a change of clothes, but that's it."

He bumped his shoulder lightly into mine. "That'll get you by for now, right?" he asked, and I nodded. "We'll be making a stop during the day tomorrow I'm sure. I can help you out."

"Sure. Thanks. I mean, I'm sure it's a computer glitch or something," I hurried to add. Even though I knew Philip wouldn't judge or look down at me, I didn't want to add "can't manage money" to the list of my obvious faults. "I'll call the bank in the morning and get it straightened out."

We finished our business and got everything loaded into the car. Naomi had the sense to buy a couple of cushy pillows, and I didn't mind one bit borrowing one when she offered. I jammed it between me and the door, and sighed in relative comfort as Kyle got us going again and back on the interstate.

What a crazy-ass day. And here I was, on the way to New York City. Exciting and scary, yet after about ten minutes that faded into monotony. Since it was the middle of the night, the scenery sucked. Dark interstate, headlights and taillights, road signs, exits with gas stations and restaurants lit up like Christmas trees, and then more dark interstate.

I adjusted the pillow, closed my eyes, and let the hum of the tires lull me to sleep.

*   *   *

Philip's raised voice jarred me from a weird dream about winning the lottery then having to hide on the perm shelf in a beauty supply store because a horde of six-armed insurance salesmen were after me.

"Not the next exit. Stop *now!*"

I opened my eyes and sat up, blinking to focus. Philip was leaning forward, speaking to Kyle, face twisted in concern.

"What's wrong?" I peered out the window but saw only the same damn nighttime non-scenery. Gravel crunched beneath the tires as Kyle pulled onto the shoulder, and his worried eyes met mine in the rear view mirror.

Philip abruptly flung the door open on the non-traffic side of the car, then turned to me and jabbed the release on my seat belt. I barely had time for an *Oh, no, not again* before he seized my wrist and dragged me out. I yelped in pain as I stumbled and landed on my knees in the gravel. "Fucking shit, Philip! Stop!"

He paused, and for an instant I thought he'd obey me, but he simply spun back to snatch one of the small coolers of brains from the floorboard. As soon as he had it, he pulled me to my feet and took off at a jog toward the guardrail and the woods beyond. I clutched at his forearm to help me keep my balance and fought to dig my heels in, but my barely hundred pounds didn't stand a chance of slowing him down.

"Do something!" I yelled back at the others, then saw that they weren't exactly sitting back and observing. Kyle had the emergency flashers on and a tranq gun in his hand, while Naomi moved toward the trunk of the car.

"Too dangerous," Philip said, voice taut and strained as he continued to drag me away from the car. "Too many cars. Too many people."

"No! Philip, you have to stop," I ordered, heart pounding. What if he didn't snap out of it this time? How far would he go to "protect" me? "Listen to me. It's more dangerous away from the others!"

If he heard me it sure as hell didn't make a difference. Breathing hard and face flushed, he set the cooler down on the other side of the guardrail, bodily lifted me over, then gripped my wrist again before I could make a dash for it. He stepped over, grabbed the cooler, and once again set off toward the woods.

"Shit, stop! Goddammit!" I seized hold of his hair and tried to figure out how I could jump onto him and bite him the way I had during the mayhem at the movie shoot. Except it'd been summer then, and he hadn't been wearing a jacket. Could I bite through that, or would I have to try to yank it aside?

Luckily, I didn't have to find out. He let out a sudden low moan, stumbled, and went sprawling, taking me down with him. His hand went limp, and I pulled away from him and scrambled to my feet. My legs felt wobbly, as if I'd done a few hundred squats, and I sat back down. Probably a result of the stress and shock.

"Did you tranq him?" I asked Kyle as he loped up, though I didn't see any darts sticking out of Philip's back.

"No, he went down on his own," Kyle replied, crouching as Philip rolled drunkenly to his back.

"Philip?" I put a hand on his shoulder as he blinked up at the sky. The anxiety was gone from his face at least, though now he looked as if he had the mother of all headaches. "Talk to me, damn it."

"I'm okay," Philip said. "Head hurts. You okay, Angel?" He tried to sit up and managed it with our help.

"I'm good," I told him. "More worried about you right now."

"It was the same as at your house and the spillway." Dismay wound through his voice. "Like watching myself and having no control. Headache is worse this time though." He looked around, as if realizing for the first time that we were all sitting in the grass on the side of the interstate. Naomi remained by the car, trunk open as if she was looking for something, but she kept glancing our way, and I didn't miss the gun in her hand. "Damn. I'm sorry," he said.

"It's not your fault," I snapped. We *needed* to find Dr. Nikas more than ever. My legs were behaving now, so I stood and brushed myself off. "Let's get out of here."

Kyle and I helped Philip to his feet, and we returned to the car. Philip settled into the back seat with me again, and Kyle stuck the cooler on the floor between us.

"That was fun," Naomi said as she settled in the front. Her eyes flicked from Philip to me and back, worried.

No one spoke as we resumed driving.

"Do you have any sort of warning before one of these fits comes on?" I finally asked after a few tension-filled miles. "Y'know, like how migraine sufferers sometimes see auras and stuff?"

"I'm not sure," Philip said wearily. "There's an antsy feeling, but probably too late to do anything about it. Comes on fast." He grimaced. "It was happening when I told Kyle to stop the car, but I couldn't do anything about it."

"Guess we'll need to be on our toes then," I said. "And you still don't get to drive."

I'd hoped for a laugh or at least a smile, but Philip merely looked at Kyle's hands, tight on the steering wheel. "Locking me down would be better," he said.

I stiffened in response to the implied threat, even though he'd been the one doing the implying. "And how do you want to do that?" I demanded. "Go back to the Tribe? Or have us tie you up in a hotel room? You think you'll be cool separated from me the next time one of your fits comes along?"

"Handcuffed in the trunk?" he suggested, but it was clear he wasn't completely serious. At least I hoped not. He gave me a half-hearted smile. "We need some sort of plan. Tranqs don't always work well on me, and I'm not sure they'd work at all when I'm in that state."

"I guess we'll find out," I said and rubbed the back of my neck. I had a bit of my own headache going on. "How the hell can we plan ahead if we don't know what triggers it, we have no warning, and we don't know how to stop it?"

"The episodes are short, which helps," Philip said, but his expression grew serious. "If this happens again, I want to get locked down. I'm not kidding," he said at my stubborn expression. "Cuffed and duct taped like a mummy in the trunk would do it."

"We'll talk about it then," I said stiffly before anyone else could enter an opinion. Kyle and Naomi glanced at each other, but they recognized I wasn't in the mood to discuss this any more. I crossed my arms over my chest and defiantly closed my eyes, and before I knew it I was asleep again.

Chapter 13

The feel of the car slowing down woke me. I opened my eyes to see dawn turning the eastern sky purple and a shift in scenery as we took an exit. Sitting up, I hastily swiped a hand across my face in case I'd drooled. "Where are we?"

Philip gave me a smile. "About an hour past Birmingham. We're stopping for breakfast. Waffle Shack okay with you?"

"Yeah, I can handle that," I replied. I'd have to order off the dollar menu, but with any luck that would hold me until I had a chance to call the bank and figure out the deal with my account. Past Birmingham. A flutter went through my gut. Before this, the farthest I'd ever been from home was Talladega, twenty minutes east of Birmingham. Every mile we drove took me beyond that old record. Scary and exciting all at once, but thinking about the distance reminded me of something else I needed to do. "Crap, does anyone see a pay phone? I need to call my dad and let him know I'm okay."

Kyle looked at me in the rear view mirror. "It's best not to have any contact."

The smile I gave him was stiff. "Yeah. That's not an option," I replied. "I'm not going to let my dad think I've just fucking disappeared."

To my relief Kyle gave me a slight nod, then drove past the Waffle Shack and to a gas station where a pay phone stood at the back of the parking lot.

"You can't tell him where we're going," Naomi warned as Kyle parked. "The less he knows, the better."

"Uh huh," I said, pretending to be distracted by the search for quarters in my purse.

"What's that supposed to mean?" she retorted.

I looked up and gave her a reassuring smile. "Means I heard you," I said. "It's cool. I understand." Didn't mean I would *obey* her.

Kyle rolled down his window as I got out. "Remember," he said with his typical calm tone, "it's easier to convince someone you don't know anything when you really *don't* know anything than when you try to hide it."

Damn it, he had a good point. I nodded once, then jogged over to the phone. My dad wouldn't be awake yet, but I could wait another four hours and still not have any guarantee he'd be up, much less awake.

I hung up after the third ring to keep it from going to voicemail and wasting my quarters. It would take a few tries to wake him up anyway. I knew that from long experience. Second try and two rings earned me a "Mmmmf" that sounded like him.

"Hey, Dad, sorry to wake you so early," I said. "I called to let you know I'm going out of town for a few days."

"Angel? Wha . . . ?" I heard rustling that sounded like him sitting up in bed. "Why? Where?"

"Some of the people with my *medical condition* are missing," I said. "I have to go to, um, another city to look for them."

"Another city? What, New Orleans?" More rustling. "I don't understand."

"No, farther away. A lot farther." I grimaced. The car was on the other side of the lot, and I knew that even a tanked zombie wouldn't be able to hear the conversation, but Kyle's warning still resonated through me. "I can't really say where I'm going, Dad. It's safer for you that way."

"Safer? Ah, shit." The sleep was gone from his voice now. "What about your job?"

I smiled at that. He was so proud that I'd held a job for a whole year, and he knew how much it mattered to me, even beyond having the access to brains. "I'm calling work next to take vacation time," I told him. "It's cool. I got plenty of time saved up. I'm gonna tell them that I'm visiting a sick aunt in—" I thought quickly. "In Denver. A sick aunt in Denver."

"A sick aunt," he repeated. "In Denver. You expect people to believe that?"

"They will if you back me up," I said with a touch of exasperation. "Look, it's just gonna be a few days. Maybe a week at most."

Godalmighty, I hoped it wouldn't take more than that. "Dad, the same people who took me that time have some other zombies now."

"Shit. Why d'ya have to get mixed up with all of that again?"

I sighed. "Because if these zombies disappear, then the whole group will probably fall apart, or at least be really weakened. Plus, if the bad company wins, then all the zombies are screwed. Whaddya think will happen if they start outing us? You think the rednecks around there will look at me with loving kindness?"

"Well, I—" My dad began, then paused. The sound of a woman's murmured voice in the background sent a jolting shock through me. A second later I heard the distinct sound of the mouthpiece being covered, and my dad speaking, muffled. Then another rustling as he uncovered it again. "Sorry," he began.

"Dad," I interrupted, while I tried to keep my voice from shaking. "Is someone with you?" Damn it all, I'd been spilling my guts about zombies. What the hell had I said? How much could be heard? "Who is it? Who's with you?"

"Hang on."

More muffled sounds, then the closing of a door. Sounded like he'd left the room.

"Um, yeah, there's someone here," he said, actually sounding a bit sheepish. "It's Tammy. The lady I went out with last night."

"Did she hear what I told you?" I demanded, heart pounding. "Dad, no one else can know about this stuff!"

"Shit, Angel, I'm not stupid!" he growled. "She didn't hear nothin'."

"Sorry." I grimaced. "It's just—" I blinked, as a second horrible thing occurred to me. "Wait, did you *sleep* with her?"

"Not a whole lot of sleeping," he said slyly.

"Oh my GOD, Dad! On the first date?"

His dry laughter didn't improve my mood.

"Whatever," I grumbled. "Shit. We'll talk about this when I get back. I gotta go."

"You be careful, Angelkins," he said. "And you better call me back soon."

"I will," I replied. "Love you."

"Yeah." He cleared his throat. "Love you too."

I made my goodbyes and hung up then shuddered. I knew it was cliché to be squicked out by a parent having sex, but Ugh! Doing my best to push away all thoughts of *anything* related to my dad's sex life, I dropped the last of my quarters into the phone and dialed

Allen Prejean's number. This was *not* going to be a fun call, especially since I knew I was probably waking him up as well.

But I was wrong. When I hung up, I not only had Allen's approval without hassle for the time off, but his best wishes for my aunt—even though he hadn't yet had his first cup of coffee. How weird was that?

Too weird, I decided as I walked back to the others. But I'd take it.

Only three other cars were in the Waffle Shack parking lot, which meant we pretty much had our pick of the tables. I didn't even try to take the seat by the wall, and simply accepted that if terrorists stormed the restaurant at six a.m. on a Thursday, I'd be dead meat. I was okay with that.

The waitress came by to take our orders. I kept my focus on the dollar menu and what cash I had left, and when it was my turn I ordered coffee and a Waffle Shack Snack, whatever the hell that was.

Philip nudged my foot under the table. I gave him an *It's cool* look.

"That's all you're having?" Naomi asked with a tilt of her head as the waitress left. "The food looks really good."

Yeah, like back in high school when Miriam Carter and a couple of her friends showed up in the lunchroom with bags of burgers and fries from Bayou Burger and told me I could have some for a dollar. She *knew* how good those burgers smelled, and she *knew* I didn't have a dollar. That particular incident ended with me shoving my bologna sandwich in Miriam's face. Probably best if I didn't try that with Naomi.

"I couldn't get money from the ATM," I told her, trying hard not to sound as defensive as I felt. "As soon as the banks open I'll call and see what the deal is." *Shit. I should've asked my dad if he'd taken money out.*

She rolled her eyes and waved to get the waitress's attention. "Get what you want. We'll sort it out later. It'll probably be hours before we stop again."

I stared at her. "Did you just fucking roll your eyes at my money problems?" The waitress started our way, but I waved her off again.

Naomi looked sharply back at me. "I rolled my eyes at you *not eating* because of something we can sort out later."

Stung, I grabbed for the menu again. "Fine. Whatever." Okay, maybe I was a bit in the wrong, but damn it, so was she. Wasn't she? I didn't know what the protocol was for shit like this. My travel experience was zilch, right along with my friends-with-money experience and my how-to-embark-on-a-secret-mission experience.

"What the hell is wrong?" Naomi asked, a hair shy of demanding. Kyle and Philip exchanged glances but remained silent, obviously way too smart to get in the middle of this.

The last thing I wanted was to cause a scene—or more of a scene. With a jerk of my head toward the door, I stood and walked out, only realizing after I exited the restaurant that if she didn't follow me I'd end up looking like a jackass. *More* of a jackass.

I walked to the car and leaned against it, and a few seconds later Naomi exited and crossed the parking lot toward me, though I wasn't sure if I should be relieved. She stopped a few feet away and gave me an expectant look. Hell, I wasn't sure how to explain all the shit going through my head.

Here goes nothing. "I know you don't mean it," I said, "but when you act as if my money problems are bullshit it makes me feel like you think I'm trying to get attention or that I'm making a big deal out of nothing. It's *not* nothing to me."

She blinked in surprise, then frowned. "Hold on one damn minute," she replied. "I never said or implied your money problems are bullshit. However, it's a solvable problem in the moment, and I don't get why you have to do shit like not eat to prove whatever point you're trying to prove." She folded her arms over her chest and glowered. "I get it that the ATM didn't work for you. What I don't get is the rest of it. What's your grand plan if the bank doesn't get it sorted out? Not eat for the whole trip? Be a martyr scraping by on a dinner roll while the rest of us have steak? You think any of us are going to feel good about that? I got you covered, but why can't you put your pride on the back burner for one minute?"

"It's not *pride*," I shot back, throat tight, but then I shook my head. "Shit. Maybe it is. When you don't have anything else, sometimes pride is all that's left. When you wear the same pair of jeans to school for a week all you can do is try and hold your head up when the girls are whispering behind your back. I just . . ." I trailed off and sighed. I didn't even know anymore what point I was trying to make.

"I'm not making comments behind your back," Naomi insisted, "and I sure as hell didn't mean to make you feel bad. There's tons of other stuff going on I *can't* control, but this is something I can actually help with."

I stuffed my hands in my pockets and kicked at the asphalt. "I'm not trying to be a martyr."

She nodded. "All right, we're clear that I'm not one of the high school girls, and that you don't want to be a martyr." She angled her head. "What can we do to fix this? You need to eat. And we all need more clothing and supplies. That's part of the mission."

I folded my arms in a mirror of her pose. "Could you stop getting annoyed with me when I ask to do something like mailing the phone, or stopping at an ATM? Cause you kind of have been, and it makes me not want to mention shit like 'Oh, hey, I have two bucks to spend on breakfast.'"

"The phone thing annoyed me," she admitted. "But I got over it after you said your piece."

Sure didn't act like you got over it, I thought, but she wasn't finished speaking.

"And, it wasn't asking about the ATM that annoyed me," she continued. "It was refusing an easier alternative, and pushing it when it wasn't necessary and when we weren't planning a stop. It didn't matter much in that particular situation, but jeez."

My frustration rose. Pushing it? I'd asked once, and Kyle had okayed it. "Look, maybe you haven't noticed, but I'm in way over my head," I said. "I don't know what the hell I'm doing, and I know damn well the only reason y'all are bringing me along is because you *have* to, for Philip. So maybe when I do something wrong or that you think is fucked up you could, I dunno, cut me some slack, since I don't have training and experience and all that?"

She looked chagrined at that, and I knew it was at least partly because I'd hit the nail on the head about why I was coming along in the first place. "That's *not* the only reason you're along, but whatever," she said. "I'll do my best. But you also need to ditch the stubbornness about accepting help."

I still wasn't sure she understood the point I was trying to make, but it wasn't worth fighting about anymore. Plus, I was getting hungry.

"Fine," I said. "But if you roll your eyes at me again, I get to smack you." I smiled to show I was teasing. Mostly.

"I smack back," she warned with an answering smile.

"Yeah, but I heal faster," I pointed out. "C'mon, enough of this shit. Let's get waffles."

"Hang on," she said, expression abruptly serious. "So there's no confusion between us, a few meals and some clothes doesn't touch what I owe you."

It took me a second to figure out what she meant. *Oh, yeah, that whole saving her from Saberton baddies as well as helping Brian find a reason to avoid having to kill her outright.* I sure as hell didn't do any of that so she'd owe me, but I understood where she was coming from. Still, I made a point of rolling my eyes at her. "You don't owe me shit."

"Riiiiight," she said with a laugh. "What*ever*."

I snorted. "C'mon. Waffles." I hooked my arm through hers.

"I'm buying," she stated as we headed back to the restaurant. "What*ever*."

Chapter 14

Naomi took the wheel after breakfast. I joined her up front to let the boys take the backseat, and within less than a mile both were asleep. I tried to do the same, without much luck. The scenery was a bit more interesting during the daylight hours, but there was only so much staring out the window a body could do before crashing boredom set in.

"Are we there yet?" I whined. "How much faaarrrttthhher? I'm sooooo bored."

Naomi glanced my way, smile twitching. "Don't make me stop this car."

"Can I drive? You should let me drive. I'm a very good driver."

"No."

"I really am a good driver," I insisted. "Never even got a speeding ticket."

Naomi chuckled. "I'm sure you are, but . . ." She scrunched up her face. "You can't take this personally, okay? But if somehow the Tribe or Saberton found us on the road and tried to cause trouble, it's probably better if it's either Kyle or me driving."

"I hate it when you make sense," I grumbled.

"There are a couple of books in my bag down there by your feet," she said. "You're welcome to 'em."

I dug through what she had. "I can't believe you don't have *Passion of the Viking*."

She laughed. "Oh my god, would you believe I've actually read that book?"

"No way!"

She grinned. "Yes, way. I'm a total romance novel fiend." She nodded toward the bag. "Try *Kilted Pleasure*. It's even better."

I dug it out, and contentedly lost myself in the perils of Lady Stonewall.

Fourteen pages into the hijinks of the rogue Rory MacTavish as he tried to win the heart of the bonny Lady Fiona Stonewall—while she apparently wanted only to find out what Rory wore under his kilt—a slightly brilliant idea hit me.

"Krewe," I announced. "We can call ourselves the Krewe since we're not really the Tribe right now."

Naomi gave me a doubtful look. "Crew? Seems a bit boring. Why not gang or herd or gaggle—"

"Murder," Kyle murmured from the back seat, eyes closed. "Like a murder of crows."

"Murder? Really?" I asked, surprised. "That's what a bunch of crows is called?" I shook my head. "That's really weird, but I don't mean crew like a road crew. *Krewe*—like the groups of people who put on Mardi Gras parades. So, y'know, a bunch of people who are wild and fun and might even cause some trouble."

"A krewe of zombies," Philip said with a smile. "That actually makes sense."

Ridiculously pleased with myself, I once again submerged myself into the book.

At some point in the afternoon Naomi left the interstate in what seemed to be the absolute middle of nowhere. When I asked her where we were going she simply responded, "More supplies," and then proceeded down a narrow country highway even deeper into Nowhere. About half an hour later she pulled into a gravel parking lot in front of a building that looked even more ramshackle and run down than Randy's garage.

I peered at the weather-beaten sign and the hay stacked in a big shelter off to the side. "Maybe this is too nosy, but what the hell do we need from Gatlin's Feed and Seed?"

Naomi grinned as she leapt from the car. "Wait and see. And don't touch anything."

I clambered out at a much less enthusiastic pace, then followed Philip and Kyle inside. Gatlin's Feed and Seed was pretty much exactly like every other feed and seed store I'd ever been in, which was good since I *loved* feed and seed stores. There was something about the rich scent of mulch and soil and hay and grain that seemed to sing with life and growth.

Memories whispered to me as I trailed my fingers along the racks of seed packets. My mother had loved these stores as well. Every Friday afternoon, back when I was in kindergarten, she'd bring me to one not far from the house and let me pick out a packet of flower seeds, and then we'd go home and plant them somewhere around the yard. By the time I started first grade the yard was a crazy and glorious jumble of every type of flower that could grow in south Louisiana.

She didn't take me to the feed store as much during first grade, with weeks and then months between trips. Then one day in spring I must have asked to go once too often. That was the first time she hit me, as far as I could remember—a sharp smack across the face that left a red mark on my cheek for over an hour and a stain on my trust in her—a stain that never faded.

Yet the flowers remained, most of them perennials that stubbornly returned every year despite shocking neglect. And even though I never forgot that slap, I also could never forget how she would go and sit in the back yard, in the middle of those flowers, as if that was the only place she could find a moment of peace from the chaos in her head.

Kyle and Philip idly poked around racks of dusty farm tools while Naomi moved to a back counter and spoke in a low voice to a grizzled man with an impressive beer gut beneath threadworn overalls. About half a minute later she glanced back and beckoned to us.

I obediently followed the boys over and even gave the man behind the counter a nice smile. He returned a toothless one then gestured, with a hand missing its last two fingers, toward a door behind him. Naomi thanked him, and then we all went through the door and into a storeroom filled with what must have been every piece of broken crap from the last fifty years. Lamps, typewriters, three-legged chairs. Junk.

The hell? Mystified, I looked around, certain I was missing the point of this—especially since the other three simply stood in the middle of the storeroom as if waiting for something.

Apparently the *something* was the closing of the door. Seconds after it clicked shut, a section of the far wall swung out to reveal an entirely different variety of merchandise. I'd been to the police supply shop with Marcus a few times, but this place was that times a dozen—an absolute bonanza of tactical equipment and electronics and protective gear and clothing and all sorts of other stuff that I had a feeling was illegal to sell without all sorts of licenses and background checks, which pretty much explained the whole secret door thing.

I quietly browsed and touched things I wasn't supposed to touch, while the other three went on their secret agent shopping spree. When they finally finished, I did my best not to openly goggle at the amount of cash Naomi handed over, then I helped carry the bags—marked "horse feed"—out to the car and into the trunk. Philip quietly informed me that we'd transfer the purchases into our suitcase and duffels only after we'd been on the road at least an hour and were certain of privacy. I gave a sober nod of understanding, as if I did this only-in-the-movies shit all the time. Hell, zombies were real, so why not secret black market stores?

After we finished loading the car, the boys took the front again, and we continued on our way. Naomi reached into her purse and pulled out four new phones that were a lot nicer than my old one. "I've already loaded our numbers into each phone in the contacts," she said as she handed them out. "No calls to anyone besides the four of us unless it's an emergency." I expected a Significant Look from her, but she was nice and kept it to herself.

I waited until we were back on the interstate before asking the question that had been nagging me since we left the very odd store.

"Do we have a *plan*?" I asked. "Or are we going to go knock on Saberton's door and say, 'Yo, dude, you got my homie?'"

"Saberton Tower would be a hard nut to crack," Kyle remarked.

"We can check out some things when we get there," Naomi said as she fiddled with the charger for the computer tablet she'd bought at the secret store. "It's Thursday, and the weekend would be best for getting in there if we decide that's the way to go. Would be tough on a weekday with so many people around."

"What kind of things will we check out?" I asked.

"Kyle will see if he can pick up any info or chatter on their security channels," she said. "No point in hitting the building if nothing we want is there. Philip will look for any chinks in their system that might allow us to slip in, and I'll make some calls and see if I can track down Andrew's and my mother's schedules."

I waited a few seconds before speaking in case she had more to say. "What do you need me to do?"

"There's nothing you need to do initially," she said with a light shrug. "Not until we have some information and a direction."

In other words, I can make the coffee, I thought with a mental sigh. "What's the deal with your mom's and brother's schedules? How will that help?"

"Don't know yet, but it sure can't hurt to know where they are, at least in general," she replied, eyes on the screen in her lap. "Getting into one or both of their homes might be useful too."

"Yeah, that makes sense." I racked my brain for some way I could help and came up with nothing. *Hey, making coffee is important, dammit.* "Do you think Andrew's involved in all this?" I asked. "I guess if he's second in command, he must be."

Naomi grimaced. "I know he was involved with the zombie research before," she replied. "I saw him on those videos, right there with my mother. I wish I could say he wasn't, but . . . yeah, he probably is." She swallowed and looked out the window. "He sure is stupid for being so smart."

"I'll smack him and tell him so when I meet him," I said, trying to get a chuckle or smile from her and failing.

"I'm not going to see him, am I?" she said quietly, still looking out the window.

"You'll see him," I told her firmly. "He won't see you, but that was his own stupid choice."

"I hate him," she said, voice catching, and it was obvious she didn't mean it.

I gave her a light punch in the arm. "Yeah, I'll definitely smack him for being such a poopoohead."

"We're never going to talk again," she said, voice growing less steady. "Even after he gets smacked."

The whole thing was really hitting her hard. Now that we were heading into his turf, her loss grew more and more real. Her ties to her family were cut and gone, and the grief was beginning to set in. She was almost certainly right—she would never again speak with her brother. And I had no idea what to say to make it better.

But sometimes nothing needed to be said. I hit the release button on my seat belt, scooched over, and wrapped her up in a big, obnoxious, smushy hug. A laugh hiccupped out of her, and then it turned into a total bawling sobfest. I knew *all* about crying and emotional release and shit like that, and I kept on holding her and generally being there for her.

I felt a gentle tap on my shoulder. Philip, silently handing a packet of tissues back to me. I took them with a grateful smile, then returned to the holding and soothing noises thing.

Naomi finally sniffled and lifted her head. I had a tissue ready for her, which she noisily blew her nose into.

"Thanks." She took another tissue and wiped at her eyes. "Before, I could pretend I was off on a job, that's all. But now I'm going to where he is . . ." Her voice caught again, and she snatched at another tissue.

"I'm sorry," I said. "But I know you'll get through this. We all have your back, and you're a total pro."

She blew her nose again. "Sure, I'll get through it. Andrew got through it."

"And you're a lot tougher," I stated firmly.

Her lower lip quivered briefly, and for an instant I saw beyond the tough mask to the forlorn and grieving woman. "It might be a little hard sometimes," she said a bit hesitantly, as if afraid to admit it.

I hugged her again. "If it wasn't, I'd be worried about you."

"So instead you'll squish me?"

"I'm squishing you with my love."

"I'll take it."

Chapter 15

To my delight New York was almost exactly like in the movies. The city had the tall buildings, yellow taxis, the strange mix of people walking along the sidewalk, and food carts on the corners, even this early in the morning. It was chilly outside, but I cracked the window so I could get a sense of what everything sounded like and smelled like. Naomi gave an amused snort, and I gave her my I'm-a-tourist-so-get-over-it glare, but no one told me to close the window.

And the traffic. Holy shit, cars everywhere. Philip explained that we were arriving at the beginning of rush hour, but *damn*. Kyle drove with a lot more calm finesse then I would've in that kind of traffic. No way in hell was I getting behind the wheel in this city, that was for sure. Naomi pointed out some of the landmarks along the route—Empire State Building, the theater district, Central Park—but even I was too tired and cramped from the long drive to want to do a bunch of sightseeing. A real bed. Yeah, that was the tourist attraction I wanted to see.

After what seemed like an endless drive in bumper to bumper traffic, we finally turned onto a quieter street and pulled up in front of a hotel that most certainly wasn't the flea bag rat trap that I'd half expected we'd be staying in. A fancy awning with brass trim overhung the sidewalk with *The Fairbourne* in elegant gold letters on the front. The building itself was grey stone with all sorts of carved columns and scrollwork and other cool stuff around the windows. And the entrance! I stared in utter delight at the brass and glass and marble. The broad entrance was flanked by two solid doors and in the center of it all stood an absolutely gorgeous revolving door. Brass everywhere, and all polished to a fierce gleam. I'd seen dozens of glass and chrome hotels on our way here, but this place oozed personality and charm and *Yes, you want to stay here because I am so very much cooler than the others.*

Kyle stopped the car and killed the engine as a young man in a dark green uniform hurried up. Following the lead of the others, I got out and grabbed my stuff as well as one of the coolers, and tried not to look too out of my depth as Kyle handed the keys to the young man. Another man in a dark green jacket and white gloves approached and offered to take our things. Kyle politely declined even as he slipped what I suspected to be cash into the man's hand.

"The car will be okay here?" I murmured under my breath to Naomi.

She nodded. "I'll have them put it in long-term parking," she told me. "We won't be using it again until we leave, most likely. There are disadvantages to driving in the city."

"You mean that little bit about the drivers all being complete maniacs?" I asked as I followed her into the hotel—with only a slight delay. I *had* to make a second round in the big revolving door. When I caught up with the others, I tried really hard not to gape, or rather to gape without looking as if I was gaping, because holy shit this place was *nice*. Huge lobby with white marble floors bordered with gold-flecked black. A gigantic chandelier that sure looked like crystal and not plastic. Black leather sofas and chairs lined with burgundy velvet pillows. A fresh flower arrangement so big I didn't think I'd be able to get my arms halfway around it—though I was tempted to try. And uniformed staff all bright and cheery.

"We're staying *here*?" I whispered to her.

"That's the plan," she murmured back.

"And we're going to pay for this *how*? What is this—some kind of five-star place or something?"

"Only four stars," she said, and it was obvious she was trying not to laugh. I started to bristle until I realized I was totally playing the role of country bumpkin to a tee. I'd laugh at me too.

"I have money stashed in a dozen different accounts that nobody knows about but me," she reassured me in a low voice. Her expression grew more serious. "It'll be worth the expense to have a safe and comfortable place to stay while we plan our next steps."

With that she went up to the front desk—a massive thing of polished dark wood—while I stayed back with Philip and Kyle and tried to look as nonchalant about the whole thing as the guys seemed to be. After a few minutes she returned with key cards that she handed out to each of us, and then we trooped off to the elevators.

"It'll be a little crowded," Naomi explained after we got off on our floor and headed to the room, "but I figured as long as it had two bedrooms we'd be okay. Kyle and me in one and Philip and Angel in the other."

Wait, what? Philip and me? I started to gently prod for a clarification, but then Kyle opened the door to the room, effectively derailing my thoughts.

Following the others in, I could only stare like an idiot for several seconds before I recovered enough to put my things down and explore the suite. Swanky. Elegant. Two bedrooms—one with a king bed and one with a queen—a living room, dining area with table and chairs, a small kitchen, and two bathrooms, one with a tub big enough to swim in. *Plus* a terrace, complete with patio furniture. The place was half again as big as my whole damn house back home.

Philip transferred brains from the coolers to the fridge. Kyle hung the *Do Not Disturb* sign on the door, and Naomi flopped onto the sofa.

I picked up a big book off the coffee table. *New York: A Photographer's Memoirs.* "Aren't they afraid someone will walk off with their stuff?" I asked. My vast hotel experience consisted of one night with Randy at Tucker Point's Sleepytime Palace on our "anniversary." Everything there was taped, nailed, or glued down.

Naomi answered with a laugh. She wasn't laughing *at* me, but only because she thought I was joking.

Allrighty then. I set the book down again as Philip and Kyle joined us in the living room.

"Now what?" I asked.

Naomi glanced at the clock. "Nine thirty a.m. now. The guys are heading out to take care of business. Kyle and Philip will check the security channels, and I'm going to make some calls. Possible targets for later are Saberton Tower, my mother's condo, or Andrew's apartment."

I sat on the couch, then had to control my groan of pleasure at how soft and comfy it was. "It's Friday," I said, "which means invading Saberton is out since it'll be full of pesky employees."

Naomi nodded. "Right, and unless we turn up something juicy in the next couple of hours, I think the easiest first step is Andrew's apartment since my mother's condo has pretty tight security. It's not likely Andrew would be home in daytime hours, but I'll see if I can get anything on his schedule." She glanced around as if looking for confirmation.

"The apartment is the best option," Kyle agreed. "I assume you have keys or codes to get past security?"

"I have his building and security code," she said, then bit her lip. "Unless he changed them."

"He thinks you're dead," I said with a shrug, then winced at the brief flash of pain that passed over her face at the reminder. *Shit, insensitive much, Angel?* "Sorry, I mean he has less reason to change his codes with you dead than if you'd simply defected."

She straightened her shoulders and nodded. "No, you're right. And he's not really a super technical guy. Don't get me wrong, he's smart and savvy, but I don't think it would occur to him to change his apartment codes. After all, I was supposedly killed less than a week after I ran away from Saberton."

"We'll keep our fingers crossed," Philip said then rubbed the back of his neck. "We need rest before we tackle the apartment. I say we get cleaned up, do whatever preliminary work needs doing, then crash until one."

No one argued. Philip headed to the shower while I quickly claimed the bigger bedroom and flopped face down on the king size bed. See, I was being nice by letting Naomi and Kyle have the slightly smaller bed so that they could cuddle more. Yeah, that was totally it.

I only meant to close my eyes for a few minutes while waiting for Philip to clear out of the shower, but when I opened them again, the clock on the nightstand said 12:07 p.m. Philip lay on his back on the other side of the bed, eyes closed and face relaxed in sleep. I'd never really seen him like this, with the deep lines of pain around his eyes and on his forehead softer, less prominent.

Low voices from the other room told me the others were awake and moving. I eased off the bed, quietly gathered my things, then crept to the bathroom to shower and dress.

"If we're leaving the car here, does that mean we're taking taxis everywhere?" I asked as we rode the elevator down to the lobby. We were all rested, clean, well fed on room service and brains, and ready to take on the world. Or at least one small part of the world. Either way, everyone looked a lot perkier now.

Naomi tugged the strap of her messenger bag over her shoulder.

"We'll use some taxis, sure, but it's a lot faster in most cases to take the subway."

My mind instantly went right back to my TV-informed knowledge of subways. "Is that *safe?*"

She turned an exasperated look on me. "Really?"

Oh. Yeah. Brain eating monsters. We were probably okay. Still, I stuck close after we exited the hotel. Naomi headed down the street in a long, confident stride that the others matched easily but had me practically jogging.

"Hey, I'm working with short legs over here," I panted after half a block. "I'm going to need more brains at this rate."

Naomi glanced back, amusement twinkling in her eyes, but she obligingly slowed her pace. "We're almost at the station anyway." The amusement increased. "You're going to *love* this."

I didn't love it. Not one bit. It didn't matter that I was in a group of mercenaries and zombies, including a couple of zombie mercenaries. The subway scared the shit out of me.

First off, it involved going underground. We didn't *do* "underground" in south Louisiana, not with the water table so high. And this shit was *way* underground. Down several flights of steps through tiled corridors lit with bad fluorescent lighting, finally emerging onto a loud and dirty platform between two sets of tracks where it looked as if a single misstep could send somebody falling onto the rails to be squished by a train—which I knew for a fact really did happen every now and then.

Plus, somewhere down there was a third rail which I'd always heard could kill you with a single touch, or maybe even if you got close enough to it or looked at it sideways. It boggled me that the tracks weren't absolutely littered with dead bodies and skeletons and other gruesome shit.

And even on the relatively safe platform, there were so many people waiting to cram onto the train! Holy fucking shit, but I didn't think there were this many people in all of Tucker Point.

On the other hand, I had a feeling no one would notice if I was rotting and bits were falling off. Or maybe they'd notice but wouldn't say anything. New Yorkers seemed to be really good about making a personal bubble of "I don't care and don't fuck with me" around themselves. I guess you had to when you lived in a city with so many people.

The train finally roared up with squealing and screeching and a blast of wind before it. I kept a death grip on the back of Phillip's jacket as we boarded—which surprised me that we were even doing so since the car already looked packed to the gills. No way could I reach one of the overhead bars above the seats, so I wedged myself between Philip and Naomi, clung to a pole and the jacket and honestly didn't give a fuck that I probably looked as freaked out as a kitten during his first bath.

I couldn't see many of the other passengers from my position, but nothing blocked my sharper-than-human sense of smell. Ugh. The odors of cheap perfume, aftershave, old pee, new pee, vomit, and a variety of unwashed body parts merged in a sickening cloud. There were plenty of clean smells as well, but the bad stuff kicked their asses and dominated. I tried breathing through my mouth but that simply allowed me to *taste* the stench, and I quickly gave that up.

After about three stops the train cleared out a bit, and I didn't feel quite as "crushed by humanity," though the smell hung around like humanity's ghost. Still, I kept hold of Philip's jacket until we were back on a platform, all the while terrified that I'd lose my grip and miss getting off the train with the others and end up lost in the city forever. Y'know, completely normal and rational fears.

As soon as we emerged into open air again, I let out a deep sigh of relief and released my hold on the jacket. Naomi started off down the street as if she knew where the hell she was going, which I pretty much assumed was true. As we followed, Philip glanced at me and smiled.

"You okay, ZeeEm?"

"Peachy." I gave him a weak grin. "There sure are a lot of people in this place."

He nodded in agreement. "I prefer a little less population density."

Naomi was kindly keeping a slower pace, which gave me a chance to look around a bit. This part of the city didn't feel quite as claustrophobic. In fact it reminded me of parts of New Orleans. More trees, less traffic, lots of little cafés and shops.

"Where are we?" I asked, "and if you say New York I will slug you."

"This is the Village," he said as if that explained everything. When I gave him an exasperated *Are you fucking kidding me?* look, he grinned a bit sheepishly. "Sorry. Greenwich Village. We're on the lower west side of Manhattan now. This area used to be an artist's haven and was considered a bohemian capital. Still is, really, though it's a lot more expensive to live here now."

After a couple of blocks Naomi stopped on a corner and casually glanced around as if taking in the sights.

"See where that blond woman came out, down the street by the red car?" she said, not looking anywhere in particular. "That's the place."

I did my best to copy Naomi's casual glancing around while looking for a blond woman by a red car. And even when I found her I casually glanced around some more since the place she'd exited from didn't seem all that *deluxe*. "Are you talking about *that* one?" I finally asked with a head tilt toward the woman in question—who, thankfully, was walking the other way and couldn't see me looking as if I had a neck twitch.

"Yes, the building with the iron railing on the steps."

"He really lives *there*?" I said in disbelief. "I figured he'd live in some glitzy Park Avenue condo or something."

Naomi scowled. "It's a very nice place. And apartments in the Village aren't exactly cheap."

"I didn't mean any offense," I hurried to say, but Naomi still looked annoyed. "Sorry, I just . . ." Shit. I simply figured the next head of Saberton would live a lot *fancier,* and I started to say so then wondered if she'd think I was implying that she was the *fancier* type as well. "Nevermind," I muttered. She was under a shit-ton of stress right now because of her family situation, and the best way for me to deal with her current uncharacteristic bitchiness was to shut the hell up.

"I get it, Angel," Kyle murmured. I sent him a weak smile of thanks.

"Front door's the only way in?" Philip asked.

"Pretty much, unless you feel like climbing up a fire escape," she replied. "But that's a bit noisy and noticeable."

"Does he take the subway to work?" I asked.

She started a casual stroll down the street. I fell in beside her while the men hung back and pretended to consult with each other about something on one of their phones. "He cycles, or has a limo come for him," she said. "Depends on what he's doing."

"Did you used to ride in a limo?" I asked with a teasing smile.

She shrugged and didn't smile back. "Sometimes. Not much. I was away a lot."

Wow, she was *not* in a joking fun mood. Probably way more on edge than she wanted to admit. "How do we get into his place?"

"With the code, of course," she snapped.

"Well, yeah," I shot back at her. "That's what you said back at the hotel. I meant how does it work?"

"I'll handle that part. Don't worry about it."

Maybe I'll go back to shutting the fuck up for a while, I decided since I didn't want her to finish biting my head off. I fell back a couple of steps, though she didn't seem to notice. Kyle moved up smoothly to take my place, put a hand on her shoulder and then leaned down to murmur something into her ear. Possibly something on the order of *Chill out or you're going to fucking blow this*. But, y'know, nicer.

Whatever he said, it earned him a scowl at first, but she followed it with a deep breath and a nod. She glanced back at Philip and me.

"Sorry, Angel," Naomi said with a little smile. "Being here is getting to me." She turned back toward the building. "Here's the plan. Angel and I will go up to the door since it'll look less suspicious with only the two of us, and I'll enter the code. There's no security guard. We'll stop at the mailboxes in the lobby, then let the guys in if it looks all clear."

"I can totally look not suspicious," I said with a slightly manic smile.

Her mouth twitched. "Right. Come on, weirdo."

Strolling not at all suspiciously, I did my best to follow her example of "I totally belong here." As we approached the steps, a tall and slender woman with dark hair and striking blue eyes exited the building, gave us a cursory glance and a distracted faint smile before she turned to walk to the corner.

"That lady's a supermodel!" I whispered to Naomi, and shamelessly goggled at the woman's back. "I *know* I've seen her on magazine covers before!"

"Uh huh, she lives across the hall from Andrew," Naomi said as if it was the most normal thing in the world to live so close to a supermodel, then shot a hand out to grip my arm. "Oh, shit. Shit."

I followed her distressed gaze to see a black car pull up and stop at the curb.

"That's his driver," Naomi hissed. "Angel, duck, move, do something."

Seriously? Where the hell was I supposed to hide on an open sidewalk right in front of the building? Naomi had been nicely surgically altered, but there was a damn good chance Andrew would recognize me.

Since I couldn't possibly hide, I chose to work with the "duck" suggestion. Yanking out my phone, I pressed it to my ear and pretended to talk on it, then dropped into a crouch and proceeded to retie my shoe.

"Uh huh, right, look," I said as the door opened, faking a thick British accent since I figured my real voice might be a giveaway as well. "I can be there for two but you blokes better have the lights set up right this time." Beside me, Naomi dug in her purse. I kept my head down as a pair of suit pants above expensive-looking shoes swept down the stairs.

"Cheerio, mate. Ow!" I bit back a yelp as Naomi delivered a kick to my leg, apparently not appreciating my dramatic attempt at vocal disguise. As soon as Andrew passed I glared up at her, only to see that she'd forgotten all about digging in her purse and stared after him as he climbed into the car. She began to step that way, and I grabbed her hand to stop her. "Naomi, you can't."

A second later the door closed, and the car pulled off.

She turned to watch as it continued down the street. "He walked right by me!"

"Damn good thing too," I snapped as I stood, unnerved by the close call. "Did you want all that surgery and pain to be for nothing?" After a deep breath I continued more gently, "You look different, and he sure as hell isn't expecting to see his dead sister here."

Her breath came in hard, fierce pants, and I wasn't entirely sure she'd heard me. I gave her hand a little tug. "Hey, is this going to be a problem?" I asked, putting on a bit of a scowl. Down the street I noticed Kyle and Philip being very aware of what was going on with us without actually looking our way, though they'd progressed to looking like tourists, complete with foldout map. I almost hoped some pickpocket or mugger made the mistake of thinking they were easy marks.

"No, I'm cool," she said tightly. "I'm fine."

"Okay, then let's get inside."

Naomi pivoted and marched up the steps to the door, jabbed the code into the keypad, then jerked when the light flashed red. I kept my mouth shut as she took a deep breath and re-entered the code more slowly. This time the light turned green, and the door buzzed. Relief stark on her face, she pulled the door open and entered with me right behind her.

She moved to a bank of mailboxes and a table that held what I guessed was mis-delivered mail. Scooping up a stack of envelopes, she proceeded to flip through them, but I saw that she was also checking out the locations of security cameras.

I pretended to text on my phone. "Clear?" I asked, voice low.

"Looks good," she said, dropping the mail back to the table.

"Same old system. Not monitored." She snorted. "The building manager said that if something happens they can pull the recording, but six months ago he was still using a system that recorded on VHS tapes and used the same tape over and over."

"Cool. I'll let the boys in."

"I'll go hit the elevator."

I went to the door, opened it and peered out as if looking for a taxi or anything besides the two men striding down the sidewalk. They came up the steps, and I held the door for them as if I was simply being polite.

"Nice to see you again, ZeeEm," Philip murmured as he passed.

"Right back atcha, ZeeBee," I replied quietly.

We headed straight for the elevator. Naomi pushed the button for the top floor, and I resisted the urge to hum dorky elevator music. When the elevator stopped Kyle exited first and checked the hallway carefully before moving to a door at the end that I figured was Andrew's. He pulled a slim wallet from a pocket of his jacket, then crouched and opened it to reveal a set of lock picking tools. I desperately wanted to watch and see how he did it, but I forced myself to be a mature and responsible spy, and instead leaned against the wall in a way that would keep anyone coming into the hall from seeing what Kyle was doing.

It only took about twenty seconds for him to get the knob lock open, but I was starting to sweat our oh-so-casual lounging in the hall by the time the dead bolt finally turned. When Kyle opened the door and slipped into the apartment I moved to follow, but Philip caught my arm.

"Wait," he said softly. After a few seconds I heard a series of low beeps. "He's putting the code in for the alarm and hoping Andrew didn't change it," Philip continued, then smiled. "If the code's wrong, it's easier for us to skedaddle from out here."

"Gotcha." I grinned as I had a sudden absurd image of everyone trying to cram through the door at once.

I heard a low *ping*, and Philip nodded. "*Now* we can go in."

We entered and closed the door behind us. Philip threw the deadbolt and put the chain on, and when I gave him a funny look he simply shrugged. "Habit. I don't like worrying about someone coming in when I'm busy searching."

Couldn't argue with that. I turned and took stock of the place. The apartment was more than a little cozy, but it didn't feel at all cramped. To the left was a small and neat kitchen with butcher-block counters, glass-fronted cabinets, and an adorably tiny gas stove. Past it and down a short hall a half-open door revealed a bathroom with a claw-foot tub on blue and white tiles. To the right was a little dining nook, and beyond it the apartment opened out into a modest-sized living room, tastefully furnished with antiques—and not the pretentious kind. The entire far wall contained bookshelves, with a desk built into the middle of it. A stained glass picture of flowers hung in front of a large window to the left, and French doors to the right opened into a bedroom, tidy and decorated in warm colors.

I loved it. It was gorgeous and homey and awesome. And not at *all* the kind of place I'd expected Andrew to live in.

Naomi stood in the middle of the small living room, eyes forlorn and glistening as she turned slowly around in place. "He got rid of my pictures," she said, the hurt in her voice palpable.

"Naomi," I began, then stopped as memory rose in a choking wave of sixteen-year-old me ripping up pictures of my mother as my dad struggled to get them away from me, screaming at me to stop, that I was crazy. I'd been sixteen for a whole twelve hours when the officer came to the house to inform us that my mom had killed herself in prison, slit her wrists and bled out before anyone found her. In my sixteen-year-old eyes it was *so* obvious that he was trying to save those pictures because he loved her more than me, *so* obvious that he'd smacked me hard to get me to let go of them because he hated me for wanting to destroy them, hated me for being so angry at her for doing this with less than two years remaining in her sentence. At the time all I'd seen was my dad defending her, siding with her once again. He'd taken the remaining photos and gotten drunk and cried over them because—I was certain—he loved her and wished he'd chosen her over me and didn't give a shit that she'd gotten one last vicious lick in on me by picking that day of all days to kill herself.

And now, looking at Naomi, it felt as if a layer of dried mud crumbled away from the memory of that hideous day. My father and I didn't know how to share our grief, and so we'd used it against each other and ourselves, and gouged the wounds even deeper.

My mouth was bone dry, and I had to swallow a few times before I could speak. "Naomi," I said again, "people deal with grief in different ways." Had Andrew raged and ripped up the pictures of his sister? Had his mother? I couldn't guess how Andrew might deal with grief. I knew he was her brother, the Saber heir, and that he either tolerated or supported the zombie experimentation, but I didn't know anything about him beyond that.

"Yeah." Her mouth firmed, and I watched her push it down to deal with later. "And I have work to do."

"Where do you want us to start?" I asked.

"Angel, you and Philip can check the bedroom," she said, getting her focus back. "Bedside table, bottom dresser drawer, and shoeboxes in the closet are places he usually puts stuff. I'll go through the desk and bookcases, and Kyle can search the living room and in the kitchen."

"Got it." I headed to the bedroom with Philip. Maroon and dark green and dusky blue in this room. Bed cover, curtains, and upholstery coordinated with one another, but didn't match. Not like one of the "bedroom in a bag" deals from BigShopMart. No dirty underwear in sight, though one sock lay half under the end of the bed.

"Put everything back exactly like it was," Naomi called after us.

I dropped to my knees in front of the nightstand and began going through the books stacked on top of it. Two thriller novels, a book titled *Hungry Flesh* with a picture on the cover of a rotting zombie reaching through a window, a field guide to medicinal plants, a manual for lucid dreaming, and a big photo book of *Reefs of the World*. Interesting, but nothing helpful. The drawer held more potential, and I carefully lifted out a big stack of photos and envelopes and placed it on the bed, while doing my best to remember how everything had been arranged.

Still in the drawer were a bunch of smaller items. A little flashlight, a bottle of ibuprofen and another, almost empty, of anti-anxiety meds. Several pens, a remote control, and a hand gripper exercise thing. Oh, and a bottle of lube and several condom packets. Vaguely interesting, but probably not at all what we needed.

I picked up a large, fat envelope from the stack and opened the clasp, wincing when one of the metal prongs fell off. So much for "exactly like it was." Since I couldn't fix it, I dropped the bit of metal into the drawer then slid the contents of the envelope out onto the bed.

Photos. Tons of them. Photos of Naomi were here—some that looked as if they'd been removed from frames plus a bunch more that probably hadn't ever been displayed. There were some of Naomi—Julia—on her own, but more with her and Andrew when they were younger, both with blond hair and bright blue eyes. Birthday parties, boating, playing on the beach, holidays, and more. Plus one of two newborns cuddled close together.

They're twins, I realized with surprise. She'd never mentioned that. And it sure as hell looked as if they'd been pretty close, at least when they were younger. There were more recent ones of Julia on her own as well, including a four by six smiling headshot taken in front of a blue curtain, and "HM" followed by a six digit number printed in the lower right corner. Like a combination of a school picture and a mug shot. HM. Heather Miller, the cover name Julia Saber had lived under for the last decade, before her untimely death and rebirth as Naomi Comtesse.

Mixed in with the photos were a half dozen scraps of paper with complex and beautiful geometric drawings on them that I recognized as Naomi's doodles. I snagged my phone from my pocket and quickly took a few pictures of the collection, then carefully tucked everything back into the envelope and sealed it with the one remaining prong.

A second packet, smaller and not so thick, yielded more photos and a regular white envelope. A chill went through me as I emptied the contents onto the bed and saw me smiling up at myself from the top photo. Me, happy, exiting Paco's Tacos arm in arm with Marcus. Me loading a body into the morgue van. I spread the photos with a quick swipe of my hand. Pietro, Rachel, Jane, Brian, and others of the Tribe, plus a few people I didn't know. None of them posed. All of them obviously taken without the subjects' knowledge, and likely some taken by Heather/Naomi before she broke away from Saberton. Unsettled, I took more phone pictures. It was one thing to know photos like this existed, but actually finding them in Andrew's nightstand was majorly creepy.

The plain white envelope contained two more photos. One was of Kyle walking past the police station in Tucker Point. The other was of him as well, but in the blue-curtained school mugshot style with the initials "KG" and a number printed at the bottom.

I peered at the second one, bothered by it but unsure why.

"How are you guys coming along?" Naomi called out.

I quickly took pics of the Kyle stuff, then glanced up to check Philip's progress. He'd finished with the dresser drawers and was rifling through a neat stack of papers on top. "We still need to go through the closet," I replied. "We won't be too much longer." I slipped the Kyle photos back into their envelope and the packet with the rest of the Tribe stuff, then carefully replaced everything in the drawer and slid it shut.

"Find anything?" I asked Philip, standing.

"Nothing noteworthy yet," he said. "Social stuff. Party invitations, a wedding announcement for Audrey Robinette."

"Hey, wasn't she the lead in *High School Zombie Apocalypse!!*?"

"That's the one," Philip replied. He set items aside. "Everyone wants to hang with Andrew. Or wants his money." He let out a low snort as he held up an invitation on fancy cream card stock with raised lettering. "Charity event tomorrow night to benefit the Child Find League." He pursed his lips. "I've heard of them—founded by a Louisiana guy after his daughter disappeared." His eyes narrowed as he peered more closely at the invitation. "Shit. Check this out." He flicked a finger at penciled writing in the upper right hand corner.

"What?"

"Jane Pennington."

My skin prickled. "Let me see that." I damn near snatched the invitation from his hand as he held it out to me. *Jane Pennington. The congresswoman and Pietro's girlfriend.* "Shit," I echoed. "That sure as hell isn't his date." Back when I saw her at Dear John's she'd told me she was heading to New York for this fundraiser. I took a quick picture of the invitation, then moved out to the main room. Naomi, camera in hand, scowled at the contents of a file folder, and Kyle meticulously searched through books in the living room.

"Philip found something," I announced.

"So did I," Naomi all but snarled, eyes still glued to the folder. "Andrew's in bed with the fucking Dallas lab." Her hand tightened on one side of the folder, crumpling it.

"The zombie lab?" I said.

"Yes!" she said. "From the little bit I've scanned it looks like they're now using zombies in longevity research. And Andrew is totally okay with that."

Duh. You saw him in a zombie video with your mom not too long ago, I thought, and even started to say so, but the edge of a photo sticking out of the folder caught my eye. "What's up with the pictures in front of the blue curtain?" I asked instead, pointing to the photo.

Naomi tugged the photo free and flipped it around to show me a man of about sixty with gold wire rim glasses and a scar across the bridge of his nose. "Saberton personnel photos. That's Dr. Kerazny, the head of R&D. Why?"

For a moment I could only stare as the connection between the blue-curtained mugshot of Kyle and Saberton personnel clicked in, then I abruptly remembered I needed to be super cool. "No reason. Just wondering."

She gave me a dubious look, but before she could question me we both jerked our heads toward the front door at the sound of a key in the lock.

Kyle moved like a whirlwind, closing drawers, and shoving Naomi and me toward the bedroom. "Out. Fire escape." A hard bang on the door punctuated his words, and right before Kyle pushed me into the bedroom I got one good look behind me of a man in a dark shirt and fatigue pants as he burst the door chain. I *knew* him. *Boat Launch Guy.* He was the Saberton man at the boat launch when Philip—working undercover—dragged me from my car and held me down for their tech to draw my blood. A few days later I saw that same man at the filming of the zombie movie and slugged him with great pleasure.

Voices from the living room told me Boat Launch Guy wasn't alone. Philip had the window open and practically threw me out and onto the fire escape. "Climb down!" he ordered—unnecessarily, since I had no problem figuring that much out on my own. Naomi was a few feet ahead of me, already clattering down the narrow metal stairs. My mind whirled as I tried to remember if I'd put everything back in place in the bedroom, then realized it didn't matter since obviously *someone* had known we were there and sent the goon squad. Those guys hadn't shown up to water the plants.

Philip climbed out as soon as I was near the bottom and started down the stairs, taking them several at a time. Naomi shoved the folder into her jacket as we reached the last landing, then did something to the ladder to make it drop to the ground. As soon as it clanged down she leaped nimbly onto it with a cool move where she put her feet and hands on the outer edges and slid down like a goddamn action movie star. For a brief instant I was tempted to try it, then decided I'd end up with two broken ankles, and therefore simply climbed down as quickly as possible using the normal method. I looked up as I did and saw Kyle finally climbing out the window. I didn't see any men in black fatigues, so I could only assume he'd dealt with them. He was still hurrying, though, so apparently it wasn't a permanent "dealing with."

I hit the ground a few seconds after Naomi. She looked up to make sure both men were on their way down, then took off at a run for the end of the street, me at her heels. I heard boots hit the ground behind me but didn't waste time looking back. If it wasn't Philip and Kyle I sure as hell didn't want to slow myself down by looking.

At the corner Naomi dropped to a normally paced walk, then gripped my arm to pull me close and make sure I slowed down as well.

"Don't look back," she warned, somewhat breathless as we proceeded down the sidewalk. She pulled her phone out and did something, and when I heard the click of the camera I realized she'd taken a picture behind us. "Philip and Kyle are going the other direction," she told me. "No sign of pursuit, but we need to do some traveling before we head back to the hotel."

"To make sure we aren't being followed?"

"Right." She flashed me a slight smile. "You're getting the hang of this espionage shit."

I snorted. "Hey, illegal activity is kind of my thing, You know?"

She snorted right back at me, turned a corner and ducked down another street, then broke into a run again. I kept up with her, and this time was ready for the abrupt shift to a walk when we reached a larger avenue.

"They're in a drawer," I said as I settled into an amble beside her.

She did a quick scan of the traffic then motioned for us to cross the street. "What's in a drawer?"

"Pictures of you," I said. "Tons of them, all the way back to when y'all were babies." I gave her a sidelong glance. "You never told me you and Andrew were twins."

Naomi shoved her hands in her jacket pockets and quickened her pace slightly. "Who wants to be twins with an asshole?"

I stayed right beside her. "He wasn't always an asshole, was he?" I asked. "I mean, there were some really cool pics of you two when you were younger. Hell, even when y'all were teens, you looked really close."

"A lot can happen in ten years." Expression tight, she glanced both ways before jaywalking toward the subway station. "Andrew made his choices, I made mine, and that's that."

And what about Kyle and his Saberton personnel photo? What kind of choices did he make? The memory surfaced of Chris dead with K Y scrawled in the dirt. Had we all been thoroughly played? I felt queasy at the thought. It didn't help that I felt ready to burst with the need to talk to someone about it, but no way could it be with Naomi. She was too close to both Saberton and Kyle to see clearly. I needed to get Philip's take on the whole thing.

I stuck right by Naomi's side as we descended the subway stairs, and I even managed to swipe the MetroCard the right way on the first try. Only a couple of other people were on the platform waiting for the train, but we walked farther down to be sure we were alone and to give us a better chance of seeing anyone coming after us.

"Those were Saberton men at the apartment," I said as soon as I knew we wouldn't be overheard. "How the hell did they know we were there?"

Her forehead wrinkled with worry. "I don't know. Maybe there's surveillance I wasn't aware of." She grimaced and shook her head. "But I can't see Andrew putting up with that in his own place."

"Oh, shit, I almost forgot!" I said and smacked my forehead. "I think something's going to happen to Jane."

"Why? What did you find?"

I yanked my phone out and pulled up the picture of the invitation. "This."

Her expression grew more serious as she peered at the tiny picture. "Damn. He sure as heck has some sort of interest in her. When is that?"

"Tomorrow, eight p.m."

From down the tunnel we heard the roar of the approaching train. "Let's get our asses back to the hotel nice and safe," Naomi said. "Then we can figure out what to do."

Chapter 16

Getting back to the hotel "nice and safe" took a couple of hours by the time we rode the subway, changed trains, took a bus, two different taxis, and then the subway again before hiking five blocks. The whole time I couldn't get the image of Kyle's mugshot out of my head, but when we finally reached the hotel I figured if anyone tailing us still had us in their sights they fucking deserved to catch us, and I'd invite them in for some damn drinks.

Philip and Kyle were already there when we made it to the room, but only by about fifteen minutes, according to them. I grunted a tired greeting, then gave Philip a head nudge to follow me into the bedroom.

I closed the door as soon as he entered, poised and ready to tell him about the picture of Kyle, but the words caught in my throat when he turned, and I got a look at his face. He'd had tons of practice hiding pain, but I knew the signs. Deep furrows between his brows, his mouth drawn down a bit on the right side, and the slight squint to his eyes.

"What's going on with you?" I asked instead.

He stripped off his shirt. "This." He gingerly lifted his arm to show me his side, and corpse stench wafted over me. Mottled skin surrounded a large patch of oozing rot and exposed ribs. "The thigh is just as bad," he said, expression grim, "and my arm is close to unusable."

"Shit," I breathed as I put my hand over the matching place on my side. No, not matching. It was in the same location, but my imprint-mirrored rot was little more than a spongy patch. Gross, but not *gross*. I peered at his side in dismay. "It's getting worse."

"It is," he confirmed. "And today the pain started. Not the rot itself, but the areas around it." He rubbed the back of his neck. "Plus a killer headache came on about an hour ago and won't go away. A bad one. Goddamn MegaPlague."

Shit. It had to be bad for *him* to call it bad. "Eat some brains," I ordered. "Drink some coffee. And lots of water."

"I've been drowning in water," he said. "And Kyle's leaving now to pick up some pizza he ordered. We'll put brains on that." He blew a breath out. "It's like little needles inside my head. I've never had anything like it before."

"Then lie down," I said, firmly pointing to the bed. "It can't hurt." At least I hoped not. This whole Plague thing was so weird, I honestly had no clue what would help or hurt, especially now that it was MegaPlague.

He sat on the edge of the bed, then carefully reclined and draped his arm across his eyes. "Damn, Angel. This is bad. I'm sorry."

"Shut up," I told him gently. "You have nothing to be sorry for. *I'm* sorry you're going through all this crap." No way would I ask him about Kyle now. Another hour or two wouldn't make a difference. "Rest. You need it."

"You eat my pizza, and I'll get revenge."

"I wouldn't dream of it," I solemnly assured him. "Mostly because you always have those nasty bell pepper things on yours."

"Kyle muttered something about getting all cheese to keep it simple."

"Kyle is a very wise man."

He snorted. "Is that what you call it?" His eyes closed, but the skin around them remained tight with discomfort.

"I'm sure there are other words."

Philip mumbled something in response. I stretched out on the bed with a couple of feet between us, closed my eyes and tried to shut out the gnawing worry about Kyle and Jane and Philip and everything else.

At some point I must have succeeded, because the sound of the front door woke me from a doze. A few seconds later I heard Kyle say, "Food."

Rubbing my eyes, I got up and went out to the main room to see Kyle setting two large pizza boxes on the table. Naomi wasn't there, but the bathroom door was closed, and I heard the shower running.

"Hey. Cool. Thanks," I said.

He gave me a small smile. "Anytime. No bell peppers, right?"

"Yeah, nasty stuff," I said, surprised and pleased that he remembered my dislike of them. Or . . . maybe it was all part of the insider game. Know your players.

Really, Angel? I did a mental eye roll at my overactive paranoia. *Why on earth would the fact that bell peppers make me gag be important info?*

He flipped open one of the boxes to reveal pineapple and onion on one side and pepperoni and bell peppers on the other. "Half cheese and half ham and mushrooms on the other," he told me. "Brain packets in the fridge."

"You're awesome," I said fervently and shoved aside the nagging doubt about him. At least for the moment. I grabbed a plate and got a peppered slice, squeezed brains onto it and brought it into the bedroom. "Hey, ZeeBee," I said, nudging the bed a bit. "Food's here. You need to eat."

He groaned softly, and I realized he hadn't been asleep. "I'll get it in a sec."

I narrowed my eyes at him. "Dude, if you don't eat a couple of bites right now, I'll chew it up and spit it into your mouth which would be beyond gross for both of us since there are bell peppers on that slice."

His eyes opened, and he slowly pushed himself up to sit. "The *only* reason I'm doing this is because I believe you'd try it." He pulled the plate close and picked up the slice.

"You know me too well."

"Craaaaaazy," he said, then wisely took a bite.

"It's been working for me so far." I watched him to make sure he ate a few more bites, then gave an approving nod. "All right, eat what you can and then nap."

"You sure are bossy for a runt," he grumbled, but he kept eating.

"You sure are perceptive for a grunt," I replied sweetly.

"If I wasn't so damn nice I'd make you eat those words," he said, then popped the last bite of the slice in his mouth, wiped his fingers and carefully reclined again. "You're lucky."

"Sure am," I said, smiling to hide my worry. The lines of pain in his face hadn't faded one bit. I gently patted his cheek, then turned out the light, left the room, and closed the door quietly behind me.

Kyle stood by the window, looking out at the city lights. Naomi, wrapped in a hotel bathrobe, sat at the table, eating a slice of pineapple-onion, without brains, I assumed. I got a slice and squeezed brains onto it, then chowed down in silence. I *really* wanted to ask about the whole Saberton thing, but even more, I *really* wanted to talk to Philip about it first. Naomi was already on edge with the Andrew stuff, and she was prickly enough to jump down my throat if I happened to suggest or even imply that her boyfriend might be the insider.

Kyle turned and reached for his jacket. "I'm going to head down to Saberton Tower and see what the security looks like."

Shit. Too late to get Philip's take on this, but I didn't like the thought of Kyle and Saberton going out on a date tonight without a chaperone. I stuffed the last bite of pizza into my mouth. "I'll go with you!"

Naomi gave me a *What the hell?* look, but Kyle simply shrugged and shook his head.

"No need," he said as he tugged his jacket on. "It'll be more conspicuous with two."

Damn it, this little recon expedition sure would be a convenient way for an insider to pass information along to Saberton. I struggled to think of a plausible excuse for why I should go with him, but totally failed to come up with a single damn thing.

I forced a laugh. "I'm that noticeable?"

"Not you," he said as he checked placement of hidden weapons. "Two people."

Double damn. I really didn't want to wake Philip unless it was an emergency, but I didn't seem to have a choice. I carefully kept my scowl hidden and reached for another slice.

Kyle started for the door, then glanced back. "You could hang on the next street over, but I wouldn't want to leave you on your own."

I dropped the slice back into the box. "I can handle myself well enough for hanging out," I replied quickly.

He dipped his head in a slight nod. "Get your coat."

"Angel, what are you doing?" Naomi regarded me, brows drawn together. "There's no point in you tagging along."

"I want to go," I said with a shrug. "What difference does it make?"

Her mouth thinned. "It forces Kyle to keep you in mind in any tactical plan, and he doesn't *need* you there."

An unspoken *You'd be dead weight* hung in the air like a flashing neon sign. My throat tightened, and for reasons that had absolutely nothing to do with suspicion of Kyle. This wasn't her defending him. She simply had zero faith in me. And why should she? So far I was barely managing to keep up with the others.

"Yeah, sure," I croaked out. "I'd better go check on Philip." I spun and hurried out of the room, then detoured to the bathroom and closed the door. No reason to wake Philip until I got control of my dumb angst and hurt feelings.

I heard Kyle say something to Naomi, but I couldn't make out the words, and I didn't really try. I turned the water on and splashed some on my face, then jerked at a light rap on the door.

"Angel, get your jacket." It was Kyle.

Damn it. Now I felt like an idiot, since this was obviously a pity invite. Fuck it. I'd take it. Maybe if I hung around he wouldn't be able to do any Saberton business—whatever the hell that might be. He wouldn't want to blow his cover, right? Right.

I shut the water off, then grabbed a towel and wiped my face before exiting the bathroom. I didn't want to look at Naomi, but I couldn't help but sneak a quick glance on my way to the closet. She had a piece of pizza in her hand but she met my eyes, and I didn't think I imagined the *I really shouldn't have said all that but I'm too wrapped up in my own stuff to fix it, and you'll forgive me, won't you?* in them. I gave her a tiny nod then got my jacket and followed Kyle out.

Kyle didn't say anything, and I wasn't about to start a conversation. He remained placidly silent all the way down in the elevator and through the lobby. He finally spoke once we stepped outside. "You mind walking a few blocks before we get a cab?" he asked. "Air feels good."

"Don't mind one bit," I said. "I like seeing all the stuff here."

He glanced right and left before crossing the street, and I fell in beside him, grateful that he kept his stride short enough for me to walk at a comfortable pace. We skirted a tiny plot of grass and trees, then continued down a cross street while I drank in the whole New-York-at-night vibe. A crowd of well-dressed drunk men who couldn't be much older than me clustered in front of a bar as they conversed in loud, cheerful voices. They went silent and parted as we approached, instinct telling them to make a clear path for us, for Kyle, and as soon as we were past the boisterous conversation resumed, louder than before. I glanced at Kyle, but his expression remained as unruffled as ever. He was either oblivious or so completely used to that sort of thing it didn't even register anymore.

Scaffolding in front of a building created a tunnel, and the sound of honking taxis and music bounced crazily as we passed through it. On the other side of the building a food truck was parked in a narrow lot, with a line of what had to be about fifty people patiently waiting to be served. Smelled fantastic, whatever they were selling, but my stomach was too tight with nerves to offer even a token rumble. I snuck a quick glance at Kyle. It wasn't that he *looked* dangerous, but he certainly *felt* it. He'd killed people. Lots of them, I had no doubt. Hell, anyone who had a signature move such as "a garrote looped twice" surely had a long list of victims.

Not for the thrill, though. I didn't see that in him at all. Murder was part of the job, a task to be performed in order to accomplish a goal.

Whose goal was he working toward now?

"Something bothering you?" he asked, tone as mild as ever. But it was clear he'd seen or felt all of my little glances.

I groaned under my breath. "Um, no. Everything's cool." Holy shit, was this ever a fucking stupid plan. Hell, it couldn't even be called a plan, since an actual *plan* required a bit of thought.

He veered down a narrow sidestreet and proceeded until we were in the near dark, a few feet beyond the reach of the streetlights, then stopped and looked at me expectantly.

Good job, Angel. Go for a walk in a strange city with the super highly trained operative who you think might be the insider. For extra points, make sure you do it without any of the others around, and top it off by following him into a deserted area with crappy lighting. "Maybe I should head back to the hotel," I suggested, darting my eyes toward the busy street. "Naomi was right. You don't need me here."

"You have an issue with me," he said, voice soft yet clear.

It wasn't a question. My mind whirled with ways to deny it, to say anything to return to the relative comfort of a minute ago. Nothing felt right. Nothing but the truth, since I knew he'd see right through any lie. "I saw a photo of you at Andrew's apartment," I said, trying to ignore the sick flip-flop of my stomach. "A Saberton personnel photo."

He simply nodded, a tiny motion, eyes on me and face utterly expressionless. The shadows where we stood seemed to grow darker, and the air thicker.

"How—" I gulped and tried again. "How do I know you're not the insider?"

He remained still and silent for several long seconds. Some sort of insect skittered across the sidewalk behind him. A car horn honked in the distance, followed by a yelled curse. The breeze shifted to replace the scent of cooking meat with the odors of old piss and rotting garbage.

"You don't," Kyle stated. He shifted against the darkness, and I imagined him slipping a garrote from his pocket.

My heart hammered so hard against my ribs, I was sure he could hear it. Freaked out, I took a super casual step back. "Okay, c'mon, y'gotta give me something here." I laughed, but it was shaky and too high. "Do you still work for Saberton?"

Kyle took a super casual half-step forward, which, with his long legs, was pretty much a full one of mine. "What do you think?"

Forcing myself to hold my ground this time, I jerked my chin up. "I think you're scaring the crap out of me, and I don't fucking appreciate it." Damn it, that would have sounded a lot tougher without the stupid little trapped-mouse squeak in my voice. "Either give me a straight answer, or . . . or do what you need to do and get it over with."

I tensed, ready to fight anything he came at me with. His eyes stayed on me a moment more, but then he pivoted and moved several feet away. He stopped with his back to me, a dark shape vaguely silhouetted by the dim glow of streetlights at the far end of the block.

"You know your way back?" he asked, voice quiet and utterly flat.

I stared at the shadow that held him. "That's it? Seriously?" *Wait. Did I really say that?* Resisting the urge to thwack my forehead with my palm, I sucked in a ragged breath as I fought to get my churning thoughts in order. I wanted to scream, *I don't want you to be the goddamn insider!* "What the hell?" I said instead. "If you won't even defend yourself, what am I supposed to think? C'mon, Kyle, I fucking *like* you. I think you're cool and nice and scary in all the right ways. Except right now," I amended. "Help me out here."

"There's no one here to *like*." No anger. No sadness. No sense of hurt or betrayal. Nothing but stark emptiness. "Go back to the hotel, Angel." And with that he moved off down the street.

It didn't feel finished, not by a long shot, but I didn't try to follow him or chase him down. He'd have no trouble getting away from me. I watched until he turned the corner, then I savagely kicked a can to skitter across the pavement with a loud clatter. *Fuck!* If he was innocent, I'd pissed him off by not trusting him— not that he'd bothered to stand up for himself or anything. I groaned. *Why should he have to?* I was supposed to be his ally.

But if he *was* guilty . . .

Ice crept down my spine. What would he do now that we'd uncovered his Saberton connection? Disappear? Bring a team to take us at the hotel? Why the hell didn't I talk to the others about this first?

Hunching my shoulders against the chill, I turned and hurried back to the hotel.

Chapter 17

Naomi was lounging on the couch, the remote in one hand, when I made it back to the room. Though she flipped through channels, she didn't seem to be paying much attention to what was on the TV. The door to the bedroom was closed, and I figured that meant Philip was still asleep. Then again, I'd been gone less than half an hour. It hadn't taken me long at all to stir shit up.

There was no point in dodging her any more. I dropped my jacket on a chair and moved between Naomi and the TV. "What's the deal with Kyle?" I demanded, annoyed that I still heard a faint quaver in my voice.

She hit the Off button and sat up. "Which deal? What happened?"

"He works for Saberton, or he used to," I told her. "I saw a personnel photo of him in Andrew's apartment. And, when I asked him about it, he got real scary and quiet, then told me to go back to the hotel."

Naomi stared at me as I spoke, but she didn't look surprised. She shook her head when I finished, expression pained. "Is *that* why you wanted to go with him? You thought he might be doing something with Saberton?"

"Put yourself in my shoes, okay?" I crossed my arms over my chest and glowered. "I saw the Saberton picture, and then suddenly he wants to go scope out Saberton, so yeah, my suspicion-meter went off. And I didn't have a chance to talk to anyone about it. You knew about this?"

"Yes, I knew. He's not with them anymore."

"Then what's going on? Why did he get so *weird* when I asked him about it? He didn't even try to deny it."

Her pained expression deepened. "What did you ask him?"

"I asked him how was I to know he wasn't the insider." I jammed my hands into my jeans pockets.

"Shit." Naomi slouched back and blew her breath out through her teeth. "Before Kyle was a zombie he was a field operative for my grandfather. Military and civilian espionage and operations. I don't know the details, but I know he went through some crap from Rachel when he joined the Tribe." She tugged a hand through her hair. "He'd done some mercenary-type work that set her against him, and she stirred up some other Tribe members." She dropped her hand and sighed. "All I know is that it was a hard transition, and he had to prove himself every step. It's why it was so easy for Rachel to believe the murder setup without Brian around to run interference. Old grievances die hard."

"Was that when he became a zombie?" I moved to the other end of the couch and sat. "And why did he leave Saberton?"

"I shouldn't even know that story," she said, voice low, then gave me a faint grimace. "You know how you guys open up to me?"

I nodded slowly. Brian had described it as, "She's really easy to open up to," but even that didn't quite cover it. It was more like, when you talked to Naomi, you sort of *wanted* to tell her stuff that bothered you, though for some unknown reason it only worked with zombies.

"He told me what happened, but I can't repeat it." She paused. "It's not my story to tell, and I'm sorry if that sounds corny."

"It's cool. I'd be pissed if someone blabbed my private shit." My shoulders slumped. "I must have struck a pretty big nerve for him to go off on his own." *Or struck the truth?*

"Don't worry about it. He's a loner by nature. I'm sure he went on to check out Saberton."

"Do you trust him?"

"Of course I do," she replied with a frown.

"That's good enough for me," I said, lying only a teensy bit as the last shred of doubt hung on. "Between the Saberton connection and thinking about Brian, I had myself all worked up. I never in a million years would've thought *Brian* would fuck us over."

She stared at me, then gripped my forearm so hard her fingernails dug in. "I wouldn't have either. I knew him pretty well."

"Ow!" I twisted free and rubbed my arm. "Sometimes people can fool you. No point in kicking yourself over it."

Doubt shimmered in her eyes. "What if Kyle—?"

I shot to my feet. "Stop," I ordered. "Naomi, let *me* be the asshole in this scenario, okay? I jumped to conclusions. Don't listen to me."

She managed a smile. "You're right. I'm on edge with everything. I *do* know Kyle, and I know he's not dealing with Saberton." She reached for her jacket and pulled it on. "I need to get some air. I'll see if I can spot Kyle and do my own bit of recon."

She didn't sound convinced. My chest felt tight as guilt wormed its way in. I'd spoiled something in their relationship, like the well-meaning friend who tells a woman her husband might be cheating on her. Whether it's true or not, the doubt and worry and fear linger.

Still, I nodded. "Lemme know how it goes, okay?"

"Sure thing." Naomi tucked away weapons then headed for the door. "Back later."

The door closed behind her. I listened to her soft footsteps fade away, then let out a curse. *Jane!* I'd forgotten about the fundraiser during all of the crap with Kyle. I needed to get word to her to stay away from the event. I checked the time and groaned. Her cell number was in my phone in Louisiana, which meant I'd have to call her office to get in touch with her. No way to do that at this hour.

I put Jane on the mental to-do list for first thing in the morning, then went in to check on Philip. He still lay with his arm covering his eyes and didn't move when I opened the door. In the light that spilled from the other room, I watched the slow rise and fall of his chest and heard the soft sound of his breath. Sleeping, finally.

After I eased out and closed the door, I pulled a chair up to the window in the main room, leaned my arms on the sill, and watched the city go by.

The click and whoosh of the main door startled me out of my mopey gazing, but when I caught Kyle's reflection in the window rather than Naomi's, I didn't turn around. Most of me wanted to apologize for pouring salt into an old wound, but the rest of me still wondered. "Hey," I said.

Kyle closed the door and said, "Angel," in a flat way that acknowledged me without inviting chitchat.

"Naomi went looking for you."

He stopped halfway between the door and me. "Why?"

"I told her I brought up the insider stuff," I said, unsuccessful in my attempt to make out his expression in the reflection. "She was worried."

"Worried," he said, and a glimmer in the glass told me he'd bared his teeth. "You mean she doubted me enough to wonder if I was off having tea with the Sabers."

"Shit. I dunno," I said. "She didn't say that."

He stripped off his jacket and dropped it over the back of the chair on top of mine. "I know her. No other reason for her to go."

I stood and turned to face him, folded my arms across my chest. "It was when I brought up Brian that did it. If he could turn, then—"

"Then maybe I could too," he said in that same scarily emotionless voice he'd used in the sidestreet.

"But she knows you," I insisted, "and never would've thought that, if I hadn't brought it up."

He shook his head. "If it hadn't already been brewing with her, she wouldn't have gone out." He pulled his phone from his pocket and started texting, I assumed to tell Naomi he was back.

"Look, I'm still sorry I said anything to her," I said. "And I'm sorry I came at you like that with nothing more than a picture."

"A picture along with part of my name scrawled by Chris Peterson's grave. I get it. It looks bad." He picked up a pizza box from the table and moved toward the sofa. "Apology accepted," he said as he sat. "Wasn't the first time I've been accused. And how do you know you aren't right?"

"I guess I don't, really," I admitted, more than a little off-balance by his attitude. He wasn't exactly doing backflips to clear his name. "But I know how much it sucks to have people always thinking the worst of you. I should've gotten more info before confronting you. It wasn't fair."

"Not much is, Angel," he said. He placed the phone on the coffee table, then flipped the box open, held it out toward me. "It blindsided me. I overreacted."

I snagged a slice of the ham, mushroom, and brains, then sat at the other end of the sofa, still uneasy. "Naomi told me you used to work for Richard Saber and that Rachel gave you shit when you joined the Tribe. But Naomi didn't know the details."

He settled the pizza box on the cushion between us and lifted his eyes to mine. "I killed Rachel's father," he said without hesitation.

It took me a moment for his words to register. "Oh," I managed. I cleared my throat and put the slice of pizza back in the box. "Killed as in, accidentally in a car crash?" I asked, forever the optimist.

He shook his head. "I garroted him."

"Oh." I shrank back against the arm of the sofa. Whatever I'd expected when I started this conversation, this wasn't it. No wonder Rachel had it in for him. If it'd been my dad, forgiveness wouldn't be at the top of my list. "Why?"

He shifted, picked at a piece of ham. "Both of us were deep into black ops for different organizations," Kyle said with slow weariness as though dragging the words out. "We clashed. He died."

I kind of wished Philip would wake up. "Okay," I said doing my best to keep my tone even. The way he said it, I doubted he'd provide details—which was fine with me since I didn't really want any. I tried for a nice neutral change of subject. "How did you come to work for Pietro?"

Kyle went still and silent, his eyes on me like a cat watching a mouse. Suddenly, being anywhere but under his gaze seemed like a really good idea. I shot to my feet, about to blurt out that I really *really* needed to go to the bathroom. His eyes followed me, and he spoke in a voice so soft there was barely any breath behind it. "Why do you want to know, Angel?"

My throat tightened. Was everything a touchy subject with this guy? "I . . . I was curious," I said, baffled. "I'm sorry. I wasn't trying to imply anything." Not that I had any idea why I was apologizing or what I could have possibly implied. All I knew was that everything I said triggered this you-went-too-far scary reaction. I turned away. "Nevermind. I'm sorry I asked."

"Angel," Kyle said quietly.

"I swear, I wasn't trying to start any shit."

"Angel," he repeated.

Out of nowhere, my vision got all blurry with tears. Totally embarrassed, I swiped at my eyes, keeping my back to him. "What?"

"Angel, please. It's me, not you. I'm sorry."

I pivoted to face him, utterly bewildered and out of my depth. The uncertainty and craziness of the day seemed to crush the breath out of me, and the tears spilled over for real. "I don't understand *anything*, and I keep doing the wrong thing or saying the wrong thing, and I'm scared to death here." I swept a frantic gesture toward the city beyond the window. "I'm slowing everyone down. Now I've stepped into shit again with you—"

"Whoa whoa whoa," Kyle said, thankfully putting an end to my word vomit. "Here. Sit down."

I sank back to the sofa and bit my quivering lower lip. Why was I such a weenie?

A faint smile played on Kyle's mouth. "This is about me, not you, remember?" The smile faded as he drew a deep breath and released it slowly. "Saberton and origins," he said with a shake of his head. "Both hard topics for me."

Wiping the tears away on my sleeve, I did my best to push down my own stupid insecurities. "You don't have to tell me. It's none of my business."

"No, I don't, and no, it's not," he said. He picked up a slice of pizza, took a bite, chewed and swallowed. "But things are different after these last couple of days. And since Brian . . ." As he said the name he hurled the slice of pizza back into the box. "He left. The fucker left. For *Saberton*." His fist clenched, and he spat out the words, though his eyes reflected deep sadness.

"Yeah, it sucks. He fucked us all over. Why does that piss you off so extra much?"

Kyle remained quiet for an endless moment, then spoke softly, "He's the one who turned me."

That was *not* the answer I'd expected. "Oh," I said as a delaying tactic while I tried to figure out a way to ask what happened without sounding super nosy. I gave up. "What happened?"

"I was dying," he said, a new intensity in his voice. "So very close. And he turned me."

"Um. That's usually how it works," I said. "Dying. Get turned. Become zombie. I'm sensing there's more to the story."

"You don't always have to be dying," he corrected with a shrug. "But I was. Saberton had about killed me with an experimental combat stimulant. It caused an aggressive lymphoma, and I was in the final stages."

When he paused, I filled in, "And Brian saved you." That didn't sound like a bad thing to me. "I'm missing something, aren't I?"

Kyle's shoulders curled forward, and he looked away. "I didn't *want* to be saved, Angel," he said, voice low and shaking with emotion.

"You mean you didn't want to become a zombie." I totally got that.

"No, I didn't want to live at all."

That slowed me down. "Then why did he turn you?"

"He was under orders to recruit me."

Speechless, I could only stare as I processed his words.

"Angel," Kyle said, his voice tight. "I'd waited my whole life to die."

I licked dry lips and found my voice. "I don't understand."

He brought his eyes back to mine. "Nobody does. *Nobody*." Sad emptiness filled his posture, his eyes, his words; thick and cloying, it sucked me closer.

"Kyle. Give me a chance to try, okay?"

He didn't speak for a moment. "Have you ever wanted to be dead?"

My gut clenched, and my fingers went cold. "Yeah," I said, barely able to force the word out.

Kyle gave a little nod. "That was me as long as I can remember."

I drew my legs up, wrapped my arms around them. "Why?"

He shook his head, eyes focused on nothing. "I never felt as if I belonged. Not anywhere. Not even in my own skin." He leaned forward, planted his elbows on his knees. "I was ten years old, dreaming about leaving."

"And when you finally were," I said slowly, "Brian took it away from you."

"I've never been suicidal," he told me. "There's a difference between wanting to *leave* and being suicidal. I know it's hard to see the difference, but—"

"No," I said. "I get it."

He let out a soft breath. "I was ready. I hated Dr. Kerazny for how it all came about, but I was more than ready to go. Everything was set."

We sat in silence for a time as the full magnitude of the violation sank in. "Sonofabitch. He turned you against your will and put you to work." I shivered.

"I tried to kill him during the process. Tried to kill myself."

"But why did you come work for Pietro? I mean, shit. What he and Brian did to you was *awful*."

"Normally, I wouldn't have," Kyle replied. "But once Mr. Ivanov understood enough, we spoke at length. He needed me, and I agree with his goals. I decided that if I had to stay on this goddamn planet, I didn't mind working for someone at odds with Saberton."

"You really do hate Saberton, don't you?" The level of emotion in his voice was impossible to fake.

"I hate what Saberton has become in the last decade, ever since Richard Saber teamed with Dr. Kerazny and set up the Dallas lab. Mr. Saber withdrew after that. A few months later the zombie intel came in from Naomi." He met my eyes. "I brought in their first zombie test subject for the Dallas lab four years ago. A man from Portland." He gave a sharp shake of his head as though to clear a bad memory. "Then came Mr. Saber's battle with cancer and his sudden death."

I processed that. "You think his cancer was related to the lab shit?"

"I don't have proof of anything, Angel," he replied.

"But you suspect it."

He nodded.

"Thanks for being willing to share all that with me."

His gaze drifted to the window. "Naomi doesn't understand," he said. "About me wanting to leave."

"No," I said after brief consideration. "She wouldn't. She's too into life and excitement and new experiences. She's probably convinced that if you could see the world the way she does, you'd be all right."

"Mr. Ivanov accepts it. Brian knows." He ground his teeth. "Even though I could never forget what he did, he always had my back. We'd come to an understanding. Then he goes and turns traitor, just like that."

I had a feeling the two had a strong tie despite the rocky surface. "We don't know the whole story of what happened with Brian," I said, though I had no idea why I was defending him in any way. "What he did to us sucks ass but, shit, maybe he was blackmailed or something. I don't know."

Kyle closed his eyes, dropped his head back against the sofa. "I'm so tired, Angel," he said and it was as if life drained out of the space around him with each word. "He had my fucking back."

That simple sentence defined so much. "This probably doesn't mean much," I offered hesitantly, "but I'll have your back, if you want." Crap, that sounded dumb coming from me. "I don't have skills like you or Brian, but . . . I get it."

He opened his eyes and stared at the ceiling. "It's good to know you've got my back, Angel."

The sincerity in his voice actually startled me. He wasn't simply saying that to be nice. He meant it and, damn it, I meant it as well. I *would* totally have his back. "Really?" I asked, to be sure.

"Yeah."

"Thanks." I let my thoughts circle a bit before I spoke again. "You were a lot braver than me."

"About what?"

"About wanting to leave. I didn't do anything directly, but I started doing more and more stupid and destructive shit. You kept on going, until it was time."

"It has nothing to do with being brave," he said, turning his head to look at me. "You and I, we're not so different. I said yes to one of the most dangerous careers out there. Thing is, I'm honest with what I do. It's not in me to screw up just to buy an easy ticket out, and I'm good at my job. So, here I am."

"For what it's worth, I'm glad I've had the chance to know you."

He didn't expect me to say that. A bit of the warmth returned to his eyes and to the room.

"Did you learn anything when you checked out Saberton?" I asked to fill the silence.

"Nothing useful other than the entrances. Front door. Underground parking with van loading dock and service entrance. Elevator and stairs to the garage."

"What, they don't have a big flashing sign saying 'Zombies R here'?"

Kyle gave a rare, dry laugh. "Sadly, no. I'm disappointed in how unhelpful they were."

I smiled a bit more. "I'm going to check on Philip and grab some Zs."

"Sleep well, Angel."

Chapter 18

I woke with an arm around me and a warm body against my back. *Comfy*, I thought with a sleepy smile, and instinctively snuggled back. The warm body behind me murmured something in a low sleep-filled voice, then pulled me closer.

That's not Marcus. The realization shot me straight to eyes-wide-open awake. Hotel room, daylight filtering through curtains, faint aroma of coffee. Philip asleep and cuddled up against me. He wasn't cupping a boob or anything, but *damn*.

Moving slowly, I began to squirm my way out from beneath his arm—not easy since his arm was big and strong and heavy and wrapped pretty much all the way around me.

Crap. "Philip?" I said softly.

"Hmmf?" He shifted and began to tug me close again, then apparently woke enough to realize what he was doing. "Oh. Sorry." He pulled his arm away, gave me a sleepy smile, and rolled over.

I scooched off the bed, amused at both of us—me for expecting the cuddling to turn into a flood of awkward embarrassment, and him for being so utterly matter-of-fact about it. So matter-of-fact that he was already asleep again. He looked a bit better, I decided. Or maybe that was wishful thinking.

After tugging on one of the fluffy bathrobes hanging in the closet, I headed out to the main room, delighted to find coffee ready, along with an assortment of bagel sandwiches. Naomi and Kyle were out on the terrace and, after getting coffee and a bagel, I joined them for a pleasant half hour of meaningless conversation and people watching. On the street below two joggers went by with long, matching strides. A flock of pigeons took to the air as they passed, then settled again. A shabby man shuffled in the other direction, dog on a rope leash walking beside him. On the corner, a woman sold candied nuts from a cart to a couple of teens. They walked off, sharing the nuts, their conversation punctuated by cheerful animated gestures.

After I finished my bagel I returned inside to shower, but the sight of the widening yucky rot patch along my ribs threatened to kill my good mood. My cheery attitude took another hard hit when I went to dry off and managed to scrape a layer of flesh off the patch with the towel. Dismayed, I stared at my reflection and the ugly nasty blotches along my left side. The rot on my ribs was the largest, but the patch on my thigh was gaining ground.

One thing at a time, I told myself after I finished some intensive deep breathing therapy in the form of screaming into a towel pressed to my face. *One thing at a time.* We *would* find Pietro and Dr. Nikas and get all this taken care of, but there was a lot of other shit to deal with along the way.

I took another moment to compose myself, then dressed and returned to the bedroom. Philip was awake and out of bed to claim the bathroom, and if he'd heard my towel-screaming he didn't say a word about it. Then again, he had plenty of reason to do his own screaming, with or without a towel.

After refilling my coffee, I settled in to work on figuring out how the hell to contact Jane on a Saturday when my list of contacts was sitting on my phone in a box at—I hoped—the St. Edwards Parish Coroner's Office.

It took about half an hour to even get hold of a human, and another ten minutes to find someone willing to take my "I'm a friend of Congresswoman Pennington. No, really I am!" even vaguely seriously. At long last the woman grudgingly agreed to take my number and let the congresswoman know I *needed* to speak to her. I expected an absolutely endless wait for the message to get through and for her to call back, but to my delighted relief my phone buzzed only a few minutes later.

I snatched it up. "Jane?!"

"Angel? Is everything all right?"

"Oh my god, I'm so glad you called back. Look, this is going to sound kind of crazy, but I need to know if you're still going to the Child Find League event tomorrow evening."

"It's been on my schedule for months," she replied. "It's the main reason I'm in New York."

"I need you to *not* go."

"What do you mean?" she asked, clearly taken aback. "Why on earth not?"

"Well, I think something bad might happen," I said, completely aware of how batshit crazy that sounded, especially coming from me and not from some super duper security specialist. I groaned. "Shit, I know this doesn't makes any sense. I can't really say more right now, but I don't want you getting hurt."

"Hurt? Me?" she said, alarm in her voice. "Why? Angel, you have to tell me what's going on. Who told you this?"

"Oh, god, it's so complicated." Crap! The stuff about getting hurt was totally *NOT* in my practiced speech. Clearly, I needed to scratch *Become President of the United States* off my bucket list. I gave Naomi a desperate look, but she simply rolled her eyes and threw her hands up in defeat. "Just . . . please, Jane, don't go to that party. Trust me. Please."

I heard her take a deep breath. "Angel, I do trust you, and I know that your intentions are good. I simply don't understand."

"I know, and I'm sorry," I said. Damn it, I was fucking this up big time. "But I really can't explain it over the phone." The whole situation sucked, but telling her the truth was out of the question. *Hi, Jane, Pietro's missing, but no, we can't tell the police, and by the way, you're probably in danger too.* That would generate one hell of an impressive shitstorm.

"I can sense this is very important to you," she said, and I had the feeling she was laying down some standard Congresswoman-to-constituent patter. I couldn't blame her. I'd be resorting to some patter as well, if I had it. "I'll see what I can do about excusing myself from the event," she continued, carefully not promising anything, I noted.

"Thanks," I said. It was better than nothing, right? "I promise I'll let you know what's going on as soon as I can."

"Are you all right?" she asked, concern still thick in her voice. "Are you in some sort of trouble?"

"No! I mean, um, no, I'm totally okay." No more than the usual sort of Angel-trouble.

"I confess, you have me worried," she said. "Is Marcus with you?"

Damn it. It took me a second to get past the pang. "No. He's looking for apartments in New Orleans." I paused. "He got accepted to Loyola law school."

"That's wonderful!" she cried. "Pietro must be so pleased. I know he's encouraged Marcus to apply for quite some time."

The ache rose higher. "I haven't had a chance to talk to Pietro." I stepped away from Naomi and out onto the terrace, pretending it was to look out at the view. "Marcus and I . . . we broke up."

"Oh, no! What happened?" She was all girlfriend now and not congresswoman.

"Jane, I didn't even know he was applying to law school," I said, voice rough and eyes on the pigeons. "Then, out of the blue, he says, 'Hey, we're moving to New Orleans!'"

She sighed. "I'm so sorry."

"Thanks." I wiped a stupid tear away with the palm of my hand. She understood, or at least it felt that way to me. "Sorry. I didn't mean to dump on you."

"Don't you worry about that," she said, then, "Hold on." I heard her cover the receiver, and then some muffled talking. "Angel, I'm sorry but I need to go."

"That's all right. Thanks for calling me back. Please be careful."

"Don't worry about me. I'll be back in Louisiana next week. Maybe we can have coffee."

I smiled weakly. "That'd be great. Thanks. You take care."

We made our goodbyes. I lowered the phone and leaned on the rail. On the street below I watched a bicycle with a flashing light as it weaved recklessly through traffic, and heard the horn of a taxi as the cyclist cut in front of it. Distant sirens blended with the low thump of music from a passing car. On the sidewalk, a well-dressed couple in long coats walked arm in arm, heads bent toward each other in smiling conversation and carefully avoiding eye contact with a panhandler.

"Damn it, Angel."

Startled, I turned to see Naomi standing in the doorway with her arms folded over her chest. "You should have told me about Marcus," she said, annoyance in her tone, but worry and hurt in her eyes.

I slumped. "Sorry. There really hasn't been a good time to tell you. I didn't want to do a 'I need to pee. Can we take the next exit? Oh, and I broke up with my boyfriend.'"

"Well, crap," she sighed. "What the hell was he thinking springing a move to New Orleans on you?"

"He wanted to surprise me, I guess." I moved inside to the couch and flopped down. "Apparently he didn't figure I had all that much tying me down in St. Edwards Parish."

She flopped beside me. Had to admit, it was a nicely floppable couch. "I want all of the details, every single one of them," she stated firmly. "But first, what did Jane say?"

I filled her in on everything I could remember, along with the frustrating sense that she was going to attend the function anyway.

"It was the best you could do," Naomi said, but she obviously shared my frustration.

"What the hell do we do now?" I raked a hand through my hair. "I think she's still going to go, and there's not a damn thing I can do about it."

Naomi abruptly stood, then grabbed my wrist and hauled me to my feet. "Yes, there is." She stepped back and swept a gaze over me. "We find you a dress."

Chapter 19

"I look like a kid playing dress-up," I said, regarding with uncertainty my reflection in the long mirror in our suite. I couldn't deny that Naomi had great taste and knew fashion. Growing up a Saber would do that, and as irked as I'd been earlier about her warped view of money and income, I had to admit it was damn convenient that she had plenty of money stashed away, and that dropping a godawful amount on dress, shoes, and accessories was barely a blink of an eye for her.

But actually *wearing* a dress that cost what I made in a month felt weird as all hell.

"No, you don't," she replied absently as she gave me an appraising look. "It'll look better once I get your hair and makeup done." She frowned. "Put the shoes on," she ordered.

Sighing, I obeyed. The entire day had been a lot like this. After her *We find you a dress* announcement, Naomi had hauled me up and down the length of Manhattan to try on what seemed like every dress and shoe in the city. It had been fun for the first couple of stores, but after the seventh or eighth it all became a blur of silk and taxis and snooty clerks. Not to mention, Naomi refused to let me dawdle and gawk at *anything,* except for one brief stop to watch a group of teen boys doing some insanely cool gymnastic dance moves—and the only reason she let me stop for that was because I plopped my butt on the ground like a three-year-old having a tantrum and told her if she wanted me to move she'd have to carry me.

Meanwhile, Philip and Kyle were off doing recon. At least that's the story they gave Naomi. I envied them, especially since I had a dark suspicion part of their "recon" involved a sports bar.

That said, Naomi had redeemed herself with the last stop before we returned to the hotel: a sleek and fancy salon where smiling women trimmed and buffed and polished my fingers and toes, and a slender man with spiky black hair and a thick and fake French accent adjusted the color of my hair to pale blond instead of over bleached and trimmed it into something other than a scraggly mess. At one point I thought the outing would end in bloody violence as Naomi fended off Mr. Fake French's attempts to style my hair, insisting she'd do it herself later. Fortunately the man seemed to realize it wasn't a battle he could possibly win.

However, it was the dress Naomi finally decided on that redeemed her the most. "You have to look as if you *belong* there," she'd stated, and with this dress I totally would. Dark blue with three-quarter sleeves to cover my rot patch, it had a V-neckline and fitted bodice that skimmed down my hips to flare out into a floor-length skirt—wide enough to walk in easily without being so much fabric it would get in my way. But my favorite and the most awesomest feature of the dress were the billion sheer fabric petals and tiny sparkly beads sewn all over the skirt.

With the shoes on—pretty and glittery peep-toe pumps—I stepped in front of the dressing room mirror and examined my reflection again. The heels on the shoes weren't skyscraper-high like some of the ridiculous things I'd seen women shove their feet into, but even a modest three inches was more than I was used to.

"I'm sorry," Naomi said when I whined about the height, and it sounded as if she really meant it. "Any lower and the dress will drag on the floor, and there isn't time to get the hem altered. Now, take all that off, put the bathrobe on, and sit."

"Don't mind me," I said as I carefully hung the dress up. "I'm a little nervous." A lot nervous. Talk about being out of my depth. This was a five-thousand dollar a plate event. A year ago I lived in a house with a driveway paved in crushed beer cans.

She moved behind me after I sat, gave my reflection a smile and started doing stuff with my hair. "I get it. Don't worry, I'll do my best to make you look utterly awesome while blending in."

"But how am I supposed to get inside in the first place?" I asked, watching her as she smeared gunk into my hair and proceeded to twist and comb and pin and do all sorts of weird shit.

"Kyle and I will take care of that," she said with such absolute confidence in her voice that I didn't dare question further. She smiled to herself as she shifted in front of me and continued to Do Stuff to my hair. Finally she stepped back to let me see the result.

"How the hell did you do that?" I blurted. It was amazing. Somehow she'd worked my hair into awesome little finger waves, giving it a terrific twenties vibe but totally elegant. I started to lift my hand up to my hair then yelped as she smacked my fingers.

"Don't touch it," she ordered. "I haven't sprayed it yet. Close your eyes." Once I did, she proceeded to lay down what I thought would surely be a few inches of shellac, and was pleasantly surprised to find my hair not at all crunchy. "Keep your eyes closed," she said once she finished spraying. "I'm going to do your makeup. And stop squinching your eyes!"

Sighing, I did my best to relax my face while she glooped and smeared and painted and who the hell else knew what. But once, again, when she allowed me to see my reflection, I could only stare in astonishment.

"I look . . ."

"You look amazing," Philip put in, smiling from the doorway.

I blushed. "Well, I was going to say I don't look anything like myself, which is a good thing. But yeah, I look amazing too." I smiled at Naomi. "Thanks, babe."

Naomi preened as she put away the makeup and hair stuff. "I had to do enough socialite bullshit growing up that I developed a few skills besides asskickery." She unzipped the garment bag that hung behind the door. "And now for the rest."

It only took a few minutes to get me into the dress, but it was almost half an hour before I could walk comfortably and confidently in the dress-and-heels combo without looking as if I was, indeed, a kid playing dress up. At long last, Naomi seemed satisfied with my appearance, demeanor, and my overall attitude. She handed me a little purse that contained my phone and the usual crap women carried in little purses like this.

"The car is waiting downstairs," she told me. "It'll take you right to the Norrington Plaza Hotel, but you need to stop outside as if you're waiting for someone. We'll be less than a block away and will bring you an invitation to get inside."

I clutched the purse and allowed myself to be bundled into the sleek black sedan. Once there I remembered to let the driver open the door and help me out, then couldn't help but gawk a bit. The hotel dominated the corner, marble and glass, and dizzyingly tall when I craned my neck to look up. On the main street, beautifully dressed people exited vehicles and flowed toward the doors, or paused in clumps of three or four to talk and laugh. I casually wandered toward the small sidestreet that ran beside the hotel and did my "looking for my date" act. A Road Closed barricade stood at the entrance to the sidestreet, and a battered sawhorse and orange plastic fencing marked a night-quiet worksite about a half a block down. A chilly breeze funneled down the street, and I pulled my beaded angora wrap close, glad Naomi had pressed it into my hands at the last minute.

"Look bored and a little annoyed," Naomi said from a few feet away, startling me. I hadn't even noticed her there. She was tapping away at her phone and looking like a hipster chick with plenty of disdain for the gowned crowd.

Bored and annoyed. I could do that. Easy enough to turn my nervous jitters into annoyed foot-tapping.

"I'm up," Naomi murmured, then stuck earbuds into her ears, turned, and walked toward the arriving guests. I tried hard not to be obvious about watching her, but I couldn't resist. If I hadn't been paying fairly close attention I'd have never seen it. Naomi, with her eyes on her phone, bumped into a tall blond woman in a skintight dress. Surprise and apologies, and as Naomi backed away she bumped into a man, then turned and stumbled into the woman again. More apologies, followed by Naomi continuing on her way down the street headed away from me.

The whole incident took barely five seconds. The man she'd bumped into continued my way in an unhurried pace. Kyle, I abruptly realized. When he reached me he slipped a stiff postcard-sized piece of embossed paper into my hand.

"Hurry and get inside before Miss Chastity Turner discovers she has a menu for Chinese takeout in her purse," he murmured and continued walking as if he hadn't paused at all.

I quickly headed to the entrance then followed other guests across the lobby and to a set of double doors. Once there, I gave the security guard who checked my invitation a smile that I hoped didn't look too manic, passed through the metal detector, then slipped into the crowd even as I heard a woman's strident voice behind me, insisting that she was Chastity Turner, and she shouldn't even have to show an invitation because didn't the guard know who she was?

Couldn't be all that special since I had no idea who she was.

Hundreds of people milled and chatted in a gold-wallpapered room about the size of a basketball court while servers in starched white shirts and black ties passed through the crowd with trays of weird-looking bite-sized things and tall, skinny glasses of champagne. I took some champagne and pretended to sip as I mingled and searched. Soft classical music flowed over the crowd and through the hum of polite conversation. Huge posters covered with images of missing children lined the wall near the entrance to the main ballroom, and a sign with "Child Find League" in gold letters hung over the door. It wouldn't be long until the guests abandoned the reception area and headed into the ballroom to eat and listen to boring speeches, and once that happened any chance I had to pull Jane aside and get her out of there would be gone.

I kept a smile on my face and my mouth shut as I clutched my champagne glass and wound my way through the crowd. The last thing I wanted to do was draw attention to myself by saying or doing the totally wrong thing, and I had no doubt my accent would stick out like a sore thumb.

Finally, I spied her listening to a stick-thin man with untidy grey hair, an interested look on her face as he intently explained something that must have mattered a great deal to him, judging by his intense and excited expression. She looked fantastic as usual, in an elegant sleeveless black gown with a subtle drape of fabric on the right hip. Fighting the urge to bull right on over and drag her out by brute force, I instead did my best oh-so-casual saunter to get behind her conversation partner and into her line of sight. Once there, I gave a small wave to get her attention. She flicked a glance my way, smiled politely and then returned her attention to the man. *Crap.* She didn't recognize me now that I looked like a respectable human being.

I edged forward a bit more, then gave a bright smile. "Dr. Pennington!" I chirped, focusing hard on *not* sounding as if I'd just left the farm. "It's so good to see you again!"

This time her head snapped around. Her eyes widened in shocked recognition, but she recovered quickly and looked back to the thin man "Would you excuse me for a moment?" Without waiting for a response, she disengaged from him then took my arm to steer me away. "My goodness, I didn't expect to see you here!"

"Yeah, well, I kind of had no choice," I replied. Shifting my body to block the view of anyone looking our way, I pulled my phone from my purse and brought up the picture of the invitation with her name on it. "Don't ask me how I got this, please, but there's a lot of shit going on, and I'm really worried about you."

Her forehead creased as she looked down at the picture. "But why would any of it put me in danger? Angel, why on earth are you in New York? And have you been in a fight? It looks as if your jaw is bruised."

My hand flew to my face. *No no no.* Shit! It wasn't a bruise. I clearly felt the weird and spongy texture of pre-rot. *On my face.* I pushed down my horror as much as possible. "No, I slipped on some stairs, that's all," I said, then bulled ahead to get her attention off my jaw. "Have you tried to get in touch with Pietro in the past couple of days?"

"Yes," she said, apparently accepting my lie, at least for the moment. "His assistant told me he was tied up with an unexpected business trip to Italy."

I shook my head. "No, he's in trouble, and this," I tapped the image on my phone, "makes me think you might be as well."

Alarm flashed through her eyes, but she quickly masked it. "What kind of trouble? Where is he?"

"It's really hard to explain," I said, all too aware how weak that sounded, "but it's why I'm in New York." I took a deep breath and set my mouth in a stubborn line. "Look, I'm not going to budge from your side until I make sure you get out of here safely with your own security guy."

She tried to hide her worry, but it showed in the creasing of her forehead. "Victor is right over there," she said with a slight nod to her left. I glanced over to see a broad-shouldered man in a dark suit looming silently not far away, his eyes hard upon me. "I need to meet with the Sabers, and then I can leave," she continued. "I can excuse myself with a migraine."

I shot a hand out to grip her arm. "No, don't meet with the Sabers!" Victor took a step forward, and I quickly released her. "Or if you do, don't go anywhere private with them."

Jane blinked at me, then frowned. "Angel, I'm going to trust you on this," she said slowly. "That you're in New York at all tells me there's something serious afoot. I'll have Victor with me while I see them here, in this room, and then I will leave." She fixed me with a hard look. "And then you will tell me *exactly* what is going on and what happened to Pietro."

"Yeah, sure thing!" I said, totally lying. Hell, right now I'd promise my soul to the devil if it would get her out of this place safely.

I wasn't sure if she believed me, but at least she didn't protest. She gestured Victor over. "I'll see you outside then?" she asked me.

"All I want is to be sure you're safe," I said, not directly answering the question.

Jane simply nodded. "I'll be out in five minutes." She gave Victor a smile as he reached her side, murmured to him that she had a headache and would be leaving soon. It was clear he understood it was fiction, but he simply nodded, pulled out a phone, and called for the driver to bring the car around.

I slouched in relief as Jane moved off, and let my gaze drift around to the rest of the event. People were beginning to filter into the ballroom where I could see tables laid out with expensive-looking china and crystal, and decorated with gorgeous centerpieces of white flowers. Jane moved through the crowd with ease to where a tall and stylish blue-eyed woman with honey-blond hair stood with a younger broad-shouldered man. He had the same blue eyes and honey-blond hair as his mother. Nicole and Andrew Saber, both talking to a man with his back to me. Nicole wore an off-the-shoulder, dark red gown with a beaded top and a flowing silky skirt. Andrew wore a tux that sure as hell wasn't a rental.

Edging slightly closer, I heard Jane greet Nicole warmly, then watched as Jane gave a slight wince and put a hand to her temple, apologized for a headache and her need to leave soon. Damn, but she was smooth. My admiration for her grew.

Jane shifted her attention to the other man with them, and the surprise in her expression gave me only a whisper of warning before he turned and swept his gaze my way.

Brian. I froze, and my gut gave a horrible lurch. Brian, standing here dressed in a goddamn tuxedo, talking to the Sabers as if they were old friends.

His eyes rested on me briefly, narrowed, and then he continued his casual look-around as if he hadn't seen me, while my pulse raced like an Olympic sprinter. Was he going to sell me out to the Sabers? Or did he simply figure this was too public a place to take me down? Either way, I knew the risk for Jane had abruptly shot up.

"Congresswoman Pennington," I heard him say. "It's a pleasure to see you, as always."

"Mr. Archer," Jane replied. "I didn't expect to see you here. Is Pietro here as well?"

"No, ma'am, he's not," Brian said. "I'm up here on my own."

Nicole looked from Brian to Jane. "Pietro Ivanov?" She tilted her head, smiled. "Oh, yes, I remember seeing something about you two dating. What a shame he couldn't be here. The chef they brought in for this event is outstanding."

Jane looked as if she wanted to press Brian for details about what was going on, but she simply gave Nicole a bland smile. "Yes, we've been dating for a while. Don't you remember? We ran into you at the Gourmet Gala in Louisiana." Then she lifted a hand and made a dismissive gesture. "But I can understand if it slipped your mind. I'm sure you have far more pressing *worries* than remembering the details of a random congresswoman's social life." Jane's smile remained fixed and her eyes hard on the other woman. The "worries" was no doubt a reference to Saberton's money troubles. It was clear Jane didn't care for Nicole Saber one stinking bit.

Nicole's hand tightened on her champagne glass. "Yes, the Gala. How could I have forgotten something so *unforgettable*." She jerked her attention to where her son stood silently watching the exchange. "Andrew, finish with Mr. Archer while I have a word with the congresswoman."

Jane's bodyguard stood a few feet behind her. I quickly moved to him, angling as best I could to be on the side away from Brian and the Sabers. "You need to get her out of here," I told him in a low, urgent voice. "Please, trust me."

Victor glanced at me and frowned, but to my relief he didn't question or protest before moving to Jane's side and touching her arm.

"The car is out front, ma'am," he said. "You should probably leave before your headache grows worse."

She met Victor's eyes, then looked past him to me. I gave her my best *Gah! Shit! You need to get the hell out of here 'cause there's danger!* look—but in a calm and socially acceptable way, of course.

"Thank you," she murmured to Victor. "Yes, I should be going." She returned her attention to Nicole. "I'm so sorry, but I'm simply not feeling well at all."

Nicole darted a look toward Andrew and Brian, and gave Jane a smileless smile. "Certainly," she said stiffly, clearly not at all happy to let Jane go but unable to physically stop her. "You take care of yourself. Perhaps we can do lunch tomorrow?"

"Perhaps," Jane echoed. "Have your people call mine. Have a good evening." And with that she turned away to allow Victor to guide her to the exit while I quietly died of relief.

Jane paused by me, leaning close and lowering her voice. "I expect you to explain all of this as soon as we're outside."

"Yeah, you got it," I said with a firm nod, though my attention remained on Brian. He was watching me again, but at the moment I'd take that as a good thing since it meant he wasn't going after Jane. I tore my gaze away from Brian long enough to check and see that yes, Jane was at the double doors and leaving, then allowed myself a brief sigh of relief. Now I simply had to get myself out of this mess.

Chapter 20

I felt Brian's eyes on me like a knife sliding through flesh. He was obviously up to some shit with the Sabers, but I had zero desire to stick around and confront him. Yet at the moment he was between me and the doors, which meant I needed to find another way out.

The crowd had abruptly grown thick as everyone began working their way toward the ballroom—where I most certainly did not want to go. Gut tight, I turned and started swimming upstream through a river of overdressed people in the direction of a side door. Someone stepped on my toe, and I resisted the urge to drive an elbow into their ribs to get them off me. I settled for their hasty apology, quickly lost in the chatter and music as I slipped between bodies, grateful I was slim, and even more glad I was short enough to get lost in the crowd.

Didn't matter, as a glance behind showed Brian heading my direction. He didn't seem to have any problem getting people out of his way without making a scene. I tripped on the hem of my skirt, seized it up while cursing the stupid heels and barely avoided crashing into a tittering woman. I finally made it to the side door and burst through it, then had to stop for a second to get my bearings and figure out where the hell I was.

Restrooms. And down at the end of the hall was a sweet and glorious EXIT sign. I still couldn't run without attracting a bunch of attention, and I certainly didn't want to risk being stopped by security, but I did a goddamn Olympic speed walk in my pretty, sparkly shoes toward that sign.

Less than ten feet from the exit I heard a door open behind me, accompanied by a brief outpouring of music along with voices and polite laughter. A quick glance back as I hit the bar of the exit door confirmed it was Brian, and right before I slammed the door behind me I saw him start my way. A quick look around told me I was on the deserted sidestreet near the sewer worksite I'd seen earlier, and nowhere near where I was supposed to come out, which meant that none of my people were anywhere around. I knew I only had seconds before Brian caught up with me, and I used two to kick off the shoes then pelted barefoot toward the main street.

The sound of the door echoed along the buildings. "Angel!"

Shit! I tried to pour on the speed and instead got my legs tangled in my skirts. To my horror I went sprawling, scraping palms and knees as I slid a few inches in some nasty gunk on the pavement. I was like one of those stupid teenagers in a slasher movie, with extra grossness.

Before I could scramble to my feet Brian was on me, literally, with a knee in the middle of my back, pinning me down firmly as I twisted and struggled.

"Angel, I'm not going to hurt you," he said, voice urgent but low. "Don't run away from me. We need to talk but first we need to get away from here."

"Get *off* me!" I snarled as I fought to get out from under him, which only served to grind the yuck more thoroughly into the dress. "I swear to god, I will scream bloody murder."

"Angel, *stop!* I'm trying to get Mr. Ivanov back, and I know you are too."

I twisted my head to glare at him. "You're fucking up the dress! And I *saw* you being all friendly with the Sabers here, just like I *saw* you kidnap Dr. Nikas. I watched the video!"

Shifting off me, he seized my upper arm and pulled me to my feet. "I was trying to determine if the Sabers would work a deal to release Mr. Ivanov," he said, maintaining an iron grip as he slapped my purse into my hand. "And, yes, I kidnapped Dr. Nikas. It was that or risk Saberton abducting him as well. He wouldn't get into the car, and I couldn't let him stay."

"How did you know he was at risk?" I snarled. Maybe I could bite him and make him behave the way I made Philip behave? Desperate, I lunged at him, teeth bared.

"Jesus Christ, Angel!" Brian growled as he evaded my bite, then twisted my arm up behind my back. "Would you *stop?*" He glanced back over his shoulder at the door we'd exited from. "I knew he was at risk because ten minutes earlier I defused a bomb under my Escalade, then tried to call Mr. Ivanov and got only voicemail."

I stopped struggling, bit my lip hard to try and stop the damn tears of frustration, but I felt a couple sneak their way down my cheek. How did all this get so fucked up? "Why didn't you tell anyone?" I asked, voice quavering.

He began walking me toward the main street while he continued to shoot wary looks behind us. "No one to tell. No one to trust. There's an unknown insider. At least one. And you need to get away from here."

"You couldn't even trust me?" The hurt in my voice wasn't faked one bit.

He sighed. "I'm sorry," he said still moving toward the street. "With Dr. Nikas in my care, I couldn't risk contact with anyone." He glanced behind him again. "Who's here with you?"

I set my mouth stubbornly. "How do I know I can trust *you?*"

The sound of the door echoed off buildings again, followed by running footsteps. Brian released my arm and gave me a little shove. "Angel, *run.* Now!" He turned and sprinted to a building across the street, leaped up to catch the fire escape ladder, pulled up and began climbing. I didn't waste time watching him. I saw the men pelting my way. I grabbed my grimy skirts and *ran.*

Kyle was leaning against the building about fifty feet away from the corner, but he pushed off and immediately scanned for threats the instant he saw me running toward him.

"We need to get out of here!" I gasped.

"Slow down," he ordered in a low voice. "Look normal and walk." He took my arm casually, though we continued to walk with purpose. My pulse gradually returned to a more normal pace. There were a lot of people on the sidewalk in front of the hotel, and I doubted Saberton's goons would try and grab me in public. Plus, Kyle would totally kick their asses.

"I had to lose the shoes," I said through a clenched-teeth smile. Not sure how normal I was able to look with a grunged-up dress and no shoes. And my makeup was probably smeared to hell and back. Oh, and the weird blotch on my face.

"What happened?"

I gave him a quick rundown of everything—warning Jane, seeing the Sabers with Brian, the incident on the sidestreet, and everything Brian told me. "I don't know what to think about Brian," I confessed as Kyle hailed a cab.

He made a noncommittal noise as a taxi pulled to the curb. He folded himself in after me, then told the driver, "One twenty-seventh and Lexington." I hadn't been in New York long, but I knew that was way the hell from where we were staying. I didn't question it, though. Everything was so fucked up now it didn't really make a difference. I tried to brush some of the yuck and grime off my feet, then gave up and wiped my hands on one of the few remaining clean spots on my dress. Didn't help. I'd only succeeded in spreading the dirt around. I clenched my trembling hands together and tried not to think about how crazy I must look to the taxi driver. Then again, this was New York, so they probably saw worse several times a day.

"He let you go," Kyle said quietly after a few blocks.

"Yeah, he did." I exhaled. "At least Jane got away."

"Saw her come out," he said with a nod. "Good work." His phone rang, but when he pulled it from his pocket he frowned. "It's your number."

Baffled, I yanked my purse open and dug through it. "Shit. It's not in here." Gulping, I looked at the phone in his hand. "Answer it."

Kyle hit the answer button but didn't say anything. After a second or two my zombie hearing picked up Brian's voice.

"Is this Kyle?"

Kyle remained silent another couple of breaths before speaking. "Hello, Brian."

"Do you have Angel?"

"Yes."

I heard Brian exhale. *"Thank god. I know you think I'm guilty. I'm not. We need to work together, or we'll end up bumping heads as badly as almost happened tonight."*

Kyle remained impassive. "Do you have Dr. Nikas?"

"I do. He's safe."

"I'll need to speak to him."

"Let me talk to Angel."

Kyle shifted his eyes to me and handed the phone over.

I took it. "Brian?"

"Hey, Angel, you okay?"

"Yeah, except some jerk stole my phone."

"I needed to be able to contact you since you weren't in the mood for calm conversation," he said. "Plus, we sort of ran out of time."

"Yeah, whatever," I grumbled. "Where's Dr. Nikas?"

"He's here with me," Brian said, and then my heart leaped as I heard the lilting accent of Dr. Nikas in the background.

"Let me talk to him," I demanded.

"Hold on." I heard muffled voices, and then Dr. Nikas came on the line.

"Angel, I'm so sorry."

It was him. It was definitely him. "Oh god, are you okay?"

"I'm fine," he said, though he sounded tired. "What about you and Philip? I didn't finish the procedure."

"Yeah, something weird's going on with that," I said, then gave him a quick recap of Philip's overprotective fits and the weird rot patches. "Look, I need to know if I can trust Brian." It suddenly occurred to me that Brian could be right there listening in on the conversation and holding a gun to his head or something like that. "If I can, um, tell me why Jacques needed the duct tape." No way would anyone who wasn't there for the procedure know that.

"I trust him with my life," Dr. Nikas said, a smile in his voice. "And the duct tape was to keep you from rolling your stool around."

Heaving a sigh of relief, I gave Kyle a thumbs up. "Awesome. So, can you fix this thing with Philip and me?"

He muttered to himself for a few seconds. "Perhaps. I have very limited supplies. I need some time to consider the problem. For now, take two tablespoons of blue-green algae along with three thousand milligrams of vitamin C twice daily with plenty of water. That should even things out for now, especially for Philip."

Algae? Ugh. I listened carefully as he gave some more instructions, including specific brand names. Fortunately, Kyle could hear everything, and he gave me a nod to let me know he'd help me remember. "Okay, got it. Thanks," I said. "Can I talk to Brian again?"

"Certainly. Take care, Angel."

Brian came back on the line. "What did you tell Dr. Pennington? Does she know Mr. Ivanov is missing?"

"I told her as little as possible," I said. "Only that he was in some trouble and that she needed to get the hell out of that place." I quickly explained about finding the invitation at Andrew's apartment, and why I'd figured she was in danger.

"She's going to be worried," he replied. "Which means she might make waves."

Make waves? Didn't he think it was important to make sure she was safe? "Well, it's tough to tell her too much without giving it away."

"One of us is going to have to contact her. She *can't* tell anyone."

"Yeah, I know that," I said, annoyance rising. Did he think I was an idiot? "I'll get in touch with her."

"Call me back when you do," he ordered, "and better to do it sooner rather than later."

"No shit, Sherlock," I said sharply. "And it'll be oh-so easy to call you back since you have my phone."

"You have a fucking phone in your hand," he snapped. "I'm sure it will work just fine. Let me talk to Kyle."

Throat tight, I shoved the phone at Kyle. When he took it I crossed my arms over my chest and stared out the window. The dress was ruined, the shoes were lost, and I didn't know what the hell I was doing. I saw Kyle's reflection in the window as he looked over at me. I knew he could see my reflection as well, and that I was crying, but there wasn't a damn thing I could do about it.

"Kyle here," he said into the phone.

"Angel's going to connect with Dr. Pennington to keep her from doing something dangerous," I heard Brian tell Kyle, because apparently I couldn't be trusted to pass that information along. *"Once that's done, we need to coordinate."*

"Understood."

"I have to go. More later."

Kyle lowered the phone after Brian hung up and gave me blessed silence for several minutes as we made our way north.

"You can let us out at the corner," Kyle said, leaning forward to pass the driver money. I knew we weren't anywhere near the address he'd given, but I didn't argue. He seemed to know what he was doing. He bundled me out of the cab, slipped an arm through mine, and walked me half a block down a side street before hailing another cab.

"He can be a dick," Kyle said after we were in the second cab and on our way to yet another address I'd never heard of.

"He was right," I said with a sigh. "I'm being stupid. Anyway, as soon as we get back, I guess I need to call Jane."

"Face to face would be better."

"I need to clean up first, and get this *thing* off my cheek."

After a few more minutes Kyle stopped the taxi and paid the driver, helped me out and walked me to the cross street. "Start with hot water and brains," he said as he hailed a third cab. "Once we get back I'll find a pharmacy and get the algae and C. And you should take my phone for now." He deftly slipped it into my purse.

"Thanks," I said, then looked up and met his eyes. "Thanks." I didn't even know how to say how much it mattered that he *got* why I was so upset. I wasn't even sure I completely understood it myself, but I really felt that he did.

He gave me a hint of a smile, then opened the door of the cab that pulled up. "No worries."

This time he gave an address that was actually in the vicinity of our hotel. We rode in comfortable silence, and once we arrived he escorted me to the door, quietly making sure that I was safe and okay before striding off down the street, somehow managing to look like an unassuming nobody who didn't require a second glance.

I wasn't quite ready to head inside, so instead I crossed the street to the little park across from the hotel. Up close and at night, it wasn't all that pleasant. Two of the benches had homeless men on them, and a couple of people wearing hoodies and baggy jeans huddled together on the far side of the fountain. Something changed hands, and the two walked off in opposite directions. Common sense told me to return to the hotel, especially since I was still in the battered evening gown and barefoot, but I didn't give much of a shit about common sense at that moment.

A guy with scraggly hair and a pinched face, with the desperate eyes of a drug addict, began to sidle up to me. I snarled at him and made a mock-lunge, and he scampered off. I swept my gaze around to make sure no one else assumed I was an easy target, but the others seemed to sense the monster beneath and kept their distance. Or maybe I simply looked totally crazy. Either way worked for me. Satisfied, I checked the time. Only nine-thirty back home. I punched in my dad's cell phone number.

"*What?*"

The snapped-out question caught me briefly off guard before I remembered my dad didn't have this number in his contacts. "Um, Dad?"

I heard a quick intake of breath. "Angel? *Angel?*"

"Yeah, it's me." I had to work hard to control the slight tremble in my voice as a wave of homesickness swept through me. "Just calling to check in, y'know? Make sure you're doing okay." I saw the scraggly druggie returning, and I bared my teeth at him.

"Yeah, sure. I'm okay," he replied. "How 'bout you? You still, um . . . You still in Denver?"

"Sure am. Staying in a real nice hotel. Four stars." I laughed, but it sounded strained. The connection was crappy and cutting in and out, but it was damn good to hear his voice, even with static. "Nicest place I've ever been." His words abruptly registered. *Why did he specifically say Denver when he knew it was a cover story?* My worry rose. "You okay, Dad? Are you at the house? Is someone there with you?"

"Yeah. I mean, no. Shit! That was a lot of questions, Angel," he grumbled. "I'm fine. With Rick at his house."

I grimaced. Rick Belluci. Bad enough my dad went on a double date with him, but Rick's house was where some of the worst drinking used to happen. "You sure that's a good idea? He can put down a six pack in about an hour."

"I ain't seen him drink yet," he told me, "and that don't matter anyway. Not with him taking me in like he did."

"Wait. Taking you in? Why?" I shook my head as if that would help things make sense. "You're sleeping there?"

"Well, I spent last night here and prolly gonna stay tonight as well."

I reached up to grip my hair. "But you *hate* going to his house!"

"Huh? I ain't never been here before. You should know that. You sure you're okay?" He paused. "Uh, maybe you need a . . . snack?"

"What? No! I'm not hungry. Not like that. You're the one I'm worried about." I scowled. "Every time you get back from Rick's house you complain about how it stinks like old cabbage and how he keeps the TV full blast and how the toilet's always clogged."

He made an aggravated noise. "Shit, Angel. Why the hell would I be at Rick Belluci's house? I ain't been to his house since he got busted for drunk driving his four-wheeler through the Tucker Point High School homecoming game, and his ex-mother in law moved in. I'm at *Nick's* house."

That still didn't make any sense, and my poor brain refused to help me out. "Nick? Nick who?"

"Jesus fucking Christ," he muttered. "Your Nick. From the morgue."

"Why—" I needed a couple of seconds to completely shift my thinking. Not that it helped. "Why the hell are you at my Nick's house?"

My dad took a deep breath. "'Cause he came to our place to check on me 'cause of the fake lawyer and your phone, then there was a car out front that left when a cop car drove by, so I came here."

I fought to understand any of that but finally seized onto the "phone" part. "Oh! My phone! It made it to the coroner's office? And what fake lawyer?"

"The fake lawyer that came looking for you at work. Supposedly she wanted to give you a bunch of money from a trust fund or some shit like that, but because your phone rang, the other guy, um," I heard someone speaking in the background, "Huh? Oh, okay. Allen. Yeah, Allen didn't fall for it and didn't tell her nothin'."

With anyone other than my dad I'd have thought they were fucking with me. Once again I dug through the nonsense. "Someone was looking for me? And what was the deal with the car and the cop?"

He made an exasperated noise. "You're makin' this hard, Angel," he said, and in that moment it was a damn good thing he was over a thousand miles away. "Your phone rang in the box and they figured something was wrong, 'cause phones don't usually show up in the mail there. When the fake lawyer turned up, Allen saw right through it and didn't tell her shit. Then Allen and Nick figured someone should check on me, so Nick came out. That's when the car stopped out front being all suspicious and mysterious-like, and Nick called the cops. With the, er, trouble going on and everything," he cleared his throat, "y'know, I figured I needed to get outta there. I was gonna go into town, but Nick brought me here instead."

"Oh." Holy shit, I actually understood him. "You're staying with Nick?" And I still sounded like an idiot. "That's really cool. Can I talk to him?"

"Sure. He's right here."

I heard some rustling and then, "Angel?"

"Nick!" The homesickness ratcheted up a notch. "What's the deal with my dad?"

"I went to check on him, and a suspicious car stopped out front," he said, automatically slipping into the cadence of giving a report or testifying. "He told me there'd been trouble before, and with you mailing the phone to yourself, and the woman looking for you at work, I thought it best to bring him here."

"You're so fucking awesome," I said with a smile. "You have no idea how much I appreciate this. What did the woman look like?"

He cleared his throat. "Athletic-looking black woman with braids that reached to mid back. She had a business card, but there's no firm by that name."

Rachel Delancey, Tribe security second-in-command. Not a Saberton person. "Okay. I know who that is. I can't imagine you'll have any more trouble from her." I doubted Rachel would do anything to hurt my dad. She was after Kyle, not me. "Are you *sure* you're okay with my dad staying with you?"

"It's no trouble. I have plenty of room." Nick paused. "Are *you* okay? Your dad won't tell me anything."

Relief and regret coiled together. Nick was a good guy and would watch over my dad like his own, but there was no way I could let him know what was really going on. "I'm okay," I told him. "I promise. I'm here with some other people. And, well, I can't talk about it. Sort of a nondisclosure thing, y'know?"

"As long as you're okay, that's all that matters," he replied, voice upbeat but with a layer of stress and worry he couldn't completely hide. "And you're going to *stay* okay, right?"

I couldn't help but smile. "I will, I promise."

"Good. Dr. Leblanc misses you, so come back soon."

"As soon as I possibly can." The homesickness swelled up again, and I had to quickly scrub at my eyes. "I miss you guys too."

I caught a whiff of the scraggly druggie even as I saw movement out of the corner of my eye, and only my zombie reflexes made it possible for me to twist away before he could snatch my phone. "GET THE FUCK AWAY FROM ME, YOU GODDAMN LOSER!" Growling, I slammed the palm of my other hand into his chest to send him staggering back to fall on his ass. "And take a fucking *bath!*"

I heard someone frantically calling my name then realized it was Nick. I yanked the phone back up. "Hey, sorry about that, Nick." I raised a fist and took a threatening step toward the druggie as he scrambled up. He backpedaled, then finally had a smart idea and hurried off. "Some dickwad here, uh," I quickly shifted what I was going to say since telling him that someone had tried to steal my phone probably wouldn't go over well, "he, um, keeps wanting a handout."

"Angel, where *are* you?" he asked, worry thick in his voice.

"Across the street from my hotel," I said glibly, avoiding a direct answer. "It's all cool. Can I speak to my dad again, please?"

"But . . ." He sighed. "Sure."

My dad took the phone. "What happened?"

I scowled. "Some fucking druggie tried to take my phone, so I knocked him the hell down. Stupid jerk."

"Kick his fuckin' ass!" He gave a quick cough, and I easily pictured his guilty glance at Nick. "I mean, that's what he deserves, y'know."

I laughed. "I got it covered. Don't worry." I wanted to tell him how messed up everything was, but I knew it would only worry him more. "It's really good to hear from you. I love you and miss you."

"Love you too, Angelkins," he said, with a rich warmth in his voice that brought tears to my eyes again. "You know when you're coming home?"

I winced. "No. Not yet. I'm sorry."

"You call me again soon, y'hear?"

"As soon as I can."

I hung up after we said our goodbyes then made my way across the street again. To my surprise the doorman gave me a very nice, "Good evening, ma'am," as he opened the door for me, and didn't bat an eyelash at my bedraggled appearance. Made me wonder what the hell *would* earn an eyelash-bat.

Yet, as I entered, I caught a glimpse of a shadowy figure leaning against a building about half a block down the street. Kyle, who'd obviously seen my complete lack-of-common-sense park visit and had stuck around to be sure I remained in one piece. I smiled and continued inside while Kyle pushed off and headed the other way.

Naomi was in the process of hanging her jacket in the closet when I came in. Her eyes swept over me and widened in shock. "What the *hell* happened?" she demanded. "I thought everything went down as planned. Jane came out, and then we got the signal to return to base."

I trudged toward the bathroom. "Well, the good news is that I found Brian," I said, peeling off the fucked up dress as I went, noticing barely in time that Philip was in the room as well.

"What?" Naomi hurried me into the bathroom then helped me with the zipper. "Did you take him out?"

I explained what happened as I stripped down and scowled at the various scrapes on my forearms and knees. "And now I need to get cleaned up so I can go talk to Jane even though it's late as hell." I grimaced. "Sorry about the dress. And, I lost the shoes when I was making a run for it."

She peered at the ruin of the gown. The rip at the knee could maybe be dealt with by making the dress a *lot* shorter, but the stain on the front was such a combo of street-grime that I doubted there was any way to get it out. "Yeah, you sure did a number on it." Then she smiled and shrugged. "No worries. You're in one piece, and that's way more important."

She gave me a quick hug, then went out to get a change of clothes and a slice of brains for me. About the time I finished cleaning up, Kyle returned with a brown paper bag containing a big jar of loose algae and two bottles each of algae capsules and Vitamin C.

After taking a whiff of the loose stuff, I opted for the six capsules. It wasn't that it smelled *bad*, but props to Kyle for having the foresight to get pills. I choked down the algae and three C's with a full bottle of water, and in ten minutes the spongy rot on my face faded to a patch of odd discoloration that I could cover with makeup—or at least make it less *OMG what the hell is that on your face?* I checked the places on my side, arm and thigh as well and was enormously relieved to find all of them significantly less icky. Meanwhile, Philip had mixed the loose algae with water to create something resembling industrial sludge and slammed it down. Hardcore.

"You can barely see it," Naomi reassured me after I peered in the mirror for the umpteenth time.

"Not fair," I said, glancing past her to Philip and the matching blemish on his jaw. "It makes *him* look tougher."

"No, it makes him look like he missed a patch shaving," Naomi corrected with a grin.

"As long as he looks equally silly," I said.

Philip gave a long-suffering sigh. "Are we done destroying the last shreds of my self-esteem?"

"For now." I punched him lightly on the upper arm. "C'mon, let's go see Jane."

Chapter 21

Jane was staying at the Langston Arms Hotel which, I was told, was as nice as The Fairbourne but smaller and more low key, and apparently better for security purposes.

The lobby was fully carpeted in patterned royal blue, and along with cream colored walls and off-white cushy chairs, had a light, cool feel. The desk clerk didn't bat an eye when I told him I was there to see the congresswoman, and obligingly called up to the room. I had little doubt my reception would've been far different—probably involving burly security guards—if I hadn't phoned Jane to let her know I was on the way over for a midnight rendezvous.

"Someone will be down momentarily to escort you to her room," he informed me, then gestured toward a bank of elevators.

Philip and I moved that way, and a few minutes later Jane's bodyguard, Victor, stepped out of the elevator. He held the door while he looked beyond us and around, then beckoned us in with two fingers.

I hurried to get in but Philip simply glanced at Victor and stayed where he was. "I'll keep watch down here, ZeeEm."

I hesitated, then nodded. Better to keep it as simple and nonthreatening as possible. Once the doors closed Victor slid a key card into a slot, then put in a code on a keypad. He remained silent, gaze steady upon me as the elevator rose, and when the doors opened he led the way down the hall to a set of double doors. Once again he used a key card and a code for entry, then proceeded into a suite about the same size as the one at The Fairbourne, but with tons of dark wood, antique-looking furniture rather than the modern style of ours.

Jane stood beside the sofa wearing rich blue velour pants and a top that looked comfortable and elegant at the same time. She turned as we entered. "Angel! I tried several times to call the number you gave me but it kept going to voicemail." She looked worried and stressed and off-center—not at all her usual self. "What on earth is going on?"

"A lot of shit," I said with a grimace. "I'm sorry. I lost my phone."

She sat down but didn't relax. "Where is Pietro?" she asked, tone firm. She wasn't going to put up with evasions any longer. "He doesn't answer his phone, and his assistant will only tell me that he's away on business. But why is Brian here if Pietro is in trouble?"

I glanced at Victor and then back to Jane. "Um, any chance we could talk in private?"

Jane looked to the grim-faced bodyguard. "It's all right, Victor. Could you step into the bedroom please?" He opened his mouth to speak, and she lifted a hand. "Yes, you may leave the door open."

Victor gave me a dark look, then stalked into the bedroom, positioning himself on the far end of it, but still with a line of sight that allowed him to glare at me. I couldn't really blame him, but it bugged me that he might still be able hear our conversation.

I sat on the sofa beside Jane and lowered my voice. "Can you trust him not to repeat stuff he hears? Even if it's kind of weird?"

"I trust him completely," Jane said, matching my low volume. "But what do you mean by weird?"

"Well, for starters, Pietro's been kidnapped, and Saberton's behind it."

Shock swept over her features. "Kidnapped? When? Why? What are the authorities doing about it?"

"Wednesday. Three days ago," I said, "and we can't call the authorities."

"Why on earth not? Does this have something to do with the defense contract?" Her eyes narrowed. "Is that what the Sabers wanted?"

"Huh? No." I shook my head, though now that she'd said it I wondered if maybe there was more going on here. "It has to do with a . . ." What the hell, I'd try the same approach I used with Randy. "A medical condition he has. And I have. Brian and a bunch of others too."

That caught her off guard. "Medical condition?" Her eyes narrowed. "Is it related to the blotch that appeared on your face?" She peered at my jawline, clever eyes noting that it was still there beneath the makeup.

I automatically lifted my hand to my jaw, grimacing. "It's related. Kind of. Saberton wants to, er, find out more about how the condition works, and I think they wanted to kidnap *you* earlier today in order to put pressure on Pietro." My thoughts returned to her comment about the contract. "But I might have been wrong," I confessed. "I think maybe they might also want to pressure Pietro and, in turn, you, to get them that defense contract they want so damn badly." I considered it for another couple of seconds then blew out my breath. "Yeah, that actually makes a *lot* more sense, though I'm still glad I got you away from them."

"So am I, to be honest," Jane said. "But what could they possibly want to pressure Pietro about?" Her gaze remained steady upon me, and I had to fight not to squirm beneath it.

"Um, about the medical condition. And his organization, I guess."

She leaned closer. "And *why* aren't the authorities involved?"

Damn it, I was utterly out of my depth. I felt my shoulders hunching. "The medical condition is . . . it's pretty weird."

She straightened and pressed her lips together in obvious annoyance. "Angel Crawford," she said, snapping the name out with more authority than my third grade teacher ever had, "that is the second time you've used the word 'weird.' This is *Pietro*," and the unspoken *My* came through with that. "I need to understand, because right now I want to pick up the phone and call the FBI."

I groaned. "Okay. Shit. Shit." Damn it, Brian would kill me but at this point what the hell choice did I have? I stood and moved to the little kitchen area of the suite, and a couple of seconds of digging in the drawers produced a small knife. I tested the edge with my thumb. It would be sharp enough for what I needed to do. Good thing I had a little packet of emergency brains in the side pocket of my cargo pants.

Knife in hand, I began to move back toward Jane. She stood up in alarm, even as I registered a blur of motion to my left.

In the next instant my face met carpet, with Victor on top of me and my breath somewhere in the Hudson River. In less than a second he had the knife out of my hand and secured somewhere on his person. My face was squished against the floor, but I managed to squawk out, "I wsnt ging to hrt her!"

"Angel!" I saw Jane—or rather, from my angle, Jane's shoes and lower legs—take a few hesitant steps toward me. "What were you going to do with that knife? Victor, let her up, please."

Victor shifted off me and gave me some not-very-gentle help

getting to my feet. I narrowed my eyes at him, but not because he'd pissed me off. Hell, he'd done exactly what he was supposed to do, and I'd been a fucktard for coming at Jane with a knife, or at least looking as if I was about to.

Yes, Victor had done his job very well. *Very* well, and the speed with which he'd made it from the bedroom to me had been pretty darn impressive. He met my gaze with an expressionless one of his own. I took a slow step toward him, pleased when he didn't retreat—not that I expected him to flinch. But even better, he didn't pull back when I leaned close, inches from the side of his face, and *sniiiiffffffed.*

"What the *hell* is going on?" Jane demanded, baffled frustration heavy in her voice. Okay, I totally understood how the part where I sniffed her bodyguard was the final straw.

A muscle in Victor's jaw twitched as I straightened, but when he met my eyes he gave me a very tiny confirming-though-grudging nod.

"I'm about to show you," I said to Jane, then shifted my attention to Victor. "If I stand ten feet away from her, will you let me have the stupid knife?"

He clearly knew what I wanted to do, and he gave Jane a measuring look first, no doubt considering whether he should protect her from the knowledge I was about to give her. Apparently he came down on the side of *Jane can handle it.* He produced the knife from a pocket within his jacket, handed it to me, then stepped back.

It wasn't until I gripped the knife and stuck out my left arm that I remembered this sort of thing really hurt. I hadn't thought that far ahead. I almost asked Victor if he'd do it for me, but one glance at him and the look in his eyes told me it *might* not be such a great idea to ask him to cut me.

"Okay, Jane," I said. "I'm about to give you a crash course on my weird medical condition." I lifted the knife, looked down at the carpet, then backed up a few feet until I was on the tile of the kitchenette, all while Jane watched me as if I was insane. She probably wasn't far from wrong.

Before I could chicken out, I stuck the point into my forearm, then pulled it down and across to slice a deep gash. "Fucking shitballs," I gasped as the pain shot up my arm in a burning wave.

Jane sucked in a sharp breath. "My *god!* Angel!"

Thankfully the pain dulled after only a couple of seconds. I dropped the knife and grabbed a towel off the counter to catch the worst of the blood, then pulled it aside to make sure Jane could see the gash was real and not some sort of sleight of hand special effects bullshit. Yet I also didn't want her to freak too hard at the sight of me standing here bleeding in the kitchen. Besides, that wasn't the point of this. With my other hand I yanked the little baggie out of my pocket, opened it with my teeth, then gulped down the contents. Within seconds the gash began to close at the edges. I wiped the blood away with the towel again so that she could see it continue to close. Within half a minute the gash was only a red line, and after a dozen more seconds even that was gone.

I looked up at Jane with more than a little trepidation, silently praying I wouldn't see disgust on her face. Wasn't sure I could handle that from her. But she simply stared, utterly dumbfounded. As I watched, a realization spread across her face.

"That's how . . ." She trailed off and sat heavily.

I turned to the sink and washed the blood off, then cleaned up the floor. Figured she needed a minute or two to process everything anyway. Once everything was spotless I moved to the sofa and sat a few feet from her. "That's how what?"

She took a shaky breath, still staring at my arm. "That's how Pietro and Brian walked away from the car wreck that should have killed both of them, isn't it?"

Only a few months ago she'd had a broken leg, and Pietro had been sporting a wrist brace I knew damn well he hadn't needed. "Yeah, it's kind of hard to kill us," I admitted.

She took another breath, deeper this time and much less shaky, visibly pulling herself together and regaining composure. "I don't understand. What kind of medical condition is this? And why is it secret? It's *miraculous*." She shook her head. "Pietro could have told me."

"It's secret because . . ." I fidgeted. "Well, because the way we stay alive is kind of gross. The stuff in that baggie was—" I shot a desperate look at Victor and got a *You're on your own* one in response. Sighing, I turned back to Jane. "It's brains."

The poor woman once again looked dazed. "What kind of brains?"

My shoulders hunched. "Human brains," I said, voice small. "It's why I work in a morgue—so I can get them and survive."

She paled and pressed a hand to her stomach. "You *eat* human brains? *Pietro* eats human brains?"

"Only after they're dead," I insisted and tried not to think about the two times I'd helped someone along to being dead enough to be my dinner. "We call ourselves zombies, 'cause it kind of fits, y'know?

But we're not bad people. I swear." Mostly. Shit. "Please, just try to think about what you know about me and Pietro and Victor."

I realized my mistake the instant the name was out of my mouth, but by then it was too late. Jane's gaze snapped to her bodyguard. "*Victor?*"

Oooh, if Victor's look could have killed I'd have been a smoking pile of ash on the carpet. Jaw so tight I thought his teeth would break, he pulled his attention to his employer. "Yes, ma'am," he said after only a small hesitation—no doubt while he was trying to decide if he could quickly wring my neck and then claim he had to do so because I was obviously stark raving insane and no, of course he didn't eat brains because that was ludicrous, right?

At this rate I was going to get a gold medal at Fucking Up. "Sorry," I mumbled to Victor.

Jane folded her hands into her lap and crossed her legs at her ankles, visibly donning her armor of Cultured Southern Woman. She had a spine of steel, this one.

"And the Sabers know about all of this," she said slowly. "And they have Pietro. But," her brow furrowed, "Brian was with them."

"Brian managed to get to one of our other guys before Saberton did," I explained. "He told me he was at the party trying to get info about Pietro. I'm not a hundred percent sure, but I'm pretty sure we can trust him."

Her hands tightened in her lap. "I knew I had a good reason to hate Nicole Saber."

"Yeah, well, she's pretty cold-blooded," I said.

"And of course you can't go to the authorities, since there's too much chance that the detail about, ah, human brains might come to light." Her lips pursed as she put the pieces together.

I grimaced. "Pretty much."

Jane lifted her chin. "I assume you're in the city to find Pietro?" At my nod she continued, "How can I help?"

That took me aback. I hadn't really thought past this point. "I don't really know, though I'm sure you can." Have a congress-woman on our team? It didn't suck. "I should probably call Brian and let him know what the deal is."

With her eyes still a tad glassy, she looked relieved to have a few more minutes to process all the weird shit I'd just dumped on her. As I moved over to the window, I gave Victor yet another apologetic look. His expression told me I probably wasn't going to be on his Christmas list this year.

Brian answered on the first ring. "Archer."

"Hey, it's me. I just talked to Jane."

"Angel." He exhaled. "I'm sorry about being an ass on the phone earlier. It's been, well . . . I'm just sorry."

"Yeah, it's cool," I replied with a shrug.

"What happened with Jane?" he asked before I could feel too awkward.

"She's on board," I said. Crap. He might go right back to being mad at me after this.

"Okay, good," he said, sounding relieved. "How did you leave it with her? She's staying away from the Sabers, right?"

"Erm, no, I'm still with her, at her hotel," I said. "And, she's on board. Like, totally." I fought to keep my shoulders down and totally unhunched.

Brian remained silent, and I had the weirdest sense that if he'd known my middle name he'd be using my full and proper legal name like a mama calling a misbehaving kid downstairs to face the music.

"It's about damn time," he finally said.

My knees actually wobbled briefly. "Oh, shit, really?" I plopped down into a nearby chair. "I thought you'd want to kill me." Kind of like Victor probably wanted to do. Did Brian even know he was a zombie? Probably, I realized, since Pietro had arranged the security for Jane.

"She's needed to know for a while now, in my opinion," he said. "Mr. Ivanov made me swear I wouldn't tell her."

"Yeah, well, luckily I have no damn judgment," I said. "Anyway, she wants to know how she can help."

"Since she knows, she needs to cover her ass," he replied. "I don't know what the Sabers have planned, but anything she can do to create a political counteroffensive to Saberton's interests would be called for. Something she can hold ready if needed."

"Right. Hang on." I covered the phone and repeated it to Jane. Her eyes went hard, and she nodded.

"I'll take care of it," she replied with an edge to her words that made me *extremely* glad she still liked me. Jaw set, she stood, moved to the office, then began making calls.

After that, Brian wanted to talk to Victor. I handed the phone over, and Victor moved far enough away that I couldn't hear him. Judging by the dark looks he shot my way I had no doubt he was tattling about my accidental outing of him. Damn. That was a bad fuckup on my part, and it could've been really ugly. A few minutes later Victor returned and handed my phone back.

"He wants to talk to you again," he said. I wasn't sure, but I thought that maybe he wasn't glaring *quite* as hard at me.

"Hey, Brian." I grimaced. "I guess he told you about my latest fuckup?"

"Yes, he did," Brian replied. "It's serious, but I don't need to tell you that. You're a smart woman. He says you need training, and I told him you weren't security or an operative. But here you are, in the thick of a huge crisis."

I turned toward the window. "I'm trying my best," I said, voice cracking.

"I know you are," he said gently. "Shit happens sometimes to all of us. Say the wrong thing. Do the wrong thing. Make the wrong choice. All you can do is learn from it and move on."

I fought back a sniffle, warmed. "Okay. Thanks."

"Thank *you*, Angel, for what you're doing. You didn't have to put yourself out there like this."

The warmth continued to spread like a tingly hug. "Yeah, I did."

"Exactly," he said, a smile in his voice. "That's what makes you *you*. Once we get out of this shit, we'll make sure you have the basics. More if you want it."

A vision of my *sensei*'s pained face swam through my head. "Sure," I said. "If you think you're up for it."

"Bring it on," he said with a low snort.

"Thanks, Brian. I'm really glad you're not a bad guy anymore."

He laughed. "Me too." And with that he hung up.

Feeling about a thousand times better about everything, I turned back to see Jane still on her phone in the office and Victor standing by the sofa, with arms folded over his chest, silently regarding me.

"I'm sorry I outed you," I said, grimacing. "I swear I didn't mean to."

Some of the tension in his jaw eased, and he gave a slight nod. "Understood."

Jane returned from the office, set her cell phone on the coffee table, then *flopped* onto the sofa with a sigh. I held back a grin. *She's a flopper too!*

"There's more to do, but the groundwork is laid," she said. Barely a second later her phone buzzed on the coffee table. She sat up and glanced at it, then narrowed her eyes at the caller ID. "Damn it. It's that horrible woman. At *this* hour."

There was only one horrible woman she could mean. "Answer it," I said quickly, before she could send it to voicemail.

Jane hesitated, then hit the answer button and lifted the phone to her ear. "Jane Pennington," she said with total calm.

Silence for a second, then, *"Jane! It's Nicole Saber,"* I heard clearly, and there was no mistaking the surprise in her voice. *"I'm so sorry, I didn't expect you to answer. The event ended a short while ago, and I thought I'd call and leave you a message. I was worried after you left so suddenly and wanted to wish you well. I do hope you're feeling better?"*

Jane's smile was frosty, but none of it showed in her voice. "Why yes. I think it was simply a touch of jet lag. I'll be right as rain after a good night's sleep."

"I'm so glad to hear it. I'd love to take you to an early lunch tomorrow so that we can continue our conversation. Racchelli's Cucina Italiana at eleven?"

"Lunch would be lovely, but I think my calendar is booked. I'll check." She lowered the phone and covered the mouthpiece, looked out the window with zero move to check her calendar.

I made frantic motions. *Do it*, I mouthed. *Yes! Take the lunch!*

Jane gave me an *Are you inSANE?* look, at which time we proceeded to go through a silent yes no yes no back and forth, with me growing increasingly more frantic in my motions.

Finally Jane threw up her hands in defeat and returned the phone to her ear. "It seems my ten o'clock appointment cancelled," she said. "How fortuitous."

I grinned in triumph, but Jane simply rolled her eyes, which only made me grin more.

"Excellent," Nicole all but crowed. *"I'll see you then."*

As soon as Jane hung up I made a couple of fist pumps in the air. "This is perfect," I said. "She's going to lay down a threat about hurting Pietro, and we—I mean *you*—can simply tell her to cut to the chase."

Comprehension dawned on her face. "Take the wind out of her sails."

"And then we have the advantage."

Chapter 22

After nowhere near enough sleep, I once again allowed Naomi to dress me as she pleased, this time in jeans that fit me like a glove, long sleeved black shirt, and boots made for kicking butt. I was almost starting to like being her personal Barbie doll. However, I had a feeling Nicole Saber would probably have a different B word in mind when I showed up uninvited to the lunch meeting.

Since having Jane pick me up at The Fairbourne would be like waving a big flag and shouting, "Yo! Saberton peeps. You can find us right here!" Philip accompanied me to a pre-arranged meeting place near Battery Park, and carefully didn't laugh when I knocked my breath out on the subway turnstile after I forgot to swipe my MetroCard.

A black sedan with government plates pulled up to the curb only a few minutes after we arrived, and a back window rolled down to reveal Jane. As I moved toward her, a black Escalade that reminded me of Pietro's vehicles slid in behind the sedan, and I damn near had a heart attack until I caught sight of Victor in the passenger seat. Made sense that Victor would be in a position to keep an eye on everything, and it was likely easier to do so from a shadowing vehicle.

I gave Philip a friendly punch on the arm then jogged to the car. He, Naomi, and Kyle would join up and keep an extra watch outside the restaurant. I slid into the back seat of the sedan, where Jane gave me a warm smile and a quick hug that worked wonders to dispel the last little niggling doubts I had about spilling the beans to her about the whole zombie thing. She still liked me, even though I ate brains. That was pretty cool.

As if by mutual agreement, we kept the conversation light and generic on the way to the restaurant. There'd be plenty of time for the serious shit later. And I decided it was a good thing the driver knew where to go, because I'd have gone past the restaurant at least ten times and never found it. Tucked behind another building, it definitely wasn't the sort of place that got a lot of tourist traffic. To get there it was necessary to walk through a narrow but tidy courtyard and then down a staircase to a dark red door that opened into a café of about a dozen tables and some amazingly appetizing smells. With black and white tiled floor, wood chairs, and white tablecloths, it reminded me a bit of the Italian-American restaurant in *The Godfather* where Michael kills Sollozzo, and I had to fight the urge to go and check the restrooms for hidden guns. Silly, because I was quite sure Victor had plenty of his own with him, and the two tough-looking men in dark suits against the back wall surely had theirs as well.

And, in a twist that really didn't surprise anyone, every table was empty except for the one right in the center of the restaurant. Nicole sat on the other side of the table in a dark red suit paired with a gold-colored blouse. She leaned back and crossed her legs, very obviously trying to appear calm and relaxed, though the quick tap-tapping of her fingers on the side of her leg showed the true state of her nerves.

For her part, Jane looked cool and collected and not at all as if everything that was on the line was, actually, on the line. I did my best to look as cool as her and finally settled for being absolutely amazed that she looked as chill as she did. My gaze roamed the restaurant and over Nicole's two men, then snapped back to the one on the right. Fairly good-looking, jet-black hair, wide shoulders, and narrow waist. Too far away to see his what color his eyes were, but I could tell that the eyebrows above them were *perfect*.

Motherfuckingshitballs. This was one of my guards from when Charish held me captive, one of the assholes who'd helped McKinney strip search me. His eyes met mine, and his mouth curved in an ugly smirk. A sick chill went through me, but I deliberately rolled my eyes and looked away as if he wasn't worth my attention. Which he wasn't, of course. Asshole. I shoved the memories aside and focused instead on the awesome smackdown about to take place.

Nicole smiled at Jane, but her smile froze at the sight of me. I fought down a manic grin and instead smiled back without showing teeth. There'd be plenty of time for teeth later, I figured.

With me right behind her, Jane approached the table, but instead of taking the seat the maitre d' held out, she leaned forward, eyes locked on Nicole's. "We both know why we're here," she said with quiet force.

Oh, this was going to be fun. I pulled a chair from another table and stuck it to the right of the one the poor maitre d' was still holding, plopped down, then grabbed a breadstick from the basket on the table and took a bite.

Smile still fixed and disgust thinly masked, Nicole's flicked her focus to me before shifting it back to Jane. "Of course. We're discussing your support for Saberton to be awarded the defense contract."

"Discussing? No," Jane said. "You intend to threaten to hurt or even kill Pietro in order to force my cooperation."

That caught Nicole off guard. She lost the smile, expression tightening. "Will you at least sit?" She hissed the last word.

Jane turned and graciously thanked the poor maitre d', then took her seat as if it had been completely her idea. I resisted the urge to lean back and put my feet on the table. That would probably get me kicked out, but damn I had a feeling this was going to get good.

Nicole took a deep breath as Jane sat, regaining a tiny bit of composure. "Congresswoman Pennington, would you care to explain your *unexpected* comment?"

Jane's expression hardened to *uncompromising*, but when she spoke her voice was as cool as frost on a junebug's ass. "Cut to the chase, bitch. No games. I have something you want, and you have something I want."

Holeeeeee shit, but I wanted to jump up and cheer. How the hell had I not seen how amazingly strong this woman was? Her normal manner was so laid-back refined it was easy to underestimate her. Now I understood how she handled herself in Washington so well.

Nicole's face flushed red and went to stone. Hot and angry stone that was super pissed she'd been outmaneuvered. No more advantage of surprise for her. She took a sip of her water then carefully set the glass back down. "Very well," she said, voice brittle. "You have something I want." She leaned back and did her best to look relaxed, but the jiggling of her leg betrayed her tension. "Deliver the contract to Saberton."

Jane tilted her head slightly. "Or what?"

Now Nicole's smile turned nasty. She reached into her purse on the floor and pulled out a small box—the kind that might hold a tennis bracelet, though I had a gut feeling there weren't any diamonds in there. She placed it on the table, then pushed it toward Jane with one finger.

Jane dropped a brief and dismissive glance to the box then returned her gaze to Nicole's face. "A toe? A finger? His balls?" Jane said without making any move to take or open the box, cool demeanor not slipping a smidge. She tilted her head in my direction. "I have an expert advisor on what you can do, have done, and will do to zombies." With one finger, she pushed the box right back to Nicole. "What is your threat?"

Nicole shot me a *furious* look, clearly livid that her grand gesture fell flat and that once again she'd been caught off guard. She snatched at the box and shoved it back into her purse, though the disgust on her face told me that, whatever piece of Pietro that was, it was going to end up in the first available dumpster.

"Simple," Nicole snapped out. "You go call in favors, exert influence, spread rumors, and do whatever you have to do to get us that contract, or I'll deliver a hundred boxes like that." Her eyes glittered with contempt. "I'm sure your *expert* advisor can tell you those creatures still feel plenty of pain."

Jane didn't even flinch. "No, darling," she replied smoothly. "It doesn't work like that."

I snagged another breadstick. This shit was good.

Nicole blinked. "Excuse me?"

"I may be new to Washington, but I've made my mark," Jane said, tone still pure silk. "It's why you chose *me* to coerce. You thought I'd be cowed by your threats, and I'd go off as ordered and use what influence I have to get you what you want." She paused, leaned back as casually as Nicole had tried to do earlier. "But I'm not cowed. And here's *my* promise."

Nicole's mouth worked soundlessly before she closed it with a sharp snap. Her right hand clenched into a fist on the table.

"You harm Pietro in any way, and I will take your teetering corporation to the ground, then bury it," Jane said, exuding power and confidence. "This isn't the only contract that matters to you. And, before your little mind moves to taking me out to cut your losses, you should know I didn't get much sleep last night. Burning the midnight oil to set up failsafes in case I meet with an untimely accident or disappear."

The blood left Nicole's face as Jane spoke, then her cheeks flushed hot, lips white as she spoke. "If you think I'm simply going to turn him over to you and get *nothing* in return, you're sadly mistaken."

"I never said you would get nothing," Jane replied. "I said I will ruin you if you harm Pietro. Not the same thing. I will consider supporting *this* contract if you meet my conditions."

I munched breadsticks and watched Nicole's internal battle to keep from telling Jane where she could shove her conditions.

"Go on," Nicole finally managed.

"First off, after the contract is awarded, Pietro is released to me—unharmed in any way."

I glanced at Jane, surprised that she wasn't asking for Pietro to be released immediately, then realized Jane knew damn well the answer to that would be No. Nicole wouldn't give up her ace in the hole before she had what she wanted, and Jane had no desire to lose ground by asking for the impossible. Damn, I felt as if I should be taking notes.

Nicole's nostrils flared. "What else?"

"Second, within three hours from now you will make arrangements for us to see and have complete freedom to speak with Pietro, including physical contact."

Nicole gave another stiff nod, her hand clenched so tightly it surprised me that blood wasn't trickling out from her nails on her palm.

"And you tell us who the insider is," I put in.

Nicole shot me a scathing look. "For all I know, *you're* the insider."

I regarded her with suspicion. It was *possible* she didn't know, but I didn't trust that calculating look in her eye. Then again, "calculating" could be a permanent part of her expression.

Jane eyed Nicole, then glanced toward me. "Anything else, Ms. Crawford?"

"Yeah, she and her thugs can stay the hell away from me, my dad, and my Krewe."

Nicole's eyes remained on me for a moment more before returning to Jane. "Anything else?"

"I believe we're complete," Jane said.

Nicole seized her purse and stood so quickly she toppled her chair, but she didn't even glance behind her at the clatter. "I'll contact you in three hours." Her jaw tightened. "You will get us that contract."

"I will exert all possible influence," Jane said, still seated and not looking at all intimidated by having to look up at Nicole. If anything she seemed more like a queen indulging some commoner. God, I loved this woman.

Nicole planted her hands on the table and leaned forward. "You're a tougher woman than I expected, Jane Pennington, but I'm sure you understand that if we don't get that contract, I'll have little left to lose." She straightened and began to stalk off but Jane's voice stopped her before she reached the door.

"And I'm sure you understand, Nicole Saber," Jane replied without looking toward her, "if I lose Pietro, I'll see you burn in hell."

Nicole slammed out the door with her men right behind her, and as soon as they were gone it was as if the entire building breathed a sigh of relief. Jane waited a moment, then stood gracefully and moved to the door. I scrambled to follow, then paused, looked at the maitre d' as he righted the toppled chair.

"Can I get some of those breadsticks to go?"

Chapter 23

Jane returned me to Battery Park and promised she'd call as soon as she heard from Nicole. Philip sauntered up a few seconds after Jane's car pulled away as if he'd been waiting there the entire time, then he and I proceeded to take a convoluted route back to the hotel, during which—using the miracle of conference calling—I gave the entire Krewe, along with Brian, a recap of the lunch discussion and the plan to see Pietro.

Naomi let out a low whistle when I finished. "Damn, Jane Pennington has giant, shiny brass balls."

"She certainly does, and it's an opportunity to be seized," Brian agreed, a note of admiration in his voice. "That said, I don't intend to go with you. I'm not comfortable leaving Dr. Nikas for that long, and it would be foolish to make it so easy for Saberton to grab all of us at once."

"That makes perfect sense," I said and heard murmurs of agreement from the others.

"Kyle and I will pick up a couple of things and meet Angel and Philip back at the hotel," Naomi said, then disconnected.

"Angel, Dr. Nikas says he has a treatment made up for you and Philip," Brian told me. "I'd like you to meet me at a place in SoHo—Betsy's Bakes, on the corner of Grand and Greene, in six hours."

"Sounds good," I said. "We should be done by then, and I know how to get in touch with you if something goes wrong."

"Don't jinx yourself," he chided, but his tone remained upbeat. "I'll save a brownie for you."

"Save two."

"Deal."

I stood perfectly still as Naomi rigged up the earpiece comm thing that would allow her to monitor and advise. And I only winced a little when Kyle made a thin slice on my side above my hip and slipped a tiny GPS tracker beneath the skin. If the worst happened, and I got captured again, I wanted the Krewe to be able to find my scrawny ass. The others each had one for the same reason. The zombies' were beneath the skin, like mine, and Naomi's . . . well, I didn't really need to know where Naomi's tracker was hidden.

Kyle held the incision shut as my parasite did its weird and tingly work to heal the wound and conceal the tracker. Philip handed me a cup, and I slurped down a thin slice of brain to help my parasite out and to stay as tanked. Craning my neck, I peered down at the cut. Nothing left but a faint red line, and after a few seconds even that was gone.

"Done," Kyle murmured, straightening.

Philip tapped out something on a computer tablet then gave a nod. "It's working." He was dressed in dark grey fatigue pants and a close-fitting black crew neck shirt under a lightweight black zip-up jacket, which was as much for concealment of weapons as for warmth. My outfit was similar, though about ten thousand sizes smaller.

"You'll need to present as strong an image as possible," Naomi had said when she produced the clothing. "You need to look confident and capable, with a *don't fuck with me* aura."

I didn't argue with her. I'd wear purple feathers in my hair if they could make up for the fact that I was a not-very-intimidating petite twenty-two year old. Naomi and Kyle were dressed in totally normal jeans and t-shirts and hoodies, but that was because they'd be staying outside to monitor and had more need to blend in. That said, I knew damn well each was still armed to the teeth.

Philip passed the tablet to Naomi, then retrieved a cloth bundle from a canvas bag and fixed his attention on me. "Marcus said you were getting to be a pretty good shot," he said as he unfolded the cloth to reveal a small black pistol about the size of my hand. "This is a Glock 27. Forty caliber, holds nine rounds. It's like the one Marcus let you practice with, but smaller."

I stared at the gun in his hand for several seconds before I found my voice. "You want *me* to carry a gun?" I squeaked.

"Only if you want to," Philip said. "There's no wrong answer here, Angel. If you're not comfortable with it, that's fine as well."

My thoughts tumbled crazily. *They trust me with a gun. This shit is so damn illegal. We need to present as strong an image as possible. They trust ME with a gun?* And then: *I could kill someone with this.*

The last thought quieted all the others. I could kill someone with this. I didn't want to do that, but the truth was I had, in fact, killed before. Twice—each time when I'd felt there was no other choice. The gun was simply another way to do so.

Gulping softly, I gingerly took the gun, then—remembering what Marcus had drilled into me countless times—kept my finger clear of the trigger, pointed the muzzle at the floor, ejected the magazine, then pulled the slide back to check for a round in the chamber to verify for myself it was unloaded.

"She passes!" Naomi crowed. I jerked my gaze to her in surprise.

"Wait, this was a test?" I blurted.

Laughing, she shook her head, then shrugged. "Not *really,* but since you actually know basic gun safety, we'll even give you bullets."

I wasn't entirely sure she was joking.

Philip produced a holster that attached to my belt at the small of my back, and for the next twenty minutes I practiced drawing the unloaded gun from the holster until I stopped fumbling awkwardly and could actually draw it with relative ease.

Finally, the others pronounced me ready enough. I loaded the magazine, chambered a round, then secured the gun in the holster. It was heavier loaded, though I wasn't sure how much was simply my imagination. *I'm wearing death on my butt,* I thought, then coughed to cover the slightly hysterical giggle that bubbled up.

"Remember, we're keeping our eyes and ears open for anything and everything that could be useful for a later extraction of Mr. Ivanov," Philip said as we made last minute adjustments to gear.

"Got it." I fought the urge to scratch at the place on my side, and settled for rubbing the itchy spot on the crook of my arm instead.

Naomi checked a few more things on the tablet, then slid it into a backpack. "Kyle and I will be in front of the Saberton building, keeping tabs on everything from the car," she reminded us. I managed not to roll my eyes at the mention of the car—a sleek hybrid SUV that had rolled off a production line less than a year earlier. Apparently the combination of spy work and way too much money meant that

Naomi had a half dozen vehicles stashed around the country in long term storage. Not in south Louisiana, though. No, that would have been way too easy. "If you see any problems, vocalize them if at all possible since I can't see what's going on," she continued, oblivious to my internal snarking. "Any questions?" When no one had any, she gave a crisp nod. "Let's do this thing."

Naomi and Kyle left as soon as Jane called to arrange for us to meet her at Washington Square near the arch. Philip and I waited about five minutes, to give the pair time to get into position, then we headed out.

Philip shifted from foot to foot in a very uncharacteristic show of nerves as the hotel elevator descended.

"You okay?" I asked.

A worried look passed over his face. "I'm still not sure it's the best idea for me to go in."

"Cut that out," I said sharply. "You haven't had any problems since we started taking the stuff Dr. Nikas recommended. Not to mention, you actually know what you're doing. I sure as hell can't do this by myself."

"I'm still having some dizzy spells. Kyle could go in with you," he said, but it was a weak protest. We'd already hashed this out several times. Naomi couldn't go in since there was too much chance she'd be recognized, and it didn't make sense to split her and Kyle up when they worked so seamlessly together. Philip grimaced and rubbed the back of his neck. "Sorry. It keeps surfacing. The worry."

"You're my partner," I told him. "Not my romantic partner," I hurried to add in case he'd misread me. But the smile that twitched at his mouth told me he understood perfectly fine and found it more amusing than insulting that I'd felt the need to clarify. "I *mean* you're more than my damn zombie kid or any shit like that," I went on. "I got your back, and I know you got mine." I smiled and bumped him with my shoulder. "It's cool, ZeeBee."

He returned the bump and the smile as the elevator doors opened. "Got it, ZeeEm. I'm good."

We took the subway to Washington Square without incident, and Jane's black sedan pulled up shortly after we arrived, with Victor and the Escalade only a second behind it. Philip took the front seat of the limo, I slid into the back, and we were on our way.

"Damn, you look awesome, lady," I said as I swept an appreciative gaze over Jane. With a perfect updo, sleek navy suit, white silk shirt, and current no-nonsense expression, she pulled off sophisticated power perfectly.

"Even with the circles under my eyes?" she asked, but she smiled as she smoothed out a fold in the skirt.

"Oh, please," I said with a snort. "It's obvious you're ready to kick ass and take names. Again."

Jane's expression turned to southern ice. "I'll do whatever it takes to get Pietro out of there." She looked down at her hands, folded them gracefully on her knee and exhaled. "He asked me to marry him."

"Oh. Wow." I didn't quite know what to say after that, and I made myself take a few seconds to gather my thoughts before blurting out something really stupid. "I'm sure he'd've told you about him being a zombie," I finally said. "I mean, if you said yes. Before you, er, did it." Okay, only partly stupid. Jeez.

She glanced at me. "I did say yes. We were going to wait until I was bit more established in Congress before making it public." She shifted her attention to the sights beyond the window. Traffic was lighter than usual, though still way more than I was used to. Yellow taxis meandered uptown with us, and a bike messenger with a thick chain slung across his shoulders expertly wove between vehicles. "I'd like to think that he would, indeed, have told me," she continued, "but right now none of that matters. What does matter is that bitch has my husband, whether it's official or not."

"Damn straight," I said with a firm nod.

Jane closed her eyes and leaned her head back, but I doubted she was taking a nap. She looked more like a warrior preparing for the battle of a lifetime, psyching herself up and doing whatever meditation or calming mental exercises would help her win the day. Meanwhile, I tried not to fidget in my supposedly badass outfit. Philip looked like an action movie hero, while I felt more like a kid in a costume.

I pulled out a packet of brains. We'd already tanked up, but a little extra edge couldn't hurt for a situation as serious as this, right? I zipped off the top and sucked down the contents. A few seconds later a delicious tingle swept through me, colors sprang to life, and everything looked as cool as a 3D movie, but sharper.

Philip glanced back at me, forehead creased in concern as he noted the empty brain packet in my hand. I gave him a reassuring *I know what I'm doing* smile. We'd be done with this crap and out of there long before I needed some crash time. He gave a slight nod and returned the smile, but a whisper of worry remained in his eyes as he faced front again. He was most likely tense about this whole excursion, I decided. There was no reason in the world for him to be worried about me when it came to brain consumption. I'd been managing my own supply for over a year now, and I knew better than to waste them.

The car came to a smooth stop in front of the Saberton building, and Jane opened her eyes. She looked calmer, more centered. I needed to learn that trick.

Victor and Philip were out first and kept a sharp watch on everything while the driver came around and opened the door for us.

"Ready?" Jane asked. Her light smile stood in sharp contrast to the steel in her eyes.

"Sure, what the hell," I replied with a fatalistic shrug.

Jane stepped out with elegant ease. I climbed out behind her and tried not to trip on the curb. As if we'd practiced, the three zombies fell in around Jane like an undead human shield.

The back of my neck prickled as we walked up to the broad glass entrance. I had no doubt we were being watched, but I hoped it wasn't through a rifle scope. After the packet in the limo I felt badass enough to tear through the milling humans on the street like a fox in a henhouse, but none of that would help me if a sniper bullet blew out my brain stem.

Philip moved in beside me and gave my shoulder a nudge, eyes fixed straight ahead though a faint smile played on his face. *I'm with you*, his nudge told me. *I got your back.*

I nudged him right back. *Ditto.*

As we approached I caught sight of the reflection of our foursome in the glass that fronted the building. We looked damn good, I decided. Jane and the Zombies. *Sounds like a punk band*, I thought with a stifled laugh, though I had to admit that Naomi had been right—we sure as hell didn't look like a group to be fucked with. Still, I breathed a sigh of relief as we entered the building, and was amused to hear it echoed by the others even though we all knew the relief was short-lived. We were in the dragon's den now and far from anything resembling safety.

I caught myself gawking as we continued moving. From outside, the building didn't look all that special, but inside, trees, glass, and at least three floors of open space above made it feel as if I'd walked off the street into a different world. A curved reception desk of polished wood and glass stood in the center of the gleaming marble floor. The whole place was empty, and it took me a few seconds of wondering before I remembered it was Sunday. To the right, a stairway curved up to the mezzanine, and to the left, a sitting area with uncomfortable-looking chairs occupied its own garden of potted plants. A security guard dressed in dark pants and a light blue shirt stood beside a smaller desk near a short corridor with a bank of elevators, his gaze on us. Another man in a charcoal grey suit approached from the direction of the elevators.

I recognized Andrew Saber from the Gourmet Gala and the party the other night. Tall, with an athletic build, he had a strong, square jaw and wary eyes. He strode toward us, cool and calm with a hint of swagger as though he owned the place—which he did, of course, or damn near.

Jane walked up to him while the rest of us hung back a few steps. "Andrew, it's so nice to see you again," she said with a gracious smile as if she'd been invited for tea.

"Congresswoman Pennington, it's truly a pleasure," he replied with equal warmth, while I wondered how the hell these people could fake such niceness. He bestowed the same genuine-looking smile on the rest of us before returning his attention to Jane. "If you would all please come with me?"

"Of course," Jane murmured, still smiling as he turned and headed to an elevator set apart from the others. Yet a flicker of uncertainty in her quick glance my way made me wonder if her stomach had the same butterflies as mine.

Andrew pulled a set of keys from his pocket and pressed a thumb-sized piece of grey plastic on a control panel beside the elevator door. A light flashed green, and the doors slid open. As soon as we entered he ran his thumb over a scanner like the ones we used at Dr. Nikas's lab, then pressed the "10" button. Nobody said a word, but the message was clear: Shit was real now, yo.

"Your mother has filled you in?" Jane asked placidly as the car began to rise.

Andrew flicked his eyes toward her. "She informed me that you wish to see and speak to Mr. Ivanov for yourself, Dr. Pennington."

That didn't really answer her question, I noticed. Nicole Saber had probably told her son as little as possible of the humiliating scene at lunch.

"What is your opinion of his condition, Andrew?" Jane pursed her lips. "Your mother tends to, ah, not always give a clear picture."

The elevator stopped, and the doors opened. Andrew stepped off and held them to allow everyone to exit. "He seems tired, ma'am," he said, "but I assure you he's being fed well and is not being abused or sleep deprived." His expression flickered ever so briefly before he regained his cool, professional mask. "Right this way, ma'am." He gestured down the hallway.

Before he could turn, Jane stopped him with a voice that could cut steel. "Other than amputating a body part, you mean?" Silently cheering Jane, I watched Andrew's reaction. There'd been *something* in that box at lunch, something Nicole had hoped to shock Jane with. And it sure as hell hadn't been a tennis bracelet.

A brief flash of annoyance swept over Andrew's face. "Yes, ma'am," he said, voice thick. "Other than that." He straightened his shoulders, jaw firming. "Right this way," he repeated and started off down the hall. Jane glanced at me then followed, Victor right at her side.

After a couple of turns, Andrew opened a set of dark wood double doors and entered a large conference room. Jane and Victor followed him in, but I paused, shoulders prickling as I scanned the area within. No windows and no other exits, with four security guards in navy blue uniforms spaced around the room, each paying *very* close attention to our every movement. One of the guards was Mr. Perfect Eyebrows and another was Boat Launch Guy, both of them hard-core assholes, as I knew all too well. A uniformed woman stood a bit separate from the others, demeanor calm and professional. Muscled without being bulky, she had light brown hair in a sensible but attractive chin-length cut, sharp blue eyes, and a jaw a bit too square for her to be conventionally pretty. She had on the same style of navy blue tactical pants as the others, but her shirt was a dark grey, she wore two radios on her belt, and an air of authority surrounded her. Probably the head security person, I decided. And, of course, all the security personnel were armed, with regular guns *and* tranq guns ready in their holsters.

I weighed the odds. Three tanked zombies and five human security guards. Easy pickings if things got ugly, except for the damn tranq guns. I didn't need a buttload of tactics training to know that it would be insanely easy to trap us in this room.

But Nicole won't get Jane's help if she does that, I told myself as I moved on in. I knew without a doubt that Jane had spoken the absolute truth when she said she'd taken precautions that would ensure Saberton went down in flames if anything happened to her— which was great, and sounded like strong insurance. Except, I couldn't help but think it was like a restraining order: only as good as a person's fear of it.

Yet the risks all seemed worth it at the sight of Pietro Ivanov sitting at the far end of the table. He looked wiped out, shoulders slumped. His left hand was wrapped in gauze, but he was alive, and in mostly once piece. My eyes went back to his hand. That answered the question of which body part Nicole had chopped off, but why the hell was it still bandaged? With brains, it should have grown back.

I masked a scowl. Obviously they weren't feeding him as well as Andrew claimed. Pietro was likely getting barely enough brains to maintain, but not enough to heal. Except . . . why not fix him up for this show-and-tell? It didn't make sense.

Mr. Perfect Eyebrows stood beside Pietro, and I gave the guard a hate-glare. He gave me an ugly smirk in return then made a point of raking his eyes over me in an obvious *I've seen you naked* look. Fucking asshole.

Pietro lifted his head slowly and with effort, as though it weighed a hundred pounds. My confusion grew. With that sort of lack-of-brains fatigue, he should've been showing signs of rot, yet I didn't catch a whiff or see any sign of it.

Pietro's gaze went straight to Jane. A smile flickered, yet deep worry formed lines of tension in his face at the sight of her here in the heart of enemy territory.

Before we had a chance to do much more than look at each other, Nicole Saber swept in like a queen at her own ball. She closed the door behind her and smiled tightly. "And now here we all are. Congresswoman Pennington, I've kept my side of the bargain."

Jane cast a contemptuous glance at Nicole, then moved to the end of the table with me right on her heels. "Pietro?"

He stood as she approached, movements painfully slow and deliberate. "Jane, you shouldn't be here." His voice was rough, thready. His eyes flicked briefly to me before returning to Jane.

"I had to see you," she replied. "I had to be sure you're all right."

"I've been better, but I've been worse," he said then tilted his head toward Nicole. "Why did she let you in here?"

A smile brushed across Jane's lips. "I made her an offer she couldn't refuse."

Understanding lit his eyes. "The contract," he began, but Nicole cut him off.

"Enough chit chat," she snapped. "You've seen what you came here to see."

The look Jane gave Nicole could have burned a hole through concrete. "I told you I wanted to see Pietro and determine his well-being," she said coldly. "I've yet to do so." Dismissing her, she returned her attention to Pietro. "Are you getting enough to eat?"

"Adequate. You don't need to worry about that." He reached and took Jane's hand with his unbandaged one, yet once again his eyes returned to me. Was he trying to tell me something? Or maybe he was sending some secret zombie message? If so, I was totally failing to get it.

"Your hand is like ice," Jane murmured, so softly that I doubted any non-zombie in the room could hear it. She stroked her thumb over his fingers. "Are they giving you sufficient brains?"

Pietro's attention snapped back to Jane, alarm flaring in his eyes before they dulled with fatigue again. "You . . ."

She took his hand in both of hers while I did my best to be very very very uninteresting and not worthy of notice. Pietro wouldn't have to think very hard to figure out who let the cat out of the bag.

"Yes, Pietro," Jane said. "I know, and I understand."

Pietro sank back into the chair. Jane kept hold of his hand and pulled another chair close so that she could sit as well.

"Jane," Pietro said, distressed. "I'm sorry. I—"

"*Enough* of the pathetic zombie love display!" Nicole snarled, a brittle edge to her voice.

Jane ignored the woman. "Don't be," she told Pietro. "I'm going to make sure you come out of this all right." She leaned in and brushed her lips across his cheek, and only the fact that I was barely a couple of feet away with tanked up zombie hearing allowed me to pick up her fierce whisper. *"I will gut this bitch if she harms my fiancé again."*

A low shudder went through him, then he slid his cheek against hers in a gesture so tender it made my chest ache. "Don't compromise, my darling," he responded, voice as soft as hers. "She'll never let me go, no matter what the agreement."

Nicole made an odd strangled noise. "*Gentry!* Get him out of here."

"Mother, please calm down." Andrew stepped forward and reached to take hold of his mother's arm, then jerked his hand back, like a child remembering not to touch a hot stove. "The contract isn't worth more trouble," he said, and it sounded as though it wasn't the first time he'd done so.

Jane stood, a deeply pitying expression on her face that was surely calculated to be as insulting as possible to Nicole. Mr. Perfect Eyebrows—Gentry—moved in on Pietro's other side and yanked him to his feet. A hiss of pain slipped out of Pietro as his bandaged hand smacked against the edge of the table, but the ugly pleasure on Eyebrows/Gentry's face told me the table-smack hadn't been an accident. Total fucking asshole. But two could play that game. I took a step forward and made a point of scenting the air near him.

"Nice brain," I murmured and bared my teeth in a feral smile.

Pietro's eyes abruptly snapped to mine, sharp and clear, without any evidence of the earlier fatigue and pain. "You see this guy on the street," Pietro jerked his head toward Gentry while keeping his eyes locked on mine, "don't kill him. His name is Pierce Gentry, and his brain is *mine.*"

I blinked, more than a little taken aback by the sudden clarity, though in the next instant I realized I was the only one who'd been in a position to see it. Was he faking the fatigue and weakness? "You got it," I replied.

Sneering, Gentry yanked Pietro's arm again and hustled him out of the room. Pain shot through my hand, and when I glanced down I saw I had it clenched like a vise on the back of a chair.

Jane turned to Nicole, once again totally composed. "Why do I not have confidence that he will be well-treated and maintained?"

Nicole's nostrils flared, and her eyes flashed with dangerous, barely controlled desperation, like a cornered mountain lion. "You have no choice but to trust me!" she said through gritted teeth. "We have a deal, and I'll keep my end of it. You got what you wanted. Now get out of my building and give me my fucking defense contract."

Behind her Andrew opened his mouth then shut it. His lips pressed together, anger in his stance that was clearly directed at his mother.

No way could I argue against Jane's doubts, not with Nicole's eyes shining with all kinds of crazy and Pietro's statement that she'd never let him go. Jane needed to get the hell out while Nicole held the door wide open. I knew damn well that the second I took my eyes off Nicole Saber she'd do something fucked up, and I fully intended to keep Jane covered until I knew she was clear. Plus, I had an insane idea of my own hatching, and this bitch hadn't tasted my flavor of Louisiana crazy yet.

"Ms. Saber, you're absolutely right," I said with a confident smile. "You've kept your side of the deal. Jane Pennington will keep hers."

Nicole gave me a puzzled look, taken somewhat off guard at the way I'd spoken for Jane. She drew a breath, but I spoke before she could.

"The congresswoman and Victor will leave now," I went on as if

I was the one running the entire show, "and Philip and I will remain here with you until we're certain you've allowed her to leave without any further harassment."

Nicole narrowed her eyes, but I shifted my attention to Jane. "You and Victor head on out," I said, doing my best to appear totally self-assured and in control. "Philip and I will check in with you later." I smiled as though all was right with the world. Victor met my eyes and gave me a slight nod filled with gratitude and worry. He'd sensed the same thing about Nicole and knew I was playing a risky game. Once Jane was out, we'd be little more than a doomed rearguard and would have to rely on Nicole Saber's sense of honor and fair play and . . .

Honor? Fair play? Yeah, this was going to get ugly, but I sure as shit didn't intend to be *doomed*.

Chapter 24

"Angel, what are you *doing?*" Naomi said in my ear.

"It's all good," I said to both Jane and Naomi.

Jane opened her mouth to protest, and Andrew stepped forward. "That's an excellent idea," he said. He didn't want Jane to stay any more than I did. Sure, our reasons were different—I was worried about her well-being, while he was worried about his own ass if Mommy Saber did something even *more* stupid to a member of Congress—but right now our goal was the same. "I'm sure you have a very busy schedule, Dr. Pennington," Andrew continued and gave a nod toward one of the security guards—Boat Launch Guy. "Edwards will show you out."

Victor took Jane's elbow. "This way, ma'am." He began to move her toward Edwards and the door.

Jane shot me a distressed look, and I gave her my best *get the fuck out, and we'll stay on it* smile in return. "Maybe we can do lunch tomorrow," I told her. "I'll have my people call your people."

Her lips twitched in what I knew was a smile forced for me, then Victor hustled her through the door, and she was gone.

Andrew and the security guard followed them out. The door closed, and the world abruptly felt smaller. What the hell was I thinking stranding Philip and me alone in the middle of Saber Land? Then again, Philip hadn't argued with my decision to stick around. Either he and I were on the same page, or he had a plan of his own brewing—though somehow I doubted his was quite as psychotic as mine. He was probably considering something sane and logical, such as trying to get more info about where Pietro was being held.

He met my eyes, expression grave and determined. Pietro was in deep trouble, that much we knew. We might never have another chance to gain some sort of advantage. We were deep in enemy territory, in the lion's den, the mouth of the dragon, up shit creek, whatever the hell you wanted to call it. But that simply meant we were in the perfect position to fuck up Saberton's world. I was more than ready to deliver some southern smackdown, but I needed to hear that Jane was out of the building first.

Fists planted on her hips, Nicole glared at the door, as if blaming it for allowing Jane to leave, then swung her attention to me, her expression an ugly mix of anger and disgust. "What a disgrace to this country that a nest of *zombies*," she sneered the word, "can enthrall a U.S. Congresswoman."

"Yes, it is," I said agreeably. And slowly. This was me, stalling for time while looking for an opening. Hell, she thought I was a hick anyway, so might as well lay down some serious southern drawl. "But, lucky for you, it's going to get you closer to that defense contract you want, right?" *C'mon, Naomi, tell me Jane's out.* I flicked a brief glance to Philip, then very casually waggled the fingers of one hand toward Nicole in the desperate hope he'd pick up on my scheme. With only two guards and Nicole in the room, we wouldn't have a better opportunity.

Philip made a quiet strangled noise in the back of his throat. *Oh, good. He figured it out.* Yet on the heels of that thought, worry and doubt surged in. It was one thing to risk myself in a totally crazy and spur of the moment plan to seize Nicole Saber and hold her hostage in exchange for Pietro, but I'd sucked Philip in as well, with zero warning or time to plan. And what if he thought I had some *other* ridiculous plan in mind? Damn it, this whole thing would be easier if the zombie parasite came with telepathy.

Nicole pursed her lips, and some of the anger left her eyes. "*If* she follows through," she huffed, but it was clear her confidence was making a comeback. She still had Pietro, and now she'd seen for herself how much Jane treasured him. A cold smile curved her mouth, and I knew it was because her desperate and clever mind was contemplating the many things she could accomplish with the congresswoman in her control.

Not on my watch, sweetheart. Not with my favorite woman in the whole fucking world.

"Oh, she'll follow through," I assured Nicole as I edged closer. Shitfuckingdamn, wasn't Jane clear yet? I tried to remember how much time it had taken us to walk from the limo to the conference room. Surely it had been at least that long since Jane and Victor left? "Of course, Jane has some serious ways to get back at you if something happens to Pietro," I continued, "but there's no need to worry about that since you're keeping your side of the deal." *Ha! Yeah, right.* "Jane simply wants Mr. Ivanov back, not revenge. She'll give you the influence you need."

Nicole gave a sharp nod. I shot a quick look toward Philip. His attention was locked on the two guards, which worked well enough for me. Even better, both guards were fully focused on Philip since he was obviously more of a threat than I was, badass clothing or not.

"Jane's out," Naomi murmured in my ear. "Are you about to do something Angel-like?"

"Absolutely," I murmured as I focused on Nicole and psyched myself up. I could do this. I could totally take a hostage. I simply had to draw my gun, grab Nicole, get my back to the wall, and then demand Pietro's release. Easy. Even a caveman could do it.

Heart pounding, I slid my hand to the small of my back, closed it around the butt of the little Glock and began to draw it—

The door opened, and I startled, a bit *too* focused on Nicole. Andrew stepped in, and I yanked at the Glock as I watched my window of opportunity begin to slam shut. *Shit!* The gun was caught on the holster somehow, but no one was looking my way yet, which meant I still had a chance. Except Nicole was turning toward the door as if to leave, and Andrew was almost between us. If I could just get the fucking gun out . . .

Weirdly enough, the sound of the gunshot didn't surprise me. It was one of those moments where you *see* shit going wrong, but you realize it an instant too late to actually change directions or slam on the brakes or, well, stop fumbling at the damn gun before you accidentally pull the damn trigger.

The sound might not have surprised me, but the line of fiery pain that streaked across my left ass cheek sure as shit did. The stupid gun came free of the holster, but by then my mind had leaped to "I shot myself in the ass!" instead of sticking with "Hold the weapon in a safe manner!" and the gun went sailing under the conference table. Pain instead of *pain* told me the bullet had only grazed me, and already I felt the numbing tingle of my parasite doing damage control. Good thing, since I had only fractions of a second to come up with a gunless Plan B.

The humans in the room were startled by the gunshot but had yet to fully react. Nicole was several steps away by this point, therefore I went with the option right in front of me. With a snarl, I lunged at

Andrew, gripped his wrist and dragged him toward me. If I couldn't have mama, I'd settle for mama's boy.

Zombie jiu jitsu powers, activate!

Or not. A chill went through me as a strange piercing cry split the air. *Philip*. I caught a blur of movement as he descended on the nearest security guard, and I heard the thud as he slammed him hard into the wall. My peripheral vision told me the other guards had their guns out, but I had zero chance to do anything about it. As I pulled Andrew's wrist, he did a neat twist that yanked me forward and nearly onto my face. Apparently the dude knew some moves. Goddammit.

"Braddock! Stop them!" Nicole yelled at the head security woman, even as I struggled to maintain balance and made a totally unsuccessful attempt to reverse Andrew's move into an *osoto gari*. It looked more like I was dancing with him, which left me with my back fully exposed to Braddock, who had no need of Nicole's suggestion. Braddock already had both guns trained on me, and I had a feeling the only reason I wasn't already full of holes and tranq darts was because she was waiting for the instant where she could shoot me without risking hitting Andrew. Good thing for me the tranqs were pretty much instantly lethal for humans—like giving a kitten a dose meant for an elephant.

Braddock never got the chance to shoot me. Philip sprang from a crouch toward her, and though she tried her best to bring the gun around to do some good, she never had a prayer against that tanked up zombie speed. Philip caught her wrist and yanked her arm straight, then delivered a surgically precise blow to her elbow. The ugly sound of the dislocating joint mingled with Braddock's sharp cry of pain, and the tranq gun tumbled from her hand to land a couple of feet from me.

Andrew flinched at Braddock's cry, which was all the distraction I needed. I drove my knee up hard into Andrew's groin, and he obligingly crumpled to the floor. Screw *jiu jitsu*. Sometimes a girl had to fight dirty.

A gunshot slammed through the room. Philip staggered but kept hold of Braddock's wrist. I scrambled on top of Andrew, clamped one hand on his throat and dug the fingers of the other hard against his belly.

"Nobody move, or I'll rip his guts out!" I yelled, eyes on the guard who'd shot Philip. I even jabbed a bit at Andrew's stomach as if I was about to make good on my threat, and he rewarded me with a convincing cry of pain and genuine fear. I was totally bluffing, of course. Sure, as tanked as I was I could easily gut him, but I figured my Ideal Plan B would probably work better if I didn't play horror-show-macramé with his intestines.

Fortunately the bluff worked, and the guard slowly lowered his weapon. "Put both your guns on the floor!" I ordered, keeping my grip tight on Andrew's throat as the guard slowly complied. I reached to snatch the fallen tranq gun with my other hand, even as my peripheral vision caught Nicole fleeing the room. So much for motherly love and protection.

Philip relieved Braddock of her other gun, then shoved her away. I had to hand it to the woman—she could keep her head in a crisis. Her face was white as a sheet, and her forearm dangled like a broken toy, but she kept enough focus to press a button on one of her radios and gasp out, "Code white," right before Philip ripped the radio from her and hurled it against the wall.

I jammed the tranq gun into Andrew's gut and released his throat. "You know you're dead if my trigger finger twitches," I told him as I shifted off of his chest.

Andrew gave a very small nod, eyes on the gun in my hand. Saberton had developed the high-powered zombie specific tranquilizer. He knew better than anyone how lethal it was for a human.

I quickly reassessed. The trade-a-hostage-for-Pietro plan didn't look very solid at this point since Nicole Saber either valued keeping Pietro over her son's safety, or else had a better plan in the works.

"You're going to get us the hell out of here," I growled at Andrew. "Now get your ass up." I climbed to my feet, tranq gun on him. I felt good, clear headed, but the thrill of being tanked on brains had subsided to a mild buzz, burned off by the adrenaline-charged exertion and the healing of my bullet-grazed butt. I remained plenty fast and strong, but a part of me missed that sharp and awesome feeling. "I'm getting hungry," I added, "so don't try anything stupid."

Andrew paled but didn't freak. He stood, keeping his hands well away from his body. "I'll walk you out," he said. "No troubles."

"Yeah, that's a real good plan," I said and hoped Naomi was listening. "Is that a real good plan?"

"Sounds good since I don't know what the hell you're doing," Naomi said in my earpiece. "We'll meet you at the service entrance in the parking garage."

"Gotcha. Philip, you okay?"

"Angel, down!" he ordered.

Zombie reflexes still in high gear, I dropped into a crouch without even thinking, dragging Andrew with me. A fraction of a second later, Philip leaped over us and onto the guard he'd slammed into the wall earlier, wrenched a tranq gun from his hand and smacked his head into the floor hard enough to stun but not dent him.

Philip straightened as I did, then strode to the guard who'd dropped his weapons. Moving with brisk efficiency, he put the guard on the floor and ziptied his hands behind his back, then retrieved my gun from under the table and tucked it into my holster. "We're good now," he said with a satisfied nod.

Andrew's mouth had dropped open at the entire display, and I grinned despite everything. Apparently he'd never seen tanked zombies in action. "How's the bullet wound?" I asked Philip.

"Handled," he said, patting the side pocket of his pants, which told me he'd already downed some brains.

"Excellent." I gripped the back of Andrew's collar. "Let's get moving. Parking garage service entrance."

Andrew's throat bobbed. "This way," he said as he moved toward the door, still carefully keeping his hands out to his sides. Philip fell in behind us, gun in one hand and a tranq gun in the other. Though we made it into the hallway without incident, I didn't need zombie senses to know more guards lurked right around the corner. Andrew started toward the elevators, but I stopped him with a quick yank.

"Wait," I said. "I'm not real happy about going in an elevator. Is there another way?"

"There are stairs a little farther down," Andrew replied, words clipped.

"Stairs are good," Naomi confirmed.

I glanced back to see Philip with his gun trained behind us. If I had to be on the bad guy side of a hostage situation, at least I was doing it with an experienced operative. "Okay, heading that way now." I had Andrew as my human shield, but a big chunk of our safety depended on how much of a shit Nicole gave about the life of her son, and so far I wasn't impressed by Mommie Dearest. I shook Andrew by the collar. "They'll keep the way clear for you?"

"Yes. Yes, of course," Andrew replied, though I caught the faint hesitation in his tone.

"I don't know about that," Naomi said.

"Yeah, I'm with you," I said. Andrew flicked a glance back at me, only now realizing I was talking to someone else as well. I gave him a tight smile. "Keep moving, Andy," I told him and took twisted pleasure at the angry annoyance that flashed in his eyes at the nickname.

We made it to the stairs without incident, and Philip checked to be sure it was clear before we went in. "It's too damn quiet," I said as we started down the ten flights, voice shaking as nerves and stress threatened to get the better of me.

"We're pulling into the garage now," Naomi said. "Don't see any threats yet, but watch yourselves."

"You know they'll have the exit covered." I prodded my hostage in the back with the gun. "You ready to do some fast talking for us, Andy?"

"I want out of this in one piece as much as you do," he retorted, then blew out a frustrated breath. "Thea Braddock's out of commission—the one whose elbow Reinhardt broke." Andrew glanced back at Philip as we clattered down the stairs. "That's the only reason this way isn't already blocked."

I hustled him down as quickly as possible without tripping and going splat. "Great. Wonderful," I snapped. "I'll send flowers to her, but right now I want to get the fuck out of here."

"If he goes right at the bottom, you're golden," Naomi said. "If he goes left, it's a setup."

"Got it," I said as we came around the last turn in the steps. "Which way, dude?"

"As soon as we get through the door we go right," he replied to my relief. "Straight down the corridor to the warehouse and loading dock." His hand went into his pocket, and I gave him a hard yank on his collar.

"Keep your hands where I can see them!" I ordered, then saw the pad beside the door.

"I'm getting my fob out so I can *open* the door," he said through clenched teeth.

Somewhere above a door crashed open, the sound echoing heavily in the stairwell. My heart gave an ugly lurch like a stripper who found out her pole was greased. "Jesus. Hurry!"

He glanced up at the sound, then shot me a black look. Too slowly, he pulled his keys from his pocket and swiped the fob across the panel. The light flashed red.

"It's not working," he said. "They must have disabled my fob."

"Lying sonofabitch," I hissed. "You didn't *swipe* it in the elevator." I snatched the keys from him and pressed the fob solidly to the panel. The light flashed green, and the latch clicked. I tossed the keys back to Philip. "Try a stunt like that again and I'll—"

Philip cut off my threat of doom as he moved forward, pushed the door open, and shoved us both through. The door swung shut with a heavy click behind us, and a quick look around told me we were in an industrial grey cinderblock corridor lit by glaring fluorescent lights along the ceiling.

"Keep moving," Philip said in his I'm-not-fucking-around voice.

"You're out now," Andrew protested, his feet planted. "Let me go!"

"We're not *out*," I shot back and gave him a hard push toward the double doors at the end of the corridor about fifty feet away. "What's next?"

Anger flushed Andrew's face, but he didn't fight me. "A small warehouse for goods reception," he said tightly, gesturing ahead. "Then a door to the parking garage."

Philip loped ahead toward the doors, pausing only to check that a side corridor was clear of bad guys.

My comm crackled in my ear. "We're at the dock," Naomi said. "It's clear for now, but you need to hurry."

"We have people behind us," I told her as I prodded Andrew into a jog. I sure as hell didn't want to be caught in the corridor when those guys came out of the stairwell. We had zero cover if they started shooting. "Philip's checking out the doors into the warehouse now. We'll be out in a sec."

Philip gave me a nod, pressed the fob to the key pad and opened the door. A moment later we passed through and into a warehouse filled with stacks of crates and boxes. A brightly lit EXIT sign hung over a regular door next to a large rollup bay door on the opposite wall. I herded Andrew onward but stopped halfway there and turned at the sound of *ca-chunk ca-chunk ca-chunk ca-chunk* behind us.

It was Philip as he pumped the lift handle of a pallet jack loaded with cases marked, "Economy Copy Paper." He shoved the whole thing toward the double doors we'd come through and, after maneuvering the jack into position, lowered it to set the pallet as a barricade against the doors. "It won't stop them," he said as he hurried my way, "but it'll slow them down."

I got Andrew moving again. "Good enough," I said. "All we need is time to get out and into the car."

When we reached the door, Philip pulled out Andrew's keys and again pressed the fob on the control panel. As soon as the latch clicked, I shouldered the door open and hustled Andrew out into the chilly air on a loading dock in the underground parking garage. The dock was probably meant for vans and smallish trucks since it was only a short drop from the platform to the pavement, and the garage didn't look anywhere near roomy enough to handle an eighteen wheeler. To our left a ramp began a sloping descent toward the lower levels of the parking garage and, off to the right, daylight filtered down the incline that led to the street above.

About twenty feet beyond the edge of the dock, Kyle bailed out of the passenger seat of Naomi's car and opened the back door, ready for us.

Andrew jerked against my grasp. "Now will you let me go?" he asked, jaw clenched.

"Are we all safe?" I snapped, patience worn thin. "No. Didn't think so. Now stop fucking asking me that and move!" I glanced at the steps by the end of the dock, then wrangled him straight toward the edge. No time to waste.

Andrew opened his mouth to protest, but a moan from Philip cut him off. I looked over in horror as Philip's legs buckled.

"Philip! Shit!" Could the MegaPlague possibly have worse timing? Muffled shouts and banging on the warehouse double doors sent my heart soaring into my throat, even as I swayed from the wave of plague fatigue that rolled over me. Though it only lasted a couple of seconds, it was all Andrew needed.

He slammed a fist down on my forearm, sending the tranq gun tumbling to the pavement below, and I yelped, more from surprise than pain. Taking advantage of my brief shock, he shoved me off balance, then jerked out of my grasp and spun toward the shouts. I didn't fall, but my brief stagger gave him enough time to dash back to the door. Recovering, I launched myself at him in a flying tackle as he yanked the door open, but I only managed to knock him into a stumbling sprawl halfway through the doorway. I crashed hard into the wall and went down, my breath rushing out in a painful whoosh. As Andrew scrambled to get up, I struggled to suck in air, to shift to my hands and knees.

A heavy thud followed by a *screee* of metal on concrete echoed from inside the warehouse as the pallet jack barricade gave way. We had only seconds before the Saberton guys were on us. My mind whirled. Maybe it would be better to cut our losses and let Andrew go? *But* we still weren't out, and though we couldn't count on Nicole Saber's motherly priorities, having Andrew as a hostage had kept us whole to this point.

Even as I came to that conclusion, Kyle bounded up in a blur of zombie speed, flung the door fully open with one hand and grabbed the back of Andrew's suit jacket with the other. In a smooth, swift action, he shifted his grip, hauled Andrew up by collar and waistband and flung him like a sack of potatoes toward Philip.

Andrew let out a strangled cry of shock but managed to keep his limbs tucked in as he landed. He'd be bruised and banged up but not broken.

"Philip!" Kyle cried out. "Grab him and get to the car!"

"That's Griffin!" a voice said from inside the warehouse.

Kyle yanked me fully upright and shoved me hard between the shoulder blades to propel me toward Philip and Andrew. "Go!" he ordered, then wheezed a sharp cough.

"What's wrong?" I tried to turn and look at him, but he shoved me again as the door clanged shut behind us. Philip shook off the MegaPlague greyout enough to drunkenly grab Andrew and roll with him off the edge of the dock.

"Go," Kyle gasped as he staggered into me and gave me a hard double-handed push that sent me careening over the edge.

I tumbled down and only avoided a faceplant because Naomi was right there and helped break my fall. She'd pulled the car closer to the dock, and I saw that Philip and Andrew were already in the back seat.

"Kyle! No!"

I jerked my head up at Naomi's anguished cry. Kyle lay crumpled on his stomach, partially body-blocking the door like a meat doorstop. Two darts protruded from his shoulder and neck, and I realized he must've tried to go back to block the door when he realized he wouldn't make it off the dock before collapsing.

He still had enough control to shift his head to look at us. "Go." I couldn't hear it, but I saw it on his lips.

"Kyle!" Naomi screamed and lurched toward him, but I grabbed her and wrapped my arms around her to drag her back.

"You can't!" I yelled. Already the door opened and crashed into Kyle, and I knew the Saberton dudes would be happy to tranq the rest of us as well. A heartbeat later, Edwards squeezed out, tranq gun in hand. Naomi stopped fighting me, and I released my bear-hug, though I kept a hand on her arm. "We'll come back for Kyle," I told her as I pulled her toward the car. "We have to go. *Now*!" A dart whined past my ear as if to punctuate my words, and I clamped down on a shriek.

She ran with me to the car, eyes full of anguished determination. "Get in!"

I didn't need any more encouragement. I dove into the passenger seat and slammed the door as another dart whacked against it. A second later Naomi took the driver's seat, shoved the car into reverse and squealed tires out of the dock area. I set my foot against the dash, bracing myself as she threw the car into drive and gunned it toward the exit.

"Sonofabitch!" Naomi yelled, and I looked up to see three cars blocking the exit. Her face twisted in a storm of rage. "*Hang on!*"

I clung to the seat as Naomi slammed on the brakes. Cold dread wrapped around me. "Now what do we do?"

"Everyone get seatbelts on, NOW," Naomi snapped out as she yanked her own on. I hurried to obey and hoped Andrew was smart enough to do so as well.

Naomi shoved the car into reverse and hit the gas again, then did *something* with brakes and the wheel and who the hell knew what else, and suddenly we were going forward in the other direction, down into the garage.

"Did you just do a bootlegger turn?" I yelled in a weird mix of terror and excitement.

"Sure did," she yelled right back, then did a sweet as hell high-speed drift around a corner before accelerating again.

"That's too fucking cool!" Damn, this chick knew how to drive. I clung to my seatbelt as she took another tight turn at obscene speeds. From the back seat I heard manly cries of alarm. "Where the hell are we going?" I asked.

"To the bottom," she told me, eyes narrowing in grim focus. "There's a hatch with access to service tunnels. We should be able to get out that way."

I didn't see any vehicles in pursuit yet, but that was probably because a) Naomi was driving like a well-trained maniac, and b) Saberton likely figured they could take their time since they had the only exit blocked. Still, it wouldn't take them long to determine we'd found a way out.

"I know the tunnels really well," she said after another turn. She opened her mouth to say more but stopped. I had a feeling she'd been about to spill *how* she knew the tunnels then remembered Andrew was in the car.

A final screeching turn. This was the bottom floor of the garage, a dead end. "There's the hatch."

I peered ahead and saw a hinged metal hatch, a bit larger than a manhole cover, in the pavement a few feet from the far wall. "Stop the car right in front of it and leave the engine running," I told her. "I have an idea."

She didn't question or ask for details and brought the car to a rubber-burning stop directly in front of the hatch. Philip threw the back door open and dragged Andrew not at all nicely out of the car.

I jumped out on my side, and together Naomi and I managed to haul the heavy metal hatch lid up and open to land on the concrete with a heavy clang. I peered into the exposed shaft to see a ladder fixed to the wall, its bottom lost in shadow.

"No way to lock it from the inside, right?" I asked.

"Nope. C'mon, let's get moving."

"You go down first," I said. "Andrew and Philip next. Then I'll park the car over the hatch. I'm skinny and can squeeze under to the hole."

"Jesus," she breathed. "I think that'll work. Slow them down enough for us to lose them." She set her hands and feet on the outside of the ladder the way she'd done at Andrew's apartment, and slid down into the gloom. A menacing growl from Philip got Andrew moving, though he climbed down in the more traditional manner, as did Philip.

I didn't stick around to watch. A low rumble from above told me the Saberton team was on their way. As soon as Philip's head was clear, I drove the car forward until it covered the hatch, killed the engine, set the emergency brake, then climbed out and locked the doors. Headlights washed the far wall as I shimmied my scrawny ass beneath the car, but instead of an easy crawl to the hatch, I found myself wedged between the undercarriage and the pavement. *Stupid low clearance car!*

Hot metal against the back of my lightweight jacket went from warm to painful in seconds. I thrashed, trapped, but the squeal of tires on the last curve fueled my determination. No way in hell would I let them capture me again. Not in a stupid way like this. I blew out my breath and managed to wriggle far enough to get my hand on the lip of the hole, then dragged myself forward. It took a few heart pounding seconds to make an awkward transition to the ladder, but I began to clamber down as a car slid to a stop a few yards away. With each movement, fiery pain like the worst sunburn ever flared across the back of my shoulders, and Hunger twisted inside me as my parasite sought resources to heal the damage.

At the bottom of the shaft, a dim bulb brightened pitch darkness to gloom, but it was enough light to see that we were in a grungy tunnel about eight feet wide. Pipes and conduits ran along the ceiling, and more bulbs dotted the tunnel every fifty yards or so.

I noted with grim satisfaction that Andrew's hands were cuffed behind him. Philip looked unhappy, but I assumed it was simply the usual we're-in-really-deep-shit until I saw Naomi sitting against the wall, face contorted in pain as she clutched her ankle.

"I landed wrong," she blurted. "God, I'm so *stupid!* There's a broken place on the ladder. Shit."

I echoed her curse then turned to Philip. "Can you carry Naomi?" He nodded and moved toward her. I reached for Andrew's arm then froze and inhaled deeply. The scent of his fresh human brain filled my senses, and I began to salivate like a dog at a barbecue. *Shit.* I didn't know a lot about this spy business, but I was pretty sure eating a hostage wasn't cool.

"Burned myself under the car," I told Philip through clenched teeth. "I don't think it's serious, but it hurts like a mother. How many packets of brains do you have left?"

"Two," he replied. "And you still have two, right?" I nodded, and he continued, "Better eat one on the move. The pain could screw you up if we get in trouble."

If we get in trouble. What the hell did he think we were in now? But he was right. Pain along with brain-hunger would distract me at crunch time. I fished a packet from my side pocket and grabbed Andrew's arm. "Naomi, you said you know these tunnels. Where to?"

She hissed out a breath as Philip lifted her. "Go down to the third junction and take a left, then right at the next one after that."

A screech of tires from another car filtered down from above. I ripped the packet open with my teeth and tightened my grip on Andrew.

"I'd rather get lost than captured," I said. "Let's move."

Chapter 25

"I think we're clear," I said, peering behind us. Or rather, I couldn't see, hear, or smell anyone in pursuit. We'd been fleeing for close to half an hour, taking turns as Naomi directed and blindly trusting that she knew where the hell to go. I wasn't even sure we were in New York anymore, but Naomi insisted that a hatch we'd passed about a minute earlier was close to the Lincoln Center.

Philip looked back and gave a nod. "I agree." He carefully set Naomi on her good foot and helped her to sit on the floor of the tunnel.

I pointed to a spot that looked fairly clean. "You. Sit," I ordered Andrew. A wave of queasiness shuddered through me as he complied, and barely a second later Philip turned, stumbled several steps away and retched.

"You okay, Philip?" I asked as I did my best to keep my own nausea from showing on my face. It had to be the MegaPlague imprint shit if I felt it as well. A few seconds later my queasiness faded, and Philip straightened, wiping his mouth.

"I'm fine now," he said, voice strong. I glanced at him as he returned to us. His eyes looked hollow, but he was doing his best to maintain a tough façade in front of Andrew.

I turned and crouched by Naomi. "We need to get your boot off before your ankle swells too much."

"Right." She clenched her hands into fists as I loosened the laces and removed the boot as carefully as possible.

"Oh, man." I winced at the sight of the mottled purple bloat that was her ankle. "That looks pretty awful."

"That's a great bedside manner you have there," she said with a strained laugh.

"Sorry. My patients are usually dead." I resisted the urge to poke at the swelling. "It looks bad, but I don't *think* it's broken." Not that I had a clue, but I didn't want her even more worried. "I think the boot saved you from fucking it up more," I added. Felt weird not to say, *Chug some brains, and you'll be right as rain!*

"Can't walk on it either way," she said with a black scowl. "God! This is *stupid.*"

"Yeah, I'm usually the one to do stupid shit like this," I said and gave her a crooked smile. "Why the hell are you stealing my thunder?"

She tried to smile back, but her face twisted instead. I knew it wasn't because of pain.

I lowered my voice. "We'll get Kyle back. I promise."

She bit her lip and nodded. "He's tough. He'll . . . be okay until we get there."

"Of course he will." Neither of us wanted to speak the truth. He was a former operative for Saberton, and even though he hadn't sold them out, it was doubtful they'd see it that way. It was tough to kill a zombie, but it was easy to torture one.

"We need to call Brian so we can get out of this mess," I told her.

She nodded, pulled her phone out of a pocket and hit the speed dial for Brian's number. A few seconds later she frowned and shook her head. "Straight to voicemail. He must have it off."

"Try my number," I suggested.

She gave me a puzzled look, then grimaced and nodded. "Right. I forgot he had yours and you have Kyle's." She made an annoyed noise as she hit the speed dial for my phone. "Damn, I'm really off my game."

"Gimme a break," I replied, a little sharply. "No one who's off their game could've managed that awesome bootlegger turn *and* remembered all the twists in these tunnels."

A corner of her mouth twitched up as she held the phone to her ear. "Yeah, that was all right." But a few seconds later she lowered the phone and shook her head. "Straight to voicemail."

"Shit," I muttered. "Maybe it ran out of charge."

"Both of them?" Naomi said, brows puckered.

"Who the hell knows," I replied. "Doesn't matter. I still know where and when to meet him. It's possible he turned the phones off for security."

Andrew shifted and made a low noise in the back of his throat.

I shot him a glare. "You got a fucking problem?"

He glared right back. "I need to take a piss," he said through clenched teeth.

"Oh." I blinked, then looked over at Philip. "Um, can you take care of that?"

Philip's lips twitched, and I *knew* he was resisting the urge to suggest I "handle" it, and only because it was probably poor form to joke and tease around a hostage. But just knowing he wanted to joke helped lighten my own mood a tiny bit.

Philip helped Andrew to his feet and walked him down the tunnel until they were lost in the gloom. Naomi let out a shuddering breath, gaze following the pair.

"He doesn't know me," she murmured, an odd combination of grief and amazement playing over her face. "This close, and he doesn't know me."

"You don't look or sound like his sister," I reminded her. "Not to mention, he thinks his sister is dead. He's not expecting to run into her." I punched her lightly in the arm. "Especially not in a sewer."

"It's a steam tunnel, not a sewer."

"Whatever. It has bugs and rats, and it smells funny."

She let out a choked laugh, but tears welled up in her eyes. "I was holding it together right up until now." She dashed away the tears and looked up at me. "I don't know if I can keep hiding myself from him."

I grimaced. "Babe, you *have* to. At least until we're safe."

She blew out her breath and visibly composed herself. "Right. And it would be a shame to waste all this plastic surgery."

"Absolutely." I reached for her hand and gave it a squeeze. "We *can't* risk your mother finding out you're still alive."

Naomi shuddered at the thought. "No way. She's—" She stopped as I held up my hand at the sound of returning footsteps. A few seconds later Philip and Andrew stepped from the shadows.

"Everything cool?" I asked as I stood.

Philip nodded then sat Andrew down about ten feet away from Naomi, making sure to position him so the light was between them. With Naomi mostly in shadow, it would be almost impossible for Andrew to see more than a vague shape. No need to give him more opportunity to recognize her.

I motioned for Philip to come with me farther down the tunnel. "I need to go meet Brian," I said in a low voice as soon as we were out of human earshot. "Everything will be easier once we hook up with him, and then we can get Naomi's ankle taken care of properly."

A frown creased his forehead. "I don't like you going out alone."

"I know," I said. "But with Kyle gone, we can't let Andrew go free. We *have* to hold onto him as a possible ace in the hole if we want to stand a chance of getting back in to rescue Pietro and Kyle."

"And with Naomi injured, someone needs to stay with her and keep an eye on him." He grimaced. "I'm getting worse. The weakness is constant now, and when it flares I can barely lift my head."

"That's why I want to go sooner rather than later."

He obviously wasn't happy about it, but he didn't continue to argue. "All right. Make sure we have a way to get him," he jerked a thumb toward Andrew, "out and to wherever Brian and Dr. Nikas are, without too much of a scene."

"Andrew's trouble waiting to happen," I said. "Probably need to secure him more and have a gag ready in case anyone happens to come down this way."

"I'll take care of it." Philip sent a chilling look in Andrew's direction.

"I'll be back as soon as possible."

He pulled me into a hug. "You be careful, you hear me?"

I returned the hug, let the comfort of it peel away a bit of the worry and stress. "You know me. I'm always careful."

"Let's not go there." He gave me a squeeze then released me and dug in the side pocket of his pants to produce a map of Manhattan. "You'll probably need this."

"Y'think?" I smiled. "Now you can double down on your awesomeness by showing me where I'm meeting Brian and which trains to take."

He chuckled softly, then spread the map against the wall and patiently showed me exactly where to go and how to get there. To my relief there was no need for me to change trains or anything that would stretch my redneck brain.

"Now get going," he said. He folded the map again—successfully, which amazed me—and stuffed it into my side pocket. "I'll hold down the fort."

With a parting smile, I turned and loped off down the tunnel to the Lincoln Center hatch.

Chapter 26

A crisp wind ducked between the buildings and snuck beneath my light jacket, bringing with it the scents of bread and coffee and some sort of greasy who-knew-what from a food cart on the corner. I pulled my hood up and hoped the wind would take some of my own stench away in the process. Hours of running and sweating and all sorts of anxiety-making activities hadn't left me feeling as fresh as a daisy. Fortunately, it seemed New Yorkers weren't the type to pay attention to a scraggly waif in their midst or, at least, didn't feel obliged to say anything about a little stink.

I had no doubt I looked like the greenest tourist in existence as I worked my way through the touch screen menu to get a MetroCard, but I finally managed to pay my fare and board the train I needed without having to ask the homeless guy sitting against the wall for help. A small crowd was already waiting for the train, but I continued farther down the platform and managed to score a car with only a few people in it. An Asian woman sat at the far end, headphones on and lips moving as if silently singing along to her music. A few seats away a black man in a business suit knitted something blue and complex. A man with reddish-brown hair and wearing sunglasses sat in the middle of the car, a German Shepherd sitting quietly at his feet.

The dog lifted its head and let out a low growl as I sidled past. I froze.

"Hush, Marla," the man murmured, and the dog subsided and laid its head on its paws again. "It's because you're a pretty girl," he continued, not moving except to speak. "Marla gets jealous of pretty girls."

All right, so apparently he wasn't blind since he knew I was a girl. Though maybe he *was* blind since I was far from pretty at the moment. "Yeah, well, tell her I'm not your type," I said, probably a bit more grumpily than I'd intended, but blind or not, the dude creeped me out a little, though I couldn't put my finger on why. I tugged my hood a bit lower, quickly continued to the end of the car and stood by the door before looking back at the pair. The man hadn't moved and still seemed to be staring straight ahead, but Marla watched me intently. When my stop came I hurried off, weirdly relieved when they remained on the train.

Maybe Marla used to be a cadaver dog? I mused as I trotted up the steps of the subway station. Ed Quinn's girlfriend, Marianne, had worked search and rescue with a dog who'd been trained to find corpses. Ed had used the dog's ability to smell rotting flesh to find zombies, who he'd then stalked and murdered.

I shuddered, glad to emerge from the subway even though the sun had set and I didn't know the turf. It was beyond unlikely that some random guy on a subway in New York would figure out I was a zombie—or even know about zombies in the first place—but the encounter still left me weirded out.

At the risk of looking like a tourist again, I consulted the map and peered at street signs to get my bearings. Fortunately, I looked raggedy enough that I didn't make a tempting mark for pickpockets or muggers. Or maybe the ever-so-faint scent of rot wafting off me kept assailants at bay. Hey, whatever worked. Stuffing the map back into my pocket, I tugged my hood down low again and slouched east on Canal Street. Surely Brian would have enough brains with him that I could top off. It wouldn't solve my spongy patches, but I'd take what I could get at this point.

After another quick peek at the map, I continued for several blocks on Canal—which wasn't much like the Canal Street in New Orleans at all—then headed north on Greene. After half a block I slowed my pace and let myself drink in the charm of the area. With wrought-iron lamps, cobbled streets and granite blocks instead of pavement, the street instantly gave off a vibe of *sedate and classy*. Narrow buildings four or five stories high crowded together on either side, many with carved and columned store fronts, and with fire escapes painted the same color as the rest of the structure. The occasional bit of graffiti dotted a wall, but less frequently as I continued up the street. It was quieter along here, and even the thrum of car tires over cobblestones seemed almost melodic.

And, best of all, I spied the sign for Grand Street at the end of the block, as well as one for Betsy's Bakes.

Hot fucking damn, I actually found it. I smiled. *Look at me, getting the hang of this big city shit.*

An elderly man strode by, humming softly to himself. A cyclist wove between cars and darted through the intersection with a Fuck You to traffic laws. A couple of young women exited Betsy's Bakes, and a man talking on his phone on the opposite corner watched them for a few seconds before turning away again. The man's bomber jacket looked like poor Chris Peterson's, and a tug of grief went through me.

The man turned his head to glance down the cross street, and my heart gave a quick double-thud as his profile registered. *Boat Launch Guy*—Edwards, the security guard at Saberton who'd helped escort Jane out. He wasn't in uniform now, but rather a dark green sweater, khaki slacks, and the jacket stolen from a murder victim. But I didn't believe for a second that he was off-duty.

Pulse racing, I stopped and pretended to consult something on my phone while I continued to scan. *Saberton.* Did they have Brian? Or had Brian sold me out? Were they waiting for me?

I had no answers, and I also had no way of knowing if any of the other pedestrians were bad guys. No way was Edwards here staking this place out on his own, but he was the only one I recognized. And if I didn't get the hell off the street, it was only a matter of time before they recognized *me.*

Doing my best not to appear suspicious, I ducked into the nearest shop and quickly closed the door behind me. Some sort of antique shop or interior design place, judging by the furniture and knick knacks and décor shit. I edged past a settee and a table full of globes to where I could peer out the window, angling so that I could watch Edwards on the corner as well as the entrance to Betsy's Bakes. Another man ambled toward the intersection from farther up the street, and I caught the quick glance he exchanged with Edwards before he crossed. He had his hands tucked into the pockets of a tan trench coat. I had no trouble imagining weapons in them.

"Are you in some kind of trouble?" a clear voice asked.

Startled, I spun around to see a sharp-featured, thirty-something man in a dark grey suit regarding me with a wary expression. "I don't want any trouble in here," he stated, then pointed toward the door. "Take it outside."

I shot a quick look at the man in the trench coat, pulse quickening as he began strolling toward the shop. *Shit!* Had he seen me? Or was he simply walking and patrolling, or whatever it was called when bad guys did it? Either way, my level of "I'm fucked" was rapidly climbing.

I quickly moved away from the window and toward the shop dude. "I'm sorry," I mumbled even as I cast another furtive look over my shoulder. I couldn't see where Trench Coat had gone. "You got a back door I can use?" I asked him, not faking the desperation in my voice one bit. "I swear to god I'm not running from the cops."

His eyes narrowed as they raked over me, and I had no illusions about what he saw. I looked like a homeless waif, possibly a drug addict. And not from New York either, not with my southern accent waving the not-a-Yankee flag. I half-expected him to reach for a phone to call the cops, but to my surprise he jerked his head toward the back.

"Thanks," I breathed, then darted toward the little hallway that led to the rear of the shop. At the end of the hall was a small bathroom and a storage room, and to the left was an office with a loveseat crammed in a corner and a desk against the far wall. A brass coat rack held a black wool coat and a tweed fedora. But I didn't see a back door anywhere.

I turned to Shop Dude in time to see him click the lock on the front door and flip the sign to *Closed*. That done, he turned and headed my way, an ugly smile on his face.

I'd almost been raped once, though I was drugged at the time and managed to almost die before it could happen. Since then I'd processed the various thoughts and feelings about that incident any number of times and wondered what would have happened if the guy who'd spiked my drink hadn't taken that curve too quickly and died in the resulting car wreck, wondered what would have happened if I'd survived the cocktail of drugs in my system and he'd done the shit he'd wanted to do to me. I still had the occasional nightmare, even though I survived the experience in every way that mattered.

But all that shit came swimming back up to the surface as Shop Dude came toward me, confident and cocky. He was about to get himself a piece of southern tail from the pathetic homeless waif who'd wandered into his shop late on a Sunday afternoon. He knew he was in control. Maybe he'd threaten to call the police if I fought back, accuse me of theft or prostitution. He looked like a fairly respectable man, not at all sleazy or smarmy. Cops would believe his side of it, no doubt.

"C'mon, man, where's the fucking back door?" I said, then

ducked into the office as I saw Trench Coat walk past the shop. Shit. Maybe I was reading the whole situation with Shop Dude wrong. Anything was possible, right?

"What's your hurry?" he asked, stepping into the office. He closed the door behind him, eyes traveling over me with a combination of distaste and nastiness in them.

Nope. Wasn't reading the situation wrong one little bit. Damn it. I backed away out of pure instinct, stopped when I came up against the desk then lifted my chin.

"Seriously?" I loaded my voice with exasperation, though it sounded high and shaky to my ears. "Is this where I have to give you a BJ to get out of here?"

"For starters," he replied, then reached behind him and locked the office door, a move that I knew damn well was meant to intimidate me.

I pushed the hood back from my face and bared my teeth. I had a gun, but a gunshot would bring the Saberton guys running. "You do this often?" I asked. "You see girls in trouble and figure you can get some action?"

He shrugged as he unbuckled his belt, eyes remaining on me in a way that made my skin want to crawl off and take a hot shower. "All I see right now is you," he said, unzipping.

I looked down at the semi-hard cock that flopped out of his pants. "I'm gonna take that as a yes," I said, then returned my attention to his face. "No way is this your first time."

"Suck my dick, you little whore," he sneered, "or I call the cops and tell them I caught you shoplifting."

Even though I'd *known* he was going to say that, it still robbed me of my breath for an instant. My pulse raced as old fear yammered in the back of my head, trying to tell me I was weak and small and couldn't possibly fight back against this guy. Old insecurities joined in, adding that I wasn't worth fighting for, that it would be easier to let it happen and try and put it behind me later.

I heard a low growl and realized it was coming from my own throat. Fuck the fear and fuck the insecurities. I was worth fighting for. *Every* woman was worth fighting for. Didn't matter if they were trash or addicts or rich or popular. Didn't matter if they dressed like a homeless waif, or in tight skirts and heels, or in jeans and flannel. No one deserved to feel helpless and worthless the way this goddamn asshole wanted me to feel and, I had no doubt, made other girls feel.

"If you're going to call the cops to report a crime," I said, flexing my hands, "it should be for something more interesting than theft."

A flicker of hesitation passed over his face, but he recovered and let out a chuckle before giving his stupid cock a couple of strokes. "You think I'm scared of a little whore barely half my size—"

The rest of his sentence died in a gurgling cry of pain as I punched him as hard as I could in his pretty nose.

He staggered back against the door, hands automatically going to his face and the gush of blood. I fell back into a stance and *without* a broken hand, which meant that my success with Carol Ann at the bar hadn't been a fluke. *I guess all those drills on the punching bag paid off!*

This guy wasn't a weenie like Carol Ann, though. It only took him a couple of seconds to recover, anger burning through the pain. He pushed off the door to grab me, one hand reaching out like a claw.

Time didn't slow down or any crap like that. I didn't have a cloud bubble above my head with my *sensei* telling me what to do. But I still grabbed that extended wrist with one hand, seized his shoulder with the other, yanked his balance onto one foot, and then executed the prettiest damn *osoto gari* any martial artist had ever seen.

Okay, it wasn't actually all that pretty, since the office was cramped, and Shop Dude had no idea how to fall properly—shame on him. But I did manage to sweep his leg—to my unending shock—and sent him crashing to the floor. And if I happened to lose my balance and land on him with my elbow in his solar plexus, well, shame on me.

His breath whooshed out, and he turned some pretty shades of purple. I replaced the elbow with my knee and grabbed his throat as I knelt on top of him, then reached my other hand down to grab hold of his balls. A part of me wished I could bring myself to bite his damn cock off, but, *eeew.*

"I'VE HAD A REALLY SHITTY DAY," I yelled, my face inches from his. "And then you come along, and you try to make it worse? Are you fucking kidding me?"

He made a strangled sound, and I loosened the grip on his throat a bit—just enough to keep him from turning blue.

I silently counted to ten in order to regain some calm. Or at least the Angel-version of calm. "Let's try this again," I said, keeping my voice nice and even and friendly-like. Well, maybe not all that friendly, since I had my fingers dug into the sides of his neck, and the grip on his balls . . . well, that wasn't friendly at all. "Listen close, asshole. I want to be damn sure you understand what I'm about to tell you."

His eyes met mine, and for the first time I saw doubt and, yes, fear. Hunger coiled hot and tight in my gut, and I inhaled deeply, nostrils flaring at the scent of his brain beneath the fear. I wasn't hungry enough to be out of control, but that didn't mean I was unaware of the Food beneath my hand.

"I know all about monsters," I purred, face close to his. Sweat broke out on his upper lip, and he made a quick attempt to throw me off, but I simply tightened my grip on his throat until he gasped and coughed. "Shh . . . We're talking here. You're being rude." I relaxed my hand enough for him to suck in a breath. "You get off on being a monster. How many girls have you done this to?" His eyes darted around the room, and I shook my head. "Nevermind. Doesn't matter. You won't tell me the truth anyway."

He saw it in my eyes, saw what a real monster looked like. The fear wafted off him like bad cologne. I could kill him, eat his brain. On the surface it sounded like a great idea. The guy was a piece of shit, and society would be better off without him.

But the reality was a lot stickier—literally, in some ways. Killing him would draw all sorts of attention, and—so far at least—I wasn't a cold-blooded killer. I'd killed two men in my life. One was William Rook a.k.a. Walter McKinney, whose skull I'd smashed after he shot me a bunch of times. I didn't feel any guilt about him whatsoever. He was a despicable and horrible person who'd killed plenty of people who hadn't deserved it one bit.

The other one . . . Every now and then, that one kept me up at night. He'd been a Saberton man sent to retrieve Naomi—back when she was still Heather—after she broke her brother's nose and ran. During a firefight out on a deserted highway he shot me as I came at him. In response, I took a baseball bat to his head. In the heat of that moment, he'd done what he had to do, and so had I. But I couldn't console myself with the idea that he was a terrible human being, so it was okay to kill him. None of this shit was black and white, and everything had consequences.

I released the dude's throat and balls, then stood. He rolled to one side and tried to cradle his nads and his nose at the same time. "You broke my nose," he whined. "Jesus Christ. My nose."

"I let you off easy," I said sharply, then stepped past him, unlocked the office door, and peered cautiously out. No sign of any Saberton guys hanging around outside the shop. I eased to the front and peeked around the globes. Edwards and Trench Coat were nowhere in sight, and I didn't see anyone else who could remotely be a security type in disguise. I decided to be cautiously optimistic that no one had seen me.

Shop dude was still curled on the floor when I returned. "What are you going to do?" he asked, voice muffled by the hand he held to his bleeding nose.

I gave him a disgusted look. It pissed me off that I couldn't *do* anything to this guy except leave him with a broken nose, but all the other options would draw a bunch of unwanted attention to me. "I'm going to *leave*, you fucking prick."

Anger and fear danced across his face. His eyes flicked from me to the door, as if unable to believe it could be that simple.

I wanted to make it as unsimple as possible, but I only had a few options at the moment. I prodded him in the lower ribs with the toe of my shoe. Hard. "Gimme your wallet," I ordered.

His jaw tightened, but he pulled his wallet from his back pocket and slapped it onto the floor in front of him. I crouched and checked out the contents. Looked like over four hundred in cash, and an absolutely ridiculous number of credit cards. I yanked his ID out and peered at it. "You're a piece of shit, Jerome Womack." I wanted to leave him with some sort of threat about how I'd deal with him later, but at this point I needed to get the fuck out of there even more. In a perfect world I'd be able to take care of all my other shit, then return here and exact glorious vengeance for every woman this shitstain had abused or taken advantage of. But this wasn't a perfect world. I knew that from hard experience.

Straightening, I jammed the wallet into the pocket of my jacket then grabbed a rubber band off the desk. "Have fun cancelling all your cards, asshole."

With that I grabbed the black wool coat off the rack and tugged it on, slapped the fedora onto my head, and left.

Chapter 27

As soon as I was a couple of blocks from Greene Street I removed the cash and chucked the wallet and its credit cards into a trash can. The fedora I stuffed under my shirt, then I raked my hair back with my fingers and tied it back with the rubberband. Finally, I buttoned the coat up—which reached to my ankles—stuck my fedora-padded tummy out, and pretended to be pregnant. A glance in a shop window had me fairly satisfied with the result. I sure as hell didn't look like a homeless waif anymore. Or like Angel Crawford, for that matter, which was also fine.

Yet my mind whirled with worry and confusion as I made my way to the subway station. How the hell did Saberton know about the meet with Brian? I knew it was possible to listen in on cell phone conversations, but supposedly the phones Naomi bought were the kind that couldn't be spied on. Plus, Saberton would have to know where either Brian or I was at to do so, and if they knew that, then they could've simply grabbed us instead of listening to a stupid call.

The train for the return uptown was crowded, and I gave a distracted no-thank-you shake of my head to an older gentleman who tried to give me his seat. By the time I remembered I was supposedly pregnant, he'd sat back down, and it was too late. Probably for the best since I'd have felt a bit guilty taking a seat from someone I'd normally give one to.

Instead I gripped the pole and continued to fret about Saberton showing up at the meet. *Someone tipped them off.* It was the only possible answer, and I hated it. A miserable dread clung to me as the train continued on its way. *I* sure as hell hadn't told anyone besides the Krewe about the meet, but that meant it *had* to have been one of the others. Had Kyle's impassioned story, explaining his hatred of Saberton, been an elaborate pile of bullshit? I tried to consider the possibility that his capture had been fake, but why would he have gone so far to make sure the rest of us escaped—and *with* Andrew Saber? If Saberton's plan was to allow us to escape so that we would then lead them to Dr. Nikas, why not simply, oh, I dunno, let us fucking escape instead of chasing us into the sewer?

Or maybe it was Naomi/Heather/Julia? My misery deepened at the thought, but the truth was that she had the deepest ties to Saberton. Maybe her whole defection had been a long con to get Pietro and Dr. Nikas. But why tip off Saberton about the meet if the goal was to get to Dr. Nikas? Naomi wasn't stupid. It would make more sense for her to wait until we all joined up with Dr. Nikas and Brian and *then* let Saberton know where we were. And the same argument applied to Philip. He was at the bottom of the suspect list, but I had to consider the possibility that he'd been subverted during the time he was undercover with Saberton.

Wrapped up in my thoughts and worries and stress, it wasn't until I saw signs for "168th Street" that I realized I'd totally missed my stop. I scrambled off the train with far more speed than a pregnant me should've had, then peered around in confusion until a woman took pity on me and showed me how to get on the train going the other direction.

By the time I emerged from the subway at Lincoln Center, I still hadn't come up with a brilliant explanation for how Saberton knew about the meet with Brian. *Nothing* made sense. I stopped at a little grocery and bought snacks, sandwiches, ibuprofen, bottled water, and vitamin C with Jerome Womack's money, then took the slightly rumpled fedora out from under my shirt and stuffed it into the bag before heading to the sewer hatch. Yet as I climbed down the ladder my stupid, neurotic, and paranoid brain tried to insist that the tunnel would be empty and the others gone, either because Naomi-or-Philip was the insider and had thrown Philip-or-Naomi to the Saberton wolves as soon as I left, OR because Naomi *and* Philip simultaneously decided that I had no clue what I was doing, was obviously dead weight and would get them all killed, and it would be best for them to cut and run while they had the chance.

Thankfully, my stupid, neurotic, and paranoid brain was quite wrong about all of this. Naomi was in the same spot, eyes closed and face drawn, apparently dozing. Philip sat against the wall a few feet away, and his unfocused expression told me the MegaPlague had attacked again. Andrew was the only perky one. Well, his eyes were, at least, as they glared at me above the gag shoved into his mouth. The rest of him was bound in a secure hogtie.

"Naomi? Philip? I have stuff to eat and drink." I set the bag down between Naomi and Philip. Naomi muttered something and sighed without waking, but Philip opened his eyes.

"How'd it go?" he asked.

My throat tightened. "He wasn't there. I'll explain in a minute."

His forehead creased in concern, but he gave me a slight nod. "When you can," he said, with understanding in his voice even though he had no way of knowing all the shit that had happened.

How the hell can either of them be the insider? They were my friends. If one of them had tipped off Saberton, it would mean that friendship was bullshit. I honestly wasn't sure if I'd be able to handle that. Both of them were too damn special to me.

Still unsettled, I let Philip take care of getting the stuff out of the bag while I shifted over to Andrew and pulled the gag from his mouth. "Sorry," I said as I undid the hogtie. "Do you need something to drink?"

"Sorry? Really?" He struggled to a sitting position, mouth twisted in contempt. "Somehow I doubt that."

All possible sympathy for him evaporated in a flash. After the monumentally shittastic day I'd had so far, that one pissy remark sliced right through the last remaining frayed thread of my self-control. "Listen to me, Andy-boy," I hissed. "I'm not like you and your people. I don't do shit like this without provocation. So don't you get all high and mighty and morally superior with me, whining about how I'm not *sorry* enough." I poked him in the chest with my index finger. "*Your* people kidnapped my dad and then me, and put me through all kinds of fucked up hell in Charish's lab." My voice rose as the pent up anger and fear and frustration came spewing forth. "*Your* people ran a bunch of experiments on innocent civilians. *Your* people do horrible shit to zombies. And *your* people kidnapped Pietro Ivanov and three of his men, murdered Chris Peterson, tried to kill Brian Archer, and now have Kyle." I was shouting now, right in his face. "So you can take your goddamn *doubt* and shove it up your fucking ass!"

"You're lucky we don't expose you," he snarled. "There'd be bounties on you monsters in a heartbeat."

"At least your shit would be out in the open then as well," I shot back. "You're lucky we don't expose *you*. And you've got a lot of nerve calling us monsters." Fury trembled through me. "Hey, I have an idea. Maybe I'll show you what it's like to be a monster. Maybe

I'll turn *you*, make you one of us! Let's see how you feel when you're the one trying to scrape out survival when everyone is trying to fuck your world up!"

He went white as a sheet and recoiled as if I really was a slavering monster. "You wouldn't," he gasped, eyes darting back and forth in a desperate search for escape.

"Wouldn't I?" The cloying scent of his fear wound around me. I let out a nasty laugh, caught up in the glorious thrill of being in control of this prick, this slimeball who was responsible for so much bad shit. Deep down I knew I couldn't lay it all on him, but I was cocked to the full pissed-off position, and he'd made the mistake of pulling my trigger. "You know damn well I'm capable of it," I growled. "Call *me* a monster? You're the monster! Only fair to make you one for real!" I grabbed his shoulder, and he let out a panicked cry and fought to twist away. "Whaddya say?" I shouted, distantly aware that someone else was yelling my name. I tightened my grip and gave him a rough shake. "It'll only hurt a *lot!*"

Eyes wide in panic, Andrew struggled against the cuffs, feet scrabbling as he tried to get away from me.

"Angel! Stop it!" It was Naomi yelling at me. Out of the corner of my eye I saw her struggle upright.

"I'm not a monster!" I screamed at Andrew, shaking him. "I'm not! You're the monster. It's your fault. All of it!"

"Angel, *stop!*"

The knife-hard edge in Naomi's voice was like a slap in the face. I turned my head to see distress and pain twisting her features as she stood on her good foot, one hand on the wall for balance and the other holding a tranq gun leveled at me.

Philip let out an ominous growl and lurched toward Naomi, but his legs buckled before he reached her, and he had to grab at the wall to avoid falling in a heap.

The panic in Andrew's face retreated as he took in the situation, and he sniggered. "Oh, this is rich. The zombie-loving whore protecting the lowly human from the crazy hick zombie while the cripple tries to stop her. Worse than the Three Stooges."

I jerked my hand away from him and stumbled back as the insults struck home. Naomi's hand shook as she held the tranq gun, but she didn't resist when Philip fought his way up to take it from her. Her hands dropped to her sides, and she slid down the wall, meeting my eyes with a look of *OMG what did I just do, this is all fucked up and damn this hurts.*

I took another unsteady step back from Andrew, from the others.

My chest ached with tension and a mild nausea that I knew was only partly because of the MegaPlague. The whole situation was fucked. Andrew was right. We were bumbling around like idiots, and I didn't have the slightest idea how to fix any of it.

Swiping a hand across my face, I turned and hurried off down the tunnel, away from the others. I heard Philip's voice behind me, angry and intense as he spoke to Andrew.

"Say another word, and I'll take you around the corner to piss and give you some pain you won't believe—without leaving a mark on you."

I stopped about fifty yards away in a shadowed section of the tunnel and sat, crying and attempting to be quiet about it.

Naomi's voice carried to me. "I may be a zombie lover," she growled at Andrew, "but I'm *not* a whore, you dick." Then she peered into the darkness toward me. "Angel?" she called, worry in her voice. "You okay?"

I didn't answer. I wasn't ready to talk to anyone right now, not while the utter humiliation of what I'd done still had me in its grip. Why the hell had I threatened him like that? He was a prick, yes, but the whole " I'm being held hostage by creatures who might eat my brain" thing had to be pretty fucking stressful. No wonder he'd lashed out.

"Angel?" Naomi called again.

"Annngellll." A second voice from the gloom in the opposite direction, like an evil echo of Naomi's voice.

I scrambled to my feet, heart hammering. That second voice hadn't been an echo, but it sure as hell seemed familiar. "Who's there?" I demanded, voice thin as I backed toward Naomi and the light.

The only response was a low groan, followed by the sound of something hitting the floor. Something soft and heavy. Like a body.

I continued to back warily as Philip staggered up to me.

"What do you have?" he asked, peering past me.

"I heard something," I told him, holding my freakout down with supreme effort. "There's someone down there. Someone said my name." I had the weirdest sensation I'd heard that voice before, but I couldn't quite place it. Maybe the echoes in the tunnel were messing with my head?

Philip gave my shoulder a squeeze, then moved slowly forward, tranq gun in his hand, while I stayed bravely behind him. He was steadier now. Hopefully he'd stay that way until we dealt with whatever was down the tunnel, whether it was a Saberton guard or a giant talking rat.

"There's someone there," Philip murmured.

"A person?" I peered cautiously around him and barely made out a form on the ground, but I couldn't see enough to rule out Giant Talking Rat just yet.

"Yes, a person." He continued forward then let out a soft curse. "Saberton uniform."

Every muscle in my body tensed. "They followed us. They found us."

Philip paused, drew a deep breath through his nose. "I don't hear or smell any others."

I sniffed as well, then frowned. "Wait. I don't smell this guy either." That made no sense. I was definitely hungry enough to smell human brains.

Curiosity overrode my weenieness, and we closed the distance. The man lay crumpled on his side, either unconscious or faking it really well, and most definitely in a Saberton uniform.

Philip flipped open his phone and shone the feeble light on the man's face.

"It's Gentry," Philip said, following it with a curse as he continued to scan around us.

Mr. Perfect Eyebrows? I owed him a few dozen knees to the balls for mistreating Pietro. I moved closer, baffled. The voice had sounded a lot like his, and it sure as hell looked like him, though for some reason his eyebrows didn't look as precisely pruned as usual. I crouched and sniffed, then sniffed again. "This doesn't make sense," I said. "There's no way this is Gentry. It can't be." I looked up. "Philip, this is a *zombie*."

Frowning, Philip used the toe of his boot to roll him onto his back. "Angel, that's Gentry," he insisted. "I worked with him long enough to know him, and I'm pretty sure he doesn't have an identical twin. Certainly not one who works at Saberton."

I shook my head, baffled. "Then he must've been turned? But that doesn't make sense either."

Philip rested a hand on my shoulder briefly as he crouched beside me, this time more to steady himself than for comfort. Lowering his head, he copied my sniff-examination. "You're right, he's a zombie. He must have been turned." He mirrored my own WTF expression. "By Mr. Ivanov? Kyle?" He sat back on his heels, face drawn in thought.

"But we saw this guy a few hours ago, and I *know* he wasn't a zombie then," I stated. "Even if he got turned right after we saw him, it doesn't seem as if there's been enough time for him to be up and about now."

"Well, he did collapse," Philip pointed out.

I gave a grudging nod. "Okay, but how is he *here*? How did he find us?"

"No clue, but we need to secure him," Philip said. "My only set of cuffs is on Asshole." He stood, then had to grab at the wall as he swayed. I hurried to steady him.

"Hey, Naomi," I called, "you got any zipties?"

"Always," she replied, squinting in our direction. "What's going on?"

"Sit back down," I ordered Philip. "You can keep an eye on Gentry from right where you are." As soon as he complied I ran back to Naomi. Andrew had been gagged and blindfolded, which pleased me tremendously. "It's a Saberton guard, Gentry," I told her. "He collapsed, so we need to secure him." I didn't want to say yet that I thought he was a zombie, mostly because I didn't want to risk Andrew hearing.

She dug zipties out of a side pocket and passed them to me, "Gentry? Shit. Are there any others?"

"I don't think so, but I'll let you know the instant that changes." I started to turn and run back, then stopped and gave Naomi a quick hug. "Sorry about earlier."

"It's cool, babe," she said. "We're all stressed to the max." She gave me a light shove. "Go."

I returned to Philip and passed him the zipties. "We absolutely can't let Andrew know Gentry's been turned," I said in a low voice. "Especially since we have no clue *how*."

"Agreed." He shifted to a crouch and quickly secured Gentry's hands behind his back, but when he stood he had to stop and catch his breath.

"I'll help you haul him back," I said and took one of Gentry's arms.

Philip gave me a warm smile. "What would I do without my Angel?"

I chuckled, absurdly cheered at the simple statement. No matter what else went to shit, my friends were still my friends. Fuck the whole insider suspicion for these two. There was another explanation. There had to be.

Together we drag-hauled Gentry back to the circle of light. Jeez, but the dude was a helluva dead weight. If he'd been conscious, the strain on his shoulders would have been agonizing, but I didn't really give a shit about his comfort at the moment. I resisted the urge to drop him on his face, and instead set him against the wall a few feet beyond Naomi.

Philip lowered himself to sit. I looked around, even though I knew too damn well what our situation was. *Two* prisoners now, Naomi barely mobile, and Philip all fucked up by the MegaPlague. What the hell was I supposed to do now?

"We're stuck," I murmured to myself, but Philip lifted his head.

"What happened with Brian?" he asked.

I hesitated only an instant before spilling the entire sordid tale to him, including how I'd disguised myself as a pregnant woman.

"Ah, I'd wondered about the coat," he said but then gave me a pained look. "You're right. We're stuck, for now at least." He sighed. "You and I are the only ones mobile. And I'm not reliably so."

"We need supplies until we can figure out a plan," I said, struggling to think. "Stuff for Naomi's ankle, splints and painkillers. That sort of thing."

"Probably need duct tape and blankets. Baby wipes to clean up, and some clothing."

"Deodorant," Naomi put in. "For the love of god, please get deodorant."

"I need to make a list," I muttered. I glanced over at Andrew, smiled and snagged the pen from his pocket. It was a really nice one, heavy and sleek, and it wrote like a dream even on the grimy scrap of paper I picked up from the floor of the tunnel. "Blue-green algae. More food and water," I continued as I jotted down the list of items.

"Definitely water," Philip agreed. "I could drink a gallon right now."

"Got it." I folded the paper and stuffed it into my pocket. "We'll figure out what to do after I get all this."

"Get the supplies, then we both need to hydrate and rest," he corrected. "Once that's done, we can secure our two prisoners, leave them with Naomi, and you and I will go recon options."

"Glad you have a clue," I said, giving him a light shoulder punch.

"Don't jump to conclusions," he replied with a wink. "Be careful."

"Always," I said automatically, then damn near jumped out of my skin as the phone buzzed in my pocket. My heart leaped when I saw the caller ID. "It's Brian! I mean, it's my number which means it's Brian since he had my phone." What if he'd been captured? What if this was really Saberton? Not yet daring to feel relief, I hit answer and then the speaker button so Naomi and Philip would be able to hear in case he said anything suspicious. "Brian! What happened? There were Saberton people crawling all over the place you sent me."

"Angel," he said, voice oddly flat. "I know it's you. You're the insider."

Chapter 28

His words sliced through me like ice cold razors, leaving me frozen and shattered at the same time. In my peripheral vision I saw Philip visibly jerk in surprise.

"Wh-what?" I managed.

"You're the insider," Brian repeated, slowly and clearly. "Every leak came from you: Mr. Ivanov's schedule and the meetings with Dr. Charish, the change in routine from lunch to dinner for him and Dr. Nikas, the new codes to get into the lab, even the location of our meet today."

I felt as if I was in one of those horror movie shots where the focus zooms in on the victim while everything else retreats into the background. "No. No . . ." My blood pounded in my ears. "Brian, how can you even think that? I swear, I didn't betray you or anyone else!"

"Saberton would have had better intel and a smoother abduction plan if it had been one of my security team leaking info," he said, eliminating Rachel, Kyle, and Naomi in a single sentence. Philip too, even though he wasn't on Brian's security team. "They heard it through someone with peripheral contact," Brian continued. "*You.*"

Naomi let out a small gasp. Philip stood, eyes widening. "Oh my god," he murmured. "He's right."

I spun to face him as the nightmare sensation tightened its grip. "What? No! No, he's *not* right!"

Philip took a step toward me, hand extended and eyes on mine as if trying to calm a wild horse. "Angel, relax," he said, then, louder, "Brian, I have this. We'll call you back."

I fought the urge to drop the phone and flee. "I'm not the insider," I insisted. "I didn't leak info. I swear!"

Philip gently took the phone from me, closed it and slipped it into a pocket. "Angel, it's okay," he said, tone soothing, but then he shifted his attention to Andrew, crouched and pulled the gag and blindfold from the man. "And *he* saw no need to tell us."

The word "baffled" probably had my picture next to it in the dictionary. "Huh?"

Philip straightened, put his hands on my shoulders, then leaned in close to whisper in my ear. "You're bugged."

I jerked in shock and drew back to meet his eyes. "How?" I finally managed to get out.

"I think I was a party to it," he said, voice going dark and dangerous. "Wasn't I, Saber?"

I spun toward Andrew and saw the glowering expression of a man who's been caught doing something really sneaky. Realization smacked me like a shovel to the face, and I slapped my hand over the crook of my left arm. "Shit!"

"The boat launch parking lot," Philip said. He took my wrist and pulled gently to straighten my arm.

My distress shifted to white hot fury. A few months ago, back when Philip was still undercover, he and some Saberton goons attacked me at the Tucker Point boat launch then held me down while a tech took blood samples from me. At one point the needle had felt like a ball point pen being shoved into my arm . . .

We'd never been able to figure out why they'd taken blood and then simply let me go. But now it all made sense. It was brilliant. I had to hand it to them. A lot of information got dropped in my presence, and all they had to do was wait for the perfect moment.

My lips pulled back from my teeth. "Get. It. Out."

Face set, Philip palpated my arm and finally paused with his thumb over a spot a couple of inches below my elbow on my inner forearm. "I think this is it." Philip flicked open a folding knife, met my eyes briefly, then made a careful slice through the skin. I clenched my jaw as the pain burned up my arm before receding. "Sorry," he murmured as he carefully worked his fingers into the gash. "I don't want to risk cutting any blood vessels, low as we are on brains."

"It's cool," I reassured him, then glowered at Andrew. "Y'all heard everything?"

He paled, but I decided it was more at the sight of Philip digging in my forearm than because of my accusation.

"That's how you knew we were at your apartment," I continued, pissed, then exhaled in relief as Philip withdrew a slim plastic and metal tube about an inch long and about an eighth of an inch wide. Cripes, no wonder my arm had been itching and bothering me so much.

Philip dropped it to the floor and ground it beneath his heel. I turned to Andrew and enjoyed his wary frown as I untied his tie and pulled it free of his neck. His eyes widened with shock and dismay as I proceeded to wrap the silk around the gash in my arm.

"That's an Ermenegildo Zegna!" he sputtered.

"And now it's a Band-Aid," I snapped. "How come you didn't have people waiting at your apartment for us when we broke in?"

He pulled his gaze away from the ruined tie, scowled. "It was intermittent at best after you went to the bar and got into that fight. The audio reduced to bits and snatches, and the tracker ceased working completely."

I quickly turned away and put a hand over my mouth to hold back a slightly hysterical laugh. *The stun gun.* That stupid stun gun had partially fried the bug and saved our asses.

After taking a few deep breaths to get myself under control, I took the phone back from Philip then walked a short distance down the tunnel before calling Brian back.

"It's out and dead," I said as soon as he answered.

"Good." He exhaled. "I'm sorry. I should have screened you for anything unusual after that incident with Saberton, even for a piece of lint stuck to your shirt."

"I hate that I was the cause of all of this crap."

"*You* weren't," he told me firmly. "Saberton played a good hand. Anyway, now that we have that settled we need to join up and figure out our next step."

"Yeah. Stuff with Philip and me is getting worse, and it would be darn awesome if Dr. Nikas could do something about it." I sucked in a breath. "I almost forgot to tell you! We have one of the Saberton security guards here. Weird as shit—he stumbled right up and collapsed."

"And no one has ended him yet?" Brian asked with dangerous calm.

"Er, no." I moved further down the tunnel and lowered my voice. "He's a *zombie.* And don't ask me how the hell that's possible, because he wasn't only a couple of hours ago."

"You're *certain* he's a zombie?" Brian asked, doubt thick in his voice. "It doesn't seem possible that he could be up and around so soon, even if he was turned immediately after you saw him."

"I'm positive, and Philip agrees. But I can't figure out why the hell Pietro or Kyle would turn *this* guy. I mean, he's an asshole! And Pietro hated him as much as I did." I snorted. "He even told me not to kill him if I saw him on the street—said Gentry was his."

"Kyle?" Brian asked, and I realized he didn't know Kyle had been taken. Before I could explain I heard a frantic scuffling sound on the other end of the line, then Dr. Nikas's breathless voice.

"Angel. Repeat what you said."

Mildly perplexed I did so.

"Oh, dear," Dr. Nikas murmured. "What is his condition now?"

My confusion increased. "Out cold," I told him. "We have him secured, though. Ziptied wrists and ankles."

"Is his skin icy and pale?" he asked with a strange urgency. "Check the inside of his eyelids. Are they pale as well? As if there's barely enough blood to make them pink?"

"Um, hang on, and I'll check." I jogged back up the tunnel to Gentry and checked his skin and eyelids. Philip gave me a questioning look, but I could only give him an I-have-no-fucking-idea shrug in response. "Yes, to all of that," I told Dr. Nikas. "What's going on?"

"Oh. Oh my goodness," he breathed. "Bring him. Bring him with you when you come here."

"Sure, but how—" I stopped at the sound of more scuffling, and then Brian came back on the line.

"Angel, tell me where you are."

"Right by Lincoln Center." I quickly explained where the hatch was, then brought him up to speed on Kyle's capture, Naomi's injury, and Andrew as hostage.

"Get everyone ready to move," Brian said. "I'll call you when I'm five minutes out." And with that he hung up.

Sighing, I pocketed the phone. "Time to say goodbye to the roaches and rats, everyone."

Chapter 29

When the call came, we hustled everyone up the tunnel and to the surface. Or rather, Philip carried Naomi to the ladder and followed her up as she did an awkward one-footed climb, then Brian came down and hoisted Andrew—ziptied, gagged, and blindfolded—over his shoulder and carried him up the ladder, repeated the process with Gentry, and finally I brought up the rear. Fortunately, Brian had strategically parked the big-ass SUV right by the hatch, and we managed to get everyone in without any witnesses to the fact that two members of our party were having fun with zipties.

Still out cold, Gentry took up the floor by the middle row of seats, while Andrew got the floor of the back row.

Brian drove in silence, no doubt because of Andrew's presence. Philip and I sat in the middle row while Naomi took the back in order to put her leg up on the seat. Unsettled, I kept looking down at Gentry. Why had Dr. Nikas sounded so agitated and yet so protective of the asshole? I looked up to see Brian watching me in the rearview mirror. I gave him a worried *What the fuck?* look, which he returned.

As soon as we were certain no one was following, I pulled out my phone and texted Jane an update on our status, along with a promise to call her as soon as I knew more. After I sent it, I sighed, wishing I had good news about Pietro for her. Instead we were back to square one. Hell, square zero.

On the floor behind me, Andrew made muffled noises behind the gag. "Shut up, Andrew," I said quietly but oh-so-firmly, hoping he heard the unspoken, *or I will help you shut up.*

"Yeah, what she said," Naomi added in a similar tone.

I rubbed the place on my arm where Philip had cut the bug out. Even though it was all healed up, the *idea* of it still festered. How much had they heard? The thing had been in there for months, which meant they'd been able to spy on all sorts of shit. Every phone call, every personal conversation, even stuff I did at work. Did they get a sick thrill when they listened to Marcus and me having sex? Did they laugh when we broke up? How hard did they snicker when I poured my heart out to Naomi . . . ?

Shock jerked me upright. I spun in my seat to look at Naomi, then gestured wildly at the spot on my arm and to her. Clearly baffled, she opened her mouth to speak, but I frantically waved her quiet while pointing to Andrew. I didn't want him to hear *any* of this. She frowned but closed her mouth, and I pointed to my arm then her again.

The bug, I mouthed. *They know about you!*

Her bafflement increased. *Go pout too?*

I rolled my eyes and tried again, and this time Naomi's eyes flew open wide as it hit her. *My mother!* she mouthed in reply as horror crawled over her face. *She knows I'm alive!*

I scowled and nodded, then pointed at Andrew again. *But I don't think he knows.* If he did, then he'd have also known Naomi was Julia, and he'd given no hint of recognition. None. Zip. Zero. The dude was clever, but no way was he that good an actor.

Her brow furrowed as she looked down at the bound, gagged, and blindfolded form of her brother, and I had a feeling her thoughts were echoing mine. An instant later her horror shifted to rage. *She held back intel and let him think I was dead? That fucking bitch!*

Couldn't argue with her there. She slumped back and let her gaze drift out the window as she tried to process this revelation. Suddenly exhausted, I shut my eyes and leaned my head back. Right now all I wanted was to get settled someplace that wasn't a grimy underground tunnel, where I could have a few minutes of not-worrying. Yeah, that would rock.

The overhead light woke me, and I opened my eyes to see we were in a garage with the door closing behind us.

"Where are we?" I asked, rubbing grit out of my eyes.

"Queens," Brian said. He got out, came around and opened my door. "Let's get him inside." He gestured to the still unconscious Gentry at my feet. "We'll leave Saber in here for a moment."

"Maybe you should leave the car running," Naomi grumbled as Philip helped her out.

I grinned at her comment then had to focus all my attention on helping Brian get the heavy Gentry out of the SUV, through the utility room, and into the house. It was a two story deal, and at first glance appeared to be at least four bedrooms. An older house, I figured, judging by the mild wear and tear on corners and floors and walls. Nicely furnished with nothing extravagant. Comfy.

Dr. Nikas stood in the kitchen, eyes widening at the sight of Gentry. "Oh. Oh, my. Bedroom." He gestured to a hallway. "Please bring him to the master bedroom."

"Sure thing," I wheezed. Good grief, were there any steroids this asshole hadn't used? By the time we muscled Gentry down the hall and into the indicated bedroom, I was more than ready to drop his ass on the floor. The only reason I didn't was because Brian gave me a *look* as if he knew exactly what I had in mind—probably because he felt the same way. In the end it was only because it was Dr. Nikas who asked that we went ahead and flopped the brute onto the bed.

"I hate this fucker more and more," I muttered as I caught my breath, then straightened and tried to look cool as Dr. Nikas entered behind us.

"Remove the restraints," he said. He didn't look at either one of us. He was focused fully on Gentry the Giant Heavy Deadweight.

I gave him a dubious look. "What if he wakes up?" From the other side of the bed, Brian looked equally doubtful.

"It will be all right," Dr. Nikas replied, utterly calm as he moved up to Gentry's head. He laid a hand on the man's forehead, then wiped his fingers down and over his cheek. He touched them to his tongue, using his weird zombie-taste diagnostics, then exhaled softly. "He won't hurt any of us."

"How can you be sure?" I asked. I noticed that Brian wasn't moving to cut the zip ties. Nice to know he and I were totally on the same page here.

Dr. Nikas pursed his lips and glanced at the two of us as if unsure whether to speak. "Because . . . this isn't who you think it is," he said, which of course explained absolutely nothing. He peered at the unconscious man. "You said his name was Gentry?"

My confusion increased. "Yeah. Gentry. Um, Pierce Gentry." That's what Pietro had said, right? I peered at the Saberton guard's face. It *was* him, wasn't it? The eyebrows were a lot shaggier than I remembered, but otherwise it sure looked like the same man. "I don't understand. Does Pierce have a twin who's a zombie?"

The man in question stirred, and I took an automatic step back from the bed.

"No twin." Dr. Nikas shook his head, then gestured to Brian. "*Please*, cut the bindings."

Gentry groaned. "These . . . two . . ." He dragged in a breath. ". . . tell them."

"Tell?" I stared at Dr. Nikas. Brian still hadn't pulled a knife to cut the zipties. "What on earth is going on? Tell what?"

Dr. Nikas moved to the door and closed it, then returned to the bedside, rested a hand on Gentry's shoulder, and spoke to him in a language that sounded sort of like Russian. Gentry shifted and, to my shock, answered in the same language.

I stared at them both. "What the shit?"

Dr. Nikas spoke in a quiet voice, eyes still on Gentry. "This is Pietro."

Brian's eyes narrowed in suspicion and doubt. "Step away from him, Dr. Nikas."

"What the shit?" I repeated.

Dr. Nikas stood and faced us, irritation wrinkling his forehead. "No, I will not step away from him," he said firmly. "And don't even think of tranqing me," he added with a surprisingly sharp glare at Brian. "This *is* the one you knew as Pietro."

Crap. How the hell could I doubt Dr. Nikas when he was so clear and insistent? I shifted my attention to Gentry again. "How can this be Pietro?"

Gentry opened his eyes and met mine, drew a deep and difficult breath. "Ate . . . motherfucker's . . . brain."

Well, that was something anyone pretending to be a loyal zombie would say. Besides, we'd all eaten bunches of brains without turning into someone else. I narrowed my eyes. "What color shirt was I wearing when I ran into you and Jane at Dear John's Café?"

"No idea." He took a labored breath. "What color tie . . . was I . . . wearing?"

Shit. Bastard had a point, but it only made my pissy mood pissier. "No idea," I muttered, then planted my hands on my hips and scowled. "How the hell can you be Pietro?"

"Gourmet . . . Gala." He licked dry lips. "Bitch . . . jacket. You . . . wanted to . . . slug her."

My hands dropped to my sides. "Oh, man." At the Gourmet Gala several months ago I'd worn a really cool thigh length dark red velvet jacket I'd bought at a thrift shop, and then had an unpleasant encounter with the previous owner that Pietro had witnessed. And that was *before* Saberton implanted the stupid bug.

"Brian, it's *him*," I said, then looked to Dr. Nikas. "*How*?"

Brian gave me a long frowning look, but finally moved forward and sliced through the zipties.

"He chose to morph," Dr. Nikas said as he rolled Gentry/Pietro to his back and rubbed at his wrists. "He was not planning on doing so for several more decades."

I bit back the urge to say *What the shit?* again, but the frustration nearly swallowed me whole. "Morph? But what does that *mean?*"

"He repatterned his DNA to mimic Pierce Gentry's. The process is very similar to the zombie healing, but using a different blueprint rather than the existing one."

It was a small consolation that Brian mirrored my open-mouthed stare. "We can *do* that?" I spluttered. That gave a whole new meaning to *You are what you eat.*

Dr. Nikas shook his head. "Only a very few can. The mature ones."

"Let me get this straight," I said. "Pietro didn't take over Gentry's body, but instead changed his *own* body to Gentry's shape, based on Gentry's DNA." When Dr. Nikas nodded, I continued, "Which means that the real Gentry's corpse is still out there somewhere. Am I tracking right?"

"Dead on."

I sat on the edge of the bed and peered at Gentry's face. I wasn't anywhere near as freaked out as I probably should've been. "Now what?"

"He needs water and supplements," Dr. Nikas stated, and with that he left the room.

Gentry/Pietro shifted his head to look at me with half-lidded eyes. I met his gaze and sighed heavily. "Pietro, you stole the identity of an *asshole!*"

His lip curled in agreement. "Best choice . . . available."

"At least you killed him," I said.

"Deserved worse," he replied, voice getting a bit stronger. "And I am no longer . . . Pietro. Cannot be." Regret and frustration swept across his face before he shook his head. "Cannot be. Must be Pierce now."

"Pierce," I echoed. "Got it." Too weird. But at least it was kind of close to Pietro.

Pierce's eyes met mine again. "Jane?"

"She's safe," I told him. "She got out before all the shit hit the fan. I made sure of that."

Clearly relieved, he nodded and closed his eyes again, though I didn't think he was sleeping. A few minutes later Dr. Nikas returned holding a tray with four glasses. Two looked as if they contained water, but the other two held murky, muddy substances—one a dusky blue and the other a sickly green.

"Brian, will you adjust the pillows to allow him to sit up a bit more?" Dr. Nikas asked. Brian complied, and as soon as Pierce was more upright the doctor handed Brian the glass containing the blue drink. "Have him drink this one first, then the water," he instructed, then passed me the glass of gross green stuff. "It looks worse than it tastes, but it should counter most of the symptoms of the imprint until we return home."

I made the mistake of sniffing it. "Oh, that's nasty," I said with a shudder. "Will Philip have to drink this too?"

Amusement flickered behind the weariness in his eyes. "He already has."

Damn it. I held my breath and chugged it down, surprised to find that it really did look and smell worse than it tasted. Still, it wasn't a chocolate milkshake by any stretch, and I gladly accepted the water he had ready.

Once I cleared the yucky taste from my mouth I returned my attention to Pierce. He'd finished the blue drink and the water, and didn't look quite as flattened anymore. Dr. Nikas took his wrist to check his pulse, and the faint smile of admiration and respect Pierce gave him was all the confirmation I needed that this really was the man I'd known as Pietro Ivanov.

"They have Kyle," I told him, finally able to let that worry surface. "They tranqed him while we were getting out. We have to go back for him."

Brian gave a grim nod. "We need to make a plan. Dr. Nikas, is Philip stable enough to take Naomi to an urgent care clinic for her ankle?"

"He should remain stable for long enough to accomplish that," Dr. Nikas replied as he gently set Pierce's wrist down.

Pierce drew a sharp breath. "Marcus—"

"Marcus went to New Orleans the day after you were taken," I told him, then smacked my forehead. "Shit! I meant to call him and give him an update."

He shook his head, pushed up on his elbows despite the distressed noise that wrung from Dr. Nikas. "No. No. They have him."

Shock held me in its grip for several seconds. "You're wrong," I finally managed to force out. "That's not possible. He was with me that evening."

"Angel, believe me." His eyes met mine. They were light grey rather than deep brown now, but I recognized the force behind them. "Saberton has him."

I stumbled to my feet. Somehow all the air was gone from the room. Brian said something to Pierce, face contorted in anger and distress, yet I couldn't make out the words. Dr. Nikas reached for me, worry darkening his eyes, but I took another step back then turned and rushed out of the room.

As soon as I stepped into the hallway I could breathe again, but fury spurred me on. It took me a couple of tries, but I finally found Andrew upstairs. He was dozing on one of two twin beds in an otherwise unfurnished room, shackled by one wrist and one ankle to the frame of the bed. I closed the distance between us in two steps, grabbed the front of his shirt and hauled him close. He jerked out of the doze, eyes flying open in shock as he brought his free hand up in instinctive defense.

"Your people have Marcus?" I yelled without a single speck of calm whatsoever.

"What? Shit!"

I shook him, rattling the chain on his wrist shackle along with the teeth in his head. "Do you motherfuckers have Marcus Ivanov?"

His expression went stony. "Why do you think that?"

A low growl throbbed through the room. Mine. I bared my teeth. "Don't *fuck* with me. I have a reliable source, so answer my fucking question!"

His gaze flicked around the room in an instinctive search for escape before he controlled himself. "Yes," he said. "Yes. Saberton has him."

Breathing hard, I released him and took a step back. "Anyone else there I need to know about?"

"He's the only other one in New York besides Pietro Ivanov. And Griffin now."

No way was I going to correct him about Pietro. "When did your people take Marcus?"

Andrew tugged his shirt straight. "Evening, the same day as the others. He was a secondary target since Archer intercepted Dr. Nikas before we could get to him."

A chill began to work its way down my spine. "How . . . ? How was he taken?"

"In his house," Andrew replied with annoying calm. "Not even a fight."

"What? A home invasion?" I felt almost lightheaded. "Your people busted in and grabbed him?"

His mouth twitched in faint amusement. "You want the play-by-play?"

Clenching my fists, I advanced on him again. "I am so not in the mood for your bullshit."

He drew back but recovered quickly. "Not so dramatic as breaking in and grabbing him," he said with a tight smirk. "The team kicked back in his house and waited for him to walk through the front door. Took him down with tranqs in seconds. He had no mods, which made it easy."

A desire filled me to smash a fist into that arrogant face, and I stood trembling with hands and teeth clenched for several seconds as I fought it back, only doing so because this was Naomi's brother. Besides, one nose-breaking a day was probably a good limit.

I turned and exited without another word, slammed the door behind me, then returned to Pierce's room. He was sitting up a bit more now, and already looked more stable. He began to speak as I entered but stopped at the look on my face.

"They took him less than an hour—" I paused to fight past the knot in my throat. "—less than an hour after we broke up."

Pierce glanced at Dr. Nikas and Brian, and they both exited at the unspoken request.

"Why the break up?" he asked, calm eyes resting on me with surprising gentleness.

I groped for the words to explain it. "He told me he got accepted to law school. I was so damn happy for him, y'know?" I rubbed at my eyes, not surprised to find them wet. "And then he said, 'Hey, we're moving to New Orleans, and I'll find you a job there.'" I bit my lip to stop it from quivering, then moved forward and sat on the edge of the bed again. "He didn't even ask. Didn't discuss it." I met his eyes. "It wasn't a Fuck You breakup. I told him I couldn't go with him, that I needed to—" I took a deep breath. "—needed to keep figuring myself out and that I still wanted to be friends." I cringed at how lame that sounded now. Ugh.

Pierce remained quiet for a moment, while I tried not to squirm or make an excuse to leave the room. I couldn't imagine he'd be happy with me for dumping his nephew over such a weak reason.

"A shame he didn't learn."

"Huh?" I gave him a baffled frown. "Didn't learn what?"

"Didn't learn from previous incidents of trying to rule your life," he said with such compassion and understanding that my stupid eyes started leaking again.

"He's never *mean*," I started to explain, to defend him, then shook my head. "Doesn't matter. He's still my Marcus," I said fiercely, "and I'll do whatever it takes to get him back."

"I know you will, Angel," Pierce said. "As will I. At this time I believe it will be you, me, and Brian who return to Saberton to do so."

Wait, what? My personal reality check gave me a quick, sharp poke. I could talk a great game, but now he wanted to include me on some sort of strike team? "I'm not exactly trained in this," I said, trying to not to fidget. "I don't want to slow y'all down or fuck things up."

To my surprise, he reached out and took hold of my hand. "Angel, *jiu jitsu* isn't what got you through everything that came your way in the last year."

"Yeah, no kidding," I said fervently. "That's 'cause I suck at it." I snorted then shrugged. "Look, I've been *lucky.*"

"Bullshit." He snapped the word out with such force I twitched. "You're a smart woman," he continued. "Resourceful. Headstrong."

"You forgot obnoxious, inappropriate, and stubborn."

One side of his mouth twitched up. "Tenacious and persistent."

I gave him a perplexed look. "Okay, sure, I finally managed to pass my GED. By one point." Man, that shit *still* pissed me off. "I'm a world class bullshitter, but I honestly don't know how I can be any help with y'all. Why not take Philip instead?"

"I'm not talking about booksmart," he stated. "Booksmart people are a dime a dozen. And Philip isn't stable enough yet." He drew breath as if to continue to argue his point, then let it out and simply lifted a shoulder in a slight shrug. "We need you."

He needed me? No, he needed another warm body, and I was pretty much the only option. *It's for Marcus and Kyle.* I wasn't much of an asskicker, but I could sure as hell fake it for those two. I plastered on a smile for Pierce. "Okay, sure. I'm your gal. What do I need to do to get ready?"

The door opened, and Dr. Nikas walked in with a small glass. "You will both rest," he stated firmly and handed Pierce the glass. "Drink," he ordered, then glanced to me as Pierce complied. "If you need help sleeping, I can prepare a dose for you as well. It is a zombie-compliant sedative."

The mention of sleep reminded me how incredibly exhausted I was. "I may take you up on that," I said with a weary smile.

Pierce passed the glass back to Dr. Nikas. "Angel, please send Brian in."

Brian was leaning against the wall in the hallway when I exited the room. "You okay?" he asked.

"Yeah. It's been a really long day, that's all." I rubbed my eyes "I kind of broke someone's nose when I was out looking for you."

"I'm sure he deserved it," he said.

"Actually he deserved worse, but I wasn't in a position to do anything about it." I yawned. "Pietro wants to see you before he goes to sleep." I turned away, then paused. "Oh, and someone needs to remember to feed and water Andrew."

He muttered something dark under his breath. "I'll take care of him."

"Don't hurt him. Much," I said. "Naomi still gives a fuck about the asshole."

He let out a snort but nodded. "Got it."

It wasn't a promise not to hurt him, but at that point I didn't care. I made a quick detour to the kitchen to find Dr. Nikas, downed some of his magic sleepy juice, and then found a flat and fairly soft surface in the form of a sofa to fall face first on.

Chapter 30

I blinked awake to a streetlight glowing against a night sky beyond the window. A low rumble I felt more than heard told me we weren't far from train tracks, and soft classical music drifted from the dining room, a piece I recognized as one of Dr. Nikas's favorites for busywork when he used his hands more than his head. A glance at a clock on the wall told me I'd only slept a couple of hours or so, but to my relief I felt surprisingly refreshed. Dr. Nikas made some damn good zombie drugs. I didn't even mind the metallic tang that still clung from his spicy fruity sedative concoction. *That stuff would be useful to have back home after a long night on call for the morgue,* I mused, then grimaced at the streetlight. *If* I ever got back home to work and my normal life. Normal for me, at least.

Someone had kindly spread a blanket over me, and I threw it aside and pushed up off the sofa. I didn't have the luxury of normal yet. Not with Marcus and Kyle in the hands of the Saberton assholes. Though I doubted Pierce was up and ready, I could start getting my own shit together. On the arm of the sofa lay a neat pile of folded clothing which turned out to be a t-shirt and sweat pants. Both looked large enough to swallow me whole, but they were *clean*, which mattered to me a whole lot more.

Other than the soft music the house was quiet. Gathering up the clean clothing, I crept down the wood floor of the hallway to a bathroom with seventies-era green wallpaper and a toilet in a matching color. Taped to the wall above the toilet was a note, written in Dr. Nikas's neat and lovely script, that read "Please jiggle handle after flushing." I couldn't help but chuckle at the little reminder that even the most amazing people still had to deal with the ordinary.

I set the clothing on the counter then indulged in a wonderfully vicious hot shower. It only took a few minutes to wash off the dried blood and tunnel grunge, but I remained under the spray for a while longer as the knots in my shoulders eased, and I imagined a few layers of stress being washed down the shower drain along with the dirt.

Sufficiently decontaminated, I finished my shower, pulled on the t-shirt and sweat pants and tugged the drawstring at the waistband tight, then gathered up my filthy clothes and went in search of a washing machine.

As I passed through the dining room I found Dr. Nikas sitting at the table and making notes on a clipboard. A large mortar and pestle rested in front of him, along with a variety of ingredients for whatever he was working on. He glanced up with a smile. "There's coffee in the kitchen, and washer and dryer through the door by the pantry."

"You're the best," I announced as I continued on through the kitchen. Caffeine had no effect on zombies, and I usually opted for hot chocolate these days. But good coffee had its place. I dumped the clothes into the washer and got it going, then returned to the kitchen and poured a cup. After the first sip I let out a sigh of pleasure. Whoever made this pot knew what they were doing.

"Where is everyone?" I asked as I emerged into the dining room.

"Pierce is asleep. Andrew is," Dr. Nikas hesitated, "resting." I had a feeling he couldn't bring himself to say *Chained to a bed and scared shitless*. "Philip and Naomi are on the way back from the urgent care clinic. She has an air cast and crutches, but thankfully nothing was broken. Brian is off getting equipment for the Saberton raid. I think that's everyone."

Hopefully that meant Pierce and Brian had a plan. One that I slept right through, not that I'd've had anything useful to contribute. I took another sip of coffee. "Need any help?"

"Angel, you have no idea how glad I am that you asked," he said then shoved the mortar across the table to me. "You may very well regret it."

I set my cup on the table and plopped down into the chair opposite him. "I'm pretty much always up for helping you anyway, but right now a little work will keep me from rearranging the furniture or staring at Pietro . . . Pierce until he wakes up and is ready to go." I peered dubiously at the green sludgy paste in the mortar. "What are we working on?"

He nodded toward a brown glass cough syrup-type bottle at the end of the table. "That's my kitchen lab version of a super-mod for Brian to use during the Saberton raid," he explained. "We're now compounding the carrier for it." He placed a big bowl full of different dried leaves, seeds, and other plant parts next to the mortar and pestle. "Grind all of that together. Add a little water as needed to keep the consistency of the paste."

"Y'all don't have a blender in the kitchen here?" I asked.

He gave a light chuckle. "A blender would process the materials in an entirely different way. I will also admit to being *old school*, and there are times I prefer the old methods I know so very well—especially when working outside of a proper lab."

That made sense. "Is this the mod Brian tested the day everything went to shit?" I asked as I transferred some greyish leaves to the mortar.

"That's right. It's designed to amplify desired zombie abilities for a short period of time." He pulled the cutting board to him and started to carefully mince what looked like some sort of root. "I had to modify the formula to accommodate the ingredients I have available here, but it should still be fairly effective."

I picked up the pestle and began smushing the leaves into the paste. A pungent but pleasant smell wafted up. "Abilities like speed and strength?"

"Yes, that's the idea," he said. "Plus, enhancement of physical senses as well as reflexes. It's no use having superspeed without the ability to react equally quickly."

"Right. Like a car going super fast with horribly unresponsive steering."

He smiled. "Precisely."

I worked quietly for a while, grinding, adding water and more ingredients, grinding some more before I finally asked the question I was dying to know the answer to, but that scared the shit out of me as well. "How the hell did this happen?" I tilted my head toward Pierce's room.

Dr. Nikas's hands stilled. "He chose to transform," he said, voice so soft I doubted it would carry beyond the table even for zombie hearing. "I have not heard his full story, but his situation must have been dire. He had intended to remain Pietro Ivanov for several more decades."

I took a moment to let that sink in. "You're saying that the same way there used to be an original Pierce Gentry, there was an original Pietro Ivanov?" I did my best to keep my tone cool and casual, but inside I boggled. "And Pietro—or whoever he was then—ate his brain and took over his life?"

"Yes, though it wasn't like this," Dr. Nikas said. "There was an agreement. The real Pietro Ivanov was a friend and associate whose mortuary business contributed to the Tribe's brain supply." He returned to mincing ginger. "He went into kidney failure secondary to diabetes, and our Pietro offered to turn him." He exhaled. "The original Pietro didn't want to live as a zombie. However, he came to an agreement to literally give his life over in exchange for care of his family."

All kinds of questions bubbled up about that story, but they could wait until later. "You said only a mature zombie can do this eat-a-brain transformation thing, right? How old are we talking?" I added water to the mixture and continued to grind.

Dr. Nikas shifted in his seat and glanced around as if someone might overhear. "It isn't really related to age."

"Like how I could do a control bite on Philip? That was only supposed to be for mature parasites."

"More specialized than that."

"If it's not an age thing, what is it? What do you mean when you say *mature parasite*?"

Dr. Nikas picked up the cutting board and scraped the contents into the mortar. He added a pinch of stuff that looked like black salt, then made notes on his clipboard. I was about to give up on an answer when he spoke again.

"Mature zombie," he said quietly, "not parasite."

I resisted the urge to say, "Yeah, whatever," only because it was Dr. Nikas. I wouldn't disrespect him like that. Besides, if he bothered to make the distinction, it meant there was something to it. "Mature zombie," I echoed. "What exactly does that mean?"

He weighed some milky yellow powder on the scale then added it to my mixture. "Sulfur. Grind it in to where the paste is an even color, then we're nearly done." He settled back in his chair then laid his hands flat on the table. "It means there is no longer anything distinguishable as human-versus-zombie organism. The DNA restructure is complete. A rare success."

"Uh," I said while I struggled to make sense of that. "Are you saying Pietro-Pierce-whoever isn't really human anymore?"

"Physically, none of us are, Angel," Dr. Nikas said with a certainty that sent a shiver through me. "Not once the organism establishes itself. The changes begin immediately. Pierce and I are perhaps even less human from a purely physical perspective." His eyes met mine, gentle and troubled and ancient. "I don't feel any less human than I ever have."

It took me a minute to get past his claim that we weren't simply humans infested with a parasite, and then another minute to push aside the useless worry that, if we were so changed, how could we be sure we remembered what it was like to feel human? "So it's *not* a parasite?"

"Technically, no. When I first tried to understand the science of it, parasite was my initial impression, and the term stuck." He flashed a smile. "Besides, it's easier to say *parasite* than *mutualistic symbiont with parasitic aspects*." His eyes crinkled with amusement. "In the end it's merely semantics. A new word such as *zombite* would better acknowledge its unique function, but old habits die hard."

Dr. Sofia Baldwin had convincingly explained to me that the parasite healed damage and kept zombies healthy only because it benefited the parasite to have a healthy host. If there weren't enough brains for it to do that, it saved itself and let us rot. That sure sounded like a parasite to me, but Dr. Nikas knew a billion times more about it than either Sofia or I did.

"Who's in control after maturity?" I asked. "The not-a-parasite or the human?"

"Neither," he said. "There is no distinction—a new unified entity with no loss of who one was and is as a person. However, before experiencing it, one cannot even conceive the enhancements to the senses, perception, and overall *awareness*. Pheromones, taste, global species sensitivity. It's exhilarating, even overwhelming at first, though totally natural."

No, not natural at all! I silently protested. Yet in my little zombie heart it rang true, like an instinctual knowing and acceptance on top of eager curiosity. "That sounds more like a living steroid than a self-serving parasite."

Dr. Nikas beamed. "A well considered analogy, Angel," he said. "And that is the model I work with now, rather than symbiosis. To put it very simply, the organism is the ultimate mod. It gradually optimizes its target through bio-restructuring until it gets the job done—albeit with some heavy side effects."

I peered at him. "You said you're mature too, like Pierce?"

He nodded and extended his hand toward me, palm down, unbuttoned his sleeve and pushed it up to the elbow. "Point to any spot on my forearm," he instructed.

Baffled, I reached to touch a spot a couple of inches above his wrist. I started to ask what he was doing, then could only stare, mouth hanging open. Like a slow-motion movie special effect, the skin of his forearm rippled and shifted as a scar formed, thick and white, angling across his forearm where I'd touched.

"Whoa." I stared at the two-inch long defect in the skin. "Have you ever had a scar in that spot?" I asked. Maybe it was a weird parasite-memory thing?

"Never there," he murmured. A few seconds later the scar rippled and became smooth skin again even as a long and barely healed gash appeared across the back of his hand.

"Whoa," I said again,

"I am mature, yes," he said. "Conscious control within genetic parameters."

I processed that. "In other words, you can control stuff that could change on a normal human, but you can't sprout wings?" I gave a nervous chuckle.

"That's correct," he replied. "And I can't change my basic blueprint. No higher cheekbones or blue eyes instead of brown."

It started to make a weird sort of sense. "Unless you—a mature zombie—ate someone's brain, got a new blueprint, and decided to redecorate." I watched with continued fascination as he smoothed his hand back to normal—whatever "normal" meant in this freaky context.

"Correct again," he said.

I dragged my gaze from his hand to his face. "Conscious control. Is that how Pietro made himself look like he was in his sixties? Instead of staying younger-looking like regular zombies?"

"Yes, and it has proven quite useful." He shifted and looked away "I've never had the need to transform or mimic aging. I stay away from people, for the most part."

With the way Dr. Nikas lived as a recluse in his lab, there was no one on the outside who saw him enough to realize he never aged. The thought of so few people ever knowing him sent a weird and sad pang through me.

Dr. Nikas looked in the direction of Pierce's room and exhaled softly. "I've been with him a long time. Mature zombies don't tend to stay close together, but I . . ."

"You need him, and he needs you," I finished for him.

A smile twitched his lips before fading. "He shelters me, and I keep him balanced," he said. "I was broken long ago. For all of our physical and even mental healing capacity, most psychological or emotional wounds remain untouched, even in maturity." He pulled his gaze back to mine. "Angel, you know I can't tolerate a crowded room, much less a public life. With him, I can simply be who I am."

"What happened to you?" I asked after a moment's hesitation.

He pulled his sleeve back down and buttoned the cuff, focusing so carefully on the task it was clear he was either gathering up the nerve to tell me the story or attempting to come up with a nice way to tell me to fuck off and mind my own business. "I was revealed as a ghoul," he finally said. "Zombie is a modern name. Ghoul, in various forms and languages, has been our label for centuries. Our kind were seeds for a great variety of legends of demonic association, sorcery, and macabre desecration of the dead." He drew an unsteady breath, then reached for the mortar and scraped the goopy contents of the mortar into a smaller bowl. "A very long time ago I lived as a physician and surgeon in Thessaloniki." His hands stilled, and his eyes went distant as though connecting with that past. "A mob ambushed me—the ghoul who'd been robbing the city's graves and, more recently, its fallen soldiers."

"Oh, no," I murmured, dread rising.

He finished transferring the minced root into the bowl then busied himself with tasting the concoction before adding a final touch of what looked like black salt. I didn't have to be a genius to understand that he needed a moment to compose himself. I doubted this was a subject he talked about much.

"I'll spare you the horror of the details," he said, and I suspected the short version was more to spare himself the horror of it. "The mob. People, friends and associates I'd known for years. So savage. So full of hate."

A shudder ran through me. Though what he described happened a long time ago, he might as well have been painting a picture of my worst nightmares. Louisiana backwoods justice for the monster that ate Grampa Joe's brain. "How'd they find out?"

"My wife." His voice grew thick. "I never told her what I was. When she found a cask of brains in the winter cellar, she exposed me."

Throat tight, I laid my hand on top of his. If he *had* told her, would she have been swayed to accept his way of living, or would she have turned on him then and there? It could've gone either way no matter how deep the relationship. What if Jane had turned on Pietro? There'd been no time to think about it in the moment, but damn, it could have been disastrous. Double kudos to Jane for being super cool.

Dr. Nikas's hand trembled under mine as he spoke again. "They forced brains on me as they mutilated, broke, and burned my body by every means they could imagine. And they had *vivid* imaginations."

Chilled to my bones, I squeezed his hand, silently grateful he'd decided to omit the graphic details. What words were adequate? None, and so I settled on the simple, "I'm so sorry."

He turned his hand over and closed his fingers around mine, silent for at least a full minute. "They broke me, Angel," he finally said in a voice choked with emotion, and I knew he meant far more than his physical body. "I don't know how long it went on. Forever. Eventually they piled wood and brush around me for a final burning, but it never happened."

I let out a breath I'd been holding, like reaching the turning point in a book when you know everything's going to be okay. "What stopped them?" I asked, genuinely curious about what could put a halt to a situation so out of control.

"*He* did," Dr. Nikas said with a nod toward Pierce's room. "He emerged from the darkness like an avenging angel, a mercenary captain and his company. In moments he and his men scattered the mob like dry leaves in the wind. He cut me down, told me it would never happen again. I've been with him ever since."

"Pietro. Oh, wow."

He wiped a stray tear away with the back of his free hand. "Yes. Strong, capable, fearless, and feared."

"In other words a badass mofo." A few days ago it would've been impossible for me to imagine Pietro Ivanov as a mercenary captain. But now that he had the form of Pierce Gentry I sure as hell could. And hell, what better place to get a supply of brains than a battlefield? "He hasn't budged off that badassness one little bit, has he?"

"No, he has not," Dr. Nikas stated. "The Pietro identity proved quite challenging for him, as he chose to adopt Pietro's relatively tame and passive lifestyle in order to ensure a seamless transition. It meant he had to enlist others to conduct business he would normally do himself."

My respect for Pietro expanded. He'd willingly taken on a life that didn't suit him for the sake of securing a steady—and mostly non-violent—source of brains for his people. He sure as hell wasn't a squeaky clean, shiny hero, but he was turning out to be a tried-and-true tarnished one. "With you as his sounding board and moral bullshit meter, you two seem to make a good team."

Dr. Nikas laughed. "When he listens to me." He kept hold of my hand even though the tension had eased. Between his story and what I knew of him from the lab, I had the feeling he truly *was* a people person, a healer who couldn't be around people, and probably had little physical contact with anyone. How sucky was that?

Dr. Nikas squeezed my hand then reluctantly released it. A wave of sadness swept through me as if I'd lost a comfy blanket, and I took a deep breath to shake off the feeling.

The sound of the garage door rumbled through the house, and about half a minute later Brian came in from the garage. He wore a leather jacket over dark jeans instead of his typical suit, which was so out of character I'd have probably passed right by him on the street without recognizing him.

"That was a pain in the ass, but it's done," he announced.

I stood and stretched as Dr. Nikas poured the pale blue contents of the bottle into the bowl of glop. "Did you bring home something fun?" I asked.

"Sure did," Brian said. "A cargo van and a small dumpster."

"Do I want to know what this plan is?"

"Probably not," he said with a wink.

I rolled my eyes. "How about the basics of what we're up against."

"Our best estimate is at least a dozen of Saberton's Special Security Team," Brian told me. "In general, they're hardcore pros handpicked for company loyalty and willingness to do whatever is required." A muscle in his neck briefly tensed. "Out of the SST, a select few who apparently have an extra dose of *fuck you* about human rights are assigned to work directly with zombies."

"Zombies don't even count as human to them," I said with a black scowl. The memory of my own capture was still crystal-clear, including how much Mr. Perfect Eyebrows and the others had gotten off on humiliating and abusing me. "I hate those fuckers."

"No argument from me," Brian said, matching my scowl. "Some of them use torture as entertainment. I'm ready to bury the lot."

"I'll bring the shovel," I said. "What's next?"

"A chat with Saber. Want to come with me?"

I gave him a dubious look. Chatting with Andrew wasn't exactly on the top of my list of fun things to do. "Depends. What are we talking about?"

Brian's smile faded. "I had a talk with Mr. Iv—Gentry. We need to put a little heat on Saber to determine where he stands concerning his sister."

"You mean so we know whether or not Naomi should see him in person?" At his nod I continued, "No matter what, I think he needs to be told his mother knew Julia wasn't dead. That should piss him off and rock the happy family when he goes home." *If he goes home*, I added silently. That wouldn't happen if Pierce considered him a serious threat. But Brian's broad smile told me I wa right on target. "What about Naomi?" I asked. "She needs to hav a say in this."

"When she gets back from the clinic," he said. "My hope is tha our little interview will help her decide what to do."

"Gotcha." I was totally happy to gather info to help Naomi ou especially since it was a lot like being nosy, which I was alread pretty damn good at.

"Not to mention, I figure this could be a good start to your train ing," he added.

"Training?" Was I supposed to run around the house a few time before talking to Andrew? I gave him a baffled look. "I'm lost."

"After you outed Dr. Pennington's bodyguard, I promised bot you and him that I'd cover the basics," Brian explained. "Interviev and interrogation isn't really a *basic,* but it'll help you think on you feet, and it's as good a place as any to start."

"Oh! Right." Whew, no running or pushups. Yet. "Sure, totall up for it." Especially if it could keep me from having another inci dent like the one with Victor and Jane.

Brian's expression grew more serious. "We also need to se what information can be wrung from Saber that will help us rescu Kyle and Marcus."

"As long as I get to do some of the wringing," I said with glower. "Anything besides Pietro's change-of-body off limits?"

"No, that's the only info that needs to remain completely hush hush," he said. "But you have plenty of other ammunition."

"I know lots of shit that he doesn't," I said then looked down a myself. Baggy sweatpants and a T-shirt that swallowed me. Prett unimpressive. "Let me throw my clothes in the dryer first." Th pants had a bullet hole in the ass, and the jacket and shirt wer burned and melted in the back from when I got stuck beneath Nao mi's car in the Saberton parking garage, but it would still be a bette look than my current one. I'd have to find a way to score som less-damaged stuff for the rescue raid though. Maybe I could b Naomi's personal fashion doll again.

"I'll make a sandwich for our guest while you do that," Bria said.

"Don't put anything weird in it," I replied as I trotted off to th laundry room.

Brian's chortle followed me. "Not promising anything!"

Chapter 31

With fresh clothing and a tough attitude, I headed upstairs with Brian. "Do we have a plan?" I asked.

"Get a feel for it," Brian replied as we reached the door at the end of the hall. "Follow my lead if you get stuck." And with that, he threw the door open.

Andrew startled so badly he rattled the headboard against the wall as he jerked his wrist cuff. After a few seconds of wide-eyed hard breathing he put on the toughest face he could manage, though it did little to hide how tired and scared he looked. "What now?" he rasped. "More threats?"

I followed Brian into the room, and when he didn't respond to Andrew, I realized he expected me to *start*. Crap. "We don't have any reason to threaten you," I said, doing my best cool interrogator impression. "You're in a world of shit, and you know it."

Andrew shifted to the awkward half-sit the shackle and cuff would allow. "Yes, I know it." His eyes flicked from me to Brian. His fear smelled like the tang of shorting wires, and a sheen of sweat broke on his forehead. He probably figured we'd eat his brain the instant he stopped being useful. A whisper of uncertainty passed over his face as he noted the sandwich and the glass of sparkling grape juice in Brian's hands. Probably wondering why we'd feed him if we were only going to kill him.

"Hungry?" I asked as I took the plate and glass from Brian.

He hesitated, clearly torn about whether to be stubborn and hungry, or cooperative and fed, but after a few more seconds he gave a tight nod. I placed the sandwich and juice on the nightstand within his reach, then sat on the edge of the other bed.

Andrew mumbled thanks and wasted no time in taking a bite of the sandwich. I gave him almost enough time to finish chewing, then asked my question. "Why do you hate us so much?"

He froze, then swallowed the bite and washed it down with juice. "Your people murdered my sister." His voice remained calm, but I felt the anger behind it.

Brian stepped forward. "I did that," he said. "Though from what she said you two didn't seem all that close."

Fury flashed in Andrew's eyes. "Who the hell are you to judge me on that?" he asked, not so calm anymore. "We didn't always get along, but I still loved her. She was my *sister*."

Brian's nostrils flared slightly. Scenting truth or lie. "We'll keep that in mind."

Andrew shot him a baffled look. "What the hell is that supposed to mean?"

"It means, when I'm deciding whether or not to kill you, it might factor in." Brian folded his arms. "It was a waste for that girl to die, but it had to be done." I had to hand it to Brian. He knew which buttons to push on Andrew.

Andrew's jaw trembled as his composure crumbled. "Why?"

I leaned forward, completely on track with Brian. "What part? Why was it a waste, or why did it have to be done?"

"I *know* why it was a waste," Andrew snapped. "She was talented and clever and full of life. I didn't always agree with her choices, but I respected her drive and skill." He fixed his gaze on me. "I want to know why the hell Ivanov had this goon kill her."

Well, damn. This whole faked death thing looked a lot different up close and personal. No wonder Andrew hated Pietro. Part of me wanted to cave in, comfort him, and tell him his sister was fine, but the rest of me knew I had a job to do. Other people's lives depended on my staying strong here. I drew a breath to steady myself. "Because she knew too much. She was desperate to get away from Saberton, but your mother had her so terrified we couldn't risk her going back."

For a second I thought Andrew was going to throw up, then he smashed his free fist into the headboard. His words came out between clenched teeth. "My mother is a desperate, manipulative, heartless woman, and Julia had good reason to be afraid of her."

"No shit." I did my best to kept my voice even and steady. "What about you, Andy? How'd you pick up such a cruel streak?"

He flexed his bleeding knuckles then grabbed the sandwich and took a vicious bite to cover his angry frustration. And fear. And to avoid answering. And to get some food while we were in the mood to feed him. Darn useful sandwich.

"You broke Heather's—I mean Julia's—heart," I said, correcting my intentional use of her cover name. "You know, when she watched a video of you right alongside Nicole being all okay with cutting up a live zombie."

He paled, and I thought he might crack, but he pulled his act together and lifted his chin. "It was that or abandon my grandfather's company and have no say whatsoever in its future." He placed the rest of the sandwich on the plate and shoved it away. "My mother knew Dr. Charish's Zoldiers project was a long shot, yet she wanted to mine anything salvageable from it. Saberton provided only minimal resources. There were other projects but all were beyond my ability to stop or control. I *told* Julia that."

I stood, jaw clenched tight as my calm went out the window. Those *minimal resources* had fucked up my life, terrorized my dad, crippled Philip, and killed an innocent man.

"Interesting." Brian drawled the word. "You're saying that, if you were in charge, you'd put a stop to the vivisection, torture, and experimentation?"

Andrew squared his shoulders. "If I was in *charge*? Yes." He hesitated as if about to say more, but didn't.

"Why don't I believe you?" Brian picked up the plate with the unfinished sandwich. "Your sister had a real affinity for zombies. You and your mother set her up with John Kang, then tried to turn her against him—her best friend. And you call *us* monsters."

With that he strode out of the room. I really wanted to stick around and punch Andrew, but I followed Brian instead, though I did slam the door behind me.

Brian walked a short distance down the hallway. "We'll let him simmer a bit while you get yourself together," he told me in a low voice.

"I almost lost it," I confessed. "Dude pissed me off."

"I get it," he said. "But you want *him* to be the only one off-balance. You've accomplished that. Now it's time to drop the bomb about his sister, then fish for information. We'll play it by ear as it unfolds. You lead again, and I'll take over if you need a boost."

"Got it," I said. "Learn by doing and screwing up." An odd thrill of excitement and nerves shivered through me, but I took a deep breath and made myself chill. The urge to punch someone faded, and I returned to Andrew's door and opened it gently. He still sat on the edge of the bed, his good hand locked over the injured knuckles as he glared at us.

I reclaimed my seat on the other bed. *Cool and calm. I can do this.* "The last time you saw Julia," I began, "you threatened to tell your mother that Julia helped a zombie escape and killed a Saberton lab guy. You scared the shit out of her, and because of that, she figured her only options were to go under your thumb forever or smash you in the face and run for her life." I paused for effect. "We know how that turned out."

His glare dissolved into anguish. "You don't think I feel the guilt of that every goddamn day?" he asked, voice cracking. "I'm her twin. *Was* her twin." He reached out with his bloody hand as though to touch something, then closed his fist on empty air. "I can't even let her go because it feels like she's still right here."

Was that because of the twin thing? Maybe on some level he *knew* she wasn't dead? "Andrew, we're not going to fuck with you anymore over this," I said. "Your mother is a piece of work—more than you can possibly know."

He narrowed his eyes. "What do you mean?"

"Julia knew your mother wouldn't rest until your security people caught her," I said. "Your sister didn't fear death. She was scared shitless that she'd be lab zombified and used as a specimen. The threat was very real to her, and she couldn't live like that."

"I *know*," he said, voice sharp with grief. "She should've trusted that I'd keep her safe."

"Pietro figured locking her away for protection would've been a waste, a different sort of death for her," I said, picking my way through how to tell him without blurting it out. "Apart from that, there was only one way to stop your mother from hunting her down."

Hate burned in his eyes. "What are you saying?" he asked. "Ivanov had Archer kill her out of some sorted twisted sense of *mercy*?"

"We killed Julia Saber," I said carefully. Andrew was a prime asshole, but this shit was real, and I didn't want to botch the words. "But that's only a name."

The color drained from his face. "What are you saying?" he asked again, barely able to get the words out.

"Julia Saber was only a name." I relaxed a little. "She did okay with cutting all ties with the family and the past. Except for you."

He stared at me for a moment as the implication set in, then lunged, teeth bared as he swung his bloody fist. I gave a startled yelp and scrambled backward, but in the next instant Brian body slammed Andrew back onto the bed and pinned him with a heavy hand on his upper chest.

"One more stunt like that," Brian said softly but distinctly, "and I'll lock you down so hard you won't be able to flinch when I eat your fucking brain." He leaned into Andrew's chest. "We clear?"

Andrew gasped for air and nodded. Brian straightened and stepped back. "You good, Ms. Crawford?"

I stared stupidly at him for a second before recovering. "Uh, yeah. Yes. Thanks, Brian." Or was I supposed to call him Mr. Archer? I straightened and did my best to pretend nothing had happened. "Sit up, Andrew," I said, then added, "Please."

He slowly moved to sit on the edge of the bed. "I'm not going to fall for your emotional blackmail bullshit," he snarled. "Whatever it is you want, you're not going to get it that way."

What now? I sure as hell didn't want to get into an argument about whether or not his sister was alive. I started to give Brian a *What the fuck do I do now?* look, then caught sight of Pierce eavesdropping in the hallway. Oh, right. I knew shit that Andrew didn't. I could use that.

"You've made it pretty clear you don't want to listen to me," I said with a shrug. "That's fine. How 'bout we cut the bullshit."

Andrew's shoulders eased a bit and caginess replaced the fury in his eyes, as if I'd finally stepped onto his turf. "You want Ivanov."

"Pietro? Nah." I shook my head even as I watched his face for reaction. "I guess you've been out of the loop. Your people don't have him anymore."

"I don't believe you," he said after a heartbeat of hesitation.

"Whether you believe me or not doesn't change a damn thing." I tilted my head and smiled. "Saberton had an insider, and Pietro's out. How do you think we knew y'all have Marcus?"

He quickly covered his surprise with a steely frown. "What insider?"

My smile widened. "Pierce Gentry."

Andrew stared for a second then let out a laugh. "Insider? You hauled him in here in handcuffs. God knows what you people did to him to get that tidbit of information." He snorted. "Pierce Gentry is hard core Saberton. Second generation."

With that absolutely perfect setup, Pierce stepped into the doorway. Dressed in black tactical pants and shirt, and with a big ass knife in a belt sheath on his hip, he sure as hell didn't fit the vision of a tortured prisoner. "You're wrong, Saber," he growled. "About me. About a lot of things."

It was like watching a movie and being in it at the same time. Andrew's mouth fell open, and something that was probably supposed to be "why?" came out a strangled croak instead.

"Because Saberton crossed the line when it fucked with zombies." Pierce pulled a baggie of brains from his pocket and slurped down the unmistakable contents.

Andrew drew a noisy breath as he fought to make sense of this new reality. "You . . . no. We would've known. You *can't* be one of those . . ."

Pierce's face went hard. "One of those animals? Monsters? Vermin? Freaks? I know all the shock team's pet names for 'specimens.'" He moved to stand shoulder to shoulder with Brian. "I *can* be one of them, and I *am*. Looks like you're wrong again."

Hot damn. I knew where to go with this. "Here's the deal, Andy," I said quickly. "We're going in to get our people back. And you're going to help us."

He dragged his eyes from Pierce to me. "What?"

"You heard me." I fought down a gleeful smile. "You're going to help us. Pietro's out, but his nephew isn't." I paused. "Your mother thinks forcing Jane's hand is a good business plan, but you don't."

"I stand behind Saberton," he said with a frown.

"Yeah. Whatever." I waved a hand. "You hustled Jane out of Saberton Tower before your mother changed her mind, and I could've sworn you looked relieved when I said your people didn't have Pietro anymore."

He didn't protest or try to correct me. "If Pennington pulls the strings needed to secure the defense contract, it's suicide for Saberton," he said, expression grim. "We'll make more enemies than allies in Congress, and turn our competitors into cutthroats. We might get a contract, but we'd go down hard later." He drew a breath. "When I escorted her out, I told her I'd be in touch with her shortly. I planned to offer her an alternative. Of course, that never happened."

"What alternative?"

He grimaced. "I didn't have one yet. I was trying to stall her before she followed through with the deal."

"The good news for you is that the original deal is blown now that you've lost Pietro," I said. "Bad news is that Jane isn't going to sit on her hands as long as y'all still hold Pietro's nephew. She's all set to fuck Saberton over six ways to Sunday, and you know she won't hold back."

A pained expression flashed across his face. *Ha! One point for Angel!* Pleased, I leaned back on my elbows. "Look, we both want the same thing here. So how 'bout you make it easy on everyone and work with us."

Pierce folded his arms across his broad chest. "I can get us in, Andrew, but it would be smoother with your cooperation."

"And if I cooperate?" Andrew asked, eyes narrowed. "What then?"

"You see this through, and we let you go back to your mommy." Pierce's gaze intensified to predator focus. "You don't, and we find out if there's anything special about a Saber brain."

Fear flickered for an instant, but then Andrew's jaw set in defiant pride. "Agreed," he said. "It's best done soon, before my mother decides to move them to Dallas."

Pierce gave a sharp nod. "A plan to move the prisoners is good. Except it will be *your* idea. We'll discuss the final preparations as soon as Ms. Crawford finishes with you." With that he gave me a barely perceptible wink, turned, and strode out.

Finishes with him? Oh, right. Naomi. "By the way," I said, then snapped my fingers to pull his attention away from the doorway and back to me. "Andrew, I'd bet my left tit you didn't hear all of the shit that came through that *thing* in my arm."

His mouth pulled down in a scowl. "What makes you think that?"

I let out a soft sigh. "Because if you'd heard everything, you wouldn't have accused us of emotional blackmail."

"Julia," he said softly, then shook his head. "I don't understand what the bug has to do with my sister." No anger or cockiness anymore. We'd put him through the wringer, and now he simply looked drained.

"Because anyone who listened to the whole broadcast would know that we killed the name 'Julia Saber,' but not the woman." I paused. "And, yeah, I can prove it."

"She's *alive*?" He tried to stand, then sat again heavily. "Julia's really alive? Where is she? Is she all right?"

"She's fine," I said, even as I heard a soft *thuck swish* which I suspected was Naomi crutching her way up the stairs. "Pietro made sure she was safe from your mother," I continued. "Plastic surgery, new identity, the works. But he couldn't take into account the damn bug."

New, scary anger lit Andrew's eyes. "My mother *knows*?"

"Unless someone else screened the bug and called the shots."

"Her assistant listened and provided transcripts of relevant information to her, which were then forwarded to me. Or so I thought." He forced the words through clenched teeth. "My mother called the shots and obviously passed me only crumbs. It's all about fucking control with her. I'll kill her. I swear to god, I'll *kill* her."

"Hold that thought a minute, Hero," Naomi said from the doorway.

Andrew's focus snapped to her. Emotions tumbled over his face as his worldview did a reset. "Julia?" He lurched up and yanked against the chains on his wrist and ankle. "God damn it. Get this shit off me!"

"Brian, could you? Please?" Naomi said quietly without taking her eyes from her brother.

Face expressionless, Brian moved in and unlocked the chains, then leaned in close to Andrew. "One wrong bat of an eyelash, and I will *hurt* you."

He barely had time to step back before Naomi swooped in and threw her arms around Andrew's neck. I caught the discarded crutches before they crashed to the floor, then I stepped back. *Maybe I should leave the room?* I wondered then saw that Brian remained at his spot by the foot of the bed. He looked out the window beyond the two, but I had no doubt he was aware of every sound and scent and movement. I doubted Andrew would do something stupid like try to take Naomi hostage, but it made sense to keep an eye on him.

Still, I felt like a voyeur as Naomi and Andrew blubbered over each other, even though I tried to model Brian's nothing-going-on-here face. After a couple of minutes the two finally pulled apart and sat side by side on the edge of Andrew's bed.

Andrew scrubbed a hand over his face. "Even *knowing* how Mother is, it's hard to believe she did this to me."

"To *you*?" Naomi scowled. "Look at what I had to do to myself to keep her from coming after me!"

"That's not what I meant—"

Naomi cut him off with a noise of exasperation. "None of this would've happened if you hadn't been a big bully and threatened to 'tell mommy on me.'"

He stiffened. "You weren't listening. I was only trying to shock some sense into you."

"Yeah?" She shifted a few inches away in order to glare at him. "Well you got a broken nose for your loving support."

"Plus another mess of yours to clean up," Andrew retorted.

"This time a fucking *murder*. I tried to keep your name clear of it, but she found out." He edged back from her. "I don't know what you're so pissed about. You got exactly what you've always wanted."

Naomi's eyes narrowed. "What the hell is *that* supposed to mean?"

I hid a grimace. *So much for the happy reunion.*

Andrew jerked his gaze away from her and out the window, but not before I saw the flash of pain in his eyes. "It means you coped with her bullshit a long time ago by staying as far away from her—from us—as you could. This time, you almost succeeded in making it permanent." One hand clenched briefly on the blanket. "You left me thinking I'd driven you off to your death. You could have told me you were alive."

"Right," she snorted, though I heard the guilt behind it. "And risk one of your self righteous gung-ho-Saberton reactions?"

Brian shifted, muscles in his arms tense, and I had a feeling he was poised to put a stop to the bickering. I laid a hand on his arm and gave him a slight headshake. Sometimes the best thing for old, dirty laundry was a little airing. He frowned at me then gave a grudging nod.

"*Someone* has to watch out for grandfather's company," Andrew was saying. "But you could have had a little faith in me." He turned back to her and shrugged, a hurt, bitter look on his face. "I don't know why I expected anything different. You abandoned me before. You abandoned me again."

Naomi's jaw dropped. "I never abandoned you! I was off doing my *job*."

"Which was chock full of the thrill you adored," he replied with a sneer. "It was a bonus that it happened to help Saberton." He waved a hand in our direction. "And now you're off working with the people who are trying to undermine us."

She gave him an *Are you insane?* look. "Zombies are being tortured and used. People have been *kidnapped*. My boyfriend has been captured." She returned his sneer in force. "This isn't about undermining anyone or anything. It's about righting a despicable wrong."

"Where do you draw the line at despicable?" he demanded. "Do you think it was all roses and lollipops for the people you lied to, stole from, tricked, or planted things on during your little spy games? And apparently murder didn't cross the line." She jerked as the last one hit home, and he lifted his chin. "As for zombies, Saberton wouldn't have even known about them if you hadn't stolen shit from Ivanov."

She hauled herself up and snagged the crutches. "This is all *my* fault?" Her voice remained steady, but I spied the quiver in her lip. She'd already been carrying the guilt of how Saberton discovered the zombies. "You're blaming *me* for your attitude of 'They're not like me so I can screw them over all I want'?" Tears welled in her eyes. "You never used to be so hateful," she said. "What the hell happened to you, Andrew?"

Regret shadowed his face before he steeled his gaze. "While you were off thrill-seeking, I was stuck taking care of business." He didn't have to add *stuck with Mother.* That came through loud and clear.

"Your business *sucks*." She crutched to the door but when she reached the hallway she stopped and spoke without looking back. "No matter what you tell yourself so you can sleep at night, it's not okay to kidnap people for profit. And, *yes,* zombies are people. So get over yourself, Andrew." With that she hurried down the hall.

"The business was all I had!" he shouted after her, voice shaking with long pent-up emotion. "You found a way out and never looked back. Maybe I needed—" He broke off, turned away. "Fuck," he breathed.

Needed . . . an escape? A way out? A new life? It was obvious he loved his sister and wanted out of his mother's shadow. Andrew's armor had a chink in it, though I had no idea how big of one.

I cleared my throat. "This is the perfect opportunity to walk away from Saberton, y'know." His shoulders sagged. *Maybe,* I thought. *Just maybe.*

He drew himself up and faced me, his expression all cool business again. "Walk away from Saberton," he echoed, voice stiff. "You believe this is a perfect opportunity for me to *walk away* from a career I love and my grandfather's legacy?"

Crap. Me and my big mouth. I fumbled for anything to say that could possibly salvage the moment, but in the next instant his composure crumbled, as if he simply didn't have the energy to maintain it.

"Saberton is my life," Andrew said, voice rough. "It's who I am. I can't abandon it. I *can't*—not even to get away from our mother." A soft sigh escaped him. "Julia's talents made it easy for her to stay away." He spoke with soft precision, as if trying to win an old argument with himself. "My talents bound me in close. It's simply how it is."

A sudden wave of unexpected sympathy left me at a loss for words. Julia/Naomi had left her family behind but could still keep doing the covert ops spy adventure shit she loved. She changed employers, but the job itself remained pretty much the same. It had never even occurred to me that Andrew might love what he did just as much—probably because the whole financial-business-power-tie-boardroom thing seemed tedious and dry and dull to me. Yet for Andrew to "walk away" was a much bigger sacrifice, I realized with chagrin. I didn't know a lot about the business world, but somehow I doubted he'd be able to step right into another high-level position anywhere else. Plus, anywhere else wouldn't be *Saberton*.

A quick glance at Brian told me he'd realized the same thing, though there wasn't much sympathy in his eyes. Sighing, I looked back to Andrew, but he'd managed to regain his bearing in those few seconds and spoke before I could.

"We have an agreement," he stated. "I'll help get Griffin and Marcus Ivanov out in exchange for my release. That's it. And we have that *only* because I know it's in Saberton's best interests to *not* give Jane Pennington a reason to fuck us over, even though my mother doesn't see it my way."

Best interests? My sympathy vanished like a popped soap bubble. "Whatever," I snapped. "You look like shit and need to get your ass cleaned up before we walk you into Saberton Tower."

Brian gestured toward the door. "Come on, Saber," he said. "Once we take care of that we'll meet with Gentry to make the final plan."

With that, I left the guys to their business and headed downstairs. Naomi sat on the sofa in the living room with her foot propped on the coffee table.

"Just like old times," she said with a weak smile.

"You gonna be okay?"

"Sure. Old shit. New twist." But she let out a long sigh. "We used to be so close. I played games with my grandfather that turned into real work. Andrew was the so-called responsible one, focused on boring stuff."

"Boring to you," I put in. "I get the feeling he really likes it."

A grimace flashed over her face. "Yeah, he does. Now," she added. "We were groomed for our talents—and our roles—when we were kids. I was lucky and loved mine. He learned to love his." She bit her lip. "I never thought I'd *abandoned* him, but I guess in a way I did."

"You can't beat yourself up over it," I said. "He's a grown man who makes his own choices."

"Andrew is Andrew. I'm used to it." A determined expression settled across her face, though I now suspected that Tough Determination was as much of a fake front as Andrew's Cool and Unruffled Businessman. "Once we get Marcus and Kyle back I'll have room to rant about my brother's priorities," she continued.

"Right." I gave her a quick hug. "Gotta go check in with Pierce on the plan." I started to turn away then paused. "You have any tweezers?"

She gave me a baffled look, but dug a pair out of her bag and handed them over.

"Thanks. I'll bring them back before we leave." I didn't know the plan yet, but I knew that part of it depended on Pierce passing himself off as the real Pierce Gentry.

I found Pierce in the garage. The SUV was gone, and in its place was a white cargo van. He closed the van's back doors and looked over at me.

"Angel? Is something wrong?"

Grinning, I waggled the tweezers at him. "Let's go, dude. We got some eyebrows to tame."

Chapter 32

This is what my life has become. Stuffed into the bottom of a garbage bin.

It was a clean one, at least, and pretty darn roomy, for a garbage bin. Pierce and Brian had muttered stuff about specs and load capacity and two cubic yards, blah blah. About three feet deep with a footprint a smidge smaller than a hospital bed, it was basically a big ass blue industrial plastic mini-dumpster on wheels.

I'd been curled up inside of it for the last few minutes, or ever since we crossed the river heading into midtown Manhattan toward Saberton's headquarters. The not-bad part was Brian curled up inside it as well. Spooning me, in fact, which I couldn't help enjoying on a primitive physical level even though I considered Brian to be in the special category reserved for Best Friends and Big Brothers.

In turn, I spooned a blanket-covered selection of tools we figured might come in handy, and, for a slightly lumpy pillow, I had an insulated lunch box containing a few baggies of diced brains, since we were down to only three packets remaining from the lab. *Maybe it's a good thing Philip had to stay behind with Dr. Nikas,* I mused. Philip was a pretty big guy, and I had a hard time imagining him and Brian cuddled up in the dumpster.

"Entering the garage now, folks," Pierce said, interrupting my mental wanderings, which was probably a damn good thing considering the direction they were headed. I felt the van turn, and then some bumps, followed by a sense of going down a slight incline. "We have our plan, but everyone needs to keep their senses sharp," he continued. "Anything could change at any time."

The van backed up, stopped, and the engine died. Brian shifted positions behind me slightly, and I bit down on an insane need to giggle.

"What's wrong?" Brian whispered.

"You're poking me in the butt!"

He made a strangled sound, and I couldn't tell if it was laughter or exasperation. Possibly both. "It's my gun. Sorry."

I clamped both hands over my mouth and shook with laughter. "Not *that* kind of gun, you dork!"

The back doors of the van opened, and I quickly got myself under control.

"I'll take care of this myself, sir." That was Pierce's voice. We were inside Saberton walls, which meant we were probably under surveillance already.

"Thank you, Gentry," Andrew replied. He sounded tired and stressed but holding it together.

"Can't let anything happen to the goods," Pierce said, surprising me with a sharp yank on the bin. For an instant I thought we were going to tumble out of the back of the van and onto the ground, but instead I felt only a rough bump.

The loading dock, I realized as I did my best to relax again.

"Close your eyes and go limp," Brian said very softly in my ear. "Someone could open the bin to check at any time."

Right. Play tranqed. I obediently closed my eyes and went as limp as possible. It helped that Brian had moved the gun.

I heard a jingle of keys followed by a beep and a door opening. Andrew using his fob to activate the latch, I decided.

The cart moved through the door. "Morning, Ferguson," Andrew said after a moment, as if he'd simply been out for a stroll— plausible since we figured that only Nicole and her Special Security Team would know Andrew was missing. After all, the bastards didn't want cops snooping around.

"Morning, Mr. Saber."

Another set of doors, a long roll, then the beep and ding of an elevator. Bump-bump going in, then silence while the car descended. According to Andrew, they'd converted old maintenance offices into a temporary holding area. Nothing fancy, but serviceable—a secure door to a corridor with a half dozen rooms, and a closed camera system to monitor a few makeshift cells.

"I'll take care of the retina scan, Gentry," Andrew said as the elevator doors opened.

"Yes, sir."

I kept my eyes closed, barely daring to breathe as the cart moved. Things beeped, and a heavy door swung open with a slow metallic creak. I heard a scrape of metal on plastic, then a *pop* that was Pierce jamming the latch to make sure we couldn't be locked in, and I only knew that because he'd told me he was going to do so.

A couple of seconds later we passed through. The air smelled different in here, antiseptic and rotten, along with something else that made my hair stand on end.

"Mr. Saber! Gentry!" A scrape of boot on linoleum was most likely a guard near the door. "I didn't know you'd returned."

"Now you know," Pierce replied, tone hard and clipped. "Has the older Ivanov specimen been recaptured?"

"Not yet," the guard replied. "No fucking leads either."

"Are Marcus Ivanov and," disgust filled Pierce's voice, "*Griffin* secure?"

"Locked down tight." The guard gave a sharp and nasty laugh. "Griffin's been getting a lesson in loyalty. Ms. Saber's orders. And, with the Dallas lab tech here, it's been pretty entertaining."

Brian tensed behind me while I trembled. Holy shit, did I ever want to leap out of the bin and tear off the ugly smile I heard in this guard's voice.

"I have two more," Pierce said with a note of triumph. I forced myself limp again as he pulled the hinged bin lid up and let it fall open with a loud plastic clatter. "Crawford and Archer. But we have a change of plans. We're moving them all out of here. With Pietro Ivanov on the loose, and no clue how he got out, we can't risk him returning to free Griffin and his nephew. Mr. Saber, you can arrange the plane to Dallas?"

Andrew cleared his throat. "Yes. Of course."

"Thank you, sir," Pierce said and pushed the cart farther along. "I'll check the condition of the specimens and prepare them to move."

"After yesterday's bullshit in the conference room, this one got his arms broken and no brains," a different guard said as the cart came to a stop. I carefully opened my eyes a thin crack and peered through my lashes, relieved that it was enough to allow me to see nearby people over the lip of the dumpster. A brawny, bald guard stood in front of Pierce. "He's chained up now, and a rotting mess," he added without a trace of compassion in his voice as he nodded toward the door beside him. "Griffin's another story." His smile widened, cruel and vicious. "The tech tested some new shit on him that supposedly keeps them aware *and* slows the rot when they get injured and hungry. It worked like a fucking charm."

Brian's hand curled into a fist against my back. I bit the inside of my cheek, quivering with rage.

A small frown crossed Andrew's face. "I hope my mother is taking care not to do irreparable damage. They're useless as test subjects if they become unstable, like Philip Reinhardt."

I held back a growl with effort. *Fuck you too, Andy.*

"Bring out whatever brains we have left," Pierce ordered. "We're going to need to get them into shape to move."

"Yes, sir."

As the guard stepped out of my thin field of vision, Pierce dropped a quick glance down and gave us a very slight *Not Yet* head shake. I fought to look limp and tranqed, and focused on running through the plan in my head. At Brian's signal I was to leap out with him right behind me, then he'd get through the door, mod up, and kick some serious ass. The effect of the mods didn't last very long, so activating it before the time was right would only waste it.

The bald guard returned with a Ziploc freezer bag, presumably containing brains. He handed it to Pierce then turned at the sound of the entrance door swinging open.

"Yes, ma'am." It was the head of security, Thea Braddock, and it sounded as if she was talking on the phone. "I'd just gone off duty when I heard. I came back to check it out." A pause. "Crawford and Archer, or so I've just been told, ma'am," she continued. "I'll call you back as soon as I know more."

Shit shit shit shit. She was on the phone with Nicole Fucking Saber.

Approaching footsteps. "Good to have you back safe and sound, Mr. Saber," Braddock said, sounding genuinely pleased that he'd returned. "Gentry? You're the one who got him back?"

Pierce offered a tight-lipped smile. Having Braddock show up complicated things that much more. "Yes, ma'am. And took down these two as well," he said, flicking fingers toward us. "Lost Reinhardt and Comtesse though."

Braddock peered into the bin and gave a low whistle of appreciation. She wore an emerald green hoody, a bag strap over one shoulder, and a hospital-blue sling supporting the arm Philip had injured. "Solid work, Gentry," she said. "I need to call Ms. Saber back and let her know it's confirmed. She's on her way in now."

"Leave off calling her for the moment, please, Thea," Andrew put in quickly. "With Pietro Ivanov in the wind, we can't risk staying in New York. This section wasn't meant to be anything more than a temporary holding place for specimens." He made a noise of aggravation. "I'm shocked the other two haven't escaped as well, considering how quickly this floor was refitted for this purpose. We're moving the lot to the airport for transfer to Dallas. No one escapes from there."

Braddock looked briefly pained. "Yes, sir. I understand your concerns regarding the security of this section, but I don't know if Ms. Saber will support that decision."

"She won't," Andrew said tightly. "But it's the right move in order to maintain security. I'll make sure she understands."

Pierce turned away, murmured to Baldy to open the door beside us.

"Yes, sir," Braddock said. "However, I still need to call her with an update."

She wrinkled her nose as a choking wave of rot smell poured out of the open door. A gurgling yowl and the rattling of chains followed it.

Marcus! I stiffened, and only Brian's hand tight on the back of my jacket kept me from leaping up to see him. Braddock's gaze went beyond Andrew and into the room. She took a half step back, face suddenly ashen, and for a second I thought she was going to hurl. Had she never seen Saberton's loving care of zombies?

"Of course I understand she needs to be told," Andrew was saying. "I'm making the call to Dallas to coordinate transport, but it's easier on everyone for me to wait and tell my mother face to face. You know that."

Yes, please, get Nicole in my grasp again, I seethed.

But Braddock wasn't listening to Andrew anymore. She stared into the room, her entire focus locked on its rotting occupant.

"Braddock!" Andrew snapped to get her attention. "Why are you down here anyway? You shouldn't be in this far." It was obvious he wasn't at all happy that Thea Braddock was witness to what happened behind these closed doors.

"No, sir. I mean, yes, sir," she replied, voice taut. "I had to come down when I heard the report that you were back."

"You know my mother," he said. "You *do* understand that it's best I inform her of this move in person, yes?"

She didn't immediately answer. Her gaze tracked from the doorway, down to Brian and me, then back to Andrew. "Yes, sir. I do," she finally said. The unspoken "but" hung between them. She had questions. Her instincts told her something was seriously off. Maybe she was wondering why Pierce or Andrew hadn't called ahead to let them know they were coming in with prisoners. Or maybe Pierce's mannerisms didn't match the Pierce Gentry she knew. Whatever it was, the seed of suspicion was getting a whole lot of fertilizer.

"I respect your opinion, sir," Braddock said as she took a step back and out of my view. "But it's my duty to notify Ms. Saber." I heard the soft beep of a phone.

I didn't need Brian's quick double-hand squeeze to let me know it was time to move. Baring my teeth in a snarl, I surged up and vaulted out, though far less gracefully than I'd hoped, which turned my dash to Marcus's door into more of a stagger. Brian was right on my heels, but none of us had considered the instability of the bin. Brian's weight had stabilized it for my exit, but he didn't have that advantage. The instant he came over the side the whole thing tipped to throw him off balance, then slammed back to the floor as his weight shifted off it.

Brian recovered in a zombie-speed flash, but Braddock had solid instincts and damn good reflexes. She had her gun half out of her purse even as the dumpster slammed back down. No doubt realizing Brian was the bigger threat—and apparently well aware it was pointless to tell a zombie, "Stop or I'll shoot!"—she brought bag and all to bear on him and fired twice.

I yelped and ducked as the sound of the gunshots slammed through the corridor. Brian staggered back against the wall as both rounds hit him center chest. Fortunately for him, that was the best place to get hit, considering his body armor, though I had to give an instant of mad respect for Braddock's shooting skill, especially with the purse in the way.

"Angel! Take care of Marcus!" Pierce tossed me the bag of brains, and the instant it left his hands he pulled a knife, spun, and sliced Baldy's throat open in a spray of blood.

As I caught the bag, the guard gurgled, clutched at his throat, and crumpled. Braddock got off another shot that seared a line across Pierce's shoulder, but he retaliated with zombie speed and stepped into a vicious side kick directly on her injured arm. She let out a choked cry as she crashed back into a partially open door then tumbled out of sight into an unlit room.

Down the corridor past Brian, the first guard grabbed his tranq gun and pointed it our way. I heard a dart skitter off the wall as I turned toward Marcus's open cell door. The guard fired again, and I distantly heard the *thuk* sound of a dart hitting flesh and Brian's grunt of pain. On my other side, as if from far away, I heard Andrew curse then saw him bolt toward the opposite end of the corridor and the exit door. But the instant I took in the sight of Marcus every-thing else seemed to retreat.

Marcus stood chained to the wall like a storybook ogre—naked, shackles at wrists, ankles, neck, and another chain wrapped around his waist. His arms were bent at odd angles and seemed to have too many joints. Rotted flesh peeled away from bones where the chains bit into him, and black blood dripped from a deep gash in his thigh. His breath came in ugly, wet rattles, and drool streamed from the corner of his mouth to string over his chest.

Eyes wild with hunger, he lunged at me a with wailing scream that sliced right through my core, then slammed to an ugly, flesh-shredding stop at the limit of his chains.

"Angel. Angel!" That was Pierce. "Get Andrew!" he shouted as he sprang toward the tranq wielding guard.

Cursing, I tossed the open bag of brains to Marcus, pausing only long enough to make sure he caught it before I pushed off into a sprint to chase down Andrew. Behind me I heard Marcus's growl and the *squish slurp* of him devouring brains.

I tackled Andrew before he made it to the door, then hauled him right back up with the idea of using him as a handy dandy human shield. Pierce dropped the other guard and turned our way, even as Braddock emerged from the room and ran at me, gun in hand and face twisted in pain and determination. A stupid little squeal slipped out of me at the sight of the security chief charging in my direction, and I thrust Andrew at her as hard as I could.

Braddock caught Andrew and staggered back a couple of steps which gave me all the time I needed to dash past her. She lifted her gun again, but I dodged to the other side of the blue mini-dumpster and shoved it at her to knock her off balance.

"I have this," Pierce said as Andrew went sprawling. "Check on Kyle." He gestured to the next door as he slapped our last three brain packets into my hand, then shifted his attention to Braddock and Andrew.

Hands shaking from adrenaline, I yanked a blood-drenched ring of keys from Baldy's belt and got Kyle's door open. I steeled my-self for a sight similar to Marcus: broken, twisted, rotting, mindless, and slavering—

It was a thousand times worse.

Head lowered, Kyle crouched against the wall, naked and cov-ered with areas of deep rot that showed bone and organs in places. Only one chain around his waist held him, and it took me a hideous second to process that his wrists weren't shackled because his hands had been cut off. He lifted his head, eyes full of fury and agony, and I received a second vicious shock as I saw what was left of his face. No lower jaw or tongue—nothing but a gaping and ragged hole. He breathed in wet gurgles, blood bubbling from his throat with each exhalation.

My reeling mind fought to make sense of the scene before me. With that much rot Kyle should've been mindless and hunger-crazed, yet his eyes reflected full awareness of me and his agony.

Realization shot through me. *The new drug.* The first guard said they'd used a new drug on him that slowed rot and kept him aware.

Kyle's gaze tore from mine and went to my left. I followed it to where a large metal bowl containing red and brown lumps rested in the corner.

No. Containing his hands and jaw and tongue.

A white hot scream of rage tore from my throat. I grabbed the bowl and ran to him. "Fuck. Fuck them. These fucking assholes." I seized the severed jaw first, ripped open a packet with my teeth. No way would three packets—or even all the brains we had with us—be enough to fix this. "Oh, Jesus fuck, Kyle." He wouldn't be able to eat the brains properly, I realized, and so I squeezed the paste out onto the exposed flesh of the jaw, then set it against his face as best I could. "Hold still," I said as a heavy shudder went through him, but once it passed he held himself motionless, eyes blazing with hatred and anger that I knew wasn't directed at me. My hands shook as I squeezed the rest of that packet and a second one into his mouth and throat, but fortunately the parasite seemed to know its business. Within seconds the jaw shifted in my hands as the tendons and muscle began to knit together to pull the bone into place.

As soon as I knew his jaw wouldn't fall off, I grabbed up one of his hands, ripped open the third packet and squeezed more brain paste out onto the stump of his forearm and the severed hand. I caught myself right before sticking the right hand onto the left arm. That would've been a bit embarrassing. I hurriedly grabbed up the other, brain-pasted it, and put left hand to left arm then flicked a glance up to his face. To my relief his jaw continued to adjust and knit back in place, though it sagged open still.

"I'll be right back," I said once I knew his hands weren't going to fall off. I darted out of the cell in time to see Andrew face down on the floor with his wrists zip-tied behind him, and Pierce bodily shoving Braddock into the room next to Marcus's.

"Remember that and come over to the dark side sometime," Pierce said to the security chief as he slammed the door closed and locked it. I didn't waste time trying to figure out what that was supposed to mean and instead grabbed the lunch box of brains from the bin and raced back into Kyle's room.

His hands and jaw hadn't fallen off in the few seconds I was gone, but he let out a heart-wrenching cry of pain. I bit off a corner of the baggie and squeezed diced brains into his mouth, relieved to see his tongue move sluggishly to help him swallow, though his hands didn't seem to be functioning yet.

From the corridor, I heard the crackle of a radio.

"Rutledge," said a voice I recognized as Edwards. *"What's your status down there?"*

"Mr. Saber and Gentry are in with the guests," Pierce answered in a gruff voice convincingly close enough to Baldy's to send a shiver through me.

"Davis and Gordon are running late, but should be here in five. You got anywhere you need to be?"

"I'm good. Checking new guests into the hotel. I'd pay for the privilege."

"Roger that. I'll be down to tuck them in later."

Kyle shifted. "Hate . . . them," he gurgled, deep anger boiling in his eyes.

"You and me both, dude," I muttered, hands shaking with my own fury. While he swallowed brains, I tried keys from the guard's ring until I found the one that opened the padlock on the chain.

I turned sharply at a clatter behind me. It was Pierce, pushing the mini-dumpster through the door. His eyes flicked from Kyle's jaw to his hands to the bloody bowl, and rage tightened his face as he drew the correct conclusion.

Kyle sucked in a wet breath at the sight of Pierce. "An . . . gel." Even through the gurgle I heard the alarm and warning in his voice.

Oh, right, he didn't know about Pietro/Pierce. "It's okay," I assured Kyle. "He's an ally. I promise. I'll explain later, but right now we need to get the fuck out of here."

Kyle growled low but didn't resist when Pierce slid his arms beneath him, lifted him gently and placed him in the bin with the tranqed Brian and messed up Marcus. I peered in, disturbed to see Marcus lying with his head lolling and eyes glassy. After eating the bag of brains he should have been better off, more responsive. "Marcus?"

Pierce answered instead. "He was coming out of the hunger craze then went down. Most likely due to whatever they drugged him with earlier." He placed a hand on Marcus's shoulder. "He seems stable for now."

"Stable" didn't do much to ease my worry.

The radio crackled again.

"Jenkins. Ms. Saber just got here and says she can't get Mr. Saber, Ms. Braddock, or Gentry via phone. Who's still down there with you?"

Pierce shook his head. "Can't fake Jenkins. We're out of time."

"Jenkins, do you copy?" A pause. *"Rutledge."* Another pause. *"Gentry."*

"Best for me not to answer. That way I can *surprise* them."

"How many more guards are between us and The Fuck Out Of Here?" I asked Pierce.

"Eleven to fourteen if they stick with the Special Security Team," he said grimly as he pushed the bin into the hallway and started down the corridor toward the exit. "Grab him," he angled his head toward Andrew, "and then we can get out of this deathtrap area, collect the package, and reassess."

"Package?" I gave him a puzzled look.

He tapped his chest and gave me a knowing look. *Oh. Gentry's body. The* original *Gentry, the one now missing a brain.*

I hauled Andrew up to his feet. "You promised to let me go," he said with an accusing glare at Pierce.

"You promised to see this through, and last thing I remember is you bolting," Pierce said. "Now would be a bad time to get me thinking about altering the terms of our agreement."

Andrew fell silent and didn't resist as I hustled him after Pierce. As soon as we were past the security door, Pierce and I both breathed a sigh of relief. Even though we still had a long way to go, being pinned in the Torture Zone would've been the worst case scenario.

A bank of overly bright fluorescent lights lit the concrete-walled area beyond the door. It was as if they'd tried—and failed miserably—to create a sense of sunlight underground. I turned a quick circle to get my bearings and found no noteworthy features other than an elevator and four doors: the one we'd come through, one marked Maintenance, one marked Electrical Room, and the stairwell.

Pierce called the elevator then blocked the doors open with the bin when it arrived. I sat Andrew down in front of the bin and gave him a *Don't you fucking dare move* look.

"Stairwell door," I said, "Need to block it too."

Pierce frowned. "I'll dismantle the lock on this side. That should slow them down a few minutes, at least." He dug a big screwdriver out of the bin and proceeded to destroy the lock control panel, then leaned into the elevator as if listening.

"Got any change?" I asked as I scowled at the stairwell door. "Coins, I mean."

He looked at me blankly, then nodded in understanding. He quickly rifled through Andrew's pockets, and came up with enough coins for me to penny the door. A couple of stacks of coins wedged high and low between the door and frame would jam it shut. In theory at least. It was a long shot, but it had sure as hell worked on Sissy Collard's bathroom door during a junior high prank involving a big ass spider in the sink and a rubber snake by the toilet.

"Good thinking, Angel," Pierce said with an approving nod as I prepped the coins. "I'll get the package." He lifted the lid of the mini-dumpster, reached in, and pulled out the body bag, then headed toward the door marked Maintenance. "Back in a minute."

"Got it," I said, and by the time the coins were wedged in place Pierce was back, with the loaded bag slung over his shoulder.

Andrew stared. "Who the fuck is that?"

I ignored him and peered into the bin. "Hey guys, got a body coming in. Sorry." Kyle shifted to sit up and gave me a weak nod. He'd made an effort to pull the blanket over his crotch, but his hands were still too weak to untangle the blanket from the tools and bodies. Keeping my expression even and clinical, I reached in and tugged the blanket up for him. I couldn't do much else for him, but I could at least give him a little fucking dignity. Marcus groaned, stacked on top of the still-tranqed Brian. Worried, I stroked a hand over his hair, then helped Pierce get everyone rearranged, with the corpse at the bottom beneath Kyle.

"We only have one way out," I said to Pierce after we closed the dumpster lid. My heart pounded as the weight of the situation hit me. "We lost Brian, and we can't just walk out with Andrew now."

"They still don't know what they're dealing with." He turned intense, calm eyes on me. "For now, we wait. A team will be on the way to check out why no one's responding. They'll run into a stuck elevator and blocked stairwell and realize shit's fucked up. Based on how they respond, we make our plan. They're fucked if they try one at a time through the elevator hatch. Stairwell is a better option, but ambush outside the elevator upstairs is what I'd do."

Oh, great. Ambush. That made me feel SO much better.

A dull thud and muffled voices came from the stairwell door. I spun to face it, tense, and twitched at another thud.

"It's holding for now," Pierce said from behind me.

A face appeared in the little window in the door, then the man's eyes widened, and he ducked down. More muffled voices.

I glanced back to see Pierce lowering the gun he'd pointed at the window. "*Now* they know what they're dealing with," he said as he pulled out his phone. How the hell could he be so calm? "We have a few minutes while they scramble," he continued. "I'll call Dr. Nikas to give a sit rep."

I gave him a blank look. "A what?"

"Situation report," he clarified. "Dr. Nikas and Reinhardt need to know our status and might have some new info."

"Oh, right, gotcha." I moved over to the sullen-faced Andrew and crouched just inside his personal space. "Did you see what they did to Kyle?"

A muscle in his jaw twitched, and he gave me a slight nod. He didn't look away, though a faint flush of what I sure fucking hoped was shame crept up his neck. Behind me I caught bits and pieces of Pierce's conversation with Dr. Nikas.

"No, he's out. Tranqed . . . No antidote that I could find . . . Right. Got it . . . Marcus is barely under control, and I think they gave him something as well. Weaker than he should be . . . No, Brian never got to use it . . . Right. All three syringes should still be on him . . . Yes, of course . . . No, it would take too long for him to get here . . . Griffin . . . Griffin's in very bad shape."

I kept my gaze locked on Andrew. "You're okay with that sort of thing?"

His flush continued to rise, but along with it came that damn defensive wall I'd seen before. He lifted his chin arrogantly. "It was a foolish move, given the circumstances."

"A foolish move," I repeated, almost as disgusted by his need to be superior as by his choice of words. Behind him I saw the lid of the bin lift and an arm snake out, a red line around the wrist that had yet to fully heal. The fingers moved in jerks, still not fully functional, but they worked well enough to grip Andrew's hair.

I kept my face impassive as Andrew let out a strangled cry of horror and tried to scramble to his feet.

"Fooooolish," Kyle rasped, using his hold on Andrew as leverage to haul himself up and partially out of the bin. Andrew twisted, squealing like a kid in a carnival haunted house, but with his hands secured behind him he couldn't pull free. I stood and shifted back a couple of feet to avoid getting kicked by Andrew's scrabbling feet, and bit my tongue to keep from laughing.

"Foooolish," Kyle breathed, wet and burbly, and pulled his face close to Andrew's. His stench rolled over me as blood and ichor dripped from his mouth and onto Andrew's neck. "I . . . am feeling . . . foolish." He shifted closer, and Andrew screamed. I almost felt sorry for Andrew, since this had to seem like a scene from a horror movie. Almost sorry. Okay, not really.

Then again, in the next instant, I saw he had a real reason to scream. Kyle had his teeth clamped on Andrew's ear and probably the only reason he hadn't bitten it off yet was the weakness of his jaw.

"Kyle, he's Naomi's brother," I said mildly. "Take it easy, for her sake."

Kyle loosened the bite, and I noted that the top half of Andrew's ear already hung oddly and dribbled blood. "No promises," he growled, but he released Andrew with a shove before flopping back into the bin.

Pierce hung up behind me. If he'd noticed the altercation, he'd seen no reason to intervene. "I'll get the mod syringes off Brian." As he spoke he pulled a second phone from his pocket. "Mine," he said as he handed it to me, and I realized he meant Gentry's. "Try calling Saber. Stall her or make a deal for *him*." He gestured toward Andrew without looking at him. "Do what you can."

"Got it." I turned on the phone then started scrolling through Gentry's contacts, somewhat surprised that there were only a dozen or so and none for Nicole Saber. I opened my mouth to ask Andrew for his mother's number, then closed it as I saw a contact with the name CEOILF.

CEO I'd Like to Fuck? No way.

I quickly checked the text messages between Gentry and CEOILF. "Ohhhhhh myyyyyy godddddddddd!"

Pierce turned sharply, in the process of lifting the still unconscious Brian. "What? What's wrong?"

"Dude! You were banging Nicole!"

Andrew jerked in shock. "*What?*"

Pierce almost dropped Brian back into the bin, denial in his eyes before he remembered he had to play Gentry in front of Andrew. He nodded once, tense. "Right. More info that way," he said, improvising quickly. "And she was hot for it."

Grinning, I skimmed through the texts, then checked Gentry's pics on a whim. "Oh, dude! Pics and all! In the front lobby?" I looked back up at Pierce. "You animal!"

"Just doing my job." He gave me an exasperated glare that Andrew couldn't see and continued to search Brian for the syringes. Andrew simply looked horrified.

I was more than happy to twist this particular knife, especially since the taunting was a healthier way to channel my anger and fear than, say, punching him in the nose. "Oh, snap! A crotch shot!" I crowed to Andrew. "You came out of there!" His mouth worked soundlessly, flush deepening to crimson.

"Angel," Pierce growled softly.

"Oh, right. The call. Sorry." I'd give Pierce shit later about how his persona's penis had been in Nicole Saber.

I returned to the contact list and dialed her number. Time to channel some more stress and worry into a bit of trash-talking. Luckily, I was damn good at that sort of thing.

She picked up on the second ring. "Pierce. You fucking asshole. What the *hell* is going on?"

Sounded like she'd heard the news Gentry had switched sides, and was appropriately freaked that her loverboy had duped her. Good. As much as I wanted to fuck with Andrew for not opposing the shit Kyle and Marcus went through, I wanted Nicole to fucking *suffer* for being responsible for it in the first place. "Nikki, darling!" I trilled. "It's been so long, sweetie. We have *got* to get together for coffee someday soon!" I began to gloat about the naughty pics, then stopped. I'd save those for a special occasion.

"Crawford." She snarled my name, managing to pack disdain and disgust into the one word. "What do you want?"

"Ooh! A pony? I've always wanted a pony!" I gushed, getting into the spirit of it. "Or, if I can't have that, then maybe you can clear a passage for us, and in return I won't eat your darlin' son's brain." I covered the mouthpiece and spoke in a stage whisper to Andrew, "Don't worry, I won't eat your brain." I paused and grinned. "I'll let *Kyle* eat it!"

He glared but cast a fear-filled glance toward the bin. His bitten ear still trickled blood down the side of his neck.

Nicole remained quiet for a moment. "Agreed," she finally said with icy calm. "Bring him up, and we'll escort you out."

"What about my pony?" I asked brightly. Since she had zero reason to believe otherwise, Nicole surely assumed that Gentry-the-traitor was human. She thought she was dealing "only" with zombie-me and human-Gentry. Not to mention, she figured we'd be dragging butt as we wrangled a bunch of out-of-commission zombies.

"You'll have to wait on that one," she replied, voice still cool though a bit stiff.

"Darn it! Santa says the same thing." I heaved a tragic sigh.

"Thing is, Nikki, honey, I don't have a lot of faith that you're really going to let us out of here."

Pierce straightened with what looked like a slim waist pack in his hand, then got all three zombies arranged in the bin as comfortably as possible before he closed the lid.

"I can't afford to lose Andrew," Nicole replied, loading her voice with resignation and a touch of anger. "I'll play your game."

She was a good manipulator, but I had her pegged. I covered the mouthpiece again. "Hey, Andy, she says she can't afford to lose you. Am I correct in assuming she's full of shit?"

He lifted his eyes to mine, and I saw behind his wall of arrogance, to the pain and despair that came with being a pawn in a brutal game. *Welcome to the fucking club,* I thought.

"She can't afford to lose me," he said. "But right now she can't afford to lose you people even more." He let out a shaky breath, eyes bleak. "She'd rather win with me dead than lose with me alive."

In that moment I actually felt a glimmer of sympathy toward him. To survive, he had no choice but to accept enemies as allies.

"Sorry, dude," I said quietly, meaning it. I uncovered the phone. "Hey, Nikki, honey, about this whole playing-my-game thing. See, I think you're chock full of shit. And Botox too."

"You little piece of worthless trash," she hissed. "Bring Andrew up, and you go free. Otherwise, you'll force me to take radical action."

"Hey, can my pony be white with brown spots?" I asked, but she'd already hung up on me. I *tsked.* "Jeez, rude much?"

"Angel, I have the mods," Pierce said.

I closed the phone and stuffed it into a pocket. "Cool. You need me to help you inject them?"

He shook his head. "I can't use them. They're not designed for my . . .mature physiology." He lifted the waist pack he'd pulled from Brian. "But you can."

I blinked stupidly at him. "I don't have a port."

"There weren't any ports when we first began using mods," he told me. "It'll be a raw surge, and it won't last as long, but it will work."

"But . . ." I gulped. "I'm not a trained soldier operative martial artist ninja. I'm a scrawny lightweight. What the hell will this SuperMod do for me? Make me snarkier?"

A thud from the top of the elevator pulled our attention. Scowling, I jumped atop the bin, reached up and banged my fist on the emergency hatch. "BACK OFF, ASSHOLE," I yelled. "I'M HUNGRY, AND YOU'RE ABOUT TO BE MY HAPPY MEAL!"

Silence reigned. Satisfied, I jumped back off the bin and returned to where Pierce regarded me with a bemused look on his face. "Okay, fine, so I get turbocharged. How does this work without a port? Do I eat it?"

"Stomach acid would destroy it," Pierce said. "For maximum effectiveness, it needs to be injected directly into the abdominal cavity." He pulled a folding knife and flicked it open. "It's similar to what you did to yourself when you stored brain reserves in your abdomen."

"Great," I said with a grimace. When my dad had been taken hostage I'd traded myself for him, but my ace in the hole had been brains packed in sausage casings and stuffed into my gut. "That shit was *loads* of fun."

"It will be a much smaller cut," he promised.

"You're giving me this mod so I can take out any guards we run into, right?" *Take out*. Nicer and easier way to say *kill*. A shiver crawled through me.

His eyes met mine. "Yes," he said with an evenness that told me he understood my angst and didn't find it odd or misplaced. "War isn't pretty. Ever. Nicole Saber has declared war on our kind and will move heaven and earth to keep us from making good our escape. Her Special Security Team will be well armed and, with only two of us functional, we'll need as much speed and strength as possible."

"Wouldn't using guns be better than jumping their asses?"

"Guns have their place," he said, "but in some situations, especially close quarters, we waste our zombie edge if we stand off and shoot. We can take damage humans can't, which gives us a psychological advantage when we're in their face, kicking ass despite their weapons."

"Got it," I said, grateful that he'd bothered to talk this out with me. Then again, this probably wasn't the first time he'd given a soldier a pep talk right before a pitched battle.

A scrape of metal made us both look toward the stairwell again. "Shit," I said. "They're trying to flush us. Let's fucking oblige and get this done."

"Lift your shirt," he instructed, then went on one knee before me as I obeyed "I'll make the cut and insert the syringe but won't inject. Once you press the plunger, it'll take a few seconds to kick in, then you'll have two to three minutes at the most before you lose the effect." He glanced up at me. "It'll probably be best to hit the mod right before the elevator stops."

I licked dry lips. "Sure thing. Sounds like a great plan."

"Put the other mods in your pocket," he said as opened the waist pack. Within it were three enormous stainless steel syringes, much like the kind used to marinate meat and hefty enough to deliver a load of the thick SuperMod goop. I took two and dropped them into the side pocket of my pants, heart already beginning to race in anticipation and dread. "Once I've made the cut I'll give you the knife so that you can administer the other doses if needed."

"Got it. I'm totally ready," I lied.

Either he believed me or it didn't matter to him. He set the point of the knife halfway between my belly button and my sternum then, without a lick of warning, drove the two-inch blade in to the hilt. I gasped and stiffened at the sharp burn of pain, then clenched my teeth as he pulled the knife to make the gash wider.

"Almost there," he murmured. He removed the knife and slipped the first syringe into the gash until only half its length and the plunger protruded. "Hold that there."

As soon as I had it, Pierce moved to Andrew and hauled him to his feet.

"I'm cutting the zipties," he growled, "but if you *fuck* with me again or try to run, our agreement is null, and your ass is mine. Understood?"

Andrew gave a tight nod. "Understood."

Pierce pulled a much larger knife from a sheath on his belt—the same knife he'd used to kill the two guards in the holding area. "Good deal. I suggest you take cover behind the bin when the shooting starts."

Andrew paled, but he nodded again.

Pierce lifted his chin. "Let's roll."

Chapter 33

We pushed the bin fully into the elevator and readied ourselves to fight our way out. The metal syringe buried in my gut felt like ice in my fingers, and I forced myself to breathe deeply and keep my hand steady.

"We're going up one floor and then out," Pierce said in a low voice, holding the door until Andrew could hunker behind the bin, and I could crouch on top. "No other choice since this elevator only goes between these two basement floors." His mouth twisted in annoyance. "She'll have her team waiting for us, but the one possible bright spot is that there are probably only a dozen or so left."

"Only a dozen." I laughed weakly. "Awesome."

He nodded toward the syringe in my hand as the elevator began to rise. "Show time."

"Right." The word came out as a squeak. I cleared my throat and tried again. "Right," I said, then took a deep breath and pressed the plunger.

I felt nothing for a second. And another. And—

"Oh, sweet Jesus," I gasped. Warmth raced through me as if every neuron in my body was waking up for the first time. My vision snapped into razor sharp focus, colors intensified, and every noise grew distinct. The thud of Andrew's pulse. The hiss of Pierce's breath. A shift of flesh in the bin beneath me. The scrape of fabric against metal above me, and a bolt sliding back. I jerked my eyes up to the outline of the service hatch, and my lips pulled back from my teeth. "Zombie Super Powers, *Activate*," I breathed.

I surged up from the crouch and slammed the palm of my hand

into the hatch. It flew open and smacked the unlucky security guard in the chin on the way, giving me a split second of advantage, which I seized along with his collar. He scrabbled for purchase, but gravity remained on my side as I used my weight to pull him down through the hatch and to the floor. Also on my side was the sudden stop when I smacked his head into the corner of the bin, and it took only two more Angel-assisted skull-meets-industrial-plastic blows to split it. I dug my fingers in and ripped his head open like a kid tearing into a Christmas present, yanked the brain out of its nice warm home, then lifted the lid of the bin and dropped the brain in.

"Breakfast in bed, y'all!"

Pierce's eyes rested on me as I resumed my perch on top of the bin, but he seemed to approve of my actions. He turned toward the door as the elevator stopped, grip tightening on the knife in his right hand. Muted growls and wet sounds of slavering came from within the dumpster, and I smiled. Hungry zombies were hungry.

"He had this," Andrew said.

I looked down to see him still cowering behind the bin, his face flecked with blood from the guy who turned into breakfast. In one hand Andrew held a canister about five inches long, with a pin still in place. Smoke bomb or tear gas, I figured. Maybe a flash bang. Whatever it was, I'd stopped the bad guy before he had the chance to use it. One point for Angel.

"Thanks." I plucked the thing from Andrew's grasp and handed it off to Pierce, then focused on the elevator door. My blood hummed through my veins, and the scent of the men outside coiled through the widening opening.

"Six," Pierce murmured, but I was already in motion. I leaped from the bin, pushed off the right side of the elevator door to launch myself at the first guard on the left. He tried to shift the aim of his tranq gun, but I grabbed his head and snapped his neck before his finger could tighten on the trigger. Beside me, Pierce moved quickly to bury his knife in the chest of a guard. He wrenched the blade up and threw the man aside as my guy dropped. A blond man with a scraggly soul patch fired a real gun at me but the bullet simply grazed my hip. I leaped forward and snapped a kick hard into his knee, spun and smashed my elbow into his face, wrenched the gun from his hand, then spun back again to ram the butt of it into the throat of a third man.

I held back a manic laugh. No way would I be able to pull off these moves without the mod. Everyone seemed to move so *slowly*. Taking them out was like dancing through people trapped in mud.

Pierce broke the wrist of another guard even as a round took him in the thigh. Unfazed, he slashed his knife across the shooter's throat. The last standing guard brought a tranq gun to bear on Pierce, but I dove at him, grabbed him by the face and smashed the back of his head into the wall. He slumped to the floor, leaving a trail of blood on the cinderblock.

I swung around to deal with the next opponent, only to see that there wasn't one. Six guards littered the floor, at least three quite dead, with the others definitely not posing a threat anymore.

Pierce cleaned his knife on the shirt of one of the guards, straightened and slid it back into its sheath.

"Good work, Angel." He gave a nod of fierce satisfaction as he surveyed the carnage, then pulled Gentry's radio from his belt and flipped through frequencies.

My skin prickled, and I clenched and unclenched my hands. I'd come down off enough highs to know I didn't have much longer as a superzombiebadass. I pivoted to the guy whose head I'd smashed into the wall, gripped him by the face again, cracked his skull open and scooped out his brain. I repeated this with the other two dead guards, then split one brain in half, handed one chunk to Pierce, then took the other two full brains back to the elevator. Andrew had pushed the bin forward to block the elevator door, and now sat slumped against the back of the car, eyes slightly glazed. I gave him a grin, then lifted the lid and chucked in the two full brains. Kyle lay curled on his side atop the body bag. He growled and awkwardly pulled one of the brains to him with his forearms. Brian stirred sluggishly, still heavily under the effect of the tranq. Marcus groaned and shifted but didn't look up.

My elation shifted to worry. "Marcus?"

"Still out," Kyle mumbled through a mouthful of brains. He swallowed awkwardly with his screwed up jaw and tongue, then bit off a piece of brain, spat it into his hand and stuffed it into Marcus's mouth. "You take care . . . business out there," he slurred. "I'll take . . . care of business . . . here."

I released a shaky breath. "Thanks." Frustration clawed at me despite his encouragement. Marcus and Kyle still had Saberton's experimental drugs in their systems, and I didn't have a clue how to counter it or help them get back to full strength. *More brains can't hurt*, I told myself. *And I'm doing everything I can to get us out of here.* That's how I'd help them. Take care of business, just like Kyle said, and get them to Dr. Nikas.

I closed the lid then crouched against the wall beyond the elevator to wolf down the remaining brain half. My hands trembled, and a slight queasiness wanted to push back against the brains I swallowed down. Yep, definitely coming down off that incredible high. Damn it.

"You doing all right?" Pierce asked. He bit off a chunk of brain, watching me carefully.

Wiping my mouth with the back of my hand, I nodded. "Yeah. Hard crash though. Need a minute."

He finished his brain and didn't bother wiping his mouth. "There'll likely be another team waiting past the next door. We need to move quickly before they realize we've taken these guys completely out."

I scarfed down the rest of the brain and got to my feet. Now I was the one who felt stuck in mud, though my little snack helped a bit.

A dart whizzed past my ear. "Angel, get back!" Pierce shouted in the same instant. I flattened myself against the wall behind the corner as Pierce dove into the elevator and took cover by the number panel. "Three," he told me, pointing down the hall. Guess they decided not to wait for us.

Well, I sure as hell wasn't going to wait for them to come to us, not in my current non-badass condition. The sound of approaching footsteps spurred me faster as I yanked the knife and another syringe from my pocket. Pierce hissed "too soon" at me, but I ignored him. If I didn't do it now it would be too late.

I jabbed the knife into my gut, eerily amazed that I'd reached a point where I could do so with relative ease. Shouts and more footsteps grew louder as I shoved the syringe in and pressed the plunger.

3 . . . 2 . . . 1 . . .

Delicious fire raced through my veins, and when the first man came close I stepped around the corner, grabbed his shotgun and slammed it up and into his face. As he staggered back I wrenched the gun from his hands, then swung the butt to clock the guy beside him in the temple and drop him like a stone. Something punched me in the side, and I swung around to see a third guard, a woman, still a good twenty feet away down the corridor. Fire leaped from the muzzle of the gun in her hand. I staggered back a step as the round smacked me in my thigh, but before I could shift my weight to charge her, her head snapped back in time with the sound of another gunshot, and she went down with a neat hole in the center of her forehead.

I spared a quick glance back to confirm that yes, it was Pierce's shot that had taken her down, then turned on the one guard still standing—the one whose face I'd slammed with his own shotgun. "Jarvis," or so his name patch read. Blood from his nose mingled with a portwine birthmark that covered the left half of his neck and disappeared under his shirt collar. Eyes wide in shock, he dropped his hands from his nose and jerked them out to his sides in a position of surrender.

"Please. Please don't kill me." His voice shook, high and thin, and his eyes darted around at the dead bodies. He didn't look much older than me, for fuck's sake. How the hell did he get tangled up in this shit?

"Get down on the floor and put your hands behind your back!" I barked at him. Or tried to bark. It came out more like a wheeze as my tanked up parasite dealt with two bullet holes, but he flung himself to the floor and stuck his wrists behind his back.

"Please don't kill me," he repeated, breath coming unevenly.

"Don't give me a reason to," I said as I ziptied his wrists together. "Stay still and be cool, and you'll be fine." Yeah, he was a cold-blooded asshole if he was on the special team, but that didn't mean *I* had to be.

He gulped once and then went as still as a statue.

Pierce approached and made a quick examination of my two healing bullet wounds as the flesh closed. "Hang on," he said, then moved over to the guard he shot, used the shotgun to smash her skull open, pulled the brain out and brought it to me. "Tank up again while you move. We still have to get to the van."

I ripped the brain in half and handed him one piece with a nod toward the bin. Understanding, he slipped the brain under the lid.

Maybe there's something to the whole concept of a zombie soldier after all? I wondered as I ate. Feeding off one's enemies seemed to be working so far.

I was more prepared for the crash when it came this time. As the prickling began I put my hand against the wall and took several deep breaths. An urge to weep filled me as, once again, the world grew dull and normal, and I bit the inside of my cheek to hold it back. The urgency of our situation clawed at me, but it was still several more seconds before I could pull my hand from the wall, leaving a bloody print behind.

I forced my legs to take me over to the elevator, and by the time I'd crossed the ten or so feet, I felt almost not-crappy. I grabbed the bin handle, then saw that Andrew still sat slumped against the back of the elevator.

"You hanging in there, dude?" I pulled the bin out a few feet to give him some room to get up, but to my surprise he shook his head.

"Shot," he said in a shaky voice then pulled his hand away from his side to reveal a red spot the size of a quarter on the left side of his shirt below his ribcage.

"Oh, shit," I breathed and came around the bin to crouch by him and peer at the wound. "How the hell'd you get shot? You stayed down the whole time, didn't you?"

"Yeah." He swallowed then nodded toward the wall and a small divot in the metal. "Ricochet." A one in a million shot had bounced perfectly to hit him.

"Can you walk? Or, um, do you need to ride?" I gestured to the bin with an apologetic wince.

"I can walk," he insisted. He struggled upright, then swayed, paling.

"No, you can't." I seized his right arm and laid it across my shoulders, then grabbed him around the waist. "Pierce, Andrew's hurt. We need to move."

Pierce turned toward us, knife in one hand and gun in the other, bloody and badass and looking as far from Pietro as I could possibly imagine without a sex change. His lips pressed together at the sight of Andrew.

"You need your hands free," he told me. "And he's safest inside the bin."

Andrew blanched and started to protest, which I completely understood since I totally got how being crammed into a rolling dumpster with hungry zombies—who probably didn't like him very much—could be the stuff of nightmares. Unfortunately, his physical state and us getting the hell out of the building took priority over his mental state.

"Sorry, Andy," I said, "but he's right." I flipped the lid up. It was going to be a pretty cozy fit with a fifth person in there, even if one was in a body bag. "Y'all be nice to your guest," I told the three zombies as they blinked up at me. To my relief Marcus was finally focusing on me, and Brian looked as if he had a little movement back. "I'll explain it all later," I added.

Andy continued to babble protests, but I wrestled him in and got the lid closed, then set both hands on the bin, dug my feet in and shoved it forward. Pierce stalked ahead, every inch the predator. I breathed deeply, but there were too many scents of blood and brains and rot for me to tell if there were any humans nearby who still posed a threat. Pierce seemed to be having the same problem to judge by the way he paused every ten feet or so to scent.

We came to a corner and stopped. Pierce listened and sniffed the air before quickly peeking around, then motioned me forward. Twenty feet down the corridor was a set of battered grey metal double doors that I recognized from my first escape from this place. "Déjà fucking vu," I muttered.

"The warehouse is through there, then the parking garage," Pierce murmured, but worry creased his forehead.

"Surely Nicole is out of guards by now?"

"There are still a couple of the Special Team I haven't seen yet," he said, and I realized he'd probably taken great care to memorize the features of every guard he encountered in the holding area. The dark flare of anger in his expression told me he'd paid especially close attention to any who were particularly cruel.

"Are you okay with me leaving that guy tied up back there?" I asked.

Pierce looked past me as if able to see around the corner to where the guard lay. "I wouldn't have left him alive if he'd been one of the more memorable ones," he said. "Though I will say he got off light with the broken nose and a few minutes of terror."

Relief flickered through me. The whole cold-blooded killer thing weighed heavily enough on what little soul I had left. It would've sucked to have my one little mercy taken away. "Is that why you didn't kill the Braddock lady?"

"Thea Braddock is the head of Saberton security but does no direct work with the Special Team's duties," he told me. "She has no final authority over them, and I fully believe she didn't know what went on behind those closed doors. She's a decent person who's on the wrong side."

Decent. That was a good word.

"Come on," he said. "I don't smell anyone out there, but we need to make a move."

Together we eased forward, extending every sense we had. Yet as soon as we passed through the double doors and into the warehouse, we stopped and exchanged a worried look.

"It wasn't locked," I said. "They know we have to come this way. They *want* us to come this way."

His expression darkened as he nodded, but he helped me get the dumpster rolling again, and we continued to the exit. At the door he tested the knob, jaw clenching as it turned easily. *Unlocked. Shit.* He opened the door a crack then scented and listened before pushing it open a foot wider. The van was still there, backed up to the loading dock. The garage was empty and silent, but a sharp edge seemed to vibrate the air.

"It's too quiet," I murmured.

"It's that bitch's last chance to keep us from escaping," he growled. "This garage is a deathtrap. A sniper or two with tranq rifles could likely take us both down." Frustration churned in his eyes as he formed and discarded plans.

I glanced back to make sure no one was sneaking up on us from behind, and something shifted in my pocket as I moved. The phone. Wouldn't do much good to call for help. We didn't exactly have a cavalry standing by—

Sucking in a breath, I shot a hand out to grab Pierce's arm. "Close the door," I said, quivering in excitement. "I have an idea."

He complied, eyebrows lowering as I pulled the phone out. "Correction," I said with a grin. "I have an *awesome* idea." With gleeful determination I selected all the naughty pics I could find and texted the lot to Philip with an accompanying message: <If you don't hear from me in 20 minutes send all pics to every website and news station in the world!!>

I fidgeted until the phone *dinged* to indicate the pics all went through, then called Nicole a.k.a "CEOILF." It connected after one ring, but no one spoke on the other end. Didn't matter. I had puh-lenty to say.

"Nikki!" I cried. "Hang on, sweetums, I have some neat stuff to send you. I know you're gonna want to take a look at this. Maybe you should have it blown up and framed to hang over the fireplace." I found and sent my absolute favorite pic of the lot—a truly artistic shot that showed Nicole's face *and* her naked nethers. "Turns out Pierce was a real photobug! And, wow, your hooha looks terrific, even after twins! Did you have a C-section? And, I *have* to know, do you do that anal bleaching stuff?"

Her sharp gasp told me the instant the photo arrived on her screen.

"This one's definitely my favorite," I prattled on, "but the one where you're bent over your desk with the Manhattan skyline in the background is a close second. That's pure *art!*" I paused for a couple of seconds to let it all sink in. "Now here's the deal, Nikki, sweetie. Because I'm *nice,* I haven't sent these to one of those spring-break-titties websites yet. Ooh! I wonder if there's a 'CEOs Gone Wild' website?"

She made an inarticulate noise, but I pressed right on. "How-

ever, because I'm not *stupid,* I already sent the whole darn package
to a buddy of mine—all the pics Pierce took, the pics you sent him,
along with the cute sexting you two did back and forth. *And* I told
my buddy that if he didn't hear from me in fifteen minutes with my
super special 'I'm Okay' code phrase, he was to spread these lovely
gems far and wide on every website and news feed that he could
find."

"You . . . you . . ."

"I know you have some nasty shit planned for us in the garage,
you fucking bitch." My voice was hard and sharp now, all trace of
humor gone. "Unless you want to be the laughingstock of the entire
goddamn world, I suggest you tell your people to stand the fuck
down. Oh, and if anything's been done to the van, it better get un-
done. Y'got me?"

Her breath came in short panicked gasps. Seemed I'd found her
weak spot. "No one will stop you," she choked out. "Get out. Get
out. Leave my son."

Pierce tilted his head, smile widening as the sound of scuffling
and muted shouts came from beyond the metal door.

"Not until we're completely clear," I told her. "Then we'll let
him go."

"Get out!" Fury and terror resonated in her voice. "Get out. *Get
out! GET OUT!*"

I disconnected while she was in mid shriek. So much for her calm
calculating crap. Pierce leaned against the doors, body shaking with silent laughter, despite our predicament.

"I think she wants us to get out," I said with a grin.

Still chuckling, he eased the door open again, even as a door
slammed on the other side of the garage. The air no longer held that
sharp edge. "Wait here," he ordered. Gun in hand, he loped to the
cargo van, made a quick circuit around it that I figured was to check
for explosives, then jumped up to the loading dock and pulled the
van's rear doors open.

As soon as he gestured to me I shoved the bin his way, and in no
time at all we had it loaded up and the doors closed. I stayed in the
back while Pierce took the driver's seat and got the van going.

"We're out and clear," he announced less than half a minute later.

"Hot fucking damn," I breathed. Shifting to my knees, I swung
the lid of the bin open. "How's everyone doing?"

Kyle lifted his head, expression grim, and his hand pressed to
Andrew's belly. "Some worse than . . . others."

"Hurts," Andrew gasped, breathing in short sips. "Oh, god."

"Shit. Help me get him out," I said before remembering that none of the zombies were at full strength by a long shot. Still, Kyle and Marcus managed to give enough push to help me get Andrew out and lay him down on the van floor without too much jarring. My eyes met Marcus's, totally relieved to see him moving and aware, but I barely had time for a smile before a choked cry of pain from Andrew pulled my attention.

"Jesus, you're pale," I muttered, lifting his shirt to peer at the little bullet wound. Barely any blood surrounded the pea-sized hole, but when I put my hand on his abdomen it was hard.

"I'm dying," Andrew gasped, fear and pain twisting his features. "Oh, god. Hurts."

He is *dying*, I realized with sick dread. "P-Pierce!" I called out, barely catching myself from saying Pietro. "Andrew's in really bad shape. I think he's bleeding internally. We need to get him to a hospital!"

Pierce glanced quickly back, cursed. "I'll call Dr. Nikas."

"He needs surgery," I insisted as he dialed. "Like, right now."

To my dismay, he shook his head. "Even if we could get him to an ER in time, we wouldn't take him. We *can't*."

"Why the hell not?" I demanded, dismayed. "Can't we, well, dump him and take off?" I shot Andrew an apologetic look, but he wasn't exactly paying attention to me.

Pierce's eyes briefly met mine in the rear view mirror. "Gunshot wounds are investigated, Angel," he said, regret mingling with firm decision. "We can't risk any law enforcement involvement." He lifted the phone to his ear. "You heard?" he said into it. "It's Andrew Saber, on the verge. Here's Angel."

I seized the phone. "Dr. Nikas. Tell me what to do!"

"Angel, send me a picture of the wound and location. Quickly," Dr. Nikas added. "He is still conscious?"

Hands trembling, I snapped two pics and sent them. "Yeah, he's conscious, but not by much. Pale, cold, and clammy. He's starting to lose it."

"And his abdomen is hard?"

"Like a rock." Damn it, I was getting a very bad feeling.

His soft sigh sent my bad feeling spiraling higher. "There's nothing medically to be done except surgery," he said gently, "and if you are still in the van it is probably too late for that. I'm so sorry, Angel."

"Oh." I swallowed past a thick knot in my throat. "Okay. Th-thanks, Dr. Nikas." Numbly, I handed the phone back to Pierce.

Kyle dragged himself up and over the side of the bin and landed in a naked, crumpled pile beside it.

Andrew gasped in a breath, flailed a hand out to clutch weakly at my arm. "Help . . . Dying." A sob turned into a cough, and panic filled his eyes. "No. Please . . ." His arm fell away, and his eyes rolled back.

Shit. I grabbed his shoulders. "Andrew! Listen to me. I can save you. You know I can." Godalmighty, I sure hoped I could. It wasn't always a sure thing, as I knew all too well. "But I won't—I won't do that if you don't want me to."

His eyes fluttered, but he managed to focus on me. "Oh, god." In that moment I didn't know if his fear of death could overcome the terror of becoming one of us, becoming a monster. "Y-yes." His voice was weaker, words slurring.

"Yes?" I gave him another little shake. "Yes, what? I need to know, Andrew! I need to know for sure!"

"Yes . . . bite." The last word died away, but it was enough. At least I hoped so. I looked over at Kyle. He understood what I needed from him, the confirmation and reassurance. His nod was slight, yet it was enough. Holy fuck, but I hoped this worked, for Naomi's sake as well as Andrew's. No time to gather my nerve any more.

Leaning down, I sunk my teeth hard into the muscle at the side of Andrew's neck. He jerked, but only barely, and his cry of pain was little more than a wheeze. *Please let this work. Please please*, I silently begged as I bit harder. I'd know soon enough if it would. When I'd turned Philip, instinct took over within a minute, guiding my body to do the damage necessary to transfer the parasite. Yet when I tried to turn another "volunteer" the next day, no instinct rose to lead me, and the man died.

My fingers dug into Andrew's shoulders as I bit and gnawed. He wasn't struggling anymore—unconscious by now, and close to death. I thought I heard Dr. Nikas's voice, distant and tinny on the phone, calling my name, but I didn't dare let my focus shift from Andrew, from the blood in my mouth and the scent of him.

Hunger rose in a wave like a cresting orgasm, a driving, snarling need to rend and rip and tear at the flesh beneath me. An eerie growl leapt from my throat as my teeth ripped and my fingers tore. Beneath the violence I wept in relief. *It's working.*

I gave myself up to the instinct, only dimly aware of the others in the van with me. Finally, I paused, lifted my head and bared my teeth. Blood dripped from my chin onto the ravaged body of Andrew beneath me.

The growl throbbed within me. *"Braaains."*

Someone shoved a hunk of brains into my hand. Kyle, maybe. Didn't matter. Instinct shifted me to the next stage, and I chewed the brains and spat them into the seeping wounds. Chew, bite, spit, repeat. He wasn't dead yet. I sensed the flickering spark of life on a level I couldn't explain. Yet he didn't wake, and the wounds didn't close. Chew, bite, spit, repeat.

More brains were pushed into my hand as soon as I needed them. The van stopped, and the back doors opened. Chew, bite, spit, repeat. I heard Philip's voice but couldn't focus on the words. Chew, bite, spit, repeat, wake up, Andrew, come on, goddammit, chew, bite, spit, repeat. Pierce spoke to the others, then he and Philip pulled the bin out, giving me more room. *Wake up, Andrew, come on, goddammit, chew, bite, spit, repeat.*

Someone, another zombie, sat near me and laid a hand on Andrew's shoulder. I lifted my head, teeth bared and a growl in my throat. Pierce gave an answering growl, but I didn't sense that he wanted to take my spawn from me. Spit-hissing, I returned to biting and braining. I *thought* that some of the wounds were starting to close, but so much more slowly than with Philip. Yet with only the one experience to draw on I had no idea if this was going wrong.

"Angel." The voice cut through to me as Philip's hadn't.

Nostrils flaring, I looked up to see Pierce spit something into his hand and hold it out for me. Brains. Pre-chewed. My human side had no problem registering that this was beyond disgusting, but my parasite didn't give a shit. My hand darted out and scooped the mush up, shoved it into my mouth, then I bit and spit some more. Maybe some spores or whatever from a mature zombie would get things kickstarted in ol' Andy.

The cycle shifted to *scoop, chew, bite, spit, repeat,* while I did my damndest to avoid thinking about how this was the weirdest possible way to swap spit with another person. And it was *Pietro*, which made it even weirder, except that Pietro was Pierce now, and wasn't some sixtyish older guy anymore. It didn't help that Pierce Gentry had been an asshole. I still had a hard time getting that out of my head.

Andrew sucked in a breath then coughed. His eyes flew open, and he gasped in more air only to expel it in an unintelligible sound. I sagged in relief and fatigue. With Pierce's help, I shifted to sit against the wall of the van and gathered Andrew close, cradled his head against my shoulder. He trembled in my arms, eyes not really focusing on anything yet.

Pierce set a chunk of brain in my hand—unchewed—and I held it to Andrew's lips. "Time to eat."

He recoiled, but even as one instinct pulled him away, a newer, stronger one had him leaning in to take the chunk from my fingers. He opened his mouth for more, and this time Pierce guided my hand to a container beside me that held chunks of brain, bite-sized and ready for feeding.

I fed Andrew another chunk and gave Pierce a weary smile of thanks. He gave my shoulder a light squeeze then exited out the back of the van and shut the doors behind him.

Andrew ate for several more minutes, eyes half-closed as he took the chunks from my hand and swallowed them. The wounds on his torso healed to smooth, unblemished skin beneath the blood and remnants of gore, and a hint of color returned to his face. He didn't look a hundred percent healthy yet, by any stretch, but he no longer resembled a day-old corpse either.

When he didn't open his mouth for another bite I knew his own parasite had enough fuel for the moment. "You need to sleep now," I said. While he slept the parasite would do its thing to make a permanent home in Andrewville.

His eyes struggled open. "Wh-what am I going to . . . do?"

"Sleep," I told him firmly. "We'll figure out the rest later."

He tried hard to form words, but at this point he didn't stand a chance against what his body and his new tenants needed. He mumbled, then his eyes closed, and he relaxed against me. Fatigue rolled over me, and I shifted him to a somewhat more comfortable position for both of us while still holding him close.

The back door creaked open, and Philip peered in, concern on his face. His eyes met mine, questioning, and I knew he was there for me but would have no problem withdrawing if that's what I needed. My hand felt as if it weighed a thousand pounds, but I managed to lift it enough to gesture him over. He climbed in and closed the door, then sat beside me and slipped an arm around my shoulders—not in a cuddly way, but more in a *You're a tired zombie* way. I gratefully leaned against him while Andrew's head lay tucked in the crook of my arm between us. I wanted to make a silly crack about how we were the weirdest zombie family ever, but instead I rested my head against Philip's shoulder, closed my eyes, and went right to sleep.

Chapter 34

A lavender teddy bear wrapped its arms around me. Shifted. Squeezed. Bled purple.

I jerked awake, and it took me a couple of seconds to figure out why a blood-covered Andrew Saber was sprawled across my lap.

His eyes darted around, confused and wild. "Hungry," he rasped, swallowing noisily as he struggled to sit up.

"Hey, careful." I tightened my arm around him and groped for the container of brains with the other. "Here," I said, shoving a couple of pieces at his mouth. "Eat this."

Distress chased away the confusion in his face, but he sucked down the brain chunks and took the others I fed him as well. Philip gently removed his arm from around my shoulders. "I'll be nearby," he murmured to me, then slipped out the back of the van.

I shot him a grateful smile as he left, then focused on Andrew. Someone had left a couple of baggies of pureed brains beside me, and as soon as Andrew finished the chunks I handed him an opened bag. He ate all of one, but then shook his head when I reached for the second.

He lifted his hands, brought them to his face. "What have I done?" he whispered.

"I gave you a medical condition that saved your life," I told him.

He shifted off my lap and crouched a couple of feet from me, shock and uncertainty swimming in his eyes. "I have to go back. To the office." His gaze dropped to the bloody ruin of his shirt. He touched one of the rips, slid his hand in to feel for the wounds that weren't there. "How . . . how can I go back now?" Distress laced his voice, but then he lowered his hand and clenched it. "Or does this mean I'm going to stay your prisoner?"

"No, you're not our prisoner," I said firmly, then reached out and took hold of his fist. "Andrew, you need to chill. We won't let you starve. We'll help you. But you really need to sit and talk with me and Pierce."

He yanked his hand away from mine. "Gentry." His voice dripped with hatred, which I could understand since he thought Gentry was a traitor and spy. And it probably didn't help that the real Gentry had been fucking his mom as well. "I can't deal with *him* right now." His lip curled. "Gentry cost us, cost Saberton *everything*."

"*He* cost you?" I sneered in derision. "Give me a fucking break, Andrew. That's like the car thief getting all pissed at the undercover cop when his comfy life of crime gets fucked up. Except that instead of cars being chopped up, it's people." I glared at him. "Don't forget, you're one of those people now. But hey, if you want to change your mind, it's not too late. It's not impossible to kill a zombie. Ask Chris Peterson."

Andrew scowled, but it was clear I'd made a solid point. "I'm not changing my mind. I don't want to be *dead*." He narrowed his eyes at me in suspicion. "Why would you let me go back?"

"Why wouldn't we? It's not like we want a pet zombie hanging around." I shrugged. "Besides, I really don't see you telling your mother—or anyone else at Saberton—that you're one of those filthy monsters now."

He gave a scoffing snort. "No, I won't be sending out a memo." He made an utterly doomed attempt to brush some of the drying blood off his shirt, then glowered and headed to the back doors of the van.

"There's a washer and dryer in the house," I said being all helpful and shit 'cause that's how I rolled. "And if you put some meat tenderizer on that blood and then scrub it in cold water, most of it'll come right out." The rips were another issue, but I figured I'd offered enough awesome advice for the moment.

A bleak expression passed over his face, and for an instant I had a glimpse of how very lost he felt. He exhaled, controlling it, then gave me a slight nod. That was probably as close to a thank you as I was going to get—and not only for the advice about blood stains.

He exited the van and closed the door. I dropped my head back against the metal wall, let myself have a couple of minutes of quiet, then headed in after him. I needed to take some of my own blood stain advice, since I was a horror show mess. Plenty of blood all over me from Andrew, but there was probably a fair amount from the guards I'd killed, as well as from my own wounds and dealing with Marcus and Kyle.

The burn of anger over how those two had been treated helped keep down the simmering guilt over the guards.

Andrew wasn't in any of the main living areas, so I figured he'd gone to "his" room to clean up. Someone had collected our stuff from the hotel room, and I dug clothes out of my bag, surprised and pleased to find my dirty stuff laundered, which was damn nice.

A long, hot shower and clean clothes did a lot to restore my get-up-and-go and clear my head. As much as I wanted to check on Marcus, I had other business I needed to take care of first. I went in search of Pierce and found him sitting in the recliner in his bedroom, an iPad on his lap.

"Hey, you got a few minutes?" I asked. "I need to talk to you."

He set the tablet aside. "Of course, Angel."

I closed the door behind me and then sat on the bed, facing him. "I need to know who gets to know about," I waved my hands at him, "the new you."

Weariness filled his eyes. "Those who know it now, of course," he said. "And I will also tell Kyle Griffin."

"What about Marcus?"

The weariness seemed to deepen, and for a moment he looked far older than the mid-thirties he was supposed to be now. "I'm seeking a way to keep him out of this. Completely out of it."

"I get that." I shifted to sit cross-legged. "But I don't get *why*, and I'm not keen on telling him his uncle's dead when he's not." I leveled a frown at him. "It really eats at him that he's not part of your inner circle. Did he fuck up somehow or do something to piss you off?"

"No." Exhaling, Pierce dropped his head back and closed his eyes. "I made a promise to Pietro Ivanov to keep his family ignorant and far from the dealings of our kind. I violated that trust once already by turning Marcus."

I mulled that over. "The original Pietro asked for that promise because he wanted to keep his family safe and happy, right?"

He lifted his head and opened his eyes. He knew where I was going with this. "Yes, and every day I debate my loyalty to a dead man versus my loyalty to Marcus—not only as part of the Ivanov family, but as my own kin." He gestured to himself, and I knew he meant zombie-kin. I also knew that none of this was cut and dried, black and white.

"Being shut out hurts him more than he ever lets you see," I said after a moment of thought. "Maybe you could look at the spirit of that promise to Pietro Ivanov and think about whether you're really doing right by it, especially since you already turned Marcus, and he doesn't have a choice except to live as a zombie."

He remained silent for a long moment, then he shook his head as if finally discarding an outdated idea. "I agree. It's time to re-adapt my priorities."

A smile spread across my face, both at his decision and at the fact that he saw me as a real person with valid ideas. "I'm really glad to hear that."

His eyes found mine. "Angel, it was easy to lie to him about being his Uncle Pietro. I was the only one he ever knew. This is not easy."

"You *are* his uncle in all the ways that matter," I told him firmly.

A light smile touched his mouth. "I'll talk to Ari. And Marcus will be told." But then the smile faded. "The best scenario for the Tribe is to have Marcus assume my former position."

An uneasy knot found its way into my chest. "But what about law school?"

True distress filled his eyes. "Do you see why this is so diffi-cult?"

"I do. I promise." I unfolded my legs and leaned forward. "But Marcus is tough *and* he's really damn loyal to you. To *you*, not the name Pietro." I peered at him. "What will you tell everyone else? Have you figured out how Pietro 'died?'"

"No. There's so much to consider, and I'm not yet as clear as I could be."

"And what about Jane?" I asked, brow creased.

Stark pain and uncertainty swept across his face. "I don't know yet, Angel."

Shit. I had zero doubt Pietro loved Jane, and I'd seen for myself how much she loved him right back. No way would he blow her off and leave the woman wondering what happened. But how the hell do you tell the woman you love that you're someone else now? "I haven't even looked at my phone yet," I said, "but I'd be shocked if she hasn't blown it up with calls and messages." I grimaced. "Is there anything I could say to, I dunno, hold her off until we figure shit out?"

He rubbed the back of his neck in a very uncharacteristic show of distress and tension. "She needs to be comforted. Reassured." He thought for a moment then exhaled softly. "Tell her I'm out of Sa-berton and safe, but I've been taken away for zombie . . . stasis recovery." A humorless smile twisted his mouth. "Not much of a lie, as I do need significant down time to recover."

The "and figure out what the hell to say to her" went unspoken.

"She won't be happy until she sees you," I told him, "but since I'm not telling her you're dead or anything, I think I can keep her from freaking out." I stood, then decided I needed to shift the heavy mood. "Does the Tribe know we're okay and that there's no insider?"

He nodded, looking relieved at the subject change. "Dr. Nikas called Rachel. He's the only one here with credibility."

The only one Rachel would believe, that was for sure. "I'm going to see Marcus now. What do you want me to tell him if he asks where his uncle is?"

Pierce's hazel-eyed gaze stayed on me for a long moment before he spoke. "Tell him the truth if it feels right," he said. "If not, tell him that information is still coming in. I'll talk to him later, in that case."

With that I left him and went in search of Marcus. I found him in a little upstairs study, lying on a futon with one foot on the floor and an arm thrown over his eyes.

"Hey." I said it softly but I still managed to startle him out of his light doze.

"Angel!" He sat up, ran a hand through his hair. The rot was all gone, but he still looked totally wiped out. "Angel," he repeated, pairing it with a smile. "When I saw you I couldn't believe you came to get me."

I started to say something flip and funny, but instead found myself moving forward to throw my arms around him, complete with full-blown bursting into tears.

He wrapped arms around me, breath shuddering. "Oh, babe."

"I didn't even know they'd taken you," I said as soon as I had enough control to speak coherently. "I called to tell you about your uncle, and it went to voicemail, so I texted and," I sniffled, "I thought everything was fine, but they must have texted me back using your phone."

He wiped away a few tears with his thumb, then seemed to realize there was no way he'd be able to keep up with my weepy flood. "It was right after I got home," he said, voice tight with lingering stress. "Never had a chance. I didn't even know *where* they'd taken me."

I put a hand to his cheek and drank in the sight of him. Even if we didn't get back together, there was no doubt in my mind that he was and would always be very special to me. "When I saw what they did to you—" My throat tightened, and I couldn't finish. I doubted he'd ever been that brain-starved before, and to have that shift into *monster* be paired with torture . . .

A shudder crawled through him. "I'm sorry you had to see it," he said, eyes haunted. "I remember them giving me an injection in the gut, then breaking my arms. I remember the rot and starting to lose control, and then nothing until coming back out of it while eating brains from a baggie." His throat worked. "It was horrific."

I reached for his hand. "I'm so damn glad you're here and safe now."

"I'd do everything in my power to see that none of us ever have to go through that again." Fierce determination backed his words. Maybe Pierce wasn't wrong at all in considering Marcus for the head position of the Tribe.

"Has there been any news about Uncle Pietro?" he asked.

Damn. It was one thing to tell Pierce I was cool telling Marcus the truth, but actually doing so was a whole other bucket of crawfish. "He's safe."

"Safe?" He sat straighter and looked past me as if expecting his uncle to stride into the room. "Where is he?"

I kept his hand in mine. Stuck a smile onto my face. "Okay, Marcus. Here's where it gets weird."

It took a while, and there were a couple of moments of almost-freakout, but Marcus finally seemed to accept what I told him about Pierce and Pietro, though by the end his jaw was clenched so tightly I thought I heard bone cracking.

"He loves you," I told Marcus. "And I think it's time for the two of you to talk things out. He's in the master bedroom, downstairs."

He leaned in to kiss me, remembering in the last instant to shift it to a kiss on the cheek. I returned the cheek kiss and watched him go, then sternly told my tired self that it didn't matter if I felt wrung out because there was still a bunch of shit to take care of.

My tired self told me to fuck the hell off, but at least allowed me to use my legs to walk out of the room.

Naomi leaned on her crutches at the bottom of the stairs, a scowl on her face, and very obviously waiting for me. My brain was too exhausted to even try to figure out why I might deserve a scowl from her.

"Hey, what's up?" I asked.

Her scowl twisted into a snarl. "I can't believe you *did* that."

"Did?" My brain finally clicked into gear. Andrew. Excuses and defensive explanations leapt into my head. *Naomi, I didn't know what else to do. He was dying, bleeding internally, and I swear I asked him if it was okay, I swear!*

I shoved down the stammering, uncertain response the old Angel would have spouted. Fuck that noise. I was at peace with how that whole thing played out. Lifting my chin, I locked my gaze with hers. "I made a decision based on how bad his injury was," I stated. "He was dying. I told him I could possibly save him and asked permission. He gave me permission." I kept my hands down by my sides so she wouldn't see how they trembled from fatigue and stress. "I don't regret it."

Her lip curled, and then she grinned widely. "Damn it, I was hoping to fuck with you." She pulled me into a hug. "Serves him right, the big ol' zombie hater."

I wilted in relief. "Oh, Jesus, you scared me."

"Sorry, I probably shouldn't have ambushed you," she said as she released me, only looking a teensy bit sorry.

I shrugged, grinned. "I'd have done the same to you."

"He doesn't know I know," she said. "He barely slowed down to wave between the shower and hiding in the bedroom, but I could feel it. You know how I am."

"Yeah, you got that sixth sense thing going on with zombies." I shook my head. "It's weird him being a zombie now."

"What's going to happen?" she asked, worry puckering her forehead. "He can't go back."

The thought that had been niggling away at the back of my head came out now. "Why not?" I met her eyes. "As long as he stays fed, how would anyone know?"

She blinked, obviously shocked and a little freaked that I hadn't replied with, *Of course he can't go back.*

"But if my mother finds out," she said, "or the lab people—" She gave her head a quick little shake of denial. "He can't!"

"Andrew's not stupid. And he doesn't *want* to stay with us." I took a deep breath. "Not to mention, with this whole Dallas lab thing going on, it sure would be cool for us to have someone on the inside."

She stared at me as if I had gone completely nuts. "You think you'd have him as an *insider?* Are you on some of Dr. Nikas's happy juice?"

"I don't mean calling us with daily updates or anything." I shrugged. "But in a perfect world that would fucking rock."

"Yeah, it would." She sighed. "But he's such a . . ." She trailed off, searching for the right word.

"Weenie? Prick? Jerk? Asshole?"

She let out a quick laugh. "All of the above, and throw in Corporate Cog. Though I guess with him being all zombified, it's more than we had before." She blew out a breath. "God, he better not get caught."

"It's up to him anyway," I pointed out. "Who knows, maybe this whole experience will change his outlook. I mean, I don't think he's really as much of a fucking nasty prick as he seems." I considered the various facets of Andrew I'd seen when he was most certainly under high stress conditions. "It's as if a bunch of his crap is simply because everyone expects him to be a big tough Saber."

"Maybe so." Her mouth twisted. "But when he's *on*, he can run with the worst of them."

I snorted. "I've noticed."

She echoed my snort, then peered into my face. "You need to get some rest. Dr. Nikas cooked up some new shit for Kyle, Marcus, and Philip. Also, Kyle wanted to see you, but I don't think it's urgent. He's in the front bedroom upstairs."

"I still have a couple of functioning brain cells," I told her. "I'll see him and then crash." I pulled her into a hug. "Thanks, chick."

She held me close, and a tremble went through her. "I know I joke and bitch, but thank you for watching out for Andrew. He drives me bugnuts, but he's still my brother."

I squeezed her then let her go. "I totally get it. It's like the stuff with my dad."

A flicker of hope lit her eyes. She knew how horrible my relationship with my dad had once been, and she also knew how much we'd repaired it. "Yeah. I guess it is." I thought she was going to hug me again, but instead she hobbled off toward the kitchen on her crutches, humming under her breath.

Returning upstairs, I headed to the front bedroom. The door was open a crack, so I eased it open and peered in. Kyle was in the bed, eyes closed and a blanket drawn up to his chin. His face still didn't seem as if it had pulled together quite right yet, and I realized that Naomi's high spirits when she'd confronted me had been a big ol' smokescreen for her own worry and anger.

He opened his eyes as the light from the hall spilled into the room. "Angel." His voice was wet, raspy, and thin.

I closed the door behind me, then needed a couple of seconds for my eyes to adjust in the gloom before I pulled a chair up by the bed and sat. A whisper of daylight snuck around heavy curtains, barely enough light for me to see, but I had a feeling any more would be uncomfortable for Kyle. "Hey," I said. "Naomi told me you wanted to see me?"

"Yes. Thank you. For coming in and getting me out of there."

My hands clenched. "No way was I gonna leave you there. I'd burn the whole building down before abandoning you to those fuckers."

"I've been through a lot before," he said, slowly and with focused effort. "Nothing . . . *nothing* like that."

"Jesus fuck, I'd hope not!" I shivered. "That was a horror show."

His gaze met mine. "You know how I am about leaving this world," he said.

The air in the room seemed to thicken around me. "I do."

He must have seen the sudden *Oh, god, please don't ask me to do what I think you're going to ask me to do, I'll do it because, yeah, but please don't!* in my eyes. "No," he said quickly. "No, not that."

I blew out a relieved breath. "Okay."

"I want you to know that I don't want to *go* anywhere until every one of those *motherfuckers* is put out of commission." He spoke with a frightening vehemence made even scarier by the quality of his voice. "Every one of them who can spend their day dreaming up a paste to innervate rot, every one of them who can smear it on and laugh. They fucked with the wrong zombie."

I leaned close. "And I'm here to tell you, if you do happen to *go* before you're done, I'll finish the job for you."

He gave the barest hint of a nod. "Then we understand each other."

"We do."

With that the dark tension seemed to leave both the room and him. "You should sleep if you can," I said. "Do you need Dr. Nikas?"

"Yes. I refused to take the sedative until I saw you."

"I'll go get him." I stood and moved to the door then looked back at him. "Thanks for having that kind of faith in me."

An uneven smile flickered. "Get the fuck out of here."

With a low chuckle, I did so, then found Dr. Nikas and told him Kyle was ready for a sedative. With that mission accomplished, I found the couch and once again introduced my face to its welcoming cushiness.

Chapter 35

After a few hours of sleep, two mugs of coffee, and another nice long shower, I once again found myself summoned to Pierce's room.

Brian was there as well, and I barely had time for a quick nod to him before Pierce asked, "How would you like to be the voice of the Tribe?" without any sort of intro like, *Hello, Angel, I hope you're doing well* or *Are you ready for me to lay some more weird shit on you?*

I gave him a blank look. "Voice of the Tribe? What, like a radio show?"

Amusement flashed across his face, but to his credit he didn't laugh out loud. "No," he said, allowing himself a slight smile. "As in speaking with authority, for us to Andrew."

My mouth dropped open. "Me?" I spluttered. Dream. Had to be. Obviously I was still drooling on the couch. Best to play along, though, just in case. "Why not Brian?"

Pierce glanced over at the implacable head of security. "Despite all of his qualities above and beyond his official role, Saber will only see him as muscle, with no real authority. Same for Philip but with even less respect."

"And how do you expect him to see *me*?" I retorted. "I'm a high school dropout, and a former felon and drug addict."

"You have street savvy, Angel, and you're clever under pressure. It has nothing to do with what you *were*, it's about who you *are*." Pierce lifted his chin toward Brian. "You already established yourself during the info gathering session, and we'll help with general effect. Brian will be at your shoulder just as he would be with me—

if I was still who I was." A faint grimace crossed his face. "Angel, I need you to do this."

The voice of the Tribe. I sucked in a soft breath. All those years of being forced to watch *The Godfather* because, according to my dad, it was the Best Movie Ever, were about to pay off. "You want me to be your *consigliere!*"

Pierce looked down, and this time I *knew* he was holding back a laugh. After a moment, he cleared his throat and lifted his head again. "In a manner of speaking, yes. At least for this."

"Okay, I'll do it." I gave a cheeky grin. "Hell, I'm his zombie mama now, so that should hold some weight."

Now he did laugh, but it was with and not at me. "Very well, let's review what needs to be said."

Once again, thanks to Naomi, I looked nothing at all like me. Black tailored jacket with matching slim skirt, white silk blouse, shoes with red soles which were apparently some sort of Big Deal, makeup that made me look mature and professional instead of the "slutty" I'd've managed on my own, and hair pinned up in an impossibly sleek style. I looked totally badass in an entirely different way.

Brian stood back and raked an assessing gaze over me, then stepped forward to adjust the drape of the fine gold chain at my throat. "Nervous?" he asked with a smile as he brushed a speck of invisible lint off the shoulder of my jacket.

"Should I be?" I asked nervously.

He chuckled. "I'm going to be right behind you, looking like this." He stood straight in his perfect dark suit, folded his arms over his chest, and put on his best Terminator face.

I burst out laughing. "Uh, yes," I cleared my throat, "quite terrifying."

He dropped his arms, lips twitching. "It is to everyone but *you*."

"Oh, all right, I guess I can see it."

Brian reached into his pocket and pulled out a tube of cherry ChapStick. "Do I need to use this?"

Laughing, I held up my hands in surrender. Many months ago I'd made a silly challenge that had ended up with Brian planting a ChapStick-laden smooch on me. "Anything but that! Fine, let's get this over with."

With a dramatic sigh of regret, Brian replaced the lip balm in his pocket. "Do you want to ambush him in his room or call him in somewhere?" he asked. "There are merits to both."

"Call him to us," I replied without hesitation. "We'll be set and ready, and that gives us the power position. It'll be like calling him onto the carpet." I paused. "Not that I know what that feels like."

"Of course not," he agreed with a totally straight face. "The parlor will work."

"There's a parlor?"

"That would be the room with the sofa you drooled on," he explained. "I'll get you settled, then go get him."

Awake and coherent, I saw it really was a parlor. Or a living room. Either way, it was perfect for what we had in mind. Simply furnished: Sofa, coffee table, wingback chair.

First order of business was a bit of rearranging for best effect and to make sure there'd be no available seat for Andrew. The sofa was already against the back wall, so we moved the wingback chair directly in front of it, and the table to my right. With the sofa effectively blocked, I plopped into the chair then had to experiment with how best to sit. Legs crossed or uncrossed? If crossed, at the ankle or the knee? Hands on the chair or folded in my lap? What looked the toughest? And why the hell wasn't there a mirror handy so I could practice my Power Zombie *Consigliere* expressions?

Fidgeting, I adjusted my jacket and finally settled on legs crossed at the knee, hands on the armrests. While waiting, I mentally ran over the main points I needed to touch on and reminded myself that if I fucked up Brian was there to bail me out.

How 'bout we not fuck up, 'kay?

At the sound of footsteps in the hall I quickly composed my face into what I hoped was a serene expression and prayed that I didn't simply look half-asleep.

Andrew stepped into the room, mild scowl on his face. He'd cleaned up and been given new clothing, but his t-shirt and sweats didn't carry anywhere near the *oomph* of my kickass suit. *I love you, Naomi!* I silently crowed.

Brian entered right behind him and closed the door, then took up the promised position behind me and to my left. Andrew clearly wasn't happy about the demand for his presence, and the ever-so-faint whiff of rot coming from him told me he was probably a bit hungry as well. He took in the sight of me all dressed up like a real person, and a whisper of a sneer began to form. I saw the moment it registered that the furniture arrangement left him nowhere to sit, and I hid my amusement as his expression settled into a solid glare.

"Andrew, it's so nice to see you again." I gave him a very pleasant smile. "Brian, do we have any brain chips left? I think those might help put Andrew in a slightly better mood." Damn, but this shit was fun.

"Yes, ma'am," Brian said without hesitation, once again forcing me to control my expression. "I'll get them."

Andrew looked even more off-balance after the "ma'am" thing, which of course was part of the reason for it. Yet even if he thought it was all a show, I knew he still had to be wondering *why*.

"Thank you for coming," I said as Brian strode to the door. "We need to hash out a few details before you go your own way."

Andrew watched Brian leave then returned his attention to me. This time the look he gave me was careful and assessing, no doubt trying to figure out what the hell my role was. "What sort of details?"

"It's hard when you're first turned," I said, sort of ignoring his question. "The hunger, I mean. You'll find that you burn through the brains more quickly if you exert yourself a lot, but otherwise you'll likely need somewhere around one brain every week and a half." Hot damn, I got through that without stumbling!

Denial and disgust swept over his face. "I don't *want* to eat a brain every week and a half. This is—" He stopped, and I had an overpowering feeling he'd almost finished with *not happening*. "This is not my life."

"I know this is a really hard adjustment," I said, keeping my voice deliberately gentle. "But you're not alone, and you're not without resources." I made a vague gesture to take in the house and its occupants. Brian returned as I did, carrying a bowl of chips and a plate with what looked and smelled like marinated and grilled brain slices. He placed them on the table beside me, then resumed his position at my back.

"Thank you, Brian," I said with a smile, then returned my attention to Andrew. "Please, help yourself. The grilled ones are really awesome."

Andrew locked his gaze on the plate like a dog staring at a bone behind a window. He licked his lips then came back to himself with a start as he realized what he was doing. Quickly swallowing, he shook his head firmly. "No, thank you."

I picked up one of the grilled pieces and took a small bite. "Pro tip: If you run too low on brains it's harder to think straight." I licked my fingers and tried to be dainty about it. "Probably smart to have a snack before any sort of negotiation." I waved toward the plate again in a help-yourself move, then finished off the piece in my hand.

Unable to resist the smell any longer, he moved forward and took a slice, then one more before stepping back. His hands shook slightly as he stuffed a piece into his mouth, relief and despair shining in his eyes.

Taking a napkin and wiping my fingers, I waited for him to finish the two slices before I spoke again. "I usually budget a brain a week for basic maintenance and to keep from smelling like a corpse." I laughed softly. "I'm thinking you don't want bits falling off in the board room."

He looked appropriately horrified. "A brain . . . a week." He dipped his head in a reluctant nod.

"You'll want to have a stash of more on hand, though," I continued, "in the event of injury or unexpected exertion. Or sex." I grinned. "Trust me, you *definitely* want to have a bit of a snack before sex."

Andrew made a gasp-choke sound in the back of his throat and turned sixteen shades of red.

"Allrighty then, we're looking at a brain a week," I plunged on, mostly because I was afraid if I didn't keep talking I'd bust out laughing at the shock on his face. "And probably, hmm, three or four brains up front as well for a stash. Does that sound right to you?"

His mouth worked soundlessly.

"That's a good start, ma'am," Brian put in helpfully.

I turned my head to give him a bright smile. "Thank you, Brian." He really did look intimidating as all hell standing there behind me. I could get used to this. Returning my attention to Andrew, I put on a slight wince. "I'm sorry, I'm sitting here blathering on and assuming that you want to get your brains from us. You got someplace else you can get 'em?"

He was trapped and he knew it. No way could he get brains from whatever source the lab used since there was too much chance he could be found out. Perhaps he could locate an alternate supplier at some point, but for now—and probably the next few months—he was well and truly stuck.

He cleared his throat, resignation settling on him like a lead blanket. "No, I don't."

Though I did a mental fist pump and happy dance, I kept my face as serene as possible. "Very well." I paused and kept my eyes on him for several seconds while I let the silence hang in the air. "What do you offer in exchange?"

Even though he had to have known it would come down to this, he was still off-balance enough from everything else that he couldn't hold back the small shoulder slump of defeat.

"What do you want?" he asked, voice hollow.

"Information. Influence. You'll be in a very good position to provide both upon your, ah, triumphant and heroic return to Saberton."

Now Andrew found his footing. He lifted his chin and set his jaw in determination. "No. I refuse to do anything that will be detrimental to my company."

Crap. Wrong tack. Let's try that again. "I didn't ask you to," I said as smoothly as possible. Setting both feet on the floor, I leaned forward. "Andrew, I'm not asking you to betray your family or your," I mentally scrambled for the word, "your legacy." *Don't blow it, Angel. You're in the home stretch!* "But you're in a pretty unique position now, and I kind of hope it'll give you a better idea of what it's like to live as a zombie and the challenges we face." I rested my elbows on my knees and clasped my hands lightly together. "Hell, I dunno. Maybe you could suggest policy and—" Shit, what was another word for influence? That was a hot-button word for him. "—guide decisions in a way that can help us out. Or at least not *harm* us."

He frowned, but at the moment it seemed more like a thoughtful frown than an *I will fuck these assholes over first chance* frown.

"And if you're not able to do any of that," I continued, "a simple heads up that shit's coming down would sure be pretty damn cool and likely make you some friends on this end." I shrugged. "Personally, I'm betting that you can rebuild Saberton to where it doesn't *need* to rely on atrocities to compete."

Andrew's gaze returned to the plate of brains. "That is not unreasonable."

"I think we'd make better allies than enemies," I said.

He gave a noncommittal chin lift that told me he didn't particularly agree with me. Then again, I knew before we started that he wasn't going to fall into our arms and be our Best Friend and Awesome Ally overnight, if ever. Baby steps, and all that.

I took a dehydrated brain chip and used it to gesture to the plate and bowl. "Have some more," I said. "No charge, no strings. I promise. You'll feel better, trust me." I watched as he moved forward to scoop up two more grillers and a handful of chips. "Do you have any questions? I know how confusing it was for me when I was a new zombie."

He shook his head as he gulped down another slice. "No. I have access to . . . information," he said, though he had the grace to look slightly uncomfortable.

"Right. That zombie research y'all have been doing." I gave a knowing nod. "You'll probably find out it's not all accurate. I mean, lab conditions aren't anything like the real world, y'know." My voice hardened. "You get your shit together and dump the Dallas lab bastards and Kristi Charish, and maybe we can look at that longevity research as a joint project." I paused as he nearly choked on a chip. "Yeah. We know about that."

He shifted his feet, clearly not liking the direction of the conversation, though I caught a flicker of interest in his eyes. "This has been fascinating," he said sourly, "but there's a board meeting tomorrow I need to prepare for."

Brian leaned forward to adjust the items on the plate and murmured names to me.

"I understand," I told Andrew. "We'll be in touch to arrange secure and discreet delivery of the brains." I stood and smoothed my skirt. "That said, it would be a really great show of faith on your part if you could give as much information as you can about the two drivers and the security guard who were taken along with Pietro and Dr. Charish: Simon Sirtis, Felicia Godwin, and Lawrence Hawkins. They're in Dallas, right?"

Andrew's lips pressed thin, and he gave a curt nod. "I'll see what I can do."

"Awesome." I lifted my chin. "Since you're *almost* in charge of Saberton, I'm sure you're aware that the movie extras your people experimented on are dying. We're taking steps to prevent more stupidly pointless deaths. I'm sure Saberton is as well, hmm?"

His eyes widened, and the color dropped from his face. "I didn't know."

"Seems to happen a lot," I said with a low snort. "That shit would piss me right the fuck off if I was in your position." I shrugged. "Who knows, maybe your mother will fill you in. She has *such* a great track record with that." I gestured to the door. "There's a car waiting out front to take you back home, and a briefcase by the door with a week's supply of brain smoothies. We'll be in touch about more."

Expression troubled, he turned to go, but before he exited I remembered one more thing. "Hey, Andy?"

He stopped, faced me again. I made a point of adjusting my sleeves before speaking. "We expect to have Chris Peterson's bomber jacket delivered to Pietro's Louisiana office no later than day after tomorrow." I kept my tone uncompromising. "And make sure it doesn't have any of Edwards's stink on it." I looked him straight in the eye. "Chris was *murdered*. He left a sister behind. I can't bring back her brother, but I'll fucking get the jacket he adored for the sister he loved."

Brief, stark guilt flashed in his eyes, but an instant later he recovered and stalked out.

I waited until his footsteps faded down the hall, and the front door slammed, then I let out a little squeal and did a happy dance. "That fucking *rocked!*"

Chapter 36

We stayed in New York until the following morning, mostly because I politely asked if we could see a few sights before we left. Okay, it's possible I whined and pointed out that who the hell knew when I would ever get a chance to see the city again, and I could hardly go back home without visiting a single tourist attraction and getting some souvenirs, right?

In a show of absolute and undying friendship, Philip gamely accompanied me while I managed to jam in visits to the Statue of Liberty, Grand Central Station, the Museum of Natural History—with DINOSAURS!—and Central Park, as well as Times Square where tourists seemed utterly fascinated by some guy playing the guitar while wearing only a cowboy hat and underwear. I didn't understand what the big deal was. They could see that sort of thing any Friday night down at Pillar's Bar. After noting how long the line was to go to the top of the Empire State Building I gave up on adding that to my list of places seen. Yet instead of returning to the house at the end of a long day of hard touristing, Philip told the driver to take us back to the Empire State Building, even though it was after ten p.m.

"Hardly any lines now," he told me with a grin, and in less than fifteen minutes we gazed out at the lights of the city from the observation deck.

Approximately five minutes after that, we both agreed that yes, the view was spectacular but damn, it was really cold and windy. We returned downstairs, climbed into the car and headed back to the house, loaded down with a truly outrageous amount of souvenirs and touristy crap.

The next morning we piled into two cars: Dr. Nikas, Pierce, Brian, and Marcus, in the vehicle Brian had driven to the city; and Philip, Naomi, Kyle, and me in the car I'd borrowed from Randy. Pierce and Marcus used the long travel time to hammer out plans and, judging by short tempers at a couple of meal stops, it wasn't all smooth sailing. Dr. Nikas, who'd assumed the role of mediator, looked frazzled before we were even halfway home.

For our part, Philip and I swapped off on the driving while Naomi stayed in the back seat with Kyle. He looked like death warmed over, and his jaw and hands still didn't work right. For his sake, everyone was relieved when we finally pulled up to Dr. Nikas's lab in St. Edwards Parish.

Naomi hustled Kyle off toward the medical section, and Philip and I went to a treatment room. Dr. Nikas gave us each two injections, then had us drink a quart of medicine-laced brain smoothie to stop the whole MegaPlague imprinting thing and put us both back to normal—or as normal as we could be at the moment. Once that was done Jacques invited me to the back to look at the growth of the heads, where I was totally psyched to see that Kang's body was almost three feet long—though still as weird and gross-looking as before—and he'd been moved to the full-size coffin tank.

I finally left the lab and headed off on my own, this time to Nick's house where my dad was still staying, according to my latest phone call to him.

Nick lived in a much swankier area than I expected, a gated neighborhood with large houses and perfectly landscaped yards. It didn't seem to fit practical Nick at all, and the only reason I didn't stop to double check the address was because the gate guard had my name as a visitor. After I pulled into the driveway of a two story house on Seraphim Circle I sat for a moment and stared at the doors of the two car garage. How the hell could Nick afford this on Coroner's Office pay, and *why* did he need such a big ass house?

I shook off the questions as I climbed out of the car and walked up to the porch. Before I could ring the bell, my dad yanked the door open. "Angel, it's 'bout damn time you got here."

Blinking, I took in the sight of him looking halfway *respectable*. Clean shaven, hair combed—and trimmed since I left—and with freshly laundered clothes judging by the Summer Breeze scent wafting from him. He lost "respectable" points due to the old spaghetti sauce stains, frayed collar on his shirt, and the rip in the side seam of his pants that he'd declared "didn't do no one no harm" when I'd once offered to sew it up for him. "Um, nice to see you too?"

The next instant he pulled me into a fierce hug. "Don't you ever run off like that again, you hear me?" he muttered, voice rough.

I hugged him back, hard. "I hope to hell I never have to," I said, a little sniffly. "I'm so glad you're doing all right."

"Yeah, I'm doin' okay," he said, then pulled back. "C'mon in." He waved a hand toward the inside as if he was inviting me into his own house.

I entered, still struck by the sense that none of the décor reflected Nick. Floor to ceiling mirrors lined one wall of the foyer, and a vase of fresh pale yellow flowers stood on a table against the opposite wall. Through an archway, I caught a glimpse of cream leather sofa on spotless matching carpet. It was all very lovely and tasteful, neat and tidy, without a thing out of place. Expensive and classy, and I couldn't for the life of me explain why it felt so very not-Nick.

"This is a really nice place," I said, because it was.

"It's comfy enough," Dad said with a bit of a shrug. Maybe he felt the same way about the décor and Nick. He gestured to a pile of books on the coffee table. "That's where Nick does his studying, and the kitchen is this way."

I followed him into a kitchen at least three times the size of mine. White tile and black appliances. "Where's Nick now?"

"Should be home soon." He opened the fridge and pulled out a Diet Coke. "With the short staff at the Coroner's Office he's had some long hours."

I grimaced. "Yeah, I called Allen yesterday. I go back to work in the morning."

He popped the top on the can and took a sip. "Allen and Nick were pretty worried about you."

"I'm sure they were," I said with a sigh, then gave him a brighter smile. "But everything's cool now." I heard the sound of the door opening.

My dad leaned in close and lowered his voice. "And I didn't tell him anything about, um, *you know*."

"God, I'd hope not!" I whispered back, then gave Nick a smile as he strode into the kitchen. "Hey!"

"Hey, Angel," he said, trying to look casual but failing miserably. Anxious delight shone in his eyes, and he cleared his throat. "I'm glad you're back safe and sound."

Grinning, I closed the distance between us and pulled him into a hug. He wasn't much taller than me, so it was a bit different than hugs from big guys like Philip or Marcus. Nick had his face right on my neck which made me glad I'd eaten recently. Nothing like getting a face full of rot smell.

Nick's breath shuddered out of him, and the hug he'd been holding somewhat awkwardly relaxed and shifted a bit closer.

I held him, deeply grateful that I had such amazing friends. "Thanks for watching out for my dad," I murmured.

I felt him nod against my neck. He continued to hold me for another couple of seconds then abruptly released me, all but shoving me away, a strangely stricken look on his face. "Yeah. Sure. Wasn't any trouble." He wiped his hands on his pants, and I had the weirdest feeling it was to remove any trace of me. "I . . . need to get some water," he muttered before hurrying out of the kitchen.

I watched him go, then glanced to my dad with a *huh?* look.

He shrugged. "Never hugged me," he replied in a low voice, "so I don't got nothin' to compare to."

I bit back a laugh. "C'mon, get your stuff. I'm taking you home."

"All right. It'll just take a minute." He headed off down the hallway, I assumed to the guest room. I heard a strange strangled sound from the direction of the living room and headed that way, shocked to see Nick leaning over the coffee table, hands clenched to white knuckles on the edge, face pale and breath wheezing.

"Shit! Nick, what's wrong?"

"Inhaler," he managed. "Bag . . . by door."

I ran to the door where his brown leather messenger bag lay slouched against the wall. I quickly dug through it to find the inhaler, then hurried back to Nick and shoved it into his hand. Trembling, he gripped the inhaler tightly and gave himself two quick puffs. A few seconds later he seemed to relax a little, and the wheeze faded.

"You need anything else?" I asked, worried. "Should I call someone?"

He gave his head a quick, sharp shake. "No, I'll be okay." He gave himself another puff, then straightened without looking at me. "Thanks. Sorry."

"It's no biggie," I told him. Poor dude was obviously self-conscious and embarrassed, but at least his color was back. My continuing to fuss over him would only embarrass him more. "I guess I'll see you at work tomorrow?"

"Yeah, Derrel isn't back until Monday, so I'll be in and out," he said, continuing to recover.

"Cool. Let's grab coffee if we can squeeze out a few minutes."

He flicked a quick glance at me, smile twitching. "Sure. That'd be great."

I hesitated, then gave him a quick kiss on the cheek. "See you tomorrow," I said as my dad came out with a BigShopMart bag in one hand. Reluctantly turning away, I headed to the door, Dad following.

I was in the foyer when I heard Nick clear his throat. "See you, Angel."

Glancing back, I gave him a smile. Something was going on with him, and as soon as I settled back into my normal routine, I intended to find out what the hell it was.

I got my dad settled back at home, changed clothes and then headed out to return the car to Randy. My car was still broken down by Top Cow Café, or at least I hoped so. Getting that taken care of had been pretty far down on my list of priorities. Worst case scenario was that the city had towed it off, in which case I intended to get the Tribe to cover the tow costs. Least they could do, right?

Either way, I'd wheedle a ride home from Randy, or if that failed I'd call my dad to come get me. Though I'd then have to explain why the heck I was with Randy in the first place, and ugh, all that crap. Maybe I could walk the hell home.

Randy stepped out of the garage as I pulled into the driveway, the crunch of oyster shells beneath the tires announcing my presence better than any alarm. He wiped grease from his hands then pulled a joint out of his pocket, lit it, and headed my way.

I stepped out of the car, closed the door and gave him a smile. "Not a scratch," I told him. "I even ran her through a car wash." The pleasant smell of a wood fire hung in the air, and an owl hooted off in the woods beyond the trailer.

Randy gave me a lazy smile. "Looks good. You got everything done you needed to get done with your people?"

"Sure did," I said. "Or at least enough for now." Getting our people back from the Dallas lab was next on the agenda, but I doubted the Tribe would need me for that, especially if Andrew cooperated.

"That's good," he said. "Win win." He held the joint out to me. "It's good stuff. Just in."

"Aw, man, I wish I could take a hit," I said with a grimace. "My medical condition, remember?" Except that, in a way, I kind of wanted to take a hit. Not for the high, but to be able to participate in this little social thing. Well, maybe for the high too.

"Oh, right." He gave a little chuckle. "Sorry. Want me to light a cigarette for you?"

"Yeah, sure." I'd settle for a fucking cigarette. "Is there any way you could give me a ride home?" I asked. "My car's still broke down by Top Cow."

"I *could* drive you home." He set the joint on a fence post, then lit a cigarette and passed it to me. "But it's probably not a good idea."

Nodding, I took a drag. "Y'mean 'cause my dad hates you?" I said with a grin.

"There's that." He chuckled, not seeming at all put out that he wasn't universally loved. He picked up the joint, took a hit. "I was more thinking 'cause your car's right over there under the big oak." He gestured with the joint.

I looked over in shock and gave a surprised laugh. "Aw, you went and picked it up?"

He smiled, leaned against the fence post. "Didn't fly over here on its own, now did it?"

"I'm guessing you fixed whatever was wrong with it too, huh?"

He let out a soft snort. "Wasn't hardly anything wrong with it. Just needed a new alternator."

"Yeah, well, I'm dumb about cars," I said. "But thanks. That was really cool of you."

He shrugged off my gratitude and hooked a thumb toward the back of the trailer. "I got a fire going in the pit. Was gonna grill up some deer sausage. Want some? Fire'll take the chill off, and you always liked hanging out by the pit."

I started to make a polite excuse, then realized he was right. I used to enjoy kicking back by the fire with nowhere to go, no one to answer to, and nothing but socializing on the agenda. But who had time for that these days? *Me*, I decided, after a quick mental review of what I needed to do, where I needed to go, and who I needed to see turned up nothing more urgent than wash my uniform for work in the morning. Why the hell did that bother me? I'd been busting my ass for the last week, so I should be happy that things were back to normal and my to-do list didn't include smashing people's heads or cutting holes in myself. And I was, I told myself. Happy.

"That'd be cool," I said.

His smile broadened with pleased surprise. "Allrighty. You grab blankets for the chairs, and I'll go get the sausage."

And as easy as that, we slipped back into an old and comfortable routine. I knew where the blankets were, and I took care of getting the chairs unfolded by the pit and the blankets spread over them. Randy's dad had used a fifty-five gallon drum to burn trash in this spot for a couple of decades, but four years back Randy had moved the trash barrel over behind the garage and put in a brick and cement pit, a yard across, in its place. A wood fire crackled under a rebar grate now, sending up sparks with each pop, and citronella torches burned in a perimeter to keep the mosquitoes at bay—not that they bothered me anymore. The whole setup sure as hell wasn't anything fancy, but it was . . . comfortable. Casual. The pit was for relaxing, kicking back with friends to enjoy a nice evening. And getting high—though of course that couldn't be part of it anymore now that I was a zombie.

Randy came around the trailer with the sausage, got it on the grill then settled in with me while the sausage hissed and spat. The aroma of cooking meat filled the air, and pleasant nostalgia helped ease the last bits of stress. The owl hooted again, and frogs chorused from the swamp nearby. I drank Diet Coke while Randy drank beer, and we joked and chatted and caught up on stupid shit. No stress to be badass or smart or clever. Only the stars overhead and the fire in front of us.

I lit a second cigarette and savored it as much as the hot sausage, even with the mild dulling of my senses. It was a little like a buzz, in its own weird way—a filter between me and the world. Randy was kicked back in his chair, mellow and relaxed after the food and a couple of joints. I suddenly envied him that. I hadn't *really* relaxed since I became a zombie—until now, though I was still nowhere near the almost-boneless state Randy was at. There were times when getting a little mellow was nice, though of course, the usual options to get to that state wouldn't work for me anymore.

Yet now I knew there *were* options for zombies, like that awesome sedative Dr. Nikas had made up. I definitely needed to get me some of that shit. And brains—not so much for getting mellow, but being fully tanked was better than a hit of Adderall.

And that SuperMod. That shit was—

"It's getting cold out here with the fire down," Randy said, breaking into my thoughts. The fire was mere embers now, to my surprise. Maybe I'd been more mellow than I thought. "Wanna head in?" he continued. "Or do you need to go?"

For an instant I seriously considered staying. Not to get back together with Randy or anything stupid like that, but simply to keep hold of this no-stress sensation. But as soon as I started thinking about it, the sensation faded. Plus I had to be at work early tomorrow. Back to the grind. Yeah, I loved my job, but it was still a *job*.

"I'm sorry, but I need to get going," I said with true regret. "Can't be late to work after being gone for so long."

He hauled himself out of the chair and yawned. "That's cool. Your car's unlocked. Key's in it."

I started to ask him where he got a key for it, then figured it was better not to. "This has been nice," I said instead, standing and reaching for the blanket to fold it. "I really appreciate it."

"It's been good," he agreed with a sleepy smile, and with that he turned and headed away from the pit and to his trailer, leaving behind blankets, chairs, paper plates, and utensils.

Some things hadn't changed at all. Laughing under my breath, I chucked the paper plates into the pit, folded blankets, then poured the remains of the beer and Diet Coke onto the embers to douse them. The rest he could clean up for himself.

As promised, the key was in the car, and it started with a smooth purr it never had before. I suspected he'd done more than simply replace the alternator. Probably a full tune-up, knowing him.

I dug a handful of brain chips out of the bag in my purse, munched them down as I pulled out of his driveway, and by the time I reached the highway I'd balanced out the mild damage done by the cigarettes. Still, I kept eating the chips, and not because I was hungry for either food *or* brains. I didn't want to be mellow anymore. Now I simply wanted to feel *alive* and awake, to get back that terrific feeling that came with being overbrained.

No way would I get that from a bag of brain chips, though. I had some stash at home, but not enough to tank me to the gills the way I wanted. I dug my hand into the bag in a search for the last crumbs of chips. Tomorrow I could go to my storage unit and get more brains out. Of course, by tomorrow I probably wouldn't feel this way, and I'd—

My fingers knocked against something hard and cold in the bottom of my purse. The last syringe of the SuperMod. Dr. Nikas hadn't asked for it back, and I hadn't mentioned that I still had it. Never know when that sort of thing could come in handy, right? But of course we were back home now, which meant I didn't really need to save it. There were plenty of real mods at the lab, and this was just a kitchen version.

I found myself at the boat launch, though it was nowhere near my house. Mod in one hand. Pen knife in my other. The mod was safe to use. I knew that. Safe, because I'd used it twice before, and Dr. Nikas knew what he was doing.

I only had the one. This was a one time thing.

Stop thinking so much.

Make the cut.

Make the cut and stick in the syringe.

Make the cut and stick in the syringe and press the plunger.

3 . . . 2 . . . 1 . . .

A shudder then a chill then the best feeling.

Lean back and close eyes. Best feeling ever.

Yeah.

Oh, yeah. Best feeling *ever*.